"Just be
that's all I'm saying."

"Good advice." She shrugged. "Except that it feels like I always have to watch my back. It's a difficult way to live. Especially when I have a child to look after and a new business to start."

"Hmm. Well, I'll volunteer to watch out for you as often as I can. You and Shelby." Noah took two steps closer, and this time ran his palms lightly up and down her arms. The unexpectedness of his move forced her to raise her head.

"Don't," she managed to choke out. "It's not right.. *We're* not right. Go home. Just...leave me be." Greer shoved his hands off her waist. She lurched sideways, then sprinted to the middle cottage and disappeared inside.

Her anxiety—over the threats to her ranch *and* the disapproval she faced—worried Noah. Greer Bell was the first woman in ages he'd had the slightest desire to be with. It was a cinch that the church board, people in town, his folks, wouldn't like the idea.

Too bad. They'd better get used to it, because he planned to go with his gut on this one.

Dear Reader,

Any time an author is invited to take part in a linked continuity, it's sure to provide fun, sprinkled with new challenges. All five of us "ranch series" writers were excited when we got the call. We'd all written about ranches and cowboys, but choosing a setting, a place to establish our town, sparked the first of many lively e-mail debates. (Thank heaven for e-mail, as we live many miles apart.)

Say "ranch" and who doesn't think of Texas? So it's not surprising that Texas with its vast diversity got our unanimous vote. With a general area settled on, the ideas flew as we built our fictional town. The result is Homestead, Texas, nestled in the heart of the beautiful Hill Country, in fictitious Loveless County. Who wouldn't want to own land there, especially if the property's free or nearly so? Ah, remember I said this is fiction!

The five of us who made up this town and populated it with our characters hope readers will come to love our families as much as we do. Every hero and heroine has a unique set of reasons for ending up in Homestead.

In this book, the fourth, I offer Greer Bell, her daughter, Shelby, and Noah Kelley, pastor of Homestead's Episcopal church. Greer's and Noah's pasts are unhappily entwined. I have my fingers crossed that you'll enjoy following their rocky road to love as much as I enjoyed helping them become a family. And I hope you'll read all five books in the HOME TO LOVELESS COUNTY series.

I love hearing from readers. You can reach me at P.O. Box 17480-101, Tucson, AZ 85731 or e-mail me at rdfox@worldnet.att.net.

Sincerely,

Roz Denny Fox

MORE TO TEXAS THAN COWBOYS

Roz Denny Fox

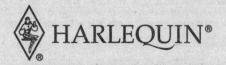

HARLEQUIN®

TORONTO • NEW YORK • LONDON
AMSTERDAM • PARIS • SYDNEY • HAMBURG
STOCKHOLM • ATHENS • TOKYO • MILAN • MADRID
PRAGUE • WARSAW • BUDAPEST • AUCKLAND

ISBN 0-373-71320-7

MORE TO TEXAS THAN COWBOYS

Copyright © 2006 by Rosaline Fox.

This edition published by arrangement with Harlequin Books S.A.

www.eHarlequin.com

Printed in U.S.A.

Books by Roz Denny Fox

Don't miss any of our special offers. Write to us at the following address for information on our newest releases.

Harlequin Reader Service
U.S.: 3010 Walden Ave., P.O. Box 1325, Buffalo, NY 14269
Canadian: P.O. Box 609, Fort Erie, Ont. L2A 5X3

We've all worked so hard to see this continuity come to fruition that I'd like to dedicate my portion to the individual editors who have shepherded our stories from beginning to end. Paula, Zilla, Kathleen, Victoria. And to the other authors, Roxanne, K.N., Linda and Lynnette, who got the tough job of tying up all the loose threads.

CHAPTER ONE

SLOWING HER RED Chevy Blazer on the outskirts of Homestead, Texas, Greer Bell passed a population sign that read 2,504. Wasn't it decidedly less than that now, at least according to the current mayor? Directly ahead in the center of town sat Homestead's most impressive landmark, the old courthouse. Its yellow granite columns and soaring clock tower told Greer she was home.

She knew that a lot of small Texas towns boasted similar landmarks. This courthouse probably hadn't changed since it was erected by a German immigrant in the 1840s; as the story went, his wife had refused to budge once they reached Loveless County. Oh, the tales that old building could tell.

Maybe returning home after ten years away wasn't going to be as easy as she'd imagined. Greer had certainly never expected her first glimpse of Post Street to bring such a mix of nostalgia and angry butterflies to her stomach. Frankly she'd assumed there'd be more visible change because of the land giveaway. She'd figured there'd be more people out and about in the middle of the week. Mayor Miranda Wright's plan to revitalize Homestead by offering land or vacant homes to families willing to rebuild the dying town didn't appear overwhelmingly successful. This was the same backdrop Greer conjured up in every dream of home during the past ten years. Maybe there were a couple of new stores. She pulled over and dropped her head onto both hands, still clutching the wheel.

She was parked in front of Tanner's General Store. Had it been revamped? Painted? Oh—down the street that sign for a Dollar Store was new. And the café.

Shelby, Greer's nine-year-old daughter, had slept on and off during their second day's journey from Denver. Stirring, the girl rubbed sleepy hazel eyes several shades darker than her mom's, which were generously flecked with gold.

"Are we there yet?" she asked for the millionth time, punctuating her query with a massive yawn.

Greer quickly raised a clammy forehead. "Not yet, honey bunny. We're in downtown Homestead. Our ranch is several miles…thataway." Greer jerked a thumb toward undulating hills barely visible beyond the courthouse, where a couple of old men sat on benches.

Shelby pressed her nose to the side window. "Then why are we stopping? Oh…is this where Grandma works?" Her voice warbled excitedly.

"My mother, you mean? Uh, no. Loretta, uh, teaches math at the high school. It's a few miles out of town." Greer's eyes strayed to her daughter's image in the rearview mirror, she noted her own deep frown. She wiped it away. After all, she'd taken many things into consideration before making up her mind to move back to the place of her birth. And yet she'd sheltered Shelby from the truth about her family—why her only grandparents were nothing but a scrawled signature on Christmas and birthday cards. But sitting in far-off Colorado—where she'd helped manage a busy guest ranch— filling out an application for a piece of Homestead's almost-free land had seemed simple. Here, facing the stark reality, even knowing it was time to confront her past, Greer wasn't sure she had the stomach for it. Still, this wasn't the moment to begin divulging the truth to Shelby. Not when so many unsettled feelings boiled within Greer.

"Groceries," she said suddenly, digging up a reason for stopping. "We need a few things to tide us over until we get to the staples I sent in the moving van. This is Tanner's," she muttered, peering at the weathered sign. "It used to be the town's only grocery store. I figured Homestead would have a superstore by now, but apparently not," Greer said, scanning the two-lane street flanked by old one- and two-story red brick or cream-colored buildings. Her stomach pitched again. She'd counted on change, but there didn't seem to be much, and now Greer wasn't sure she could get out and step back in time.

Shelby felt no such compunction. Unbuckling her seat belt, she threw open her door and slammed it shut with a bang.

Watching her energetic daughter bound over the curb onto the sidewalk, Greer emerged more slowly from the Blazer, and then took a minute to lock the doors, even though no one in Homestead had ever done so in the past.

Shelby didn't wait for her mom at the entry, but shoved open one of the peeling double doors and disappeared inside, causing a bell over the door to jingle. Such a small thing, but Greer was further catapulted back to her childhood, when she'd trailed up these steps after her dad, clutching money she'd earned doing chores around the farm. Robert Bell, always stern, invariably scolded her for spending every last penny on books, knickknacks and candy. And yet…despite his own thrifty ways, he'd never tried to stop her. The memory was a sharp reminder of all she'd lost.

A lump settled in her throat as a string of familiar scents wafted past on the breeze created as Shelby let the door bang shut. Greer knew what her daughter would find inside. Oak barrels of varying sizes, brimming with gourmet goodies.

Well, gourmet by Homestead's standards. Delicacies such as home-cured jerky, fat dill pickles, peppermint drops, or specialties like imported teas. Seasonally, Mrs. Tanner stocked spicy cinnamon-orange, or pear-and-apple blend. For as far back as Greer could remember, stepping into Tanner's had been like walking into a treasure trove. Food was the least of what they offered. Collectibles, toys, Christmas ornaments, kitchen gadgets and sundry gifts hung from the ceiling or were tucked in a myriad of cubbyholes. She'd have to bribe Shelby with a second trip to town if she hoped to pry her out of the store anytime soon.

Needing to let her eyes adjust to the dim interior after leaving the bright fall sun, Greer hesitated beside a barrel of shiny red apples. She supported herself against it to make sure her jelly knees weren't going to let her down.

Once, she'd loved this store. Loved this town. She blinked rapidly to stave off tears she thought had all been shed long ago, and attempted to locate Shelby, all while compiling observations—well-oiled dark oak floors, a painted tin ceiling, dancing wind chimes tinkling softly in the lazy breeze of a fan. Her gaze skipped over the clerk standing behind the counter. She did notice he operated a more modern cash register than she recalled.

A customer laughed at something the clerk said. Greer judged both men to be a bit older than her almost twenty-seven years. It was hard to tell until her eyes adjusted. But she was reassured that something *had* changed. Affable LeRoy Tanner, a contemporary of Greer's dad, obviously no longer owned the store. LeRoy and his wife had been fixtures in town forever, it seemed.

In her sporadic letters, Greer's mother had indicated that a number of old-time residents had fallen on hard luck and left town.

A booming voice addressed Greer by name, and she snapped her head around. Realizing it was one of the men at the counter, she squinted to see better.

Shelby abandoned the Madam Alexander doll she was inspecting to burrow into Greer's side. "Mama, that man knows you," she said in a stage whisper.

Greer cleared her throat. "I'm sorry, you…ah…have me at a disadvantage. I'm still sun-blind." She was pretty sure it was the clerk who'd spoken, yet it was the customer who galvanized her attention. A good two inches shorter but broader-shouldered than the clerk, the customer wore typical rancher garb—square-heeled boots, blue jeans and a long-sleeved cotton shirt. It was his arresting blue eyes under a worn baseball cap that gave her pause. Not your typical cowboy, but in spite of the general consensus, there was more to Texas than cowboys.

"I'm Edmond Tanner," the clerk said, rounding the counter with his hand outstretched. "My dad, LeRoy, would've been here at the time you left. I've gotta confess, your hair gave you away. I'd've known those red curls even if Loretta hadn't told us you were due to get in today, Greer." His hearty chuckle was cut short by a rib-jab from his companion.

"Oops, forgive my bad manners." Edmond cocked his thumb like a pistol. "I figured you two knew each other. Greer…Noah Kelley. Er…I reckon I oughta call him *Father* Kelley. With your dad being on the church board and all, I assumed Loretta had passed on the news about Father Holden's stroke. We're lucky the greater regional Episcopal council saw fit to let Noah fill in until his pop's back on his feet."

Greer reeled at the announcement and did a double take. Now she remembered Noah Kelley. They'd both been much younger. And he had certainly changed. Holden's son used to wear his hair slicked down. He'd looked—well, stiff in starched white shirts and the requisite Sunday suit.

Noah responded to the lengthy introduction with a dismissive shrug. "I'd probably graduated from college and entered seminary before you got out of high school, so there's no reason you'd know I ended up an associate priest at a church in Austin for…oh, more years than I care to think about. Time sure flies."

Ed Tanner stroked his chin. "You're gettin' old, Noah. I forgot your mom recently ordered a cake for your, uh, thirty-second birthday wasn't it?"

"Thirty-first," Noah said, playfully aiming a punch at Ed's bony arm. "Years come and years go. Think how long you've been an old married man, Ed. Why don't we forget age and just welcome Greer home." Noah's eyes rested on her briefly. "I do remember you," he said after a pause. "You wore pigtails and were nearer the age of—is the charming girl at your side your daughter?"

"Yep, my name is Shelby," the child piped up without a shred of modesty.

Noah's teeth flashed in a grin. "Well, I hope I'll have the privilege of seeing both of you lovely ladies again soon. At church on Sunday?"

"No, you won't," Greer shot back so quickly it surprised everyone. "We haven't even moved in yet." She grabbed Shelby's hand and hurriedly collected a shopping cart. How did she tell the local Episcopal priest that she hadn't darkened a church door since she'd left Homestead—because his dad had been instrumental in convincing her parents to send her into exile? Noah Kelley was a sneaky one. Not only didn't he resemble any man of God Greer had ever seen, where the heck was his identifying collar? How dared he go about town looking like an ordinary rancher.

"Come on, Shelby, let's start with vegetables." Greer aimed her cart toward the very back of the store where she remembered Tanner's displayed fresh produce. *Talk about bad luck.* Of all the people she'd give anything not to run into here in Homestead, a relative of Father Holden Kelley topped her list.

In the occasional letters Greer received from her mom, Loretta Bell had probably avoided mentioning Holden or any member of his church board on purpose. No surprise there, given the shouting match they'd all had ten years ago.

NOAH EXCHANGED a blank look with Ed. Intrigued, he excused himself and hurried down the aisle after the woman and girl. He caught up quickly because Shelby had stopped to inspect a rack of kids' books. "My invitation to attend church remains open for whenever you get settled, Greer. Attendance at St. Mark's fell off even before Pop's stroke. My main goal is to recapture the strayed or lost," he said, turning up the wattage on a slightly crooked smile. "I'd especially like to entice back young families such as yours." Noah's bright gaze again shifted to Shelby. "You'd be eight or nine? We have a growing Sunday school that would gladly make room for one more. Perhaps your mom remembers Debra Coleville, or she may have been Debra Rooney then. She teaches a combined second- and third-grade class."

Shelby hugged the book. "Will some of the kids be in my third grade at regular school? I just turned nine."

"I think Megan Ritter's eight. Her sister, Heather, is six or seven, and their brother, Brad, is nine. So's Callie Montgomery's sister, Brittany. And…the Gallaghers have a range of ages," he said, rattling off a stream of names.

Some sounded vaguely familiar. Greer scrabbled through her mind but was unable to place anyone specific except for Gallagher. Every Texan knew State Senator Clint Gallagher.

"Mama, if I met some kids Sunday, I'd have friends for when I start school next week."

Greer released her breath and gave a severe shake of her head. "I said no, Shelby. We need every waking hour to get the ranch cottages ready for our paying guests. Church is out of the question."

Glancing between mother and child, Noah offered what he thought was a compromise. "I understand you and your husband are probably anxious to spruce things up in order to get your business off the ground. You could send Shelby with her grandparents."

Pulling herself up to her full five-foot-three inch height, Greer let stormy eyes rake the much taller man's guileless expression. "Shelby's never met my parents. And for the record…I don't have a husband. Now, if you'll excuse us, I'd like to finish shopping so we can get out to our ranch before the movers show up."

Spinning on one heel, she sped down an adjacent aisle, uncaring that she'd been rude to a man of the cloth. She didn't let up her mad dash until she reached the bins of vegetables and began pitching items willy-nilly into her cart.

Shelby finally found her. "Yuck, Mama. We don't eat turnips. And what's that green stuff with the red edges?"

Greer frowned at her cart. "It's chard. On second thought, these greens will probably spoil before I have a chance to use them." Meekly she put back the chard and some lettuce snatched up in her hasty attempt to escape Noah Kelley. *Father Noah!*

Greer's heart tripped fast. It would be better if Noah did resemble his formidable dad. Instead the son had straw-blond hair that fell appealingly over a suntanned brow. Standing a good six feet in boots, Noah's worn blue jeans fit his long legs as if sculpted. Even at a distance, Greer had been aware of eyes the color of a Hill Country sky. Up close, once he'd taken off his cap, those same blue eyes surely saw straight into her guilty soul.

Now why would she think that? She was guilty of nothing! She threw baking potatoes haphazardly into a paper bag. Father Noah would change his tune fast enough. As soon as his ailing dad clued him in about her ignominious fall from grace.

It seemed so long since she'd raced home from college in East Texas, heartsick and needing comfort. Instead she'd endured hearing Father Holden advise her folks to send her to Denver to live with her dad's sister—so she could adopt out her illegitimate child. Oh, he'd made it plain she wasn't the first girl in their parish to be shuffled off. Any girl in her predicament set a bad example, for their congregation, he said.

Greer's dad, one of St. Mark's loyal board members, went along with it. That still hurt. Even after all these years—or so she gathered, reading between the lines of her mom's sparse letters—Robert Bell hadn't changed his stance. Greer had hoped that with the passing of time, and with her added maturity, it'd be possible to get over the past. Maybe not.

She still quaked inside as she recalled what a humiliating experience that had been at seventeen. It wasn't as if she didn't already feel like dirt over being duped and dumped by a college senior she'd thought loved her. In truth, Dan Harper couldn't shed her or his responsibility for a baby fast enough. When her parents and her church turned against her, too, that had been the worst blow.

"Mama, can I get this cereal?" Shelby ran back to the cart with a box of a kid-popular variety her mother rarely let her eat.

Greer opened her mouth to refuse, but saw shadows

lurking in Shelby's eyes that she recognized. A favorite cereal spelled comfort to a nine-year-old. Mom and child had left behind everything in Shelby's world.

Gently, Greer pushed aside her daughter's overlong bangs. "Okay, but when this is gone, it'll be stick-to-the-ribs oatmeal for a while. Or whatever Cook whips up for our paying guests."

"We have a cook?"

"Not yet. I plan to hire someone as soon as we make our guest ranch livable. We need to book guests ASAP. Until then, though, it's just you and me, kid."

Shelby hugged the box to her thin chest. "Maybe Grandma and Grandpa Bell will invite us to their house for dinner tonight. My friend, Rhonda Ann, in Colorado—she ate dinner at her grandma's a lot."

Greer winced. "Don't get your hopes up, Shel. My parents lead busy lives. You and I, ah, are going to be busy, too. Remember what I told you about Mayor Wright saying our new place is a fixer-upper?"

"Yeah." Shelby dropped the cereal in the cart next to a gallon of milk her mother had taken from the cooler. "Mayor M'randa said our place needs cleaning and painting. That's why Mr. and Mrs. Sanderson gave us a bunch of paint before we moved. So we can get straight to work, right?"

"Right. Miranda said the previous owner of our ranch let it go downhill. That paint was a very generous gift from the Sandersons," Greer added, thinking fondly of her previous employers at the dude ranch in Colorado. "I hope paint and elbow grease is all it takes to make it presentable for guests."

Shelby darted down the next aisle, where she located their brand of peanut butter. She placed the jar in their cart, and Greer tossed in a loaf of bread and some jam, sensing her daughter's desire to leave. Greer, too, was dying to see their property so she could assess what needed doing.

"Okay, Shel, I think we have enough here so we won't starve for a few days. All our talk about settling in has made me want to hurry and get there. Shall we go pay for our stuff?"

"Can I push the cart? Oh, and can I buy the book I showed you? It's about a girl who grew up in Texas." She latched on to the cart handle, all the while bouncing up and down on her toes. She did slow where two aisles intersected.

"I don't know about buying the book today. I need your help to put the house in order. I know you, Shelby Book Worm. Once you bury your nose in a story, you tune out the whole world. And how do I know? Because you're just like me." Greer tweaked her daughter's shoulder-length coppery hair. "I'll ask Mr. Tanner to hold the book for you. It'll be your special treat for helping me clean up around the ranch."

"O…kay!" Shelby was generally agreeable. "Mama, where are the other shoppers? Look at all this neat-o stuff. How come nobody's here 'cept the clerk and the man who told us about church?"

Greer secretly hoped Father Noah Kelley had made himself scarce. Shelby had always been a kid with a million questions. "You remember how, after I started working for Cal and Marisa Sanderson at Whippoorwill Ranch, we only shopped every two weeks? We drove into Denver. Those stores are huge compared to the ones in Homestead. Everything's bigger there, and there's way more people. We've come to a small town, Shelby."

"Yeah, I told my teacher I was scared to leave Colorado. She said I was lucky to be going to a small town. She said kids in small towns stay friends forever and ever. Is that true, Mama? You never talk about friends from here. But you said you were born in Homestead and lived here until you went away to college."

*How did she explain to Shelby that her good memories of
growing up in Homestead were erased by what had happened
during her first year of college? A year that had vastly
changed her life?...* "Honeybun, people move in and out of
small towns, too. And Mr. Tanner remembered me. So did
Mayor Wright. In fact, Miranda said she'll drop by to make
sure we get in okay this afternoon. If I remember correctly,
Miranda's three years older than me. So is Ed Tanner. I'm sure
we'll run into some of my other classmates, too."

"Okay." Shelby sighed as they approached the counter.
Greer was relieved to see that one particular customer had left.

"I wish you were still friends with Father Kelley. Then we
could go to his church on Sunday, and I'd hurry up and meet
kids my age."

The truth was that Greer had been hoping against hope that
Holden Kelley had been among the people who'd pulled out
of Homestead, a part of an exodus that had led to Miranda
Wright's land giveaway. The mayor almost didn't get her
program approved by the council. But Greer knew how
stubborn farmers like her dad, not to mention powerful
ranchers like Senator Clint Gallagher, could be. She could
easily imagine the difficulties Miranda had experienced.

According to the article Greer had read in the one newspaper her mom had sent, some residents resisted Miranda's
plan, calling it stupid. If not for that article, which had caught
Greer's interest, she would never have checked out the land
deal. Personally she was thankful, although she had received
a couple of unsigned letters suggesting she look at parcels
other than the Farley ranch. The mayor said to pay them no
mind. Despite the resistance of some residents, similar plans
had been successful in repopulating dying communities in
other states.

The idea made sense to Greer. The town's treasury purchased abandoned farms, ranches and homes for unpaid back taxes. Parcels were then offered to entice people to relocate. For people like her, who'd never otherwise be able to scrape together a down payment, low-cost loans could be obtained in exchange for agreeing to live on the land for a year. At times, Greer had to pinch herself to believe she might actually realize her dream of owning her own guest ranch.

As she set their groceries on the counter, Greer checked around for Father Kelley. Presumably he'd taken off.

Ed Tanner talked nonstop as he scanned and bagged her groceries. "So you haven't seen the Farley place? Jase didn't leave the Dragging F in very good shape. Did I hear right, you're planning to open a dude ranch by Thanksgiving?"

"I prefer the term guest ranch. But yes. I've been the assistant manager at a similar spread in Colorado, and my boss there thinks I'm capable of running my own place. I intend it to be a working ranch. One that lets city folks experience a bit of the real West." She made room on the counter for the milk. "I should probably research a brand. I can't imagine people would be in any rush to pay money to stay at a ranch called the Dragging F." Greer rolled her eyes at Shelby and the two giggled.

Ed laughed, too, as he handed Greer her change and offered to help tote her purchases to the car. "Farley lost a bundle of cash in that failed consortium, just like Nate Cantrell, Zeb Ritter, your dad and others. Jase's mistake was in mortgaging the Dragging F to the hilt in order to buy in. When they went belly-up, he lost it all. Everyone lost their savings, some more than others. At least your pa had his farm to fall back on."

Hating to admit she didn't know what Ed was talking about—that she hadn't known her dad was involved in a consortium—Greer murmured a response and made a mental note to find out more. Jointly owned ranches were common in Colorado.

At the Blazer, she unlocked and opened the back. "Thanks for carrying the heavy stuff out for us, Ed."

He stepped aside to let her shut the door. "Good luck, Greer. And take care. You're gonna live on the outskirts of civilization, wedged between the river and Clint Gallagher's back forty. Eight or nine years ago, a developer said Homestead could be the next boomtown. He threw up a couple of spec ranchettes, but then there was a drought and a downturn in the economy, followed by foreclosures. His grandiose plans went straight to…well, you fill in the blank," Ed said, eyeing Shelby.

That information was more than Greer had heard, too. Now the decline of Homestead made sense—droughts were the bane of a rancher's existence. "Thanks again, Ed. We'd better head out, since we have a ways to drive."

"Next time you're in town, maybe my wife'll be working and I can introduce you. Lorrie and I met at college. She's from Big Springs. My folks retired five years ago, and my brothers moved to Dallas, wanting bigger and better things. I like it here, and I'm grateful that Tanner's is still the easiest place to shop. Oh, there's a Wal-Mart on the road to San Antonio, and some like the variety they offer and are willing to make the drive. Most aren't." Ed reached the sidewalk and gave a half wave.

Greer held the door for Shelby. "I won't pretend the lack of progress makes me as ecstatic as it does you. Frankly, I'd hoped to buy supplies closer to my ranch."

"Your next investment should probably be a good commercial freezer. And if there isn't one, add a storage pantry. Jase catered to hunters, but he wasn't much on amenities."

"I barely remember Mr. Farley." Pursing her lips, Greer slid under the steering wheel. She saw major dollar signs flashing before her eyes. She had some savings and a line of credit. Big-ticket items could kill her budget if she wasn't careful.

Shelby bounced up and down in her seat, trying to see everything as Greer drove out of town. "Mama, when will our horses and sheep be delivered? Back home, Luke Sanderson had a dog of his very own. Can I have one, too?"

"I'm not taking delivery of any stock until I assess the condition of our barn and corrals. As for a dog, Shelby, we'll need to discuss that later."

"Why?"

"Because you'll be in school, and I'll have my hands full seeing to guests. Let's talk about this next summer when you're home to feed and train a dog."

"Summer?" Shelby flung herself back against the seat. "That's so far away, Mama. It was just summer. It's gonna be a long time till we have another one."

Saying nothing, Greer veered left down a gravel road. Until Ed Tanner brought it up, she hadn't given much thought as to how far from town her ranch was. And she'd expected houses to have sprung up along the Farm-to-Market road. Clearly they had not.

Braking at the end of a long gravel driveway, she drew Shelby's attention to a lopsided sign hanging from a post— a sign announcing they were about to enter the Dragging F. Excitement inside the Blazer was palpable. Maybe that was why Greer felt so let down when she stopped in front of a less-than-stellar ranch.

Shelby was the first to utter a sentiment Greer shared. "Ugh, I hope this isn't our new home. It looks…well, awful."

With a trembling foot, Greer set her emergency brake before switching off the Blazer's engine. "We knew it needed work," she ventured, attempting a cheery tone.

Shelby joined Greer outside the Blazer and the two clung together. "Listen, so it's seen better days, Shel. There's nothing a scrubbing and a few coats of paint won't fix. Let's look around." Greer pulled out a key Miranda had mailed her. Clearly none was needed. The front door had a hole where a lock mechanism should have been.

Their exploration was cut short when an older, dark-green sedan pulled in. The driver parked behind the Blazer and Greer reeled as her mother stepped out. Rollicking emotions ranging from anxiety to joy set Greer's heart banging like a tambourine. Loretta had aged. Oh, she was still lithe, trim and neatly turned out, but deep lines etched her face and neck. And her once-vibrant red hair had gone brassy.

"Is that the mayor?" a curious Shelby inquired.

Greer's throat had closed and tears hampered her ability to respond. All she could do was shake her head. *No, no, no,* galloped through her brain. She couldn't handle one more disappointment today. Not on top of seeing the town, meeting Holden Kelley's son, then finding her and Shelby's dream home so decrepit.

Loretta Bell quickly removed a mop, bucket and broom from her back seat. She slowly approached the duo standing on the porch. Suddenly, with a small cry of delight, she dropped everything and went down on one knee in front of the granddaughter she'd only seen via yearly photographs.

Uncharacteristically shy all at once, Shelby edged closer to Greer and looked up at her mother for instructions on how she should react.

Through a haze of tears, Greer noticed that Loretta had held out her arms, but then let them fall. In that one brief moment, Greer realized that it took guts for Loretta to show up unannounced, since she had no idea how she'd be received.

Releasing a sob, Greer hastily mumbled introductions. Bridging the gap, taking the initiative, she gathered her mom and her daughter into a trembling hug. Three generations of Bell women sank down on a sagging porch step. They all talked at the same time and alternately laughed and cried together until Loretta jumped up and collected her cleaning tools.

In a voice still husky from tears, she said, "I took time off work to help you make this place livable." She let a worried gaze rest momentarily on Greer. "Your father is…uh…busy cutting hay." She quickly turned aside. "The truth is, Greer," she said in an unsteady voice, "He's too stubborn to let bygones be bygones. Yet, everything that's happened has taken its toll on Robert's health. He splits his days between the farm and church work." Raising a slender wrist, Loretta checked her watch. "He'll expect lunch on the table at noon as always, so I can only stay a couple of hours. As much as I'd like to sit and talk, we need to dig in."

A stab of sadness affected Greer's breathing. She ought to have suspected that her parents still cared first and foremost for each other. Then came their devotion to church, jobs, and last to their only child. A mother herself now, Greer didn't think she'd ever subscribe to that concept. She'd never let Shelby take a back seat to anyone or anything. If ever she met a man she'd consider marrying, he'd have to understand going in that her love would be divided equally. Perhaps it shouldn't have been such a shock that her parents had shipped her off to live with a stern, rigid aunt. Greer had always been a tagalong in her parents' lives.

Following Loretta and Shelby as they chatted about inconsequential things throughout a depressing tour of the house, cottages, bunkhouse and a barn that had no door at all, Greer wondered if in coming home she'd made the second mistake of a lifetime. Had she idealized this opportunity? Was she crazy to think it spelled a future for Shelby?

True, the mayor had been a huge cheerleader for her program, but truer still, Greer had latched on to the deal with gusto.

Over the next hour as the trio worked together, her worries began to fade. Her mom's chatter spurred Greer over her disappointment with the dilapidated place.

"I have a bolt of cloth at home guaranteed to brighten this kitchen," Loretta said. "Greer, come help me measure these windows. Tonight I'll sew up red-and-white-checked valances and curtains. Add a coat of white enamel to these cupboards, and your guests will gravitate to this room."

Greer accepted one end of the tape measure. As she did so, a blue GMC pickup pulled in. Within seconds, Homestead's mayor bore down on the house, swinging a galvanized bucket swathed in a bright red ribbon in one hand; in the other she carried a steaming pie plate. Shelby ran to open the door.

A tall woman who could be called statuesque, Miranda Wright wore jeans with panache. Her mink-brown ponytail swept her shoulders as she thrust the bucket into Greer's hands. "Welcome to Homestead. I could've brought you a plant, but you'll get more use out of a hammer, nails, screwdriver, paintbrushes, gloves and assorted tools. The dried-peach pie is courtesy of my mother, Nan. Oh, Loretta, hi. You know how Mom loves to bake. I assume my able escort is none other than Shelby?" A yellow Lab trotting at Miranda's heels claimed Shelby's attention. "That's Dusty," Miranda said, then asked a question about school. As Shelby petted the dog, they discussed the local elementary. Miranda said, "How cool is it that your grandma teaches math at the high school across the street from where you'll be going?"

"I didn't know that." Shelby's hand hovered over the dog. "So maybe I won't feel so bad not knowing any kids. At the store in town, Mama met a man who invited us to church. He said I'd meet kids my age. But Mama said we can't go, 'cause we've got so much work here."

Miranda, who noticed Greer staring at something outside the kitchen window, stepped over to have a look. "Ah, I wondered what was so engaging. Looks good, huh? That's Noah Kelley, exercising one of his horses by the river. Is he the man Shelby meant? Did he mention he bought one of the two mini-ranches bordering the eastern edge of your property?"

"What?" Greer spun around, wearing a frown.

Miranda just grinned. "Yeah, I know his mom's on the Home Free committee, but the ranchettes aren't part of our package. Anyway, he didn't want to displace his folks from the rectory, since they've lived there for probably forty years. Neither did he want to move home, which I'm sure you can understand."

Feeling confused, Greer slipped out to the back porch, where she was able to identify that the rider was indeed *Father* Kelley. "I thought you said my property butted up against Clint Gallagher's grassland," she muttered.

Miranda pointed in the opposite direction. "Yes, and you'll probably need to rebuild those buckled fence sections. The senator opposed our land giveaway. Another thing—I know the guy you worked for in Colorado recommended you run sheep instead of cattle, but old-time cattlemen are never comfortable having sheep move in. Clint rents deer leases, too. I'm sure you realize hunting season's right around the corner."

"Gr…eat!" Greer blew her bangs out of her eyes. She'd rather fence off Noah Kelley, who was actually trespassing. However, if she did that, she'd cut her stock off from water. What had made this ranch so appealing was its proximity to the Clear River.

Her attention remained focused on Noah, who sat the pinto like a seasoned cowboy. Her insides curled, and Greer almost missed her mom calling from inside the kitchen that she had to leave. Hurrying to walk Loretta out, Greer saw Noah's home, visible through a stand of weeping cypress nearer the river. A long-ball pitcher could, without much effort, smack his brick chimney, which gleamed in the nearly noontime sun. Miranda whistled for Dusty, announcing that she had to leave, too, and Greer thanked both women for stopping by. As they turned their vehicles around, she wondered what had possessed her to think Homestead could be her utopia. Every bit of her old baggage, plus some that was new, had already begun piling up on her doorstep.

But Father Kelley did indeed look good....

CHAPTER TWO

GREER'S VISITORS exited her lane, headed toward Homestead and soon disappeared. Rotating her neck a few times to ease a growing tension, Greer glanced back at her ranch and sighed. Outside, the house looked no different, but somehow felt lonelier.

"When's our furniture going to get here, Mama?" Shelby skipped alongside Greer as they again climbed the steps to the wraparound porch.

"The company estimated late afternoon, honeybun. We have time to get a lot of work done before they show up with our things."

"Dontcha think this is the perfect spot to hang the porch swing the Sandersons gave us? It's in the Blazer. We can hang it now, can't we?"

"That's a great idea, Shelby. It'll put our mark on this place and make it feel homey. I'll fetch the swing. See if you can locate that package of screws Miranda brought. Then I'll grab the ladder I saw when we toured the bunkhouse."

The task of hanging the swing proved to be anything but easy. Greer had worked up a sweat by the time she got the last screw into the knotty pine planking someone had installed as a porch ceiling. But, once she'd succeeded in wrestling the slatted swing onto its chain hangers, the effect was wonderfully inviting. She and Shelby ran into the yard to admire their handiwork, all the while grinning at each other.

"I get to try it out first," Shelby shouted. She charged up the steps, then suddenly stopped short to stare into the distance at the horse and rider, once again visible by the river. "I sure do wish Mr. Kelley would ride up here to see us. That's a pretty horse he has. Do you think he'd give me a ride?"

"Shelby, you need to call him Father Kelley, not mister."

"He's not *my* father." The girl pouted a little.

"No. The title *Father* is like saying *Doctor.* It shows respect."

"Does it mean I can't ask to ride his horse?"

Greer reluctantly looked over at Noah Kelley. He'd dismounted and was letting the animal drink from a shallow spot. "It's not as if he's a friend. Even if he rides out our way, I'd rather you didn't ask him for favors. Anyway, remember the sooner we make progress getting our home livable, the quicker we'll bring in our horses. How about if I let you decide what room we start cleaning next?"

"Cleaning's no fun," Shelby grumbled. "Grandma said before she left that we need to wash all the windows. Especially the ones in the kitchen so that when she brings the curtains tomorrow we can hang them."

"Are you sure you want to wash windows? I'm going to put white vinegar in the water to cut through the grime built up on the glass. I know you hate the way vinegar smells."

Shelby wrinkled her nose. Trooper that she was, she reached for the second bucket.

"Let's do the inside first, Shel. Then I'll change the water and we can start outside. I'll tackle the taller windows that require a ladder. You wash whatever you can reach from the porch."

"Okay." Shelby ripped open a pack of sponges and plopped a green one in her bucket and a pink one in her mother's. "Grandma's nice," she remarked out of the blue, and followed with a question Greer had been dreading. "I don't understand why Grandpa couldn't come with her. Is he mean?"

Greer dropped her wet sponge, then hurriedly bent to retrieve it. "I wouldn't call him mean. Do you remember Mr. Greenfield the man who rented that cabin next to ours at Whippoorwill Ranch every summer? The artist?"

Shelby nodded. "Yeah, he was real grumpy."

Using a dry rag, Greer carefully polished the window she'd finished washing. "He did tend to growl, and he wasn't a very good neighbor. Cal said the man was estranged from his son. They'd argued. Well—" she took a deep breath "—a long time ago, before you were born, my dad got really upset with me. You know how I tell you we have to talk out our differences and not go to bed mad because it only gets harder to make up? My dad and I didn't talk. We've let ten years worth of nights go by without making up. That's why he didn't come today. I don't want you to think the way he acts has anything to do with you, Shel. It doesn't."

"If my teacher was around, she would've sat you guys down and *made* you talk. She'd say, get over it! 'Cause that's what she did when kids argued at recess."

Smiling, Greer moved to a new window. "That works with kids. Dad and I weren't kids. Adults can be stubborn and pig-headed a lot longer."

"I wish one of you would just say you're sorry, so then maybe I could ask Grandma if I can ride to church on Sunday with her and Grandpa." Shelby shoved her bucket over and started on the window in the kitchen door.

Greer's fingers stilled, then tightened on the sponge, and she scrubbed so hard she was in danger of breaking the pane of glass. Explaining this was going to be much more difficult than she'd ever imagined. Yes, Shelby had gone to church with Luke Sanderson, but their views were liberal. St. Mark's was ultraconservative. Coming here was probably a bad plan. What had she been thinking?

"Shelby, hon, chores go by faster with music. Will you run and get the portable CD player from the Blazer? And bring the CD case from under the front seat." Greer knew that would redirect her daughter. There were few things Shelby loved as much as listening to music.

Over the next hour or so, they sang along with the CDs and managed to finish the inside windows. Greer filled the buckets with fresh water. She placed Shelby's under the living room window and carried hers around the corner, calling, "I'll set up the ladder and do the side windows. Wow, it looks like all but the front one will be too high for you. So, when you finish it, hon, empty your bucket and take a break. You've worked hard today. I'm proud of you."

Reacting to the compliment, Shelby gave her mom a hug before dancing away.

Sparkling windows and a gently swaying swing made a huge difference to the appearance of the house, Greer thought as she opened the ladder and climbed up with the bucket. She'd dried the last pane and had closed the ladder to carry it around front when she heard the clippity-clop of an approaching horse. Afraid she knew who to expect as she rounded the house, Greer saw something she *didn't* expect. Her daughter stood on a wobbly porch railing, stretched full length, scrubbing a window too far out of reach.

Greer opened her mouth to shout. She might even have called out to Shelby, but her warning came too late. There was a loud crack as the rail separated from the house. Greer's yelp of distress mingled with Shelby's scream of fear as the girl fell to the ground below, tangled in wood spindles and broken boards.

Dropping the ladder, stumbling over it, Greer lost precious seconds in her attempt to reach Shelby. The girl's sobs sent fear hammering through Greer's heart. "Honey, lie still. Let me move the boards and see how badly you're hurt." She discovered that Shelby had somehow ended up beneath the four-by-four top rail. Greer was in such a state, it took extra moments before she realized a second, larger pair of hands had brushed hers aside and were even now removing the heaviest debris.

"Oh, Father Kelley, it's you!" Wild-eyed, Greer stared blankly up. Just as fast, she sank to her knees and attempted to drag her sobbing child into her arms.

"Take it easy, Greer. She's suffered a nasty fracture of her left forearm."

The minute he made the observation, Greer's eyes were drawn to a V-shaped indentation five inches above Shelby's wrist. Merely seeing it sent bile rolling from Greer's stomach to her throat. She swayed unsteadily. But looking at the terrible break also steadied her cartwheeling emotions. "We need a doctor. I don't know who's in town. Is there anyone? I used to see a doctor in Llano. He was old, so I'm sure by now he's retired or dead. Wait! There's Hill Country Memorial hospital in Fredericksburg. But it's quite a drive," she added worriedly.

Noah ignored her babble, calming Shelby by asking pertinent questions about pain, all the while carefully checking her for neck, back and leg injuries. "Greer," he said at last, "outside of the arm she mostly has superficial scrapes and bruises. Homestead has a clinic now. It's staffed by a competent physician's assistant. Kristin Cantrell—er, that *was* her name. She recently got married. Dr. Louise Hernandez comes every Wednesday to check on cases."

"You think I should take Shelby to a P.A.?"

"Yes. Will you see if you can find a magazine? It's the best I can think of at the moment to manufacture a splint. Meanwhile, I'll phone the clinic and make sure Kristin's in. On Friday afternoon if it's slow, she takes calls from her house."

Keeping a soothing hand curved over Shelby's shoulder to ensure she lay still, Noah unclipped his cell phone and punched in a number one-handed.

Glad to have a specific chore, Greer dashed off. If only her moving van had come, she would've had magazines readily available. At first she thought finding anything suitable was a lost cause, but then she saw that her mother had left a stack of old newspapers in the box with gloves and paintbrushes. Layering several together, Greer ran back with them as Noah clicked off his phone.

"We're in luck," he said, shooting her a confident smile. "I caught Kristin as she was ready to walk out the door. She'll meet you at the clinic." Relieving Greer of the papers, he fashioned a splint using several thicknesses. As he peered around for something to secure the splint, Noah noticed that Greer wore laced sneakers. He had on boots and Shelby's sneakers closed with Velcro. Greer jerked her foot back as he untied and began pulling out her right shoelace.

Once she realized what he intended, she tried to help. Only her hands shook too much to deal effectively with the knot on her left shoe. She gave up and let him do it. Greer leaned over and brushed a kiss on Shelby's forehead, whispering to her softly.

While Noah worked to stabilize the broken arm, he attempted to explain the clinic's location to Greer. "You know what?" He broke off, gazing at her with a perplexed frown. "You're in no condition to drive anywhere." Tying the second lace, he leaped agilely to his feet. "Just give me a minute to unsaddle Jasper and turn him out in your corral. I'll carry Shelby to your SUV. You and she can sit in the backseat. I'll drive you to town."

Greer started to object. But after an inspection of her hands, she realized how badly she was shaking, and quickly reconsidered. "You can't put your horse in our corral. Several rail sections are down. I'm pretty sure I have a lead rope under the back seat of the Blazer. That cedar looks sturdy, and there's plenty of shade. Will he be all right tied on a lead?"

"He'll be fine." The words were barely out of Noah's mouth before he'd pulled off Jasper's saddle and placed it on the porch behind the swing. He made short work of staking out his pinto, then hurried back to Shelby's side. "I'll be as careful as I can moving you to the car, squirt, but I won't lie—it'll probably hurt. You go right ahead and cry, if you need to, okay?"

She did, with loud gulping sobs.

Despite her earlier thoughts, Greer was grateful that Noah Kelley had appeared out of nowhere when he had. She dropped her purse twice after belatedly remembering to run in and retrieve it from the kitchen counter where she'd tossed it that morning.

"Are you all right?" Noah murmured, steadying Greer with a hand to her waist as she climbed into the backseat of the Blazer and ended up tripping over a loose, floppy sneaker. "Whoa there." He scooped up her shoe. Clasping her upper arms, he turned her to face him. "You're very pale. Are you in danger of fainting?"

"I'm fine. Well, no, I'm not. I'm queasy as all heck." She put a shaking hand to her head. "Considering Shel's a tomboy, I'm surprised this is our first incident of its kind. But it is, and it's unnerving as anything. I promise to get a grip, Father Kelley. And I won't forget I owe you for all the help you've given me today."

Noah had finally managed to settle her next to Shelby and restore her dangling shoe. He shut her door and slid into the driver's seat, and for a heartbeat he let his eyes connect with hers in the rearview mirror. He scowled as he shoved the seat back a few notches to accommodate his longer legs. "Just being neighborly," he said tersely. "No payment required or wanted."

Backing out with a spinning of wheels, Noah swung from the lane to graveled road with a bump that had Shelby crying out in pain.

"Sorry, peanut." He was more careful after that to miss chuckholes. Before long, he engaged the injured child in subjects he thought might interest her in order to take her mind off her pain. He discovered that like him, she loved horses and dogs. She nattered on about Miranda's dog, Dusty. Shelby had owned a horse in Denver, and from what he gathered she'd have another once the corrals were secure. The matter of a dog was obviously a touchier issue between the girl and her mother. Shelby pulled a sad face and announced, "Mama says I've gotta wait till next summer to get a dog. I don't wanna wait that long. I told her I can train him after school, and he can sleep on the floor in my room. He'd be good company for when I come home from school, too. Especially since I don't have any friends to play with way out here."

Greer, who was supporting Shelby's broken arm, reached over with her free hand and lightly pressed two fingers to her daughter's mouth.

But the girl kept talking. She rattled on about what kind of dogs she liked even after they'd parked and Noah carried her into the clinic. Greer tuned her out, he noticed. Either this was an old discussion, or she was still numb from the fright caused by the accident.

Kristin Gallagher met them at the door and after brief introductions, ushered them straight into a pristine examining room. Her blunt-cut strawberry-blond hair brushed the shoulders of her lab coat as she bent to remove Noah's splint.

He darted a guilty glance toward Greer. "Sorry about that. I didn't know she'd cut your laces. Maybe a store in town has spares."

"Not to worry. I'm sure I have extras in one of my moving boxes. I generally wear boots to work around the ranch, anyway." Nervous, Greer paced the small room and read the plaques hanging on the walls. According to them, Kristin possessed B.S. degrees in nursing and psych, plus was certified as a physician's assistant.

The P.A. focused her attention on her patient. "I usually see a lot of injuries like this the day school opens. But that's been a few weeks. Were you swinging on the monkey bars?" she teased Shelby.

"I was helping Mama wash windows at our new ranch." Shelby sniffled and wiped her good hand across a runny nose.

Kristin gave her a tissue, but aimed a sharp look at Greer's bowed shoulders, as if she wondered whether her new patient might be the victim of parental abuse.

Before Greer could speak, Shelby herself disabused Kristin of that thought. "Mama said the only window I was supposed to wash was the one I could reach from standing on the porch. I figured the porch rail was wide enough to hold me. It was old and rickety, I guess."

Visibly relieved, Kristin handed Greer a clipboard filled with a colorful packet of forms. "Maybe you could complete Shelby's medical history for me while I set up to X-ray her arm. I gave our receptionist and my assistant the day off."

Greer took the clipboard. "I was so rattled when Shelby fell. I'm sorry I didn't think to bring her vaccination record.

Really, she's been remarkably well except for the occasional winter cold that everyone in Denver seems to get."

"You're from Denver?" Kristin moved a portable X-ray unit from one side of the examining table to the other.

Noah, who lounged with a shoulder negligently propped against the casing of the open door, hurried to help her. He supplied a missing piece of information. "I happened to be out exercising Jasper and rode past their ranch at the time Shelby fell, so I volunteered to drive them to the clinic. Greer and Shelby are our new neighbors, Kristin. At the Dragging F."

Greer rolled her eyes. "Ghastly name. I may run a contest and have my first guests rename the ranch."

"I'm sorry this is your welcome to Homestead," Kristin said, grimacing. My father-in-law said Jase Farley was the type to get a kick out of a name like the Dragging F. I can't wait to go home and tell Ryan we now have good neighbors all the way between us and the river." She sent Noah a wide smile.

That comment caught Greer's attention. She swung her head between the two. "Oh, then you and your family live in the other ranchette? Ed Tanner said a developer had built two before the bottom fell out of the real estate market here."

"No. My husband, Ryan Gallagher, manages his dad's ranch. The Four Aces borders you on the north and east."

"Oh. Gallagher as in state senator?" Greer's eyes rose from the page she was filling out. "I, ah, used to live in Homestead. Garrett's a year younger than me, so I knew him the best of the Gallagher boys. If Trevor hasn't changed too much, I could probably pick him out of a crowd. Ryan…I'm guessing he's Garrett and Trevor's older brother?"

Kristin nodded. "Wow, so you've come home, too? Like Ryan and Miranda. And Callie Montgomery, but she'd been gone a long time. You likely haven't had a chance to eat at her café yet. Best family dining in town." Kristin removed the film plate. "I need to go develop this. There's no doubt that her arm's broken. I have to be sure the bones are aligned and that there's no restriction of blood." She smiled down at the supine child. "You lie still as a mouse until I get back. Let your mom finish those forms. Noah, you could take a seat in the waiting room. The new *Western Horseman* magazine is out there."

"Thanks, Kristin, but I'll stay and keep Shelby company. We're old buddies. We both like horses and dogs. She'll have a cast, right? Maybe I'll tell her about the time I broke my foot playing soccer and had to start my school year wearing one." He pulled up a chair and sat next to the exam table. "Casts aren't so bad. Everybody gives you sympathy, including teachers. And the kids all want to sign their names on the plaster."

If the P.A. leveled a questioning glance in Noah's direction, he was impervious. Shelby, it seemed, didn't want to talk about casts, but pumped him for information about the care and feeding of dogs. She asked about different breeds, and Noah shared what he knew. She prattled on even after Kristin returned.

"Alignment's good," the P.A. said. "But I still have to deaden the arm in order to straighten out the bones. If anyone's squeamish, you're excused."

Greer blanched but set the clipboard aside. Noah saw that pain filled her gold-flecked hazel eyes as she gently combed her fingers through Shelby's tangled hair. "Shel, I want you to hold my hand tight so Mrs. Gallagher can fix your arm good as new."

Noah rose to stand opposite her. "If you're not up to this, just say the word. I'll be glad to supply the muscle needed to hold her still."

The eyes Greer raised to meet his were glossy with tears, but he recognized in them a rock-steady determination. Reaching across Shelby's legs, Noah briefly squeezed Greer's hand. That move earned him a second inspection from Kristin, who made no remark, however, except to give Shelby permission to go right on talking about dogs. Which, of course, she did. Nonstop.

Later, Greer would think her daughter had brought up every pet a friend had owned, and remarked on every cat or dog she'd seen on the street. When Shelby's porous pink cast graced her arm from fingertips to just below her elbow, Greer's ears rang and her nerves were shot. But had Shelby run down? No. She examined the pros and cons of big and little dogs until she fell asleep on the drive home.

Noah let five minutes elapse before posing a worried question to Greer. "You've been very glum since we left the clinic. Is something wrong? Are you worried about her arm healing properly? Or is it a concern about not having insurance? I'm sorry, but I couldn't help overhearing you ask Kristin about a payment plan."

Greer leaned back and shut her eyes. "It's all of that and more. I think whoever said you could never go home again was right. I'm beginning to think chucking everything in Colorado to move here was a mistake. The condition of the ranch was bad omen number one. Shelby's accident is number two. I'm wondering what'll happen next."

"Where you went wrong," he snorted, "is believing there's such a thing as good and bad omens. Life is all about having faith in a higher power. Place your trust in His hands, Greer."

"Yeah, right! The last thing I need is a sermon." Her voice rose and woke Shelby, who started to cry, claiming her arm hurt.

Greer awkwardly gathered the gangly girl into a hug, not a simple matter because they both wore seat belts.

"Mama, will you ask Father Kelley to put in my favorite CD?"

"Shh, honey bunny, don't you remember I had you bring the CD case into the kitchen? We'll be home soon. Until our furniture arrives, I'll make you a bed on the porch swing and you can listen to music there."

"That's not going to be very comfortable," Noah interjected. "How about if we stop at your place and leave a note for your movers on the door with my phone number. You two can spend the afternoon at my house. I'm sure my living room couch is more comfortable than your porch swing. I'll ride another of my horses back to your ranch and collect Jasper."

"Thank you, but no," Greer said primly. "You've done quite enough. I wouldn't presume to take you away from the people in your congregation."

Noah could hardly miss the brittle edge to her voice. Every so often he slanted a curious glance in the mirror. Each time she pursed her lips and turned aside.

It was clear to Noah when he pulled in and stopped outside her house that Greer couldn't wait to see the last of him. Playing back the afternoon's events, he was unable to put a finger on what he might have done wrong. But he was a pretty good reader of body language. Greer wanted to carry Shelby from the Blazer to the porch swing without accepting his help. At nine, the kid wasn't much shorter than Greer. And she was all arms and legs. Shelby fretted, whined and cried, saying, "Ouch, Mama, I hurt. Please let *him* carry me. He's bigger and stronger."

The tears in Shelby's eyes moved Greer to give in, albeit reluctantly. She gathered up the blankets and pillows from the car that Shelby had curled up in on their driving trip. Bustling about, doing her level best to ignore Noah, Greer spread pillows and blankets on the swing so he could put Shelby down.

"Do you have a cell phone?"

"Yes," she said, but didn't elaborate or offer her number.

He reached for his wallet and took out a business card that listed his numbers at home and at the church office. He passed it to Greer. She stuffed the card in her purse, then abruptly went into the house. The screen door banged shut. She opened it just enough to tell Shelby, "Honey, you need to thank Father Kelley so he can get along home. I'm going to fetch the CD player and CDs."

Noah returned the wallet to his back pocket. Nothing in his beliefs said he had to hang around where he wasn't wanted. With a smile for Shelby, he grabbed his saddle from behind the swing where she now sat, her arm propped on a pile of pillows.

"Thanks for everything you did," she said, tearily. "Mama wouldn't like if I asked, but…will you come see me again tomorrow, Father Kelley?"

Hearing the woebegone tone of her request, Noah hesitated. "Maybe I'll ride over if you'll agree to call me Noah instead of Father Kelley. Tell your mom the same goes for her. Titles are too stuffy. After all, we're neighbors and I hope we'll be friends."

About that time he chanced to see Greer peering out a kitchen window—checking to see if he'd left. Her expression plainly said she wanted him gone before she put in another appearance on the porch. That meant he should backpedal on his promise.

"Actually, I may not be able to come by, Shelby. A man in my position doesn't have much free time. Tomorrow I need to work on a sermon. Saturday I coach a kids' basketball team. Sunday I have a full schedule. I know you don't feel like doing anything right now, but by Monday you'll be as good as new except for wearing a cast. And like I said, everyone you meet at school will want to sign their name on it. That's tradition."

"Will you sign it first?"

"The plaster's still too soft." Noah jogged down the steps, stirrups clanging as they slapped his leg. He slung the saddle over Jasper's back and tightened the cinch. "Kristin said if it wasn't for the fact that you broke both bones in that arm, she'd have used one of the newfangled inflatable casts. Take it from me, though, they're not as impressive as the one you got." Winking, he vaulted into the saddle.

"What's impres—" Clattering down the gravel path, he didn't hear her question.

Inside by the open window, Greer heard the entire exchange. Something cramped in her chest as she witnessed the easy, sexy way he had of mounting a horse.

Snatching up the CD player and several of Shelby's favorite disks, she poked her head out the window. "Father Kelley meant your cast is cool, Shel."

Drawing back, Greer noticed their moving van slowing to negotiate the turn into their lane. Darn, she could've used a few minutes to get more organized.

CANTERING OUT, Noah saw the big van make the sharp turn off the main road. If he was really a nice guy he'd go back and help the two men seated in the cab. Given the late hour, they'd be lucky to have everything unloaded by dark. Greer would be left with the chore of assembling beds and making them up. To say nothing of knocking together something for supper. His stomach growled, reminding him they'd all missed lunch.

He would've turned back if Greer Bell had shown the slightest indication that she'd appreciate his help. She hadn't. In fact she'd been testy almost from the moment they met. Noah had no illusions that if she'd had any other choice, she would've sent him packing when he showed up to untangle Shelby from the broken porch rail.

Crossing the point where their two property lines intersected, Noah kicked Jasper into a solid gallop, never once glancing back or letting on that he'd noticed the moving van headed into the Dragging F.

He'd have to quit referring to it as the Dragging F, especially considering the disgust Greer had expressed for the name today. Not that he wasn't in agreement. If he planned to see her again, which he now doubted, Noah would've suggested she name the ranch after the fantastic sunrises that rose daily over the river. *As if the woman would stand still for any advice from him.*

Again Noah wondered what he'd done to make her angry. Or did she dislike all men? He knew, of course, that some divorced women took back their maiden names. It was less common if that woman had kids, which Greer did. Come to think of it, what had she said earlier at Tanner's—that Shelby had never met her grandparents?

Robert Bell, Noah could imagine, since he was a crusty old guy. The type who was a law unto himself. One who took his job on the church board seriously—which also gave Noah pause. He'd refrained from telling his father that he was growing tired of the copious complaints from Holden's friends on the board about his lax style of handling church duties. Noah hadn't wanted to press a man recovering from a stroke. He knew his father well enough to figure they'd clash on other issues, too. After all, he'd lived in Holden's house for eighteen years. It was a given that they wouldn't see eye to eye on Noah's relaxed methods, his avoidance of Holden's hellfire-and-brimstone approach.

GREER STEPPED OUT on the porch carrying the things she'd gone in search of. The CD player needed an extension cord so she could plug it into an outlet and through an open window, and she busied herself doing that.

"Mama, Father Kelley said we're s'posed to call him Noah."

Flustered, Greer glowered at the fast-disappearing horse and rider. "We can't. It's not polite. Why would he say that?"

Shelby looked at her solemnly. "He said 'cause we're neighbors and he hopes that makes us friends."

Plugging the player's cord into the extension, Greer punched the on button. She straightened fast when Missy Elliott's latest hit tune exploded from the machine. The noise warred with the squeal of the moving van's brakes until she turned down the volume. "We'll talk about this later, Shel. I'm going to be very busy for the next couple of hours. If you need anything, yell loudly to get my attention."

"I need a dog," she yelled, a cheeky grin spreading over her face. "Did you hear Noah tell me he's going to get one? He's driving to the animal shelter next week. Can't we go with him?"

"Shelby Lynn Bell, no! And don't be calling Father Kelley by his first name, and I don't care what he said. Just because chance made us neighbors does not mean we'll be friends. Remember Mr. Greenfield?" Leaving it at that, Greer hurried down the steps and out to meet the movers. She wasn't quick enough, however, to miss her daughter's final retort. The girl said that Noah was nicer, younger and a whole lot cuter than Mr. Greenfield, who looked like a troll.

That observation on Shelby's part was true, and it was all Greer could do not to laugh. She didn't, though, because she sensed there were going to be further issues with Noah Kelley. Especially if he got a dog.

Later she'd make time to fortify her position on all fronts. Just now the lead mover had handed her a checklist and insisted she had to point out where she wanted each box and piece of furniture. And, he told her sternly, when they finished her check marks needed to match those on the sheet provided by the movers. It'd been a long day—too long—and now it had begun to seem endless.

CHAPTER THREE

THE LENGTH OF TIME it took the two burly men to unload the truck clocked in at almost three hours. That was partly due to a restless nine-year-old who kept wanting a snack or a drink or asking a question, which meant Greer had to take frequent breaks. Luckily the men, a father and son driving team, were understanding; they planned to pick up a northbound load in San Antonio, where they'd spend the night. The younger of the two scrawled his name on Shelby's cast before they closed up the truck and left.

"I wanted Noah to be first to sign it," Shelby admitted. "But he said the plaster was still soft when he went home. Do you think he'll come back tonight?" Shelby strained to keep Noah's house in sight as her mom attempted to help her inside.

"Watch where you're walking, Shel, or you'll trip and risk breaking something else."

"Why are you acting so grouchy?"

Greer sighed. "I'm sorry. I'm tired," she said, raking a hand through her hair.

"I'm hungry," Shelby said. "It's getting dark and we haven't had dinner."

"I fixed you fruit and cheese for lunch." Greer remembered swiping a few orange wedges—all she'd had since breakfast. "Unloading took longer than I expected. Mr. Jarvis and his son were kind enough to set up our beds. We'll have supper and then I'll find the sheets. What would you like to eat?"

"Grilled cheese sandwiches?"

"I should've known." Greer laughed. "That's exactly why I wrote griddle on the box we packed it in."

"I wonder if there's anything good on TV? You said programs won't be the same here as in Denver."

"They will be different, hon. Right now, though, there's nothing on at all. I need to call the cable company in the morning and arrange for service."

"No TV? For how long?"

"I don't know. This isn't the city." Seeing the storm brewing in her daughter's eyes, Greer tried to deflect it. "Maybe we can pretend we've just moved into the Little House on the Prairie, Shelby. You've read all of those books a dozen times and watched the series almost that often."

"That would be cool. Do we have an oil lamp I can put in my room?"

Greer opened the refrigerator and stuck her hand in to make sure it was working. She'd already transferred everything from the cooler. Unwrapping the cheese, she treated Shelby to one of her famous no-because-I-said-so-and-I'm-the-mom looks. "I said pretend. And I'm not building a fire in the fireplace and cooking our cheese sandwiches over coals, either."

"Bro…ther! If we'd gone to Noah's house like he offered, I bet I could watch TV."

Greer paused with the knife poised above the block of cheddar. "Shelby, you used to be shy around Whippoorwill guests, especially those we didn't know well. I'm surprised you're so taken with Father Kelley."

Shelby cast down her eyes and kicked rhythmically at the table leg. "Hey, this is our table."

"Did you think I'd leave it behind? And quit changing the subject." She slit open the packing box, removed the griddle and wiped it off with paper towels before plugging it into the wall socket.

"Noah's nice. He doesn't treat me like I'm a kid. In Colorado most of the ranch guests talked to Luke Sanderson and me like we were still in kindergarten."

Picking up two slices of buttered bread, Greer tested the griddle and when it sizzled to her satisfaction, she flipped the bread on the hot metal, quickly layered on cheese slices, then put another piece of bread on top. "I cut up a couple of those apples we bought at Tanner's. Granted, it's late, but we need something besides a sandwich."

Shelby slid off the chair and cradled her injured arm. She figured out how to open the fridge. As she set out the plate of sliced apples, she asked casually, "If this is where you lived before you went to Denver, does my real daddy live here, too?"

Greer's body stilled except for her heart, which kicked into high gear. So was that what Shelby's sudden interest in Noah Kelley was about? Did she figure he was the approximate age of her father? That maybe he *knew* her father? As a matter of fact, Greer thought, swallowing a lump, Noah and Daniel Harper probably *were* the same age.

Clearing her throat several times, she paused to turn the sandwiches and give her racing mind time to sort out a proper response.

"Did you hear me?" Shelby asked, staring solemnly at Greer.

"I heard. Why all the interest? Did…someone here bring up the subject?" For a second Greer's heart seemed to stop. *Holden Kelley could have told his son all the sordid details.*

"No. Luke asked if that's why we were moving to Texas. To find my dad."

"The answer is a resounding no." Greer singed her fingers transferring the hot sandwiches to plates, where she cut them in half. Setting one in front of Shelby, Greer unplugged the griddle, then sat opposite, in her usual spot. She hoped to keep this conversation brief. "I think we've done okay. I mean, you and me alone, kiddo." Seeing how her daughter poked at her sandwich halves with one finger, Greer cut them into more manageable bite-size pieces.

Shelby nibbled on one, set it back, and after she swallowed, muttered, "Noah's stronger than you. When he carried me from the car I felt…safe."

Greer started to flex her arm and show her muscle, as they used to do teasingly with Luke. He was two years older than Shelby and loved to lord it over her. There was no laughter in Shelby's eyes now, so Greer planted an elbow on the table and massaged the tight muscles gripping her neck. "I can't argue with your logic. Men are physically stronger, so women have to work smarter to make up for that genetic oversight. But I've always kept you safe, honey." Sighing long and loud, Greer knew her assurance had neither assuaged nor deterred Shelby's curiosity. "Eat. I don't know where your biological father is. He lived in Houston. That's a long way from Homestead. We met at a college way east of here. Kids often travel some distance to attend colleges and universities." She didn't identify exactly where she'd met Dan. One day, she'd answer all her daughter's questions. When Shelby was old enough to understand.

The girl chewed methodically and swallowed. "You don't have any pictures of him. I know 'cause Luke and me looked one time when you were on a trail ride and Lindsay was supposed to watch us, but her boyfriend came over."

Greer gasped. She'd thought Luke's sister was so mature. "That's right, honey. I don't have pictures of him. I'll say this once and that's all. Sometimes in a relationship people discover they aren't headed down the same path."

Shelby wrinkled her nose. Greer realized she was being far too vague. "Honey, he wasn't a man I could count on. You… me…we both deserved better."

"Then I guess he's not like Noah. We could count on him."

Having just taken a bite of her sandwich, Greer sputtered and choked. "What makes you think you can know that about the man after only a couple of hours?"

The girl munched a wedge of apple and swallowed. "I feel it," she said in total earnestness. "Didn't you, Mama?"

No danced on the tip of Greer's tongue. But some unseen, unnamed force kept her from blurting out the harsh word. Truthfully, Noah had been a rock today. He'd given no indication that he *wasn't* a person who could be counted on. Rather than say something petty, Greer slid out of her chair and took her plate to the sink. "I'm going to make up our beds and run water for you to have a bath, Shel. Kristin said to wrap your cast in plastic so it doesn't get wet. I thought you could skip your bath tonight, but you got dirty in the fall. You'll rest easier and sleep better after a soak in the tub."

Shelby yawned. "Gosh, I'm tired. Do you know where we packed my stuffed animals? It was okay not having them when we slept in motels, 'cause I shared your room. But I really want them tonight, Mama." Her lower lip trembled.

"Honey, they're in a box. But my bedroom's only steps down the hall from yours. Are you sure you need your animal friends tonight?"

Shelby nodded vigorously. "Okay," Greer said, handing the girl a glass of water and the pain pill Kristin advised Shelby take at bedtime. "Bath first and then you can sit in bed and read to me while I open boxes until your animals show up. This pill will help you relax."

"If I had a real dog instead of a stuffed one, we wouldn't have packed him in a moving box. He'd be here to keep me company."

"Enough about getting a dog, Shelby Lynn. We'll get one eventually. What's a ranch without a dog or two? It's just that there are things around here we need to finish first."

Greer ran water in a nice big tub in a remodeled bathroom her mom had scrubbed to a shine earlier. The fact that each cottage had a private bath, and even the one in the bunkhouse had upgrades, had gone a long way toward making this particular ranch more attractive to Greer than others Miranda had offered. It was also scary because the loan reflected those improvements. The local banker for the project had taken every opportunity to impress upon Greer the magnitude of the debt she'd taken on. She had to be open for business and bringing in an income by Thanksgiving. She simply *had* to, or her dreams would go the way of others that had failed here.

"Water's ready," she called to Shelby. They laughed together over wrapping the cast in clear plastic. Yet when it came time for Greer to actually help with Shelby's bath, the girl grew modest. Greer knew being bashful was partly Shelby's age. If nothing else, it forced her to see how the years had flown past.

"Shel, I want us to be real partners in this ranch. You're okay with us leaving Colorado and coming here, aren't you?"

"Yeah. But I'm just a kid. You want me to be like Chuck Hazlett? Luke Sanderson said Chuck's his daddy's partner in Whippoorwill."

"Chuck invested money in Cal & Marisa's dude ranch. He's what's called a silent partner."

"I didn't like him. I'm glad you only went dancing with him twice, 'cause he didn't like me, either."

Greer helped Shelby stand and climb from the tub. Wrapping her in a towel, she gave her a big hug. "That was more than enough reason for me to tell Hazlett to take a hike. You're number one in my life, Shelby."

Getting into a nightgown with the cast wasn't easy, but Greer finally figured it out. When she brushed bright, wet hair out of Shelby's eyes, the girl ventured a question that had obviously bothered her for a while. "Mama, is there something wrong with me that my real daddy didn't like me, and Chuck didn't, either?"

Greer gasped. "Is that what you think? No, Shel! Your dad never even knew you were a girl. He left long before you were born. Honey, you've never said a word about this before. Is there something else behind your concern?"

"I guess I'm just lonely. I want a sister or brother like Luke has. But Lindsay said she heard Chuck say no man would ever marry you. I didn't know why."

Greer gathered the girl close and hugged her tight. After depositing Shelby in the middle of her bed, Greer tucked her in and dropped a kiss on her nose. "Lindsay's folks said time and again that she listened at keyholes and picked up half-truths. The real story is that Chuck Hazlett got mad at me and said things to the Sandersons to cover the fact that he tried to force me into a...compromising situation. Fortunately they didn't believe him. Oh, honey, I know you don't understand, and it never dawned on me that Lindsay would hear, or worse, repeat what she'd heard to you and Luke." She shook her head. "Here's your book." Upset, Greer straightened abruptly. "If I get married, it's going to be to the right man. Someone good and kind." Crossing the room, she tore into the first of five boxes stacked under Shelby's window.

Heaving a huge sigh, the girl opened her book. But instead of reading, she asked, "Is everything Lindsay said a lie? The day we left, she said if you didn't get married soon you'd be too old to have babies and I'd never get a sister or brother."

Greer's hands hovered over a box in which she could see Shelby's stuffed toys. She pulled out two teddy bears, a rabbit and her favorite spotted dog. Arms full, Greer rained them down on Shelby's head. "What? For the record, missy, your mom's not so old. Not even thirty. Today, women have babies into their forties. Since it's apparent you're not interested in that book, it's lights out for you, young lady."

Her mom snatched away the book, and Shelby arranged the animals around her, then flopped into the pillows. Greer had no more than flicked off the light and plunged the room into darkness when Shelby, always a whiz at math, announced, "Mama, we'd better hurry and find me a nice daddy. If you wait till you're forty to have babies, I'll be twenty-two. By then I can have my own babies."

Greer's dry response came from outside the door. "Did you switch gears and hit me with this sister bit hoping I'd relent and get you a dog? If so, it won't work."

"Nope," said the sleepy, yawning voice from the darkness. "I've wanted a sister lots longer than I've wanted a dog. It's scary in here. Will you find our bathroom night-light, Mama?"

"Consider it done. I'll be unpacking boxes in the kitchen for a while if you need me. Otherwise, I'll check on you before I go to bed."

Greer had been restoring order to the kitchen for two hours or more when she happened to glance out the curtainless window above the sink. Nothing but inky blackness, stretching as far as she could see. The night was very still. A shiver wound up her spine for no reason at all, other than maybe Shelby's remarks about being lonely and her room being scary. Crossing her arms, Greer rubbed at scattered goose bumps.

She mentally chided such silliness. The Sandersons' ranch had been equally far from town or neighbors. The difference was that Whippoorwill had a full staff of employees and cabins filled with guests. If all went according to plan, this place would be just as busy by the end of November.

Stepping to the door, Greer looked off in the direction of Noah's house. Earlier, lights had flickered through the trees. Now there was nothing but blackness. She cupped her hands to the glass and peered up at a moonless sky. The kitchen clock she'd hung said it was approaching midnight. Time to go to bed. She wasn't normally jumpy, but it'd been an eventful day. She'd be okay after a good night's rest. In addition to everything else, there'd been a lot of emotion tied to moving home.

Greer decided that for tonight she'd leave the small light on over the sink. Father Kelley claimed there wasn't such a thing as bad omens. Once again she recalled those anonymous letters. She'd initially wondered if someone at the bank or on the land application committee opposed her plan to open a guest retreat. The typed, unsigned notes suggested she'd be happier with a section nearer town. Or maybe she could turn one of the big older houses into a bed-and-breakfast.

Miranda insisted no one officially involved with the project would've sent the letters. She admitted facing opposition. It was known that Clint Gallagher had tried to raise capital to buy the whole parcel. The Dragging F would make a nice addition to the Four Aces. In any event, *someone* had sent the notes.

As she undressed and showered quickly before crawling into bed, Greer blanked her mind to those negative thoughts. She was here now, and she planned to stay, planned to build a good life for herself and Shelby. Just before the comfort of sleep closed around her, Shelby's comment about their needing to find Greer a nice man brought a faint smile to her lips. It was a fantasy that made for interesting bedtime illusions. But Greer would never admit that tonight, ever so briefly, the face of such an illusive lover bore a distinct resemblance to Father Noah Kelley.

A SOUND, a woman's scream, had Greer bolting upright out of bed, jarring her out of sleep. She grabbed the small bedside alarm. The illuminated hands showed it was just after 2:00 a.m. A cougar? No, this was the Hill Country.

A bad dream, she decided, and sank back into a crumpled pillow, hoping her heart would slow its mad gallop.

The second scream, partially muffled, ended in an eerily dragged out moan. Catapulting up again, Greer scrabbled for her robe. Seconds later, she was pounding down the hall toward Shelby's room. By now Greer's heart had lodged in her throat. Why hadn't she realized immediately that her daughter might have awakened in pain or confusion caused by being in a new place?

A pencil-slim beam of light shimmering from the nightlight in the bathroom landed on Shelby's bed. Her eyes were closed and her breathing regular. The arm not encased in the cast curled around her spotted dog and a tattered teddy bear that had been Greer's first gift to her newborn daughter.

Backing out of the room, Greer next made a cursory inspection of the house. It was when she opened the front door a fraction of an inch to scan the porch that a third garbled cry, clearly drifting up from the direction of the river, sent Greer racing back to her room to dress.

She threw on the jeans, boots and plaid shirt she'd laid out for working in the next day. This *was* the next day. However, she hadn't planned to get going on so little rest.

She looked around for some means of protection, although her mind had locked on the probability that some human or animal out there needed help.

Greer had never been a proponent of guns, but she used to carry one on trail rides, and she could shoot. Now she wished she'd brought a handgun from Denver, since they were two females alone out here.

She recalled having seen a rusty pitchfork lying in the barn; her mom had said it should be tossed in the trash before someone accidentally stepped on the tines and ended up with tetanus. Leave it to her mom to think in terms of worst-scenario accidents. Greer remembered her mother had carried the pitchfork up to the house, where she'd stood it by the green garbage can outside the back door.

Feeling her way like a blind woman, Greer located the pitchfork. Although she was armed now, what she really needed was a flashlight. It occurred to her to try to find one in a box of miscellaneous kitchen items she hadn't yet unpacked. Just as she began to open the carton, the thin, almost strangled cry wavered again.

Greer dashed out the door, torn at leaving Shelby alone for however long it'd take to trek the distance to the river. When she started to walk, she quickly found a path. Greer recalled that it zigzagged across her pasture to a small stand of cypress overhanging the river. That was where it now seemed the cries were coming from. Did people boat at night? Boys she used to know went south to hunt Lord-only-knew-what at night.

Her property sloped from the house all the way to the water's edge. If she hurried, she could get down there to see if a boater or perhaps a calf had somehow got stuck or stranded, and be back before Shelby even realized she was missing.

A desire to be a good Samaritan won out over her fears. Greer took off at a half run. By now, her eyes had adjusted to the almost starless night. All the vegetation along the path had been chewed away, probably by cattle.

It'd only been her land for seven days. One week since she'd signed the city's contract and put her name on a two-year trial mortgage held by the Homestead Bank and Trust. The fact was, Greer had no idea when Jase Farley had abandoned his ranch. No doubt he'd owned animals he watered at the river, just as she hoped to do one day soon.

The closer she drew to the dark trees, the more tightly she gripped the rough-hewn handle of the pitchfork. So tightly her palms were sweating and her fingers ached. Greer's mouth felt dry and she licked her lips.

The only sound she'd heard since she embarked on this fool's errand was the rapid *thunkity, thunkity, thunk* of her heart. The mournful cries appeared to have stopped.

Slowing her charge into the dark trees, which could be home to any number of dangerous animals or humans, Greer glanced at her house. How stupid was she, leaving Shelby alone and unprotected?

Backing up a few steps, intending to make a mad dash back the way she'd come, Greer hit something solid and warm and—she feared—very human. She wrapped her hand firmly around her feeble mode of protection, the pitchfork. Hoping the element of surprise might at least buy her running time, she spun, ready to launch a counteroffensive.

Suddenly she was blinded by a bright stream of light that burst suddenly from an industrial-size flashlight. Greer threw up an arm to ward off what she assumed was an imminent attack. She stumbled, tripped over a bulging cypress root and fell hard on her backside. A yelp of frustration mingled with her pain.

The last thing she expected was to hear a voice she recognized. "Greer, why in heaven's name are you tramping through the woods in the dead of night? Are you sleepwalking?"

Noah Kelley. *He* was behind those ghastly cries?

Greer lost no time in scrambling up. "Maybe the question should be why have you lured me down here?"

"*What?*" He finally pointed the light he carried at the ground, which gave them each a better chance to peruse the other.

Greer saw he had on the boots he'd worn earlier, and blue jeans somewhat less faded than the previous ones. His dark blond hair was thoroughly disheveled, and he was shirtless. His skin had turned dusky gold in the light. His chest was dusted with hair a lot darker than the wheat-blond locks draped appealingly over his forehead. She'd thought her mouth and throat were dry on the trek here; now she couldn't have swallowed if her life depended on it. But as Noah continued to look dumbfounded, she snapped, "You obviously hoped to frighten me, with all those woman-in-distress noises."

"That's exactly what it sounded like. I've got no idea what time it was, but a high-pitched scream woke me up. At first I thought I was dreaming, but then I heard it again. Not quite as distinct, but worrisome enough to get me out of a warm bed. Since you're the only person here, and you're female, why wouldn't I think *you're* the one out here caterwauling at the moon, not the other way around?"

The hand not gripping Greer's pitchfork curled into a fist. "There isn't any moon, in case you're too unobservant to notice. And I may be a female, but I am not the source of those cries. Admit I caught you in the act of trying to scare me into leaving my property." She sniffed disdainfully. "I suppose you sent those letters, too."

"Letters?" he echoed.

"For a college graduate, you certainly have a limited vocabulary."

Noah glared at her and shook his head. He flashed his light along the ground, illuminating the soft loamy soil for a good number of yards in all four directions. "Do you see any tracks besides ours?" he asked abruptly.

"My point precisely," she said, rattling her pitchfork under his nose.

"Stop that, you're making me nervous. If someone made that noise as a scare tactic, name one reason why a man in my position would pull such a stunt."

"Ha! Like father, like son maybe. That was clever of you today, acting as if the church stood ready to welcome me back with open arms. It was especially clever to do it in front of Ed Tanner. Shelby's accident helped you add to your pretense of good works, because now Kristin Gallagher will vouch for you, too." Greer made a few short jabs at him with the pitchfork again. Enough to send Noah into full retreat while she stomped several yards up the trail toward her home.

"I've got another news flash for you, Father Noah Kelley. Miranda told me your mother served on the Home Free committee. You Kelleys may think this juvenile bullshit will ensure I leave town and not contaminate your oh-so-pure congregation, but the truth is, I wouldn't take a million bucks to set one foot in your so-called sanctuary. It's only fair to inform you I'm not the girl who left Homestead ten years ago. I've toughened up. This is my land and I won't be run off. Tomorrow I'm going to Guthrie's Hardware, and I'll apply to purchase a twenty-two. If you check with my former boss, he'll verify I can cut a rattlesnake in half at twenty paces. So don't mess with me."

Totally bewildered by her outburst, Noah played his flashlight over Greer Bell's stiff back as she marched up the trail.

He was really confused when it came to the remarks she'd tossed out about his mom and pop. He guessed his mom was still serving on the mayor's committee in his father's stead. But letters? What letters? Noah scratched his head. The other stuff about his father—it was clear Greer must have run afoul of Holden's judgmental views. Noah understood. Raised in the Episcopal church, Noah found his dad's over-the-top conservatism stifling, too.

Watching his neighbor disappear from sight, Noah had to smile. He was certainly willing to extend a more love-thy-neighbor policy if that was Greer's concern. He sobered instantly, remembering the woman's scream he and Greer had both heard. He wasn't behind it, and he'd bet Sunday's offering Greer wasn't the culprit, either. Short of a ghost, which he definitely didn't believe in, then who? Clint Gallagher? It was no secret the old so-and-so had tried to finagle getting hold of Greer's land. Gallagher couldn't bear the thought of having anyone closer to the Clear River than his Four Aces ranch. The drought had ended, but during the worst of it, the need to ration river water had caused contention. Noah had heard that night-siphoning had caused hard feelings among men, many once good friends who'd gone bankrupt when the K.C. Enterprises consortium failed, largely due to the long drought.

Deciding there was something sinister about the cries, Noah—too keyed up to go back to sleep anyhow—set out to make a thorough search of the area. He traced Greer's boot tracks from the trees back along the path across her property. Since moving out here, Noah had witnessed Gallagher ranch hands occasionally crossing what was now Greer's land.

Tomorrow, he'd drop in and chat with Ryan Gallagher. Clint's oldest son was a square-shooter who'd been managing the Four Aces for a while. Clint, known far and wide as a wheeler-dealer, reportedly suffered from macular degeneration, a problem the senator preferred to hide. Failing health or not, maybe the old reprobate wasn't willing to lose the land. Did he still want it?

Still, this business tonight, with the disembodied scream, smacked of something childish. Too amateurish for a man of Gallagher's stature, he thought.

Although, if Greer was right and someone was trying to frighten her into leaving Homestead before she fulfilled her contract, who stood to gain the most from her departure? That was a million-dollar question Noah couldn't answer.

He backtracked to the river again and came across a spot between two flat rocks, where a deep indentation in the sand might have been made by a small boat tying up. There were enough granite slabs between the riverbank and the small copse of trees that a person or two could've jumped from rock to rock without leaving footprints.

Noah did that, taking a route designed to keep him out of sight of Greer's place. Some people were aware he'd bought one of the ranchettes, but he didn't think it was widely known. So what if his crashing in from the southeast had prematurely upset the perpetrator's plans to draw out and frighten Greer? He refused to think it might be anything worse.

A tree-by-tree search netted him something lodged in the fork of the largest cypress. This gave Noah immense satisfaction, but left him thinking that his second visit tomorrow morning, after Ryan Gallagher, would be to take his find to Sheriff Wade Montgomery. Dump this in Wade's lap and see what he made of it.

GREER FELT NOAH'S eyes monitoring every step of her retreat as she hotfooted it home along the lumpy cattle track. Had she not been so furious, his laser-blue eyes would've had a paralyzing effect. He'd tried to act so darned innocent. Greer didn't for one minute believe he was.

She took the pitchfork inside and stood it next to her bed, in case sometime between now and daylight she needed it again.

After locking the kitchen door, she checked to see that the front door missing its locking mechanism had remained shut—that the chair she'd shoved under the knob hadn't been disturbed. Finding everything as she'd left it, she looked in on Shelby and was profoundly relieved to see that she was still fast asleep.

Greer couldn't have gone back to bed if her life depended on it. Her nerves felt too ragged.

Remembering that she'd unpacked the box with her herbal teas, she put a kettle of water on the stove and sorted through an assortment of teas one of her favorite guests had given her last Christmas. Julie Masters and her contingent of Western writers happened to be the group Greer hoped would initiate her facility. The women had confessed that they loved exploring new places. Especially spots representative of the Old West. And bless the Sandersons, they'd urged Greer to get in touch with the women as soon as she'd set her opening date. Marisa and Cal both thought Homestead, Texas, would appeal to the writers as the site of their next retreat.

Choosing chamomile tea from the redwood box, Greer passed the kitchen window on her way to nab the kettle before it could whistle and risk waking Shelby. She saw a light in the distance, bobbing along the bank of the river, and stopped short. At first she thought maybe she was looking at the person responsible for waking her up in the middle of the night. Then the person holding the light turned and flashed it up into the trees, where it cast an umbrella over him. Noah.

The pot whistled and Greer absently grabbed it and turned off the burner. She poured water into her cup and dunked her tea strainer up and down as she watched the man who obviously hadn't gone home when she had.

What was he doing? Was he setting up more dirty tricks?

When her tea was dark enough, she put the strainer in the sink and snapped off the light, plunging the kitchen into darkness. As she sipped her steaming drink, it became apparent that Noah was conducting a grid search of the area that ran from the riverbank and into the trees.

Did that mean he'd told the truth? That he wasn't the person behind that scare tactic? If not Noah, then who? And why? Greer shivered. The lack of an answer to that question made her feel a lot more uneasy than if she'd been able to pin it on Noah.

Her appetite for tea or anything else was lost as a sick feeling invaded the pit of her stomach. Feet glued to the kitchen floor, Greer stood chewing on her lip until the bobbing light moved from the cypress grove and made a beeline toward Noah's house. If he'd found anything important, wouldn't he have come to share the information with her? That was what she would've done in his place. She was back to not trusting the younger Father Kelley. Either Father Kelley.

Tomorrow, after visiting the hardware store to fill out paperwork to purchase a firearm, Greer supposed she ought to stop in at the sheriff's office. And say what? Would anyone take her word over that of the charming priest?

CHAPTER FOUR

SLEEP EVADED GREER for the rest of the night. She slipped out of bed a number of times to check on Shelby. And to rattle the doors and windows and to listen in the kitchen for any caterwauling, as Noah Kelley had described the cries. She was haunted by the fact that the first sound had seemed so human. The subsequent ones Greer wasn't so sure about.

When her bedside clock said five-thirty, she gave up attempting to sleep. Instead, she dressed and decided to put her restless energy to work doing something constructive, like unpacking their household.

She felt vulnerable and exposed standing in a brightly lit living room with gray layers of early dawn breaking, so much so that coverings for all the windows now headed her list of items to buy in town. She hoped the material her mother planned to use for kitchen curtains was opaque enough to leave her feeling secure.

Darn, she hated this loss of control. Hated the way the person or persons responsible for those night noises had undermined her confidence. She ran down a list of people who knew she was in town, but who might prefer she leave again. She still couldn't help thinking it was just too convenient that she'd encountered Father Kelley at the river, and there'd been no sign of anyone else. No footprints except hers...and his.

Greer had the living room unpacked and set up much the

same as their cabin at Whippoorwill had been by the time Shelby wandered out of her bedroom, still clutching a stuffed animal.

"Good morning, honeybun. How's the arm today? Let me check your fingers. Kristin said we should keep an eye on them to make sure they don't get puffy."

"I can wiggle them and it doesn't hurt." Shelby skipped over to show her mother. As she crossed the room, her eyes widened and she grinned. "Did elves come in the night and make this room look just like our old house?"

Greer laughed. "Elf Mom deserves all the credit. While you snored away, sleepyhead, I've been busy. But Elf Mom needs a break. How about if I go fix pancakes and bacon for breakfast?"

"Can we have slices of the peach pie Miranda brought yesterday, instead? Grandma put it in the pantry, and we forgot about it last night."

"You're right. It slipped my mind because it was so late when we had supper. But Shelby, pie's not what we eat for breakfast."

"Why?"

"It's too sweet. Pie is for dessert."

"Peaches are fruit, Mama. And the syrup we put on pancakes is sweet."

"Honestly, twerp, I've never known anybody who argued all the angles the way you do. I swear you're going to be a lawyer when you grow up." She ruffled Shelby's sleep-flattened curls. "You know, pie does sound good. Who says we can't break from tradition? We make the rules. You run and get dressed in the clothes I laid on your chest of drawers. I'll make my coffee and pour you a glass of milk."

"What'll we do after breakfast? If we clean cottages, I'll have to do stuff with one hand.

"I have something else in mind. Think you can hold the tape measure while I measure all our windows?"

Shelby nodded. "Why?"

"Because I don't like not having our windows covered up at night. I thought we'd go to town, and I'll see if the hardware store stocks louvered blinds."

"Didn't Grandma say she's sewing us kitchen curtains?"

"Yes, but I started thinking that with guests having free run once we open, we'll want our privacy. I believe there are blinds that fit behind curtains."

"That's okay then. 'Cause we don't wanna hurt Grandma's feelings."

Greer caught the child close for an impulsive hug. "You're a good kid, Shelby-girl. Do you know that?"

The girl wriggled loose. "You're who taught me it's not nice to hurt people's feelings, Mama. You musta forgot yesterday, 'cause you weren't very nice to Noah."

"Father Kelley," Greer reminded, a frown replacing her indulgent smile.

"He likes Noah better. We're just s'posed to call him Father at church."

"Shelby, didn't you hear me say we're not attending his church?"

"But I want to. Noah told me about lots of kids my age who go there."

Shaking her head forcefully, Greer nevertheless saw that her protest was useless. Shelby dashed down the hall and disappeared into her room.

Lord, but she was a stubborn kid. Greer wondered if that was a trait Shelby had inherited from her dad? Then again, maybe it came from the Bell side of the family. Certainly her dad was bullheaded enough.

Greer washed the breakfast dishes by hand, as well as the

ones left from their evening meal. It was a chore she didn't mind. She'd had the movers leave a still-crated commercial-grade dishwasher in a cookhouse that needed repair. Once the dishes were dried and put away, she finished writing her list.

On the drive to town, Shelby was her usual chatterbug self. Greer had a habit of listening with half an ear so she could respond appropriately when necessary. Like now, as Shelby leaned forward and asked loudly, "Can we eat at the café Dr. Kristin told us about? Callie's café."

"Call her Kristin, honey, not doctor."

"Why? You said we hafta call Noah Father Kelley."

"Kristin Gallagher is a doctor's assistant, not a licensed physician." Glancing over her shoulder, Greer sighed. "Shelby, must you always *question* everything I say?"

The girl lunged back against the seat. "My old teacher said asking questions is good."

"When it pertains to schoolwork, yes. Did you know that when I was your age, a parent's word was considered law? My mom and dad's stock answer was *do it because I said so.*"

"Well, your mom's a teacher so I guess that's why. Mama, what does my grandpa do?"

"He farms. He used to grow squash. And kept sheep that he sheared for wool. Pigs, which he marketed twice a year. He raised chickens he sold as fryers, but he also maintained a flock of hens strictly for laying eggs."

"No horses or cows?"

"I had one saddle horse. Dad didn't raise beef. We didn't have the grazing land. It wouldn't have been worthwhile when he could raise enough sheep to make it pay."

"Is that why we're getting sheep? You wanna be like Grandpa?"

Greer paused. "That's not why I decided on sheep. Cal Sanderson said they'd be easier to raise than cattle. And sheep will present our guests with a different aspect of Western life. Plus we'll shear them and sell the wool. If everything works out the way I hope, maybe later I can lease land and get a few head of cattle. Okay, Q and A time is over. Our first stop is the hardware store."

"You never said if we could eat lunch at the café, Mama."

"Let's see what time I finish all our errands. After the hardware store, I want to talk with the sheriff."

"Gosh, why? I don't want to talk to any old sheriff. They shoot people."

"Shelby, where do you get these wild notions?"

"From Luke and Lindsay. And from TV."

"I should've known," Greer muttered, thinking she'd placed too much trust in Cal and Marisa's kids being good role models for Shelby. "Here in Homestead, honey, our sheriff is a good guy."

Greer dug out her list and shepherded Shelby into another store that brought back a flood of memories. This time, the man behind the counter was the one she remembered. Myron Guthrie hadn't changed, except that his hair had gone from gray to white. He'd always been as wide as he was tall. He had no hair atop his head, but wore bushy muttonchop sideburns and a full beard. He still peered at customers over a pair of half-glasses. And he had a good memory, because he knew Greer on sight.

"Well, well, if your little gal ain't the spittin' image of you at the same age, Greer Bell. If you're wonderin' how I knew you was back, it's because I ran into Ed Tanner having breakfast this mornin' at Callie's. He said you're fixin' to spruce up Jase Farley's old hunting ranch."

"That's right. I qualified for the mayor's land giveaway program. We're going to open a guest ranch. This is my daughter. She's nine. Her name is Shelby."

"Pretty name for a pretty little gal." Myron took note of Shelby's shiny new cast as he unscrewed the lid of a squat glass jar and extended it over the counter. "I wonder if you like Tootsie Pops as much as your mama always did."

Shelby's eyes lit up, but suddenly shy, she backed against Greer and only gazed at the candy through lowered eyelashes.

"It's okay to take one." Greer nudged her forward. "Mr. Guthrie's been giving his customers lollypops from the day he opened the store." Smiling, Greer selected one with a red wrapper. She watched Shelby reach in the jar and pull out her favorite grape candy.

Myron screwed the lid back on the jar. He pointed out a waste basket near the door where Shelby could deposit both candy wrappers. Then he focused on Greer, who'd popped the candy into her mouth. "I doubt you stopped in just to pass the time of day. I see you've got a list."

Greer cast a furtive glance at the door to make sure Shelby was still occupied. "Uh, Myron, first I'd like to fill out an application to purchase a small-caliber gun. I'd rather not let Shelby know. She slept through a situation that happened at the ranch last night." In brief terms, Greer described the screams.

He drew his bushy brows together. "Probably some danged teenage boys messin' around the river. Wade and his deputy have had run-ins with kids, or so Millicent reported in the paper." Myron opened a drawer and got out a form, which he shoved across the counter. "A woman and kid all alone that far out probably oughta have a gun. Just be careful who you go shootin' at, missy. You don't want to be the one who ends up warming Wade Montgomery's jail if you nail somebody's ornery kid."

Greer took the pen and started writing. "Jock's no longer sheriff?"

"Jock retired. Homestead's lucky to get his son. Wade's more evenhanded than his pa."

"Hmm. So, you think it was kids? I planned on going by the sheriff's to file a complaint. Maybe that's not necessary."

"Won't hurt," he said, taking her completed form. "Wade likes to keep a tight rein on his town. What with all the new folks moving in thanks to the mayor's scheme, there's bound to be new kinds of trouble."

"I guess townspeople aren't happy with what Miranda's done to resurrect Homestead."

"Me, I'm happy as a clam at high tide." The big man grinned like a boy. "Haven't had so much business in five years, what with all you kids coming home to rebuild. I meant that the town council was real divided on our Miranda's plan. You know how it is with Hill Country folks. Pa grumbles at the dinner table. His kid remembers that, so when he and his pals go hot-rodding at night, huntin' up mischief, they maybe act out Pa's grumblin'."

Greer nodded absently. She'd formed her own suspicions about who was responsible for last night. And he wasn't a hot-rodding teen. "I didn't come just to apply for a gun permit, Myron. Do you sell mini blinds?" She laid her list on the counter. "These are the inside measurements for all my ranch house windows. I'll need blinds later for the cottages, too, once I get them fixed up."

Guthrie adjusted his glasses before scanning her figures. "You're in luck, Greer. I unpacked a new order last week that includes blinds. I even got me one of those fancy cutters. I stock brown, white and ivory, but I can order blue or maroon if you want to wait. Come on, I'll show you what I have."

"Brown or ivory should do me." Calling to Shelby, Greer fell in behind the waddling, short-legged store owner.

"There's toys in aisle five if the little one wants to start making her Santa list." Myron winked. "Diversifying is my wife, Sophie's, idea. She likes to remind me every now and then that if she hadn't suggested I branch out, we might've folded like so many of the other old-timers."

Greer directed Shelby to an aisle already decked out with artificial Christmas trees. "I hope to be open by Thanksgiving, so I expect I'll give the local economy a boost. Eventually I'll need locks for the cottages, a door for the barn and materials to fix a falling down corral. The blinds and locks are all I'll order today. Oh, and I need to find a company to fix the fence between my land and Gallagher's pasture."

"Smart idee, I'd say." As Guthrie showed her the blinds and Greer made her selections, Myron gossiped . By the time he'd filled her Blazer with blinds and the hardware items she'd bought, Greer knew a lot more about the goings-on around Homestead.

"So, Shelby, you spent quite a while cruising the toy aisles. Did you start making your Santa list? Only a little over two months and it'll be Christmas."

"Mr. Guthrie's got lots of good stuff. But I decided since you won't get me a dog now, that's all I'm going to ask Santa for this year."

"Shelby, that's no fair. I know Luke Sanderson told you where Santa's gifts come from."

The girl grinned cheekily. "So? Hey, did you decide if we get to eat lunch?"

"Okay. After I take care of some business with the sheriff. That's provided you can stay quiet in his waiting room while I chat with Sheriff Montgomery."

"I will, I promise. Is the sheriff somebody you know from when you used to live here?"

"Wade Montgomery is seven or eight years older than I am. As I recall, he left Homestead after high school and went to college in Houston. I think he took a job on the Houston police force. This is the first I knew he'd moved home. Myron said another guy I used to know still lives here. Ethan Ritter. You'll be happy to hear he has a horse ranch not far from us. He runs a therapeutic riding school, and he married a woman who has a daughter about your age. They've adopted two kids, a boy and a girl who are nine. Father Kelley mentioned them yesterday, but I had no idea who he meant."

"Mama, are all the guys you used to know married?"

Greer darted a sidelong glance at Shelby. "I don't know. I suppose so. Why?"

"Nothin'. 'Cept I heard Luke's mother tell his dad that maybe you coming home would be good. She said maybe you'd marry one of the guys you went to school with."

Feeling her face heat, Greer concentrated on parking between a dusty white Ford with the sheriff's insignia on the side and a light-colored pickup truck. Once she'd successfully jockeyed into the spot, Greer unbuckled her seat belt and faced her daughter. "Shel, I want to make this perfectly clear. I'm not on a husband hunt."

The girl's thin face fell, and she cast down her thick-lashed eyes.

"You seem unhappy about that."

"Luke and Lindsay did cool things with their dad. I... hoped..." Shelby bit her lip and let her thought go unfinished.

"We do cool things together, Shel." Now Greer found their exchange uncomfortable. She prided herself on being a very good mom. Had she fooled herself into believing Shelby had never missed having a dad?

The girl slipped out of her seat belt and opened the back door. "We do okay when you're not working, Mama. I figured if I had a dad, even if he worked like Luke's daddy, I'd have twice the chance that one of you wouldn't be busy all the time." Hopping down, she slammed the door.

Greer leaped out her side of the vehicle, making a mental note to devote more hours to Shelby, even though so much needed to be done to get the ranch ready for guests. *Who was she kidding?* As a single parent and a working mom, she knew that spare hours came at a premium. She sighed, unable to see how she could juggle her schedule.

The sheriff's office was at the back of the courthouse. His dark wood walls were papered with Wanted posters. Greer assumed she'd be stuck answering a million questions once they left, as Shelby knelt on a bench, paying an inordinate amount of attention to the posters hanging at adult eye level. For a third-grader, Shelby read exceedingly well, and she retained everything. Greer hoped there weren't a lot of really horrid criminals whose deeds would give her daughter nightmares.

Greer announced herself to a secretary. Barbara Jean Steck, it said on her name tag. "I'm new in town," Greer told the woman. "A former resident, actually." She darted a glance at Shelby and lowered her voice. "Uh, last night there was an incident at my ranch I'd like to report. To Wade if he's available."

"He's in. Let me call and ask if he has time to see you, Ms. Bell."

Wade flung open his office door a moment after his clerk buzzed him. "Greer, long time no see. Come in, come in. I don't like hearing you've had an incident at your place. That would be the Dragging F, correct?"

Cringing, Greer's eyes automatically cut to the girl still on her knees. "Will my daughter be all right by herself for a few minutes?" As Wade nodded Greer noticed that he hardly looked different from the brown-eyed, brown-haired, lanky guy he'd been in high school. There was an added maturity, of course. Or maybe the official khaki pants, white shirt, boots and heavy belt loaded with cop paraphernalia gave him that commanding aura.

Wade stepped around Greer and introduced himself to Shelby. "My wife's sister, Brittany, is about your age. We'll have to get you together one of these days. Brit will be ecstatic to have another girl in town. She thinks the school here is overrun with boys."

Shelby, obviously impressed with Wade's height and hardware, sat flat on the bench. She did little but nod with wide eyes.

Turning to his secretary, Wade said, "I'll bet Barbara Jean can find a cold bottle of juice for Shelby while her mom and I have a word in my office."

Smiling, the woman removed a bottle of fruit punch from a compact refrigerator. Greer smiled with pride when Shelby remembered to say thank you for the drink.

After leading Greer into a Spartan office, he pulled out a straight-backed chair across from his desk. Wade shut his office door and made his way to a swivel chair. "Problems out at the Dragging F so soon? Didn't you just move in yesterday?"

For the second time that morning, Greer launched into the story about the screams that had awakened her in the night.

Wade rocked forward and back as she gestured and talked. He tapped a pencil on his blotter when she relayed Myron Guthrie's opinion that it'd probably been the work of kids. "What kids would be aware I'd moved in?" she asked. "Furthermore, why would kids want to scare me like that?" Greer laced her hands and nervously bounced her thumbs together.

"Did you see anything suspicious?"

"I followed a path to the river and ran into Father Kelley.

Noah Kelley," she stated, in case Wade might've heard that the senior Father Kelley had helped along her abrupt departure from town ten years ago.

"Right. Noah bought a mini ranch near the river. Surely you're not accusing him?" Wade laughed until it became apparent from Greer's scowl that she did consider that a possibility.

"Sorry, I can tell you're not joking. But even trying my hardest, I can't see Noah as a night prowler. He's about as upstanding as men come."

"Well, he was the one to point out ours were the only tracks there."

Wade gave a slight shrug. "Myron's probably right on the money. We've got boys in town who have too much time on their hands. I'll do some nosing around."

Still needing to be convinced, Greer stood. "Should I make an official report?"

"They steal or vandalize anything? Then no," he said when she shook her head. "Tell you what, Greer. Either my deputy or I will make a point of taking a run out that way after dark for the next few days. If we find anything suspicious, we'll handle it. Take my card. Should any problems crop up, call the office. After hours, my cell." He uncoiled his long body from the chair and led the way to the door.

As they exited his office, the front door burst open and a perky woman with flaxen hair and three exuberant kids piled into the room. The youngest of the children, a girl of about six, squealed happily and jumped into Wade's arms. His deep voice came from beyond the tangle of arms, legs and hair.

"Greer, you'll get to meet my family sooner than I thought. My wife, Callie. Her brother, Adam. He's eleven. Her sister, Brittany's, nine. And this pistol is Mary Beth. She's six."

Greer, already smiling at the antics of the littlest girl,

extended her hand to the woman. "I assume you're the Callie Kristin Gallagher said owns the best restaurant in town. This is my daughter, Shelby, who's nine. Ever since we left home this morning, she's been bugging me to have lunch at your café."

"We've just brought Wade lunch. The kids are bored. They want to go riding at Wade's father's place. Is that a new cast on Shelby's arm? I figured if you met Kristin, this would be why." She touched Shelby's bright pink cast.

Shelby and Brittany, after a brief period of eyeing each other, sat side by side on the bench and struck up a conversation, like instant best friends, leaving Greer to explain her daughter's accident.

"Noah happened by your place and drove you to town? Wasn't that lucky?" Callie exclaimed. "I suppose he rode over to invite you to Sunday service." She circled a finger indicating her family. "We'll be there. Brittany and Kayla Ritter's daughter, Heather, will be so happy to have another girl in her Sunday school class. Their other daughter, Megan, is eight. She's a darling. "

As they chatted, Greer edged toward the door. "The girls will see Shelby for the first time at school on Monday. I'm afraid I have way too much work at the ranch to spend half a day in church."

Shelby heard the exchange. "Please, Mama, can't we go to church? Then I can see Brittany again. Please, please, please!"

Greer pasted on a smile that didn't reach her eyes and kept shaking her head. "If you want lunch, Shel, we need to go. Callie, kids, so nice meeting you. I'm sure we'll run into each other again. Shelby and I will have more time to socialize after I open the guest ranch for business. I hope," she added.

Callie, who'd gone to stand beside Wade, turned her face up to his. "We'd be glad to swing by and pick Shelby up Sunday morning, wouldn't we, Wade? I mean—" Callie issued a little shrug "—with that arm she won't be much help working around your ranch. You'll probably accomplish more by yourself, Greer. But it's up to you."

Greer knew what the woman said was true; nevertheless her heart took a little dive worrying that her dad or others in the congregation might make thoughtless comments about her that could hurt Shelby.

Yet the girls both wore such pleading, hopeful faces, Greer didn't have it in her to refuse an offer extended in kindness. "All right. What time should she be ready? I'll unpack and iron one of your good dresses, Shelby." Turning to Callie again, Greer grimaced. "Everything's wrinkled even though it's packed on hangers in those wardrobe boxes."

Waving a dismissive hand, Callie broke in. "Let Shelby go dressed as she is. Noah's quite casual. We only dress more formally for special occasions."

"I went to St. Mark's for a lot of years. I know Father Kelley had a strict dress code. Nice dresses for women and girls. Suits and ties for men."

This time Wade intervened. "Maybe the other Father Kelley, Greer. Noah's emphasis is on showing up, not on dressing up."

Though she remained skeptical, Greer turned to leave, finally convinced that the other kids were going to be dressed in jeans or shorts.

"If you're stopping by our café for lunch," Callie called, "today is prime rib with roast potatoes and fresh vegetables. We always have grilled cheese or hamburgers. I tried a more upscale menu when I first opened. It didn't play well," she said, shrugging.

"No kidding?" Greer laughed. "This *is* cowboy country. Hey, I hope you didn't nab the only good cook. I'm going to need one to feed my guests, plus a cowboy cook for trail rides. Within a few weeks, I hope to hire an all-around ranch hand and someone to clean the bunkhouse and cottages. First, though, I have to see about cable and phones."

"I can't think of a cook offhand," Callie mused aloud. "But my dad, Dale Collins, has lived here forever. He owns and operates Buddy's Gas and Auto at the edge of town. He might know of someone."

Wade again broke in. "Callie, I'm sure Greer's met your dad. She lived here until she graduated from high school."

"Oh, well, Dad's not like you probably remember him. He's turned his life around."

"I'm happy for anyone who can do that," Greer said. "If his shop's in the same location, I know where that is. He fixed my first car when my dad couldn't get it to run."

Callie smiled. "He mostly putters with antique cars now."

Greer motioned Shelby toward the door. "Once I settle on a name for my ranch and get things spruced up, I'll drop in and see if your dad has anyone he'd recommend."

They left and took the walkway around the courthouse. Shelby was so excited about having met her first new friend, Greer could hardly get her to settle down and buckle her seat belt.

"Mama, wait! I think that's Noah taking the parking spot you just left. Can we wait and see? I want him to sign my cast."

Squinting in the rearview mirror, Greer was almost blinded by light reflecting off the windshield of a maroon pickup that zipped into her old parking space. "Honeybun, I can't stop in the middle of the street just so you can see if it's Father Kelley. Let alone wait to have him sign your cast. Anyway, would he drive a pickup? Another thing—he's a busy man, so I doubt he'd bother to visit the sheriff. "

"Why not? You visited the sheriff. I'm glad, too. Doesn't Brittany have pretty eyes? I wish my eyes were blue. Why aren't they?"

"I suppose because no one in my family has blue eyes."

"What color were my daddy's eyes?"

Greer swallowed bile rising in her throat. "I can't remember. Brown, I think, and mine are goldish-brown. That's why yours are a beautiful hazel."

"Luke says they're muddy-brown."

"Honestly, Shelby, they are not. I wish you'd told me about all these things Luke and Lindsay said and did while we still lived in Colorado. I'd have shaken them by their ears."

Shelby giggled at that. "Can I have a grilled cheese? I didn't wanna hurt Mrs. Montgomery's feelings, but I don't like ribs."

"Prime rib isn't ribs," Greer tried to explain, heading for the café, which was situated in the town's historical district in a quaint Victorian-style house. "Do you see a parking place? Wow, they're busy. Maybe we won't get in."

"There, Mama. Around the corner. A truck just pulled out."

Greer followed her directions and nabbed the spot. They got out and she locked the Blazer; she didn't want anyone walking off with her mini blinds.

NOAH KELLEY shut off his Chevy diesel's engine and stared after the vehicle that had vacated the parking spot he grabbed in the sheriff's lot. Unless he missed his guess, that was Greer Bell. He wondered if something else had happened to her.

Gathering the box of stuff he'd discovered last night, Noah shut his door. Wade would tell him if anything else had gone on out there.

He hadn't expected to find the sheriff's whole family inside. They all chatted for a few minutes. "Brit," he said, "I'm glad you convinced Ms. Bell to let Shelby come to Sunday school." He glanced at Callie. "I suspect it'll take more persuading to get Greer there."

Callie glanced at him oddly. Wade didn't notice. He had his nose in the box Noah thrust into his hands.

"What's this? An old tape player and speakers you're giving me…why?"

"Evidence," Noah said.

Callie took that as her cue to corral the kids and leave. She and Wade exchanged a quick kiss, then Noah followed Wade into his office. Once the door was closed, he launched into his version of the previous night's events.

"Did you know she was just here wanting to swear out a complaint?" Wade said, making a closer inspection of the items in the box.

"I thought that was her leaving as I drove in. Anyway, I found this wedged in a tree after she went home last night. I didn't see a soul, but the tape player was still warm, so I've got no doubt the sounds we both heard came from these high-velocity speakers. I'm guessing the perpetrator came and left by boat."

"Really? Greer seems to think you're to blame."

Noah blew out a breath. "So she said last night." His blue eyes darkened. "And she convinced you, Wade?"

Sitting, the sheriff rocked back in his chair. He drummed his fingers on the desk top. "Of course not. Probably some smart-ass boys. That's what Myron Guthrie told her, too, when Greer applied to buy a gun." Wade snapped forward and dropped his head in his hands. "I want citizens arming themselves like I want a hole in the head."

Noah crossed one knee over the other and waggled his

boot. "Could it be that guy, Craddock? The petty crook who poisoned Kayla Ritter's vineyard?"

"Nope. We're watching him. This is a kid-type prank, Noah. I'm more worried about Greer buying firearms. I sure as heck don't need her taking a potshot at somebody's little darling, even if he's acting like a juvenile delinquent."

"Greer told me she can cut a rattler in half at…twenty paces. I'll bet she can. However, she doesn't strike me as the type to shoot first and ask questions later."

"I can only hope. You're not completely sold on the notion it's kids. Why?"

"Gut instinct, Wade. You must have those, too."

"Yeah."

"Actually, it's more," Noah admitted. He mentioned what Greer had said about someone wanting to scare her off the land. He would've mentioned the letters, but he didn't have enough particulars.

"Okay, any idea who might have a grudge against Greer?"

Noah shook his head. "Me, she seems to think. My dad." He laughed at that. "Next, I plan to stop at the rectory and ask what he might've done."

The phone rang, so Noah stood up. As Wade's hand curved over the receiver, he muttered, "I'm hoping it's kids. You find anything that says different, Noah, leave it alone. Get hold of me." Finally picking up the receiver, Wade barked his name.

Noah sauntered out. He found Callie still there. She was in the lot with Kayla Ritter, who'd double-parked beside his Chevy, apparently just to shoot the breeze with Callie.

Noah waved and Kayla waved back. He indicated by a twirl of one finger that he'd like to back out. Rather than pull over to wait for his spot, Kayla said one last thing to Callie, then drove off.

Joining him at his pickup, Callie said, "Back in Wade's

office I got the impression that you've taken a shine to our newest resident, Noah. Is she in trouble?" She lowered her voice. "Like, with the law?"

Startled, Noah eyed her. "Not that I'm aware of. Why?"

She shrugged. "My own experience?" It was known that when Callie came to town, she'd stolen her siblings from an abusive stepdad and was on the run. Wade had helped them get free. "When I arrived today," she said, "Greer was in talking to Wade. I sense she's holding something back. Secrets." She shook her head. "I'm aware that she used to live here and apparently knows Wade and you from back then."

"You wouldn't be jealous?" Noah teased.

"It's nothing like that. I can't quite put my finger on what I sense." Callie sighed. "And you're not going to tell me one thing more than Wade will. Men! Too closed-mouthed. Women consider a dozen possibilities when we need to figure out answers. Maybe I'll mosey on down to the café and talk to Greer myself."

Noah's raised his head and glanced down the street. "Greer's having lunch in town? Hmm, think I'll go see if she'll let me buy her meal." He moved past Callie and jumped into his pickup with such purpose, she called, "Hey! I've never known you to buy *any* woman lunch, Noah Kelley."

He tuned her out by starting his pickup's raspy engine. He was probably being too obvious. No doubt it'd come back to haunt him, since rumors spread like wildfire in this town. On the other hand, he'd been more than circumspect in dealing with unmarried women his age thus far. He was, after all, a man of marriageable age, as his mother said often enough. So what was the big deal if he'd finally met someone who intrigued him a little?

A little? Who are you kidding? Greer Bell set funny little fires blazing along nerves he'd thought were nerves of steel.

Nudging the lumbering diesel into a higher gear, Noah did a U-turn. Why not, if Kayla Ritter had guts enough to double-park in front of the courthouse?

Noah kept his eyes peeled, but didn't see Greer's Blazer near the café. Disappointment washed over him. He almost didn't take a spot that someone had just vacated. If his stomach hadn't growled menacingly at that moment, he'd have driven on. In the end, he decided that unless he ate before he went to see his folks, his mother would insist on cooking him a big meal. Especially if his stomach made noises like it was making now.

Jamming on his emergency brake, Noah bolted up the steps of the old converted house before he could talk himself out of it. He peered in the beveled glass of the front door. The interior was inviting, thanks to Callie's good taste. The old house was really run-down when she'd acquired the property as part of the Home Free program. Noah's restless gaze homed in on Greer, and unexpected pleasure went through him. She sat with her daughter at a table under a back window. Shelby was facing him, while Greer's back was to the door. A fast look around verified that there wasn't another seat to be had, not even in the side-rooms. Nope, no openings anywhere.

Noah—afraid that people he knew, parishioners, would notice the tables were full and conclude they ought to invite him to sit—hurriedly wove his way through the tables. But when he reached his destination, unsure of the reception he might get, his bravado collapsed. *What if Greer told him to get lost?*

Luckily Shelby glanced up from her menu, saw him. "Noah, hi! Look, my cast is hard now. Can you sign it? Mama, do you have a pen?" She patted the chair beside her. "Noah, you can sit by me."

Greer's eyes held the same expression as they had last night in far odder conditions. She picked up on his hesitancy. "Shelby, Father Kelley is probably meeting someone for lunch."

"Actually, no," he admitted in a rush, even though he again scanned the room. "I don't see any seats open. I was hoping you'd let me join you." It seemed natural to pull out the chair next to the beaming child.

Aware that Greer's jaw had tensed, Noah fumbled a pen out of his shirt pocket, tested a few places on the cast before finding a suitable one. He wrote his name in a bold scrawl and might left then, except that a waitress he knew dashed up. Noah had reasons for staying put and letting the woman think he'd planned to meet Greer all along. The waitress, Janet Kaufman, had made it clear on several occasions that she had marriage on her mind and him in her sights. Unfortunately, Janet also had his mother's blessing to proceed, full steam ahead.

"Ladies first," he said blithely, bestowing a very warm smile on Greer as she gripped her menu. And as if it was an everyday occurrence, he bent over Shelby's menu and helped her choose. "I'll have the daily special, Janet. Oh, just put everything on my check."

That brought out Greer's anger. Which Noah effectively disabled by taking both of her hands. In front of Shelby, whose eyes widened, and Janet, who plainly sulked, he deliberately lifted Greer's left hand to his lips and brushed a tantalizing kiss on her knuckles.

As he'd hoped, Janet departed so fast she didn't see Greer snatch back her hand. Noah braced for the sting of Greer's wrath. Her throat worked convulsively as she tried to speak, but not so much as a peep came out. That gave him time to confide how Janet relentlessly pursued him.

"Oh, now I understand," Greer said. "In Colorado, my boss's wife shoved guys at me. Losing them was never easy. But please, warn me next time before you attack."

Noah smiled, but his mind was working overtime trying to figure out how he could engineer a next time.

CHAPTER FIVE

LUNCH WAS PLEASANT, even though Janet pretended to be too busy to refill their coffee. "Maybe you hurt her feelings in the way you discouraged her," Greer murmured.

Noah didn't know what to say. Especially when Greer set down her sandwich and asked, "Aren't men in your position looking for a wife who'll be a good hostess? Your mom taught Sunday school, directed the choir and coordinated wedding receptions. I'm sure she wants you to find that kind of life partner. I take it Janet attends your church?"

Noah stopped himself from saying he thought his mother's main role was taking on any job ordered by his father. "Church membership and attendance are not criteria for how I care to choose a wife, Greer."

She mulled that over and seemed to want to delve deeper. Yet her eyes indicated that she knew she'd started up a slippery slope, and she retreated to pick up her sandwich again.

Darn, Noah had hoped for the opportunity to add that love was his only criterion for marriage.

A truck passed their window and claimed Shelby's attention. Two big dogs occupied the passenger seat. "Mama, do you see those neat dogs?"

"Border Collies." Greer said, turning to look as did Noah, who went on to say, "I've decided to take a run out Highway

6 to the animal shelter next week. Many a barking dog has scared off a would-be intruder."

"Is that like a burglar?" Shelby asked after the vehicle with the dogs had turned the corner.

Noah set down his cold coffee. "I'm not so worried about thieves, Shelby. But some kids get a kick out of opening corrals and letting stock go free around here. I'd rather not have to chase down my horses. There's too much open territory in the foothills where they could get hurt."

"We need a dog, too. Mama, there's hills behind us."

"True, but soon we'll have staff and guests on the property. Noah doesn't have anyone watching his place if he has to be away from home." It was then Greer realized that she'd used his first name rather than Father. Dammit. For a preacher he was way too disarming.

She opened her purse, counted out money for her lunch and Shelby's, plus tip, and left it by her plate. Then she stood up. "Speaking of not leaving one's home unattended…we should go. Shel and I also have a backseat full of mini blinds that need hanging before I start painting cottages."

Noah scrambled to his feet, helped Shelby up, and handed back Greer's money.

Parroting Callie's earlier remark, Shelby said, "I won't be much help, Mama." The child shoved her cast between the adults, interrupting the tussle with money. Noah was determined to get the check.

Greer saw they were attracting interest and said stiffly, "You win this time. Thank you for lunch." She dropped the money into her purse.

"Mama, I'll bet Noah will hang our blinds."

"Hush, Shelby, we've taken enough of his time today." Greer hastened her unhelpful child up the aisle between tables.

Noah placed enough money on the table to more than cover the bill. Greer and Shelby had gotten a head start, but he caught up outside. "I heard what Shelby said, Greer. Have you hung mini blinds before? It's quite a chore. I'd be glad to help if you have things to stay busy with for a couple of hours." He checked his watch. "I planned to swing by and talk to my pop, then go pick up a load of hay I ordered from Wright's. After that I'm all yours."

Something in the way he'd said that made Greer feel a burst of excitement. She wanted to refuse and probably would have if Shelby hadn't jumped in to accept. And as the man had bought them lunch, it'd seem rude to disagree.

"Filling two hours is hardly a problem. But please don't feel obligated because this kid of mine has no brakes on her mouth." Greer thought that sounded lighter, and gave him an out if he felt pressured by Shelby.

"That's what I love about kids. They have none of our inhibitions. You could use a hand, Greer, but you never would have asked."

"Right. Because we're practically strangers, and you have your own life and a demanding job."

"Hardly strangers. We knew each other as kids. And now we're next-door neighbors. So I'll see you around, neighbor."

His heavy-duty pickup sat right in front of the café door. He'd climbed in before Greer could think of a comeback. Still, she found the thought of seeing him again far more appealing than she wanted to—or had any right to. A friendship between her and the local Episcopal priest wouldn't even rank on the suitability scale.

NOAH WHISTLED as he drove off. He couldn't remember the last time he'd felt like whistling just because his heart was joyous. Probably not something a man in his profession ought to confess. Except…who knew better than the Lord how frustrated he'd been since returning to his hometown? He believed the Lord worked in mysterious ways, so he assumed Greer Bell had come into his life for a reason.

Slowing before he reached the rectory, Noah prepared what he'd say when Pop hit him with complaints lodged by the board about his methods of running the church. Noah wasn't his father and never would be. At the time he'd left high school for college, Noah would have said that anyone who dared suggest he'd follow in Holden Kelley's footsteps was crazy. He hadn't much liked growing up a preacher's son. The expectations imposed on him by his parents and local society were confining and burdensome, to say the least. His original intent had been to choose a degree program in business administration. Church attendance had been ingrained in him from birth, so that was probably why he'd attended campus services on Sundays. In the middle of his junior year, he'd received *the call*. To be honest, he'd always thought that was nonsense. He tried to ignore the voice, first dismissing it as his conscience, then as the result of stress. He even feared he might be going insane. But the voice persisted and his campus pastor—young and forward-thinking, suggested Noah had been called to spread the Word. Relieved to learn the voice in his head hadn't meant he was losing it, he actually stopped to listen. And in listening, he heard. And he followed. After graduating with a B.A. in business, he enrolled in Austin Graduate School of Theology. Of course his folks were ecstatic. They never understood that his degree in divinity was where all resemblance between him and his father began and ended. Holden was old-school inflexible. While Noah was more liberal and relaxed. And there was certainly room in the various factions of the Episcopal faith to accommodate many different approaches.

Surprisingly he and Pop didn't butt heads the first Sunday Noah stood in for the ailing priest. But it'd been Ruth who begged her son to investigate filling in for his father. Little did any of them realize the greater area council had already been considering what to do at St. Mark's. Even though Noah had been reluctant to offer his services, he'd allowed them to persuade him…. On a temporary basis, he'd insisted.

Ruth, during the early months, devoted herself to tending to her sick husband. Fiercely protective, she didn't let anyone bother Holden with church matters. Only lately had Holden improved enough that he demanded to schedule a few visitors. That was how he'd discovered that neither his wife nor his son were filling his shoes to his satisfaction. Precisely why Noah limited his visits.

The doctor said Holden could suffer a third major stroke, and Noah didn't want to be the one to cause a relapse. Yet, neither was he going to reverse everything he'd implemented.

Ruth answered his knock, looking more frazzled than usual. As a rule, his mother personified the conservatively dressed, newly permed, small-town pastor's wife. A woman prone to blend with whatever setting she happened to be in. "Noah, forever more," she scolded. "Since when do you knock as if you're a guest?"

"Since I became an adult with a home of my own, Mother. Would you walk in unannounced at my place?"

"No, but mercy, you grew up here." She fluttered bony hands and fussed with the top button at her throat, another nervous trait Noah recognized.

"I've just washed our lunch dishes, but it's no trouble to make something for you, dear. I can warm up ham, fry potatoes and boil a couple ears of corn. They're fresh," she said, moving toward the high-ceilinged, old-fashioned kitchen.

"Don't bother, Mom. I've eaten. Is Pop available to chat or is he napping?"

Ruth turned back, her face strained. "I hope you're not planning to upset him again, Noah, like the last time you came by. Ralph Fenton, Harvey Steffan and Joe Carpenter did a good job of it this morning. I suppose that's why you're here."

"What's got those old buzzards going *now?* Don't tell me, let me guess. Harv calls me a karaoke convert because I'm using a screen during services to display scripture verses and songs via my computer. Mrs. Percelli, our organist, went to Dallas for a couple of weeks to visit her daughter, so I've been using tapes. I hear the board objects to my playing new Christian rock groups. I'll bet Joe's sounded off about the fact that I'm playing guitar for our youth choir. Oh, and Ralph, the miserable old goat, simply can't abide change of any kind."

His mom nodded after each statement like a bobble-head doll. "I didn't hear everything they said. Holden asked for iced tea and cookies. Noah…what's karaoke? Harvey says it originated in taverns and bars and is the work of the devil."

Noah exploded in laughter. "Sorry, Mom. I'm not laughing at you. He sounds like some old-time revivalist or something." He paused. "I have to admit I'm curious as to how Harvey knows karaoke originated in bars."

"Did it? Oh, Noah. It's obvious that your big-city church did things differently than we do in Homestead. What I can't understand is why you persist in antagonizing long-standing board members. Can't you do as they ask?"

"No, I can't, not if I'm going to build up a membership in shameful decline."

Ruth sliced a hand through the air. "The seven-year drought toppled ranches, and businesses were stretched thin. We lost a few members."

"Even before the drought," Noah said gently. "And more than a few. I went over the church books and budgets for the last ten years and computerized them. St. Mark's has been slowly dying for quite some time. It's got to stop."

His mom's birdlike frame seemed to crumple before his eyes and she appeared older than her fifty-seven years. "Your father worried obsessively over that. It probably contributed to this last stroke. You can't bring this up again, Noah."

"You brought it up, Mother, and you seem to be siding with the board. To get healthy, St. Mark's has to add members. Families." He didn't tell her it was a goal set down for him by the greater area council. Otherwise the Homestead property would be put up for sale. Homestead would lose St. Mark's.

"Your father needs another six months to get back on his feet. I'm doing my best to limit his time with the board. As Holden grows stronger, I find it more difficult to intervene. I'm begging you, Noah, please steer clear of controversial subjects today."

"I'll try. Do you have any idea how many times I've walked out to avoid arguing?"

"Doc Cooper explained that stroke patients are often grumpier from the frustration of not being in control of their lives."

"I understand. So, what do you think? Is Pop awake?"

She motioned for him to check. "It's time for his blood pressure pill. He asked to take it with lemonade. I'd just finished mixing a pitcher when you knocked. Would you like a glass as well?"

"Sure, as long as you're bringing him one anyway. Are you taking care of yourself? I swear you're getting thinner."

"Bless you!" She pinched his cheek. "You know what they say, women can't be too thin or too rich."

"Not true. I've counseled anorexic teens and miserable

wealthy folk. By the same token, I've known people I'd call rich who barely have two dimes to rub together."

"When I see Ralph Fenton again, I'll mention this conversation. That should prove your compassion makes you a good man, and suited to this job."

Feeling guilty because he didn't have a lot of compassion when it came to dealing with Ralph, Noah opened Holden's door and walked softly to his bedside.

His father was a once big-boned man made smaller by his recent ordeal. Holden's eyelids opened gradually and warily as if he sensed someone in his room.

Noah noticed there was a droop to his father's left eyelid, and the left side of his mouth was still drawn down. To make communicating easier, Noah circled to the right side of the hospital bed they'd brought in to accommodate his needs.

"Well, it's about time you showed your face around here." The senior Kelley pressed a button and brought the upper half of his bed into a semi-upright position.

"I've been busy."

"Yeah. Making stupid changes to a perfectly good church agenda." Some of Holden's letters were still badly slurred as he tried to form words.

"The board ought to be letting you rest. Next time, send them straight back to me. They're trying to circumvent me."

"Right. The way I hear it, they did complain to you about your liberal—" he practically spat it "—approach. You ignored their advice."

Noah dragged a chair closer and sat down. "Pop, they drop unsigned notes in the suggestion box. I announced a month ago that I won't respond to anonymous gripes. Do they think I can't identify their writing?"

"Then listen to what they say, boy. Those men were guiding church protocol when you were wearing diapers."

"Did they also tell you about all the new members we've picked up?"

Holden looked moody. Noah assumed the men had said something, but that his father wasn't impressed. As he apparently still had the floor, Noah decided to broach the subject he'd come to discuss. "Did they mention that the old Farley place got a new owner this week?"

Holden's lip curled. "Another of Mayor Wright's down-and-outers? If your mother had heeded my advice about how to cast her vote, all that land would be where it belongs. In the hands of a real land steward, Clint Gallagher."

"Well, Jase's ranch brought back a former resident of Homestead. A former church member, in fact. Greer Bell and her little girl. Robert and Loretta's daughter," Noah said, thinking his dad might not place someone who'd left so long ago.

"That girl was a blight on St. Mark's. If she's come back with the name Bell, she's still a blight. Do you hear what I'm saying?"

Noah was totally taken aback by his father's vituperative response. He might have resorted to yelling had Ruth not entered bearing lemonade and Holden's pill.

She cast a look of stern disapproval on her son. "What's all the shouting? Holden, calm down and take your medicine." She poked a small pill between his lips and held the lemonade glass, forcing him to swallow. "I told you no good would come of you voting with the mayor, Ruth," he bellowed. "Greer Bell's come back to flaunt her illegitimate kid. Did you know? Why didn't you tell me so I could've had the committee block her application? Isn't it enough that we've let in all this other riffraff?"

Ruth gave a start, nearly dropping Noah's drink. He took it quickly, unsure whether he should stay or bow out now before things went farther downhill.

"Loretta may have mentioned that Greer's return was a possibility," she mumbled evasively.

"If the girl's taken over Jase's ranch, it's more than a possibility. Listen, boy, we don't need the likes of that...that immoral woman sullying this town or our church. We're God-fearing people."

Noah shot to his feet. "What happened to *come all ye who are weak and heavy-burdened?*" His voice rose as he asked, "Since when do we sit in judgment of others?"

Holden ignored him. "I forbid you to allow it," he ranted. "Robert will thank you if you send her to the Southern Baptists on the outskirts of town. If the girl had one shred of decency or care for her family, she'd have stayed in Colorado."

"I don't believe I'm hearing this! I'm telling you both, Greer's daughter is coming to Sunday school with Wade Montgomery and his family. If I hear so much as a hint that she's been made unwelcome, I'll do my level best to see the doors of St. Mark's closed." Furious, Noah didn't look back to see how his remarks affected his father as he slammed out of the room. He'd just opened the front door when Ruth ran after him. "Noah, I'm ashamed of you. What if you'd caused your dad to have another attack?"

Noah shut his eyes and vigorously rubbed the bridge of his nose. "I can tell you unequivocally that he and I will never see eye to eye on this. Or anything else, it seems. We're not a fundamentalist church, Mother. Out in the world, times have changed."

"Not here." Ruth extended blue-veined hands toward her son. "Oh, I know Holden takes a hard-line approach on moral issues, Noah. He always has. Since...well, his mother carried on with a married man and made his father a laughingstock after she bore the other man's baby. Plus, he's ill. Would it be so awful to discourage the Bell girl and her…bastard child? That's what she is, you know."

Shocked, Noah spun away and bounded down the steps. "Shelby Bell will attend St. Mark's on Sunday."

"What does it matter to a child where she worships?" Ruth called. "If you'd rather not be in the position of refusing her, I'll talk to Loretta."

"No, Mother, you won't. Not as long as I speak for St. Mark's," he from between tightly clenched teeth.

Wringing her hands, Ruth wailed, "Holden's right. None of this would be an issue if I'd voted the way he wanted on Mayor Wright's land program. I never imagined this would tear my own family apart."

"Luckily I believe in forgiveness, Mother. What I'd like to know is when and why that particular concept slipped by you and Pop."

"Your father and the board believe we teach by example. Greer was a smart girl who obviously went wild partying and consorting with bad boys the minute she got to college. Robert and Holden wanted to visit the boy's family, to see he did right by Greer. She flatly refused. Wouldn't name the boy. *They* only sent her to Denver to stay with an aunt during her confinement. Greer ought to have given the baby up for adoption. It would've been best for…everyone."

"Enough! That's such archaic thinking, I can't even— Forget it," he muttered. "Fighting is senseless. The child has a name, Mother. It's Shelby Bell. She's spunky, happy and smart as a whip. As a mother yourself, could you have given me up for adoption?"

Ruth sucked in an indignant breath. "For shame, Noah Kelley! From the moment your father and I met, we lived by the good book. Greer Bell didn't. Her kind never will."

Noah threw up his hands. He obviously wasn't going to

change his mother's mind on the subject of Greer. "I need to cool down before I can talk about this rationally. Like I said, Shelby will attend church with Callie Montgomery. If you're planning to be there, I'll expect Christian behavior toward Greer's daughter."

"Oh, Noah. I wish you'd reconsider…."

Without another word, he marched out to his pickup. His next stop was Wright's Hayseed Ranch to pick up a load of hay. He chatted with Nan Wright, but his thoughts remained on Greer. At least now he had a clearer picture of why she took his head off that first day they met, when he'd extended a simple invitation to church. And the other night down by the river. Now he understood why she'd accused him of trying to drive her out of Homestead.

Noah wondered if their sheriff was aware of Greer's history. Had her return sparked enough resentment in someone for that person to push the boundaries of harassment? He'd considered Clint Gallagher first, because the curmudgeonly state senator made no secret of wanting more land. But he'd already paid Ryan Gallagher a visit. Six foot, eagle-eyed and straight-arrow, Ryan had taken time to ponder Noah's questions before declaring that his dad, while not above trying to obtain the abandoned properties, wouldn't stoop to illegal means of getting them.

Noah believed Ryan. So then who could it be?

After stocking up on hay, Noah headed back to town to chat with Ed Tanner. He was no help.

Deciding to take Greer's injured daughter a token gift, Noah cruised the toy aisle. Ed suggested the book she'd put back. Noah paid for it. It didn't seem enough. Yet he had no idea what Shelby already owned. A display of night-lights had him taking a second look. He spotted one he was sure would please her, but maybe not her mom. Shaped like an appealing terrier, the dog's body lit up when plugged in. If Shelby happened to wake for any reason, he was reasonably certain the glowing dog would comfort her and maybe even make her smile.

Once he left Tanner's, he went home to unload his hay. As he worked, his thoughts wandered repeatedly to his neighbor. Drenched in sticky straw, he showered and took a little time to polish Sunday's sermon. He actually considered changing it to explain what it meant to love thy neighbor. Or would that be too obvious? But he believed the best sermons were lived, not preached.

AFTER LEAVING TOWN, Greer drove into the lane that led to her ranch. She glimpsed the back of a car in her driveway, and her hands tensed on the steering wheel.

Shelby bounced excitedly in the back seat. "Grandma's here, Mama! Look, Grandma's probably brought our kitchen curtains."

It was good to be told that was her mother's car. On the other hand, what did it say that a nine-year-old had recognized the car, but that Greer hadn't?

Since Loretta wasn't anywhere to be seen outside, Greer assumed she'd gone in. Granted, there was no lock on the door yet. Not until she installed the one she'd bought at Guthrie's.

Her arms filled with mini blinds, she relied on Shelby to guide her up the steps. "Hello?" she called, stepping into the entryway.

"In the kitchen," Loretta warbled back. "I had no idea when you planned to get here, Greer. I'm not in the habit of breaking and entering," she said, her laughter warm. "I hope you'll forgive me this once. I have a roast in the oven and the Andersons are coming to dinner. I finished your curtains and couldn't wait to see them up."

Dropping her ungainly load of long boxes on the living room floor, Greer was slow to follow Shelby into the kitchen. Her mom climbed down off a kitchen chair, noticed Shelby's cast and said, "Oh, my word! Honey, what happened?" Her eyes went to Greer for the answer.

"Shelby fell yesterday while attempting to wash a window that was out of her reach. Didn't you notice the porch railing lying in pieces?"

Loretta brought a hand to her heart. "I'm sorry, no. Once I saw that your car wasn't here, I unpacked the curtains. I was determined to hang them and surprise you." She knelt to inspect the girl's cast. "What a thing to happen on your first day here, sweetie. Greer, why on earth didn't you phone me? Where did you take her? The new clinic in town?"

Shelby pointed to Noah's signature. "Lucky for us Noah rode in on his horse right when I fell, Grandma. He's so smart. He wrapped paper around my arm so it wouldn't hurt. And he used Mama's shoelaces to tie it up. Kristin cut them off, so now Mama hasn't got any way to tie her sneakers."

"I do, Shelby. I had new laces in our catch-all box."

Loretta glanced quickly up at Greer. "Noah Kelley came here? That's a surprise," she murmured. "Oh, perhaps not. He's very nice."

"Yep, Grandma, he is," Shelby piped up. "Noah drove Mama's car so she could sit in back with me. He took us to Ms. Kristin's clinic. Mama said I can't call her Dr. Kristin, 'cause she's not a doctor, but I'm s'posed to call Noah Father Kelley, 'cept he says not to." The girl heaved in a breath at the end of her lengthy sentence. "Today we met the sheriff. And guess what? I get to go to Noah's Sunday school with them day after tomorrow."

Greer's mother straightened. "Greer, do you think that's wise?"

"Wise? Whatever do you mean, Mother?" Greer knew full well, but she wasn't in any mood for this.

As usual, Loretta avoided meeting her eyes. "What do you think of the curtains?" she asked abruptly.

"I love 'em," Shelby chirped.

"They brighten this room," Greer said with a shrug. "How much do I owe you for the material and labor, and for the rods?"

"Owe me? Nothing. They're my housewarming gift to you."

"Mama bought blinds at the hardware store today for all our windows," Shelby announced.

Loretta was unable to cover her pain. "I'm sorry I came in and took over," she said, suddenly stiff. "You should've said yesterday that you wanted blinds rather than curtains."

Greer sighed. "The curtains are great. I'm going to put blinds behind them. As I explained to Shelby—although she left that part out—guests are likely to roam around as if they own the place. Most don't intend to intrude on the ranch-owner's privacy, but it happens. It's our fault, really. When guests arrive, we urge them to consider the ranch their home for the length of their stay."

"Whatever made you decide to share your home with a bunch of strangers, Greer?"

"At the time I chose this occupation, I was faced with single motherhood. My counselors in Denver were kind enough to point me in the direction of careers that would allow me the flexibility to be with my child."

Again Loretta averted her eyes. "Shelby, do you have a marker or crayon in your room? If so, run and get it and Grandma will sign your cast."

Delighted, the child skipped off.

Only after her footsteps had faded did Loretta face her

daughter. "Greer, back then your father and I made the choices we thought best for everyone. I'm sure we caused you strife. I didn't go unscathed, either. I've missed you, whether you believe that or not. But, if you don't want me in your life, tell me why you moved back to Homestead."

Greer jerked open the refrigerator door and pulled out two sodas. She handed one to Loretta. "Several times over the course of this move, I've asked myself that very question." She popped the top, listened to the hiss of escaping air, then took a long pull from the icy drink.

Her mother wiped the condensation from her can and carried it to the sink where she opened it, as if fearful it'd spew all over the floor. Or maybe she needed her back turned to say what she wanted to say. "There's nothing anyone can do to change the past. If I'd been a different woman, maybe I would've stood up to Robert and Holden. Or maybe not. They made convincing arguments in favor of sending you to Robert's sister. We thought a large city would make it easier to locate good adoptive parents for your baby. Can you stand here today and say that if you had everything to do over, you wouldn't have done things differently, Greer?" Loretta turned then and didn't flinch from the fire in Greer's eyes.

"What do you want to hear, Mother? That I'm sorry I was naive enough to fall for a smooth-talking jerk? You want to hear my main regret? It's that my family didn't stand behind me when I most needed them. I love Shelby. I'd *never* not support her. Never!"

Her mother's weepy eyes swept her from head to toe. "You're stronger than me, honey. I can't change that, either. But it doesn't mean I wouldn't like to."

The two women stood on opposite sides of the kitchen counter, both glaring, neither bending until Loretta reached for her purse. "I'll be going," she muttered.

"Mom, wait." Greer caught her arm. "I didn't sleep well last night. There were noises outside, and then I was worried about Shelby's arm so I kept checking on her. She'll be disappointed if you leave before you sign her cast."

"I hear her coming now." Pulling loose, Loretta met her granddaughter in the hall. "Ah, good, you found a permanent marker. You need to take this pen to school on Monday. You'll collect a lot of signatures."

Shelby watched with big eyes as her grandmother made fancy curlicues on her capital *L*. "Noah said I'll meet kids at Sunday school. I'll take my marker there, too."

Loretta capped the pen and gave it back. "Seems you and Father Kelley had quite a talk."

"Uh-huh. He likes horses and dogs, like me. And tons of catsup on his French fries. Noah's coming over this afternoon to help Mama hang mini blinds."

"You don't say." The older woman sent Greer a quizzical look. As she strode to the door, it appeared she'd let Shelby's last remark pass without comment. But, hand on the knob, she stopped, turned, and said, "I hope one thing you do remember about this town, Greer, is that people talk. As a businesswoman, you do have a reputation to consider."

"Meaning *what*, Mother?"

"Meaning there are those in Homestead who will misconstrue Father Kelley's simple kindness for…something else."

"Is that so? How will anyone know he's helping me install a few blinds unless you intend to gossip about it at church?"

"Consider how I heard, Greer, via your chatty daughter…" She let it go and fled the house. At the bottom of the step, she paused. "By the way, dear—you're welcome for the curtains."

CHAPTER SIX

SHELBY PICKED UP on the tension vibrating in the wake of her grandmother's swift departure. "Are you and Grandma mad at each other?"

"Mad? Uh…no." Greer just couldn't believe she'd been reprimanded like a kid because she'd forgotten to thank her mom for the gift. As for the prodding Loretta had done regarding Father Kelley, Greer's response had come from her own guilty conscience. Her mother had merely expressed the same concern Greer had felt about Noah's offer to help hang her blinds. Not only should she have thanked him politely and declined, she should also have ignored the lust sizzling in her belly, a sensation she hadn't experienced in years. Ten years to be precise.

Considering who Noah was, combined with her past history, she knew her feelings were inappropriate. *Hard work.* That was what she needed.

"Shel, grab a couple of your favorite books. I'll carry a blanket out to one of the cottages so you can sit there and read while I paint walls."

"I wanted to paint. But I guess I can't, Mama." The girl went off to find one of her favorite books to reread.

The cottages, three in all, were standard one-bedroom, one-bath units with good-size sitting rooms. They each had space for a chair, a TV and a queen Hide-A-Bed. The kitchens consisted of sinks, cabinets and counter space for coffeemakers, and an L-shaped alcove that would accommodate a small refrigerator, a corner table and chairs. They were well-built but had been neglected.

A coat of paint would do wonders, Greer decided. She'd brought several gallons of cream and earth-toned colors from Denver. At the time she hadn't known how many gallons she'd need. But as the Sandersons were redoing their cabins it would've been foolish not to take advantage of their offer to share costs.

"Will you be okay by yourself for a few minutes, Shel? I'm going to get the ladder and paint supplies."

"I wish I had a dog to keep me company while you're busy," Shelby whined.

"A dog would run all over the place making a nuisance of himself."

The child heaved a huge sigh and dropped her chin into her hands. She could be very dramatic when she wanted to make her mother feel guilty.

There were no two ways about it; Greer hated seeing Shelby unhappy. An only child herself, she'd been acutely lonely much of the time. "I'll tell you what, Shel, let's see how much I can get done in the next couple of days. If I make a lot of headway, maybe I'll reconsider getting that dog."

The girl's outlook improved markedly. And the return of Shelby's sunny smile was the only reward Greer needed after Loretta's departure had left her feeling low.

During her second trip from the cottage to the bunkhouse where she'd stored her supplies, Greer noticed a line of dust being kicked up a half mile or so in the distance. Billowing dust clouds rose in the opposite direction from Noah's house. Greer dragged out the step ladder, set it up and climbed to the top, trying to see better. She identified two men in cowboy garb trailing a line of fat cattle on ATVs. It was a reasonably large herd, being moved from one of Gallagher's pastures to another. The lead animals plodded through part of her brush and cottonwoods. Steers and cows with healthy-looking calves. Greer climbed down, lost in thought. Miranda had said Clint Gallagher wouldn't be pleased if Greer's stock strayed onto his deer leases. That consideration didn't appear to be reciprocal.

Monday, right after she registered Shelby at school, Greer intended to stop in town and locate a fence company.

Some two hours later, she'd painted half the living room of one cottage, and rested atop the ladder for a moment, admiring the change a little paint made. All at once, Shelby jumped up and raced outside, yelling, "Mama, Mama, Noah's here! Noah's here! I see his pickup in front of our house. I'm gonna go tell him where we are." The screen door banged on her noisy exit.

The paint roller Greer had just filled shook. She nearly smeared peachy beige paint on her white ceiling tile. Jittery though she was, Greer did her best to act cool. Her mother was absolutely right; she should discourage Noah Kelley's visits if for no other reason than that Shelby had gone crazy over the man. Add to that the noticeable quiver in her stomach, plus the fact that small-town residents had long memories, it all spelled trouble.

The smart way to handle this would be to take him aside today and explain her situation…and his. In the eyes of old-timers in Homestead, she had a tarnished past. Father Kelley wore a halo, for heaven's sake.

Greer felt his presence in the room the minute he stepped through the cottage door. She didn't need to hear the screen open or Shelby shouting, "I'm back, Mama. Noah's here. And guess what? He brought me presents! Get-well presents, he said, 'cause of my broke arm."

"Broken," Greer corrected, never taking her eyes from the spot she'd been working on since Shelby dashed out the door. A well-painted square, for sure.

"Yeah, Mama, that's what I said. Is it okay if I open them now?"

"Fine, honey. Did you remember to say thank you?" Greer rolled faster to keep the paint from dripping, and to steady her hand.

"Oops. Noah, thanks! I didn't know people got presents for broke arms."

"Broken." This time Noah did the correcting. "And you're welcome, squirt. It's nothing, really."

Hearing paper rip, Greer finally felt she'd reached a place where she could tactfully pause and see what was happening below. Only she hadn't expected that Noah would leave Shelby seated on the blanket tearing into her gift, or that he'd cross the room to where she was on the ladder. Too late she realized he stood directly below her, and had placed a booted foot a rung below hers. Heat from his body and the aroma of his spicy aftershave hit her like a truck. Greer was afraid she'd drop her pan and roller.

"Need help cutting in the corners?" he asked in a husky voice. "I've been known to sling a pretty mean paintbrush, even if I do say so myself."

His solid chest against the back of Greer's already fluttering left leg had her stammering, "Oh, I, uh, can't let you do anything of the k-kind. Give me a minute to finish this wall. Then I'll be ready to hang the blinds. B-but, if you have other visits to make, I'll tackle that project on my own later this evening."

Shelby's squeal of delight drowned out Noah's response. "The book I wanted! And a puppy dog night-light! Look, ev'rybody, the whole dog lights up when he's plugged in. I *love* it."

"I'm glad," Noah said, his attention torn away from Greer. "You probably have a night-light, but I saw it and bought it because…well, it's a dog. I know how much you like dogs. This one doesn't bark, but all the same it'll help you feel secure," he added pointedly, that comment obviously aimed at Greer.

"You two wouldn't be ganging up on me so I'll agree to a dog, now would you?" Greer responded dryly.

Noah's expression remained serious. Shelby, however, jumped up and ran to hug his waist with one arm. "Guess what, Noah? Before you got here, Mama said d'pending on how much work she gets done, maybe I can get a dog next week."

He looked up at Greer again. "I've definitely decided to visit the closest animal shelter next week. Probably Wednesday. Is that too soon for you? Wade's decided it *was* kids fooling around at the river, but…I'm not sure."

Noah was keeping the news of the tape player between him and Wade for the moment. Because it was really Wade's decision whether to discuss it with Greer. And unless the sheriff connected the device to someone in particular, Noah wasn't about to frighten Greer.

"Myron Guthrie believes it was teenage boys, too," Greer said. "Wade promised to have a deputy do a drive-by for the next few nights." She saw an expression in Noah's eyes, an expression she couldn't quite read. He tried to hide the look by coughing and turning away.

Suddenly the thought of having a watchdog seemed comforting. "Wednesday?" she repeated.

"Yes, would you like me to swing past and pick you up?"

"Uh…how late is the shelter open? According to the school pamphlet I got, the bus will drop Shelby off at our lane at three."

"Far as I know, it's open Monday through Saturday from ten to six. I can call them and let you know if that's not right."

Shelby galloped excitedly around. Her foot accidentally kicked the ladder and made it shudder.

"Whoa there, squirt. I know you're happy, but don't kill your mom," Noah said, steadying Greer with a broad palm clamped around her thigh. That did more to make her feel on the verge of tumbling off than did the wobbly ladder.

His touch, coupled with his deep laughter, sent a twinge of desire through Greer. Recognizing the trouble she was in, she freed herself from his grasp. "Horsing around isn't helping me get this place in shape."

Noah caught the out-of-control child and swung her high. "Give your mom a kiss, and then sit down so we can get to work, okay?"

His easy way of handling Shelby had a more profound effect on Greer than did his warm hand on her leg. None of the men she'd known in Colorado had devoted time to her daughter. Well, except for Cal Sanderson. And her long-time boss treated Shelby the same as he did his son and daughter, with discipline and affection.

Greer suddenly thought about the men she'd dated. They'd all been friends of Cal and Marisa's. Two had told Greer to her face that she acted cold and distant. A third hadn't been interested enough to offer a critique. She brought herself up short. She wasn't going to date Father Kelley! It was too bad that the only prospect she'd run across, who was both interesting and liked kids, had to be Holden Kelley's son.

Wouldn't the folks in Homestead who'd labeled her a "slut" be surprised at how few men she'd gone out with since she'd left. They'd probably never believe it. Depressing, Greer thought, reaching out to vigorously roll paint.

"I'm impressed with how much you've improved this place

already," Noah said, pausing to unbutton his shirtsleeves and fold them up before he opened the paint can. "Curtains at the kitchen windows. A porch swing. Paint. By the way, I brought my toolbox. Before we get to the blinds, I'll tackle repairing your porch railing."

"It needs a whole new section, I'm afraid. I plan to go to town Monday after I enroll Shelby in school and get someone to put up a fence between me and the Four Aces. I'll get whoever I hire to mend the porch railing."

"I guess you're aware Clint's crew drives cattle across your land from time to time?"

"Earlier I saw them driving cattle north of here. I'll need woven wire fence, anyway, because in a few weeks I'm bringing in sheep."

"Do sheep run off? Don't they pretty much stay put? Fencing will cost you a pretty penny. Sheep? I wonder if Clint Gallagher knows?"

"The fence is a necessary expenditure, even though sheep are docile unless something scares them. Yesterday Miranda reminded me that Gallagher rents deer leases. I can't have Shelby wandering in where she might accidentally get shot. Oh…did you mean that because Clint's a cattleman he'd object to sheep next door? There are already sheep in the valley. My dad raises some, as do other ranchers."

"The fence is a good idea. I hadn't thought about Shelby wandering off. I should have. Ethan Ritter's son, Brad, ran away one day and got lost. He was badly dehydrated by the time he was found." Noah motioned Greer down from the ladder and climbed up to cut in the edge between ceiling and wall. "I talked to Ryan Gallagher about the other issue. He runs the Four Aces now. He said his dad tried to convince the council to vote against Miranda, apparently with backing from the former mayor. Ryan swears that's as far as Clint went."

"I haven't apologized yet for accusing you." Guilt tinged her voice. "Wade Montgomery almost rolled on the floor laughing when I mentioned it."

Noah glanced at the blanket where Shelby had been sitting, her nose in her new book. He discovered she'd gone. To the bathroom, perhaps; he heard water running. "I had no idea why you were so hostile toward my father, Greer. Today I asked."

She hesitated, her knuckles white as she gripped the roller. Her eyes darkened appreciably. "Then why are you here?"

"You made plain what you think I'm like. But you're wrong, Greer. There are differences between Pop and me. Major differences."

What differences? Greer wanted to ask since Noah didn't elaborate. Still, her heart lurched wildly and began thudding faster, contemplating possibilities. Had Shelby not run out of the bathroom and straight to Noah, Greer would have probed further.

"Noah, the sink faucet in our bathroom is dripping water all over everywhere. Will you fix it, please?"

Greer gasped. "Shel, he's not our handyman."

He tapped a finger on the girl's upturned nose. "It's quite all right, Greer. It so happens I am handy with a wrench, and I enjoy puttering. My house didn't need much. It sat empty for a few years, but it'd never been lived in."

"That's certainly not true of this place." Greer heaved a sigh as she went to inspect the dripping faucet. "Which does *not* mean Shelby should come to you for help anytime she unearths a problem."

"Why not, Mama, if Noah likes to fix stuff? Mrs. Sanderson said the first thing you hadda find in Texas was a real good man who can work side by side with you, like Mr. Cal does with her."

Quite sure she couldn't get any redder, Greer shut her eyes and rubbed a hand down her face. She left beige tracks, and Noah told her so.

He sounded far too amused to suit Greer. "Shelby, oh— never mind. I'm embarrassed, Noah, okay? The truth is, the parent of a nine-year-old has no skeletons in her closet. A kid drags out every single one."

"Mo…ther," Shelby said, rolling her eyes dramatically. "There aren't any skeletons in our closet. You packed them in a box with the black cats and witches we put up at Halloween."

Although Noah would've loved to tease Greer about the shock on her face, he decided she deserved some slack. "Halloween will be here soon, squirt. Our church voted to have a carnival for our Sunday schoolers and others in the community looking for a safe place to trick-or-treat. You and your mom are welcome."

"What happens at a carnival?" Shelby asked.

"Fun and games. For now, the exact plans are a secret."

"I like games. And secrets. Can we go, Mama? Can we?"

"Honey, we'll see. I'm making no promises until I have this place shipshape."

Then—just that fast—Noah saw Greer close herself off. Again. Right when he thought he'd made headway in loosening her up. Hadn't he assured her things at St. Mark's were different on his watch? Unless—unless he'd read too much into the flashes of interest he thought he'd detected. Determined to operate under his original assumption, he winked. "Alas, there's no rest for the wicked. Or do you believe, Greer, that the righteous don't need any? If so, I'll just grab my toolbox and Shelby can lead me to that leaky faucet."

A red-gold sun had dipped into the west before the trio emerged from the cottage. Sweat plastered Noah's blond hair to his neck and forehead, but the faucet no longer leaked and the walls were painted. He hauled the ladder and his heavy toolbox out onto the vine-latticed porch. "Where's the lock?" he asked, setting down his load to reach back inside.

"Someone stole the door locks. I bought new ones at the hardware store, but it's getting late. I'll install them tomorrow."

"Huh, after all our work, you'd risk letting vandals wreck the place tonight? Get the locks. All of 'em. Wait—don't tell me you slept in an unlocked house last night?"

"I wedged a chair under the doorknob. After the—you know—excitement down at the river, I didn't sleep much." Her yawn punctuated her announcement.

Noah muttered something; had he not been a priest, Greer would've thought they were swearwords. His irritation spoke volumes. She hurried to her SUV and returned with the locks.

Taking the sack, Noah set about working his way methodically from door to door. Greer and Shelby stood aside and watched. Greer focused on his broad, suntanned, capable hands. She imagined how those hands, calloused—not smooth as it seemed most priests' hands would be—would feel against her skin. Her mouth grew dry as she considered other things she shouldn't fantasize about. Finally she hurried inside and came back, carrying iced tea for her and Noah, and juice for Shelby.

He tightened the screws on the last lock, the main house dead bolt, with Greer holding a flashlight, since it had grown dark. Noah tested his work. "At least hanging blinds will be a piece of cake compared to assembling this last lock. And there's plenty of light inside," he drawled. When she completely missed his meaning, she added, "No offense, Greer, but you wiggled that flashlight so much, it's a good thing you didn't try to be a surgeon."

"Funny! I said I'm tired. And will you look how late it is?" She extended an arm and tapped the face of her wristwatch. "You need to get home to bed, too, Noah. We can't monopolize all your time. I'm sure you have other obligations."

"But the blinds. I know you wanted them hung tonight."

She waved away his concern. "I'll do them tomorrow. You've been a huge help. The locks were more important."

"You carry on with painting. I have a basketball team I work with in the morning, but right afterward I'm free. I can be here by one."

She started to protest, but he said quite firmly to leave the blinds, that he wanted to hang them. Greer tucked a loose strand of hair behind her ear and walked him to the door. She lingered in the doorway as he ambled off, whistling, waving as he climbed into his pickup. *Well, you certainly discouraged him, didn't you?* As she went inside and used the dead bolt he'd installed, she told herself she had to make things plain tomorrow.

She was doing heavy-duty cleaning, and moving junk out of the bunkhouse in order to paint, when Noah showed up on Saturday shortly after noon. He was so cheerful and pitched right in to lend his muscle that she put off their little talk until this day, too, got away. It was 6:00 p.m. before she knew it. "Goodness, I've kept you so busy, Noah, I'm sure you have to leave."

He wiped his brow and took the dustpan from Shelby, who'd been hurrying back and forth to empty it in the trash bin outside the bunkhouse. "This space sure looks better," he said, leaning on the broom handle. "We're losing our daylight. Time to go inside the house now so I can hang those blinds."

"Absolutely not! Again, I've taken up most of your day. And since tomorrow's Sunday, I know you probably need time to prepare for your early-morning service."

"I pared back to one Sunday morning service. At nine. Hey, I hate to bring this up, but for the last hour or so I've been running on empty. Don't you ladies ever eat?"

"I'm hungry, too, Mama," Shelby put in as she set the dustpan in the corner.

Greer panicked. If her mom had a valid reason for saying the community might misconstrue Noah's offer to help a single mom hang blinds, what tales would circulate if Greer fed him, too?

"What's wrong?" Noah squinted at her. "If you haven't thawed anything out, we can go over to my place. I've got a bunch of microwave meals. When we come back, you can put the squirt to bed while I get started on the blinds. We should be able to finish up by nine-thirty or ten."

Her panic grew. Oh boy, would the rumors fly if she and Shelby were spotted going home with Noah after dark. "I, ah, have food," she stammered. "Including part of a dried peach pie Miranda's mother baked as a welcome-to-Homestead gift."

"Hey, sounds good. Point me toward the blinds. I'll get started and you can interrupt me when the food's done."

It sounded so simple and innocent. But the knot that had formed in Greer's stomach tightened anyway as she led him inside her humble home and pointed out the stack of blinds she'd piled in the living room.

Shelby announced she was going to her room to play. She promptly dashed off, leaving the adults alone.

Instead of hunkering down over the boxes, Noah stood in the center of the room and scrutinized the area as Greer snapped on a floor lamp and two table lamps set on matching maple end tables. The room looked inviting in the pale, yellow glow. Her overstuffed furniture, which flanked a floor-to-ceiling brick fireplace, was of good quality and solidly constructed. Nothing fragile that would scare off even a big man. Noah was by no means overweight, but he worked out, rode horses and slung around bales of hay. He also mucked out barns. He'd visited homes where he'd been afraid to sit on a chair in case his weight collapsed the spindly legs.

Spotting a frame filled with pictures on the rough-hewn mantle, he crossed the room for a closer inspection. It was a collage of Shelby's photos. In the first she was a serious big-eyed infant. At maybe two years old, she was feeding ducks almost as big as she was. In the next, at age five or six, she sat proudly on a docile horse. Her legs were so short they stuck straight out from each side of the saddle. That shot had Noah chuckling, as did the last in the series. The girl smiled for the photographer, showing off a gap where her two front teeth should be. He set the frame carefully back where it'd been and turning slowly, let his gaze roam the room, landing at last on Greer.

"Now it's my turn to ask if something's wrong." Greer had nervously watched him study her belongings intently.

"Far from it. I've just been thinking that what you've put together already is nice. Really nice, in fact. Feels…homey."

Funny, but his approval was more nerve-wracking than his disapproval would have been. Greer didn't handle compliments from men easily, and discovered it was even harder to accept one from a man she couldn't quite pigeonhole. She jerked a thumb toward the kitchen, pausing to wipe suddenly sweaty palms up and down her jeans as she edged past him. "Thanks. Uh, if you have everything you need for the blinds, I'll go get busy on our meal. Will…soup and ham sandwiches be okay? Or…gosh, maybe you need something more substantial."

"Anything's fine, Greer. I hope I haven't given you the impression I'm difficult to please."

She paused in the kitchen archway. "No, it wasn't that at all. I'm sorry if it sounded that way."

He hooked his thumbs under his wide leather belt. "Greer, do I make you nervous?"

"No! Yes." She quickly averted her eyes from his long and steady perusal. "It's just that I'm not used to cooking for a man. Leeta, the cook at the ranch where I worked, always insisted men need stick-to-the-ribs fare. She'd set out platters heaped with meat, potatoes, three or four side dishes, plus scrumptious desserts. Our male guests cleaned every platter." She gave a quick shrug. "Shelby and I nibble more than we eat big meals. But you've worked so hard today, I'd feel terrible sending you away hungry."

Noah crouched down, opened the first box and dumped out the hardware for one mini blind. It gave him time to digest what she'd said and also what might have been implied: that she wasn't an old hand at inviting guys to her house for dinner. What his folks had said—well it just didn't fit with the woman he'd been observing these last few days.

"So you're still willing to take potluck with us?"

"Soup and a sandwich will be far healthier for me than the microwave meal I'd fix if I went home. Really, Greer," he said when she continued to stand there. "Slap any old thing together and don't worry about it."

She gave in with a deep sigh.

Noah tugged at his ear and hummed softly. He couldn't help feeling he'd vaulted some major hurdle. Noah wondered whether Greer's problem was specifically with him or with men in general. If the opportunity presented itself tonight, he intended to get an answer to that question before they parted.

Climbing the rickety ladder, he measured an equal distance down both sides of the window frame, marked the holes, and with an electric drill he'd bought himself last Christmas, he set the first screws. Two blinds were up and a third almost done when Greer summoned him and Shelby to the table. "Shel, remember to wash your hands."

Noah set down his drill and coiled the cord. Inspecting his hands, he grimaced. "Better point me to a sink, too."

Greer did, but then walked into the living room to study the effect and stopped to admire what he'd accomplished. "Don't those look nice? I'd be lucky to have one done in the time you've put up three. Thank you!" She paused. "Seems I'm always thanking you."

Shelby ran up, drying her hands on her jeans. "I told you Noah can fix stuff really good, Mama. And if he washes his hands in the hall bathroom, he's gonna see that sink leaks a bunch, too."

"Shelby! Honest to Pete."

"Not Pete, Noah!" The girl giggled and darted away when her mother attempted to hush her by covering her mouth.

Greer had set the kitchen table and arranged the settings so Shelby sat at the end, between her and Noah. She hadn't allowed for his much longer legs. As they both sat and Greer ladled thick tomato soup into three bowls, their knees brushed and she almost dropped the pot.

Noah caught her wrist and steadied it. "Here, I'll hold the pan, and you dip."

She noticed he didn't seem at all bothered by the fact that their legs kept tangling beneath the too-small table. But it flustered her.

"Relax," he murmured with knowing sympathy. "Eating is something we both do every day. We're going to get through this fine, Greer. Ham and cheese sandwiches are my favorite."

"I like grilled cheese better," Shelby said, deconstructing her sandwich so she could eat the cheese first.

"Shelby, I know I let you take apart your sandwich when

it's just you and me at supper. Don't you remember I said you can't do that in public."

The girl glanced up and around the table. "But we *are* home."

"We have company," Greer said sternly. "You are not using company manners."

"Sorry. I didn't know Noah was company." She slapped the meat and bread back together.

Uttering a sigh, Greer abruptly left her seat to pour two cups of coffee from the coffeemaker that had stopped gurgling. "I'm sorry, Noah. This wouldn't be an issue if you'd had her call you Father Kelley, as I asked."

"What do guests call *you* at work?"

"Ms. Bell. I wear…or did wear a name tag."

"Should I be calling you Ms. Bell, then?" Noah ate several spoons full of soup, his eyes holding Greer's as she wadded her napkin distractedly in one hand and followed the path of his spoon, all the while clearly perplexed.

"N…no, calling me Ms. Bell while we're puttering around here would feel odd. It'd be too formal."

"I feel the same about you calling me Father Kelley. I just want to be myself Away from the church—and even at church—I want to avoid formality whenever I can."

"That's cheating," Greer said. "That gives the impression you're somebody you're not. Oh, I'm not saying this well, am I? People wouldn't be confused if you'd wear your collar. As a matter of fact, why don't you?"

Noah swallowed the bite he'd taken of his sandwich. He noticed Shelby had all but stopped eating, and her head whipped from side to side as she tracked their rapid exchange with interest. "I never thought about it, but it's probably because the collar makes some people nervous. Like you."

"Okay, but boots and blue jeans says something entirely different about who you are than a clerical collar does."

"Ah, now we're getting somewhere. You think I'm more approachable without the trappings of a priest, right?"

A short nod acknowledged his assessment.

"Then I'm succeeding. My aim is for people not to separate my faith from me. I want to make faith desirable and accessible. But I do wear the collar for important things like marrying and burying."

Shelby found his last statement terribly funny. She laughed hard and choked on her milk. That pulled Greer's attention away from Noah's comments long enough to yank her daughter up and tap her on the back until Shelby caught her breath.

When things returned to normal, table talk turned to other things. Finished with his meal, Noah carried his plate and bowl to the sink. "If you have a pencil and paper lying around, Greer, I'll jot down a list of plumbing supplies you'll need to pick up from Myron next time you're in town. As well as the faucet leak in your main bathroom, I noticed the elbow pipe under the sink is almost rusted through. I doubt I can break it loose without stripping the threads on the couplings at both ends. You need a new one."

Shelby darted away, digging out a pad and pencil from a pink backpack that sat on the kitchen counter. "This is my brand-new school pack, Noah. Mama bought it for me to start my brand-new school. Do kids in Homestead carry backpacks?" she asked, sounding worried.

"Sure, they do. And yours is going to be the envy of many. Most of the ones I see at Wednesday night Bible studies are plain black or tan."

"Oh, no! What if the other kids think I'm trying to be cooler than them? They'll hate me. Mama," she wailed and ran to bury her head against Greer's breast.

Noah sat in a state of semi-shock. "*Where did I go wrong?*" he mouthed to Greer.

She slid her chair back and consoled the weepy girl. "Shelby, honey, it's getting late and you're tired. Maybe the kids Noah's talking about are older. There's no sense crying over not fitting in when you haven't even seen what kinds of packs other third-grade girls have. You're going to see Brittany Lambert tomorrow. Ask her if pink packs are okay."

Straightening, Shelby rubbed red, swollen eyes. "All right. Can we buy me a different one if nobody else has pink?"

Noah finally figured out his gaffe. "I'm sorry. You know what, Brit's pack is purple. According to Callie, Brit's in a purple phase. If pink's out, I'll buy you a new pack myself on Monday and bring it to school. It's the least I can do for making you cry."

"Thank you, Noah." Shelby ran to Noah and flung her arms around his neck. "Luke's daddy used to do stuff like that for him all the time. Like, if Luke forgot his lunch or his school books or field trip money, his daddy brought them to school. One time I forgot. Mama was busy, so I had to borrow a book from my teacher. That's why daddies come in handy."

Noah gave her an awkward pat on the back until she stopped squeezing the breath out of him. Once she let go, he grinned. Until he saw that Greer wore a frown and her gold-flecked eyes had turned cold as brass. He sobered, too, thinking that if he wasn't in hot water with one of the Bell females, he'd landed in it with the other.

Laying the list of supplies on the counter, he muttered, "While you put Shelby to bed I'll go hang the rest of the blinds."

When Greer returned, she began to open boxes and sort out blinds to hang on the opposite side of the kitchen from where Noah was working. She turned on the CD player loud enough to discourage conversation.

Later, she watched from the corner of one eye as he gathered up his tools.

"I'll drop in on Monday afternoon and repair the sink if you have the parts, Greer. Tomorrow you might want to see whether any of the other bathrooms have anything leaking. If you pick up all the parts at one time, we can get you ship-shape in a couple of days."

Lagging behind as he headed for the door, Greer crossed her arms. "I know Shelby gave the impression that I'm woefully in need of a man. That's just the weird logic of a kid," she said dismissively. "I'm more competent than I've probably appeared."

He waited on the porch and said nothing as Greer flipped the outdoor light switch five or six times to no avail. Noah took note of her exasperation and hoped she couldn't see how annoyed he was at her idiotic statement. "You know, Greer, another attitude I try to epitomize is neighborliness. In Homestead, people can rely on each other. Tell Myron Guthrie you need an electrical switch added to that list."

He saw her go still, then tense up. At first Noah assumed she was going to tell him off. Then he realized her attention was focused on something beyond his left shoulder. Turning, he caught the flash of a light swinging left and right along a bend in the river. The light seemed to somersault in the air—it fell a foot, bounced, then was picked up and grew steady again.

Noah uttered a laugh. "That'll be Wade's deputy, Virgil Dunn, running a check just like Wade promised. Something you'll learn if you stick around…Virg is a nice guy but a klutz. I'll bet you lunch at Callie's Café he tripped over that big cypress root."

"What do you mean…if I stick around?" She edged back over the threshold and started closing the door. "I told you the other night, I'm here to stay."

"Good!"

The slam of her door cut off Noah's reiteration that he'd be here Monday afternoon at two.

CHAPTER SEVEN

NOAH DROVE across the perimeter access road, hoping to catch Virgil and ask if he'd found any sign of kids messing around Greer's place. He didn't connect with the deputy.

Greer was very much on Noah's mind after he drove home. She stayed there while he slept. He woke up in a sweat at almost 2:00 a.m. with a hard-on sure to send the current church board into apoplexy if they knew. And just where did they get off acting so self-righteous and judgmental about him or Greer, anyway?

Unable to fall back asleep even after a cold shower, he decided to do his own check along the river. Throwing on jeans, boots and a football jersey that had seen better days, he grabbed a flashlight and struck out on foot. The nights were growing cooler. A sliver of moon did nothing to illuminate dark granite boulders flanking even darker water. An east wind rattled fallen leaves as he tramped through the woods. Other than the leaves, nothing moved, although an owl hooted.

Maybe kids were the culprits, after all, and it'd been a one-time thing. If only odd things hadn't happened to other new-comers who'd come to town. Noah tended not to believe in coincidences. When stuff happened to Callie, Wade had said he didn't believe in them, either. As Noah faced Greer's ranch, expecting to see the house and cottages dark, he was shocked to discover lights blazing in the house and middle cottage. He set out at a trot, praying he wouldn't step in a pack rat hole or a cow pie in his haste.

His lungs begged for air before he reached the main house and tore up the steps. He rapped softly on the door at first, then harder, finally banging loudly and shouting.

A white-faced Greer, her springy curls flattened by a scarf and her chin streaked with pumpkin-colored paint, appeared at the corner of the house, where the porch rail lay in pieces. Once again her only weapon was that silly rusted pitchfork.

"Noah it's 2:00 a.m.!" she hissed like a cornered bobcat. "Has there been another incident? If so, tell me quick. I left Shelby in her sleeping bag in the cottage I was painting."

"No incident that I know of. Something…uh, woke me up. I decided to check along the river. I saw lights on at your place and got worried. Why are you in the cottage? Don't tell me you're painting at this hour?"

She relaxed the pitchfork. "You're worried about us? I appreciate the thought, Noah, but in future you can save yourself the trouble. We're fine. I've got a long history of insomnia. I *am* painting. I get a lot more done that way. Shelby, bless her heart, has learned to sleep anywhere. Oh, you might be interested to know she insisted we plug her new night-light in near her sleeping bag."

He smiled. "I thought she'd like that night-light. Do you need help? I mean, I'm up and awake."

"We'd probably talk and wake up Shelby. And no offense, but how would it look if you fell asleep at the pulpit tomorrow?"

He laughed, and the light from his flashlight jumped, dancing up as far as Greer's chin. "Anybody tell you you're cute when you're trying to act fierce? By the way, what color is that paint on your face?"

Her hand flew to her cheeks, then to the scarf tied beneath her hair. It was a vain gesture, unlike her, and she quickly let her hand drop to her side. "It's something called spun persimmon. Looks like plain old pumpkin in the can."

"Yeah, on your face, too."

"It's better after it dries. Well, on the walls it's mellower. I have leather furniture that'll go great in that cottage. Listen, I need to get back. Shelby doesn't usually wake up, but if she did…"

"Right, I understand. Come on, I'll walk you."

"Do you always fuss over people, Noah? Or don't I seem capable? I assure you I am. In Denver I often took guests out on moonlight trail rides."

"Mmm, that sounds like fun." He closed the distance between them, grasping her elbow lightly as he turned her around the end of the house. "Did Wade mention that…other things have happened in Homestead. Even before our incident the other night, Greer."

"What things? He never said a word."

"I'm not saying they're related. In fact, it's possible I'm worrying about nothing." Noah matched his long stride to her shorter, now flagging steps.

"Nobody's been…like murdered or anything?" She shivered and he stopped at the corner of the first cottage and turned her toward him so he could rub the exposed flesh below her T-shirt sleeves and warm her arms with his hands.

"Nothing so drastic. Since I'm not in law enforcement I could be wrong about this. In fact, I'm sure Wade's probably already considered it and discounted it, but someone's targeting newcomers to Homestead. Do you remember Ethan Ritter? His brother, Jud, and I were around the same age."

"I know of him. Haven't seen him in years. Did something happen to Ethan?"

"To the woman he married, Kayla. She moved here to find a drier climate for her daughter, Megan, who has severe asthma. That's another story. Anyway, Kayla started a vineyard. Suddenly the vines all died. Chemical poisoning from a herbicide. Wade arrested a guy named Tolliver Craddock, who has a record. A slick lawyer got him off. Ethan's always questioned Craddock's motive. They're strangers, right? So Ethan wondered why Craddock targeted Kayla. I don't know if he said it to anyone other than me, but he once brought up the possibility of someone hiring Craddock. Someone who wanted Kayla to fail. If she did, she'd lose her land."

Greer leaned her pitchfork against the siding of the cottage they'd painted earlier in the day. Moving out of Noah's reach, she rubbed her arms. "They arrested this man? But now he's out?"

"Wade told me he has Craddock under close surveillance."

"Then he can't be the person who did all the wailing and screaming that scared the socks off me."

"Maybe he has an accomplice."

"But I don't even know him. You said *things*, as in plural. What else?"

"Not long after Callie moved in, her house was trashed. That *was* kids. Angry because their dad, a guy already head over heels in debt, didn't get a parcel of land."

"That would have nothing to do with me, either. Clint wanted this land, but you believe he's not involved."

"I can see you think I'm connecting dots when there aren't any. Maybe I *am* off base. The way I remember this town, Homestead used to be a sleepy, almost boring little community. However Wade's been a whole lot busier than Jock ever was as sheriff, and he's uneasy about this, I can tell. Just be vigilant, Greer, that's all I'm saying."

"Good advice." She shrugged. "Except that it feels like I should always watch my back. It's a difficult way to live for someone who's trying to start up a business."

"Hmm. Well, I'll volunteer to watch your back as often as I can." Noah took two steps closer and this time lightly ran his palms up and down her arms. The unexpectedness of his move forced her to raise her head.

"Don't," she managed to choke out. "It's not right. *We're* not right. Go home. Just…leave me be." Greer shoved his hands off her waist. She lurched sideways, then sprinted to the middle cottage and disappeared inside.

Her anxiety worried Noah as he watched the door bang shut on her heels.

Midway through his walk home, it struck him that Greer saw his offer as a come-on. He *was* interested but he was also sincere in his concern. How had he offended her? Even though he'd been out of the dating circuit, he couldn't help being male, couldn't help reacting to her as a woman. He'd never been a monk, and for a time at college he'd cut loose and sown a few wild oats. None of what he'd done had hurt him or the women he'd been involved with. The current church board would have a fit if they got wind of his exploits, though.

It so happened that Greer Bell was the first woman in ages he had the slightest desire to be with. Too bad if she didn't cotton to the idea. It was a cinch his board and his folks would like the idea even less.

Entering his silent house, he had an answer for the lot of them. They'd better get used to it, because he intended to go with his gut on this one.

GREER SAGGED against the door inside the cottage. The unpainted walls seemed to mock her, demanding to know why she'd foolishly turned down an offer of help. She hadn't handled that encounter very well. Certainly not in the mature fashion she'd promised herself. Maybe he *hadn't* been flirting with her. He'd scared her, although he probably only meant to comfort her. He must think her an idiot.

Hurrying into the bathroom, Greer splashed cool water on her hot face. In the process of drying herself, she noticed the leak. She remembered that plumbing parts for this sink were included on a list Noah had written earlier. It seemed everywhere she turned she was bound to be reminded of him.

As she took up the paint roller again, Greer let her mind deliberately recall his features. He didn't have to work to attain good looks. His eyes alone, the color of a cloudless Texas sky, were stunning. His sun-streaked hair had a natural wave. Greer wished she had access to old high school yearbooks. Her bet would be that Noah had been an athlete. Football, most likely. He had the height and muscle for it. And didn't every boy in Texas start out with their dads shoving a football in their chubby hands? She pictured Noah with a son.

That was dangerous thinking.

Greer couldn't help picturing a little Noah Kelley. The man had a natural way with kids, and she wondered why he wasn't married with a couple of his own. His mother, Ruth, used to schedule weddings at St. Mark's. Greer had attended several. His mom fussed and fluttered, seeing candelabra and flowers placed just so, and then sat through every ceremony with a hanky in hand. Yes, Greer was fairly certain a woman like that would want her son to have a wife. A wife of whom Ruth and her husband approved, of course. That let her out.

The Kelleys had sat in her parents' living room as judge and jury, passing judgment on Greer's shameful activities, which had resulted in her—Lord have mercy—getting pregnant without benefit of marriage.

Stopping, Greer poured more paint into a new roller pan. This time a warm cream color, a perfect contrast for the pumpkin shade. Finishing this cottage and the next, and then tackling the bunkhouse—that represented her future. There was no future in expending energy trying to imagine the kind of wife Ruth and Holden would pick for their only son. Someone who was the complete antithesis of her, that much she knew.

Rejecting those thoughts, Greer doggedly worked her way around the rooms. She finished just as the sun crept up over the rolling green hills that ran along the far side of the river. She'd taken her paint supplies out to the porch, and stood there for a moment, in awe of the view. Streaks of gold and lavender and pink rained over dark-green hills, spreading rainbow ripples across the visible portion of the Clear River. With a wake-up view like that, she wondered how Jase Farley could ever call this paradise the Dragging F. If it was up to her, she'd name it Sunrise Ranch.

Greer's breath closed tight in her throat. It *was* up to her. She'd just found the name to put on her business cards and brochures. Sunrise Ranch. She wanted to tell someone, share the idea with someone. Shelby was still asleep. It was too early to call her mother. She didn't know the mayor that well. *Noah.* He was awake. At least, a thin stream of smoke rose from his square chimney. The card with his phone numbers, which he'd pressed into her hand the day of Shelby's accident, happened to be in the front pocket of the jeans she had on. Pulling it out, she flattened it. Twice she reached for the cell phone tucked in her back pocket. Twice she hesitated.

But darn it, who in town did she know better? Before she could change her mind, Greer punched in his number. She'd let his phone ring once. If he didn't answer, she'd hang up.

He did answer, with just his name. A deep, sleepy rumble

that conjured up all kinds of delicious visions in Greer's sleep-deprived brain. They were such titillating pictures, she couldn't find her voice.

"This is Father Noah Kelley," he repeated. "Speak if some-one's there."

That jerked Greer back to the present. "Uh…it's Greer."

"Greer! What's wrong? I'm just fixing breakfast. Give me a second to turn off my stove and I'll be right there. Three minutes, tops."

She laughed. "Nothing's wrong. It's more that something's right. I hope you don't want to come over and strangle me for calling with something unimportant at such an early hour, but I saw smoke coming from your chimney and, well…"

"Greer, you don't have to give me a ten-minute disserta-tion on why you're calling. It's okay. Honest."

She hauled in a deep breath. "All right, here goes. I've named my ranch. Well, I think I have. I need…want a second opinion. I just finished painting the cottage and stepped out on the porch. Shoot, being a guy you probably don't care about sunrises. I'll let you get back to your breakfast," she said, her words falling over each other.

"Hey, don't go! I bought this property for the incredible view from my back porch. It's funny, but the day you moved in I realized I'd have to quit referring to your place as the Dragging F. I almost turned back to suggest you consider watching the sun come up before selecting a name. And now you have."

"You're not just saying that to make me feel okay about phoning you at the crack of dawn, are you?"

"No, I swear. So what *are* you calling the ranch, Greer?"

She told him, and explained her idea for a brochure, then waited breathlessly.

"Sunrise Ranch," he echoed. "Simple and succinct. If I were a stressed-out New York businessman looking at a cold, snowy day it'd appeal to me. Too bad you aren't coming to church with Shelby today. The best photographer in town is Millicent Niebauer from the *Homestead Herald*. She sings in our choir and you could corner her after the service. She'd be flattered if you asked her to take the shots you'll use in advertising."

Did he know what a temptation that was, the rat? Although, really, nothing could be tempting enough to get her to attend church. "Now that would be a black mark on your record, Father Kelley. I haven't been to bed at all. I'd not only snooze during your sermon, I'd probably snore. Thanks for your approval on the name. And for the tip. I'll add stopping by the *Herald* to my list of Monday chores."

"I won't pretend I'm not disappointed you won't come to church. I'm sure Pop soured you with his hellfire sermons, but I don't preach doom and destruction. I wish you'd consider giving me a chance to entice you back."

"This is where I have to be honest with you, Noah. Getting me back to St. Mark's would take a miracle. So unless you're a miracle-worker, you're wasting your breath."

"Maybe one of these days we can sit down and talk about why you're so adamant. Faith is also about forgiveness. Of others—and yourself."

"Goodbye, Noah." The tremor that shook Greer's hand was so strong she almost couldn't press the small disconnect button on her phone.

"Mama, who are you talking to on the phone?" Shelby came out on the porch, rubbing one eye, holding her favorite stuffed toy with the arm still in a cast.

Greer rearranged her angry features into a soft smile. She ran her fingers through her daughter's rumpled curls. "It's okay, honey bunny. Did you see I finished painting the cottage? It's cool, huh?"

"I'll go look, Mama. I hope I didn't sleep past when Brittany and Mrs. Montgomery are s'posed to pick me up for Sunday school."

"No, it's early. But you almost missed the most fabulous sunrise." She turned Shelby toward the river. The palate of colors still streaked the sky, but the river had gone more silver. "When I first came out it was like the river took on the color of the sky. A bit later it turned fiery red. I thought it looked like…like paradise. I think we should call our place Sunrise Ranch. How's that sound to you?"

"Okay, I guess."

"Or maybe Paradise Ranch," Greer mused aloud. "Which sounds best?"

Shelby shrugged. "What's paradise?"

"Sort of like heaven."

"Ew…people are dead when they go to heaven."

"Honey, not heaven in the literal sense. It just means a really happy place. The happiest, in fact."

"Oh." The girl stood on one bare foot, then the other. "This isn't paradise then."

"Shelby, don't you like it here?" Greer said, sounding aghast.

"I like it okay. But I'd need a daddy for it to be the happiest place."

Greer couldn't hide her dismay. She tripped over her tongue. "Is this more of Luke and Lindsay's wisdom?"

"Nope. It's in my heart, Mama." Gazing past her mother, Shelby pointed and tugged on Greer's shirt. "Is Noah's house on fire?" she asked urgently. "Should we call the fire department?"

Distracted though she was by Shelby's shocking comment, Greer whirled. "Uh, that's smoke from his fireplace, Shel. It's okay, his house isn't burning."

"Can we go inside and build a fire? It's cold out here. I forgot my slippers."

"We, uh, we don't have any firewood, so no. I'm sorry. Guess it's another thing to put on my list for town. I'll see where people buy firewood. Maybe if we go back inside and I start breakfast, the kitchen stove will take the chill away. Go get your sleeping bag."

"And the doggie light Noah bought me. When we go on Wednesday to get my dog, I bet he'll keep me toasty warm."

Greer knew she'd have to follow through on that outing. A big bag of dog food was yet another thing she'd put on her long list of items to buy or order on Monday.

After breakfast, she wrapped Shelby's cast in plastic and helped her into the bathtub. It was harder washing her shoulder-length hair while keeping her broken arm out of the water. All in all it proved difficult. And time-consuming. They'd no sooner found Shelby a pair of nice red pants that were stain-free and a blouse to match that was a little more Sunday-go-to-meetin' than her normal T-shirts, when Callie Montgomery and Brittany knocked at the door.

Greer hurried to greet them, conscious that she probably looked a wreck.

"Hi." Callie waved over her sister's light-blond hair, fixed in a French braid today. Greer was frankly relieved to see that Brittany wore purple capris, a sleeveless matching top and white sneakers with a purple stripe. Her worry about Shelby's appearance now seemed overblown. Callie looked good in trim slacks and a feminine blouse. Wade sat at the wheel and waved to Greer. He clearly had his hands full keeping six-year-old Mary Beth inside the vehicle. Adam, typical of eleven-year-old boys, slumped in the far backseat, probably playing a handheld Game Boy.

Shelby, a bundle of excitement, exploded through the

screen. The girls ran off to the car, and Callie grinned. "Those two haven't hit it off or anything. We'll bring Shelby home around twelve-thirty."

"That soon? When I went to St. Mark's as a youngster, sermons dragged on well past twelve-thirty. Sometimes to one o'clock."

"Noah believes in finishing in an hour. I'm sure you'd be pleasantly surprised." Callie saw Greer open her mouth and held up a hand. "I know you must be snowed under with work. How's it coming? Are you making any headway?"

"Quite a bit, actually. Yesterday we painted the first of the three cottages. The mini blinds are all hung, door locks installed, and a couple of the leaky faucets are fixed. Last night I painted the smaller of the cottages by myself."

"Goodness, that sounds like a lot of work for you and Shelby to have done."

"Well, Noah came on Friday and Saturday and brought his toolbox."

"Oh, so that's where he went to. Ethan phoned Wade to ask if he'd seen Noah. He tried him at the church office and his house. Ethan operates a therapeutic riding school for children who have physical disabilities. He had a couple of questions for Noah. Oh, well, they'll catch up with each other today." She shrugged slightly. "Gosh, I didn't realize Noah was so handy. He sure kept quiet about it when I was renovating the café." Callie grinned. "But maybe Wade warned him off. Wade kept coming around, and I thought he knew there was a warrant out for my arrest."

"You're joking."

"No. My stepfather swore one out on me for kidnapping my siblings."

Wade honked and beckoned to his wife. "It's a long story, Greer. But it has a happy ending." The face she turned toward her waiting husband softened noticeably, and Greer felt a stab of something akin to envy. Especially since Shelby seemed to continually drop little remarks about how nice it'd be to have a mom *and* a dad.

"I won't keep you, Callie. Thanks for going out of your way for Shelby. My mother probably would've taken her. Or maybe not," she mused half to herself. "That's a long story, too," she said with a sigh. "Time will tell if it has a happy ending."

Callie, already partway down the porch steps, glanced back with genuine sympathy in her clear blue eyes. "If you're talking about dysfunctional families, Greer, you'd have to go some distance to beat mine. One of these days after you get settled, I'll fix us a decadent dessert and coffee, and we'll have a long chat."

"I only hope I have time for stuff like that, Callie. It'll be a while before I can leave my guests totally in the hands of staff."

"That reminds me, was my dad able to provide any names?"

"I haven't talked to him yet. I'm not in a position to hire quite yet. Soon, though. And thanks for the tip."

Callie's steps slowed. "Wade said I needed to make it plain that my dad may recommend migrant workers, and you should check their green cards. Saves everyone from getting in trouble with the law."

"If people have a steady job where someone trusts them, aren't they less apt to be in trouble with the law?"

"You and Dad will get along fine." Wade laid on the horn again. Callie cast a guilty glance at her watch, fluttered her fingers at Greer and scurried off.

Leaning against the door casing, Greer waved to the children, who waved madly back from the middle seat in the family car. Her heart lurched when they disappeared from sight. A lost feeling washed over her. She recognized it as one she hadn't experienced in a while—the feeling that some important piece was missing from her life. She told herself she was just tired from hard work and lack of sleep.

And since she didn't have long before the Montgomerys brought Shelby home, she'd better get started on painting cottage number three.

The paint colors she'd chosen for this unit were called "baked clay", which was a rust color, and "utterly beige." They went well together. Marisa Sanderson had a knack for decorating. Almost everything Greer knew about running a guest ranch she'd learned from Cal and Marisa. But that didn't ensure her own venture would be a success. It was another huge weight she lugged around. What if she squandered the savings she'd put aside for Shelby's future, and then fell flat on her face? Easterners came in droves to vacation at a working ranch outside of Denver, Colorado. That didn't mean anyone would want to visit Homestead, Texas. Granted, there were attractions in the area, like the Bluebonnet wildflower trail in the spring, craft stores galore in Fredricksburg, and Schlitterbahn, a water amusement park in nearby New Braunfels. They were a bit of a drive, but maybe eventually she could afford to transport guests.

Dreams. Oh, she'd never been short on dreams. According to her mom, dreaming of things beyond her reach had probably blinded her to the faults of the guy who'd fathered Shelby. Dan Harper's family had money. Greer frequently searched her soul, trying to decide if the fact that Daniel drove a nice car, wore fine clothes and spent lavishly on her had turned her head. She honestly believed what had drawn her to him had been his smooth words and carefree manner. Her parents and their friends were so serious all the time, and she'd wanted something different. Now, she was forced to be serious, too.

The painting went well, even though she was exhausted by the time she'd finished. She was outside between the cottages, rinsing her paint tools with the garden hose, when she heard wheels crunching on her graveled lane. The morning had flown by fast.

Hearing a car door slam, she called out to Shelby. "Honeybun, I'm in the back. Wait on the porch and I'll be right there to let you in the house."

"Don't tell me you finished another of the cottages," a deep voice said.

Greer jerked around. Noah stood on the path. Shelby skipped behind him. He had on a dark blue suit, white shirt open at the throat and black, dress cowboy boots. Greer's hand flew to her sweat-matted curls and slid down to the front of a paint-stained T-shirt.

"Mama, Mama, I met some really neat kids. Megan, she's a year younger than me. She hasn't lived here for long, either. When she came, she had a hard time breathing, but now she breathes good. Her sister Heather's my age. Well, she's not a full sister, I think Brit called her a stepsister. Heather's my age and she's read more books than me, and I read a lot. They've got a brother, Brad. He's another one of the steps. That's what he called it. He's pretty cool, and loves horses as much as me. He invited me over to their ranch to ride. I told him pretty soon I'd have my own horse. That's right, isn't it, Mama? Anyway, they go to my school. They've got different last names, but pretty soon they'll all be Ritter. Isn't that right, Noah?" She grasped his hand and looked up at him.

Greer shaded her eyes. Before she could ask why Noah had brought Shelby home, he volunteered the information. "Wade got called out on an emergency, a big pileup on the highway outside town. He generally brings his own vehicle for that reason, but wouldn't you know, today he didn't. Neighbors said they'd drive Callie and the kids home, but they didn't have enough seat belts for everyone." He rubbed his knuckles over Shelby's head and made her already flyaway hair stand on end.

"I didn't mind," he added with a big grin. "Gave me an excuse to hurry along the usual lollygaggers and complainers. I'll undoubtedly hear about that from the board before tonight's service, so I propose we run off and do something fun. I can go home and change, which'll give you time to shower."

"Mama, Noah said maybe we could go see The Cowboy Artists' Museum in Kerrville. And it's open this afternoon. He said it's neat, so can we go?"

Greer stared at the two eager faces. Frankly she was too exhausted to disappoint either of them. "Sure, I suppose we deserve an outing. Provided you won't get upset, Noah, if I fall asleep on the drive."

He stepped to the door of the third cottage and whistled. "You've knocked yourself out getting this done, Greer. Didn't you nap at all during the time Shelby was at church?"

She shook her head. "It's no big deal. I get on these tears where I don't sleep for a while and then I crash and burn. Riding in a car if I'm not responsible for driving brings that on quicker."

"I'm no doctor, but I wouldn't think that's too good for your system."

She shook her head, then closed her eyes and rolled her head around on stiff shoulders. "I've been like this a long time. It had its advantages all the nights I had to work or take care of Shelby when she was a baby, and study as well."

"She was born before you graduated from high school?"

Greer blushed. "No, between my college freshman and

sophomore years. But, I graduated from high school early. I was barely eighteen when I had her."

He acted as if he might ask another question, but noticed Shelby listening. Instead, he tugged at one ear and cleared his throat. "I'll mosey on home. How much time do you need?"

She yawned and clapped a hand over her mouth. "That depends on whether I fall asleep in the shower."

Afraid she was in danger of doing exactly that, Noah tweaked the ribbon that held Shelby's ponytail in place. "Check on your mom at the end of fifteen minutes, squirt. I shouldn't use bribes, but I see an ice-cream cone in your future if you don't let her drown before I get back."

Shelby hooted, and Greer laughed, too. It felt good, and she realized he'd driven away the gloom that had settled over her after Callie and Wade had left with Shelby.

The girl released her hold on Noah's hand. Running over to her mom, she waved a handful of papers—standard Sunday school art projects, plus another typed paper that Shelby extracted from the pile and thrust into Greer's hand.

"This is a note about children's choir, Mama. The tryouts are Thursday night at six-thirty. I love to sing and so do Brit and Megan. We made a pact that we're all gonna go. Will you take me to church on Thursday?"

"Honey, what have I been saying since we got here? I have to get things done around here so I can be open for guests before Thanksgiving. "

Shelby's bottom lip quivered and her eyes filled with tears.

Greer was helpless to drive them away. But even if she hadn't had so much to do, she *couldn't* take Shelby there. Greer remembered the role Noah's mother had always played at choir practice. Ruth Kelley had pointedly informed Greer that she wouldn't be welcome at church in any capacity; this was between the time she came home from college and when her parents had made arrangements to take her to Denver to live with her aunt. Greer had loved singing and had a fair voice back then. She still didn't understand why they made her give up choir. She'd tried to tell Ruth her pregnancy wasn't showing yet, and that no one except they and her parents knew she was going to have a baby. That hadn't mattered.

Noah stepped in now, showing far greater empathy for Shelby's situation than his parents had for Greer's. "Callie's aware that you're on a tight timetable, Greer. Before you say absolutely no, give her a call. She said she and Kayla Ritter could work out a car-pool arrangement for the girls."

"And I wouldn't have to drive at all?" Greer asked, just to be perfectly clear on what this entailed.

Noah bent to help collect the paint supplies. "I won't cross my heart and hope to die or anything. But that's what I understood. So Shelby, don't waste those tears until after your mom sees if she can figure something out with the other moms."

"Will you?" The girl's still-swimming eyes sought her mother.

Even though she felt she might be sticking her foot in a sinkhole that could drag her in over her head, she gave her reluctant agreement to make the call. Yet another thing to add to Monday's chores.

Happy again, Shelby raced to the main house, and Noah drove home to change into something more casual. Caught up in a situation she didn't seem able to control, Greer gave in and went to shower.

CHAPTER EIGHT

THE TRIP to the Cowboy Artists' museum provided an entertaining afternoon. It wasn't someplace Greer had ever visited when she lived in Homestead before. The permanent work exhibited, as well as paintings in a traveling show by a Wyoming artist, allowed Shelby to see a varied and rich depiction of ranch life before modern encroachments.

"I know she's impressed," Greer said, hanging back to look at an exquisite bronze sculpture of a cowboy on a bucking horse. "I can't recall when I've seen Shelby this quiet."

A smile danced in Noah's eyes. "She sure carried on in the pickup on the drive here. How many times did she give you a rundown on all the kids she met this morning in Sunday school? Five? Six?"

"Or more, but that's Shelby. Ed Tanner's identical twin boys fascinated her. She couldn't get over the fact that the teacher was able to tell them apart."

"Ah, but Deb's seen them since they were babies. I get the feeling Shelby's determined to figure out how to do that, too, so next time she sees them she'll know which one's Halsey and which is Hamilton without having to ask."

Greer's laughter was warm and rich, like the woman herself, Noah thought. It went without saying that with her willowy slenderness, she looked fantastic in anything she chose to wear. Today, her choice of khaki slacks and a gold sweater set brought out honey-colored threads in her dark red curls. Under the intense museum lights, Noah saw a fairy sprinkling of freckles across her nose and upper cheeks that he hadn't noticed before. Shelby had freckles galore, but then her hair was more coppery red than Greer's deep sorrel.

Noah had noticed Shelby talking to her grandmother after church. He'd been taken aback by the disapproval marring Robert Bell's face. It was evident also in the abrupt way Greer's dad set off to get the family car. Right after Shelby had skipped back to rejoin Brit, Megan and Heather, Noah's own mother, who hadn't been at the service, appeared and pulled Loretta Bell aside. The two women, deep in conversation, suddenly left via a side door that led to the rectory. Noah never laid eyes on either woman again, so perhaps the Bells had eaten lunch with his folks.

"I know this might not be a good time, Greer, but you did tell me Shelby had never met your folks. Yet I saw her go up to your mom after morning service. Robert made himself scarce, but your mom seemed to know Shelby. Care to tell me what's going on?"

"And ruin our day?" Greer dragged her lower teeth across her upper lip. Noah thought she'd elaborate. Instead, she walked on to the next exhibit. He sensed a darkness running through her from then on, and he wished he'd kept silent. His remarks had apparently thrown a damper on Greer's day.

Sticking to his earlier promise to Shelby, Noah took them to the DQ after they left the museum. He would've been fine with them eating their cones in his pickup as they drove home. Greer said, "Forget it."

"With cloth upholstery? No way. Shel, honey, there's a nice table under that sprawling old mesquite. Go on over and sit. I'll grab napkins."

She did, a huge handful. Noah thought she'd gone over-board. As it turned out, she knew her daughter best. Shelby licked leisurely. The afternoon had grown warm, so sticky ice cream dripped over her wrist and hand and onto her pants. Not even the tabletop escaped unscathed.

"Hmm. I'll store this information for future reference," Noah murmured to Greer. "No letting that girl eat in my truck until she's twenty-one."

Greer couldn't hide a smug I-told-you-so grin.

Shelby's machine-gun chatter on the ride home failed to keep Greer from falling asleep. Noah didn't know how she could nap through the child's endless questions. But she managed. That left him to answer the barrage. He got rather adept at anticipating what the girl would find along the highway to inquire about next. Too bad Greer missed his fine performance. The fact that she felt comfortable enough with him to sleep and let him deal with her daughter said a lot. He liked that she trusted him so much.

He had to shake Greer several times outside her house. "Hey, sleepyhead," he chided softly when her eyelids fluttered a few times. "I can carry you inside and dump you straight into bed, but I think the ice cream revved Shelby up for the rest of the day. She's already out in the field chasing butterflies. I doubt you'll want to nod off and leave her on her own. Come to think of it," he added, watching Greer stir, blink and stretch so that her sweater clung to the shape of her breasts. "How does a single parent manage with babies? Aren't they awake day and night for the first few months? That's a complaint I've heard from friends and parishioners who were new parents."

"The secret, you novice, is to catnap whenever their eyes shut for more than five blessed minutes in succession."

He cut off her yawn by tugging her out of the front seat and anchoring her to his side with an arm around her.

"What are you doing?"

"Keeping you from falling up the front steps while you're groggy. Who'd finish putting this place in shape for paying guests if I let you break an arm or leg or your pretty little neck?"

Greer had to loop an arm around his waist so their walking together wasn't awkward. He felt solid. And the steady beat of his heart calmed the flutter in hers. She sagged against him. "A lady could get used to this specialized curb-to-door service."

That would be fine in Noah's opinion. He enjoyed the feel of her softer body against his. Since he wasn't in any great hurry to go home, he sat on the porch swing, tumbled her into his lap and shoved off with his feet. Leaning back, he took advantage of their closeness.

Still torpid from sleep, Greer didn't try to muster the energy to stop him, although she couldn't imagine why he was doing this. Noah nuzzled her neck and acted strangely content to have her where she was—on his lap.

The next time he pushed the swing, Greer felt her hips slide back and forth across his lap. The move produced a side effect she was sure he hadn't counted on. She struggled to put distance between them without drawing attention to his... problem.

Noah dug in the toes of his boots to stop their momentum. Setting Greer on her feet, he frowned. "Something wrong?"

"You have to ask?" Embarrassment swept her cheeks as she scrambled to get up while her upper body remained curved against his. She finally managed to climb to her feet, and tugged at her slacks, then checked to see that her shirt hadn't parted from her waistband.

Rising more slowly, Noah took her hands. Bending, he smiled softly just before brushing a deliberate kiss over her startled lips. "Greer, I—" They both noticed that a car had turned off the main highway and was headed toward the house. They could still see Shelby, who was now picking black-eyed daisies.

Greer wrenched loose from his hands and made a huge pretense of looking at her watch. "Noah, our trip to the museum took longer than you said. Don't you need to get home? I mean, hadn't you better be leaving for your evening service?"

He might have responded quite differently had the car not stopped beside his pickup and interrupted what he was prepared to tell her. Greer looked even more flustered when Loretta Bell emerged from the car.

She walked toward the house with purpose. Noah saw she was already dressed in a suit and heels for the evening service. He descended two of the porch steps as Loretta reached the bottom.

"Father Kelley," she acknowledged, sounding frosty.

"Noah," he said firmly and quietly. "We're not in church, Loretta."

Paying no heed, she frowned. "I thought that was your pickup, but then assumed it couldn't be, given the time. Ralph Fenton and Joe Carpenter told Robert you left morning service very abruptly. The men left our house half an hour ago, hoping to catch you at the church for an impromptu meeting before this evening's Eucharist." She didn't chastise him for his casual attire, but the way her eyes swept him from head to toe had the same effect.

Noah owed her no excuses for leaving church earlier than usual, or for being late tonight. And he offered none. He nonchalantly took the last two steps, skirting the older woman before stopping and saying to Greer, "Tell Shelby so long. I'll be here tomorrow afternoon at the time we agreed on. Don't forget to go by Guthrie's and pick up the items we need."

Greer nodded vacantly. Her mom didn't speak to her. Not until Noah started his pickup, made a circle around her car and drove down the lane. "Greer," Loretta said coldly. "Tell me my eyes were deceiving me when I drove in. Tell me you weren't cuddled up in the swing with…with…our priest."

She might have been half asleep a few minutes ago, but her mother's stinging comment pumped hot blood through Greer's veins and jolted her fully awake. "Is this a social call, Mother?"

"Must you always be curt, Greer?" Loretta heaved a sigh. "I came to talk to you because Ruth Kelley sought me out following this morning's service. For reasons that go back to the concerns I expressed to you about sending Shelby to our Sunday school. Ruth said your decision created a rift between Holden and Noah. Because Noah sided with you and against Holden."

"I didn't ask Noah to be my champion. Why doesn't Ruth talk to *him* about this? He invited Shelby to church. He invited me. Several times, Mother."

"I just wish everyone would get along. It pains me greatly to say this. But…I feel partially to blame for encouraging you to move back to Homestead."

"Encouraging me? I don't recall anything of the kind. You said nothing, if I remember, when I asked about Miranda's Home Free ad in the *Herald*. The first I even knew you cared one way or the other was when Ed Tanner said you'd given everyone in town our arrival date. I thought when you showed up to help clean the house that you were pleased we'd come. Which is it, Mother? Are you glad Shelby and I are here or not?"

A bleakness entered Loretta's eyes. "I have mixed emotions to be honest. As I said then, I wanted nothing more than to hug my only grandchild. And I missed you, Greer, the whole time you were gone. But…your dad, and Holden, and the other church board—Ralph, Joe and Harvey Steffan—feel so strongly that no good can come to our struggling church if we relax our long-standing rules. Pious rules. They say it's as if you delight in flaunting an illicit affair. I hate to think of the uproar if any of the board members should get wind of the way you acted here today with Noah. He does answer to his board, you know."

"How did I act, Mother? What is it you think I've done wrong?"

"Don't be coy. I saw you sitting on his lap. I saw you get up and straighten your clothes, and…he…kissed you." Shock reverberated in her tone.

"Oh, and it's automatically my fault, is that it?" Hurt again, Greer reached behind her for the doorknob. "Mother, I think you should go before I say things I don't want to say to you. I moved home hoping to give Shelby the extended family she's never had. I thought…after all these years that you and Dad would have mellowed."

"I have. Your father won't if you send Shelby to St. Mark's. And unless you stop encouraging Father Kelley to…to—"

Greer held up her hand, then covered her trembling lips. Managing to control the emotion that welled up, she yanked open the door, dived inside and slammed it hard enough to shake the frame. She hugged herself tight to ward off the churning anger and the pain. And she stopped to wonder if Daniel Harper's family ever treated him like a pariah. Furthermore, why had her dad and Holden Kelley placed all the blame on *her?* Her counselors at the group home had said that being older and more experienced, Daniel was at fault for deliberately taking advantage of a small-town girl. His sole purpose in seducing her had been so she'd write his essays and keep him from flunking out of yet another university. It was graduate or his rich daddy would cut off Dan's generous allowance. Her father, Holden, and others on the board had pressured her to demand marriage. Shelby was far better off being raised without *that* dad.

To hell with the lot of them. If she made anyone uncomfortable by coming home, so be it. She hadn't been keen on letting Shelby go to St. Mark's even though in Colorado she'd attended church with the Sandersons. An Episcopal church with more liberal attitudes than St. Mark's.

Greer had decided long ago that she'd never go where she wasn't wanted. But, by heaven, she'd fight for her daughter's right to attend Sunday school with kids she liked. And just so she wouldn't change her mind, Greer picked up the phone and called Callie Montgomery to see about kids' choir practice.

"Hi, this is Greer Bell. Ah, it is you, Callie. I thought so, but I wasn't sure. Shelby came home from church all excited about the choir. She said you and Kayla Ritter, I believe, might start a car pool. I can't offer to drive, but can I contribute toward gas? Shelby has a pretty good singing voice, and she wants to go. As I mentioned the other day, I, uh, am up to my eyeballs in work."

Greer stumbled a minute, because what if Shelby blabbed about their visiting the museum today?

"I'm so glad you called, Greer. I just got off the phone with Kayla, as a matter of fact. I was worried about Megan wanting to sing. That's Kayla's daughter, who has severe asthma. It turns out singing's good exercise for her lungs. So we're set. If you want to kick in a few bucks a week for gas, we won't refuse. On the other hand, we both know it's tough to start a new business. If it stretches your budget too thin, we can work out some other kind of trade once you're making an income."

"From your lips to God's ears," Greer teased. "Do you

know how hard it is to paint walls with my fingers crossed? That's more or less what I'm doing. I have to earn money at this venture, but it won't break me to buy a few tanks of gas."

"I'm sure you'll do well once you open. You're in a perfect location to show off our beautiful Hill Country. Only Kristin Gallagher has a better view from her house on top of the hill."

"They're not living on the Gallagher home place?"

"No, Clint still lives in the big brick mansion. Travis and his wife built on Four Aces land. Ryan and Kristin are on another property altogether."

"I remember Trevor and Garrett. I should know Ryan, I guess, but I can't quite recall him."

"From what Wade's said, Ryan left home at eighteen, joined the military and almost never came home. Used to be bad blood between him and Clint."

"Boy, can I relate to that," Greer mused wryly.

"I hear you loud and clear." For a minute neither woman spoke, then Callie said, "I'd better go, Greer. Time to pop dinner in the oven so my hungry brood doesn't riot when they come in. They get panicky if they don't smell cooking."

"Right. I'm sure I unpacked a calendar. I want to write this down. Oh, here it is. What time shall I have Shelby ready on Thursday?"

"Five-thirty okay? Tryouts are from six to eight. Between you and me, the tryout thing was designed to make kids feel special when they get picked. Everyone is, if you get my drift."

"Ah. That's good. I was afraid it might be a blow to Shelby if she got turned down. Okay, I'll see that Shel eats early that night."

"How are you coming on your renovations?"

"Good." Greer described everything she'd done so far.

"Sounds like you'll be ready in no time. Are you planning

an open house for locals? Practically everyone in town has relatives living out of state. Word-of-mouth is the cheapest form of advertisement."

"I hadn't thought of that, Callie. What a good idea! My former boss has been helpful in sharing his mailing list, but your suggestion's a good one. Well, bye, and thanks again." Greer pictured how the ranch might look once she was completely finished. Maybe she could host an open house with an autumn theme. This was the perfect time to decorate with locally grown squash and pumpkins and corn shocks. Of course she was putting the cart before the horse. First she needed to hire a cook, one who liked catering social events. As she'd told Callie, it was a great idea. It had been nice chatting with her. In Colorado, Greer hadn't made many friends her own age. This felt like a friendship developing. And it filled the emptiness left over from her mother's visit.

MONDAY, Greer found herself juggling ten things at once and still felt as if she was running behind. Shelby couldn't decide what she wanted to bring for lunch. Typical.

While she made up her mind, Greer went to find Shelby's vaccination record and put it with her car keys and purse. Except the card wasn't where she was sure she'd last seen it. She dug through desk drawers, dresser drawers and finally discovered it in a side pocket of her purse. Belatedly she remembered getting it out to log Shelby's tetanus shot the day she broke her arm. At the time it'd seemed a good idea to put it in her purse so she wouldn't forget it today. Where was her mind? On overload, she supposed, racing back to toss together Shelby's lunch.

"Honey, do you want me to set it up so you take the bus home today, or shall I pick you up and start bus service tomorrow?"

"Today. That way I can see if anybody lives near enough so I can ride there when we get our horses, huh, Mama?"

"I don't know about you riding off. Noah told me Ethan Ritter's son, Brad, got lost in the hills. He was dehydrated before they found him."

"I always took water when I rode around Whippoorwill Ranch."

"Yes, well, you were all but born and raised on that ranch. This is different."

Shelby pouted, which was difficult as she also attempted to fill her mouth with breakfast cereal. "At Sunday school I met Megan, Brad and Heather. Their daddy teaches riding. I think they live near us. Megan and Brad ride by themselves to visit Cody Peters and Sara Gallagher. I didn't meet them, but I will today. Brit said Sara practically lives next door to us. And Noah lives real close. We can even see his house. You'll let me ride down to see him, won't you?"

"Shelby, no. It's riding alone I object to. With Brad and Megan, there are two of them. If one gets hurt, the other can go for help."

"Soon I'll have my dog. We still get to go to the shelter on Wednesday, don't we?"

Greer put a hand to her head. "Yes, I guess so. I did promise. But if you don't stop talking and eat so I can get you to school on time, I may change my mind."

"Oh, Mama, you're teasing me." Shelby did, however, buckle down and eat.

TWENTY MINUTES later, Greer pulled in and parked at the school. Shelby's new friends came out in a flock and swarmed around her, the girls chatty and giggly, the boys standing back with their hands in their pockets.

"I'm Shelby's mom," Greer said during a brief silence.

"I've met Brit and Adam. The rest of you are?" She let them fill in the blank—then hoped she'd remember who was who among Megan, Brad, Heather, Cody, Adam and Sara. Last names she'd worry about later. "Kids, Shelby and I have to find the office and register her. I'm sure I'll see you again, and she'll see you soon. At least those of you in third grade." Most of them darted off except for Heather, a petite child compared to Shelby. Heather had wise eyes in a serious elfin face.

"I'm assigned to take you to the office, Mrs. Bell," Heather said softly.

"It's Ms. Bell, but if it's fine with your mom, you may call me Greer. We appreciate having a guide, don't we, Shelby?"

"Uh-huh." She edged nearer her new friend. "I'm getting nervous again, Heather. I didn't think it'd be scary after I met kids yesterday. But…I don't know where my room is or who's gonna be my teacher."

Heather took Shelby's hand. "It'll be okay. Mrs. Latimer's your teacher. Mine, too. And she's really nice."

Greer listened to the girls talk until they dropped their voices and she realized Heather had opened the door to the office. Signing Shelby up was a simple formality. Her previous school had already sent her folder with grades. Greer filled in the shot record, after which the secretary turned to Shelby.

"Welcome! We love new students. A wonderful group has joined us in the past year. Heather, will you introduce Shelby and her mother to Mrs. Latimer?"

"Yes, ma'am." Heather bobbed her head and took off like a rabbit. The school, renovated from what Greer remembered, was laid out in a large U with a playground in the center and another out back. Shelby's class was quite small. And, as Heather said, Mrs. Latimer was warm and gracious.

Greer turned to leave, but spun back. "Excuse me, Mrs.

Latimer. I forgot to ask in the office about Shelby's bus. She'll be riding it home after school today."

"No problem. You live on Jase Farley's Dragging F Ranch, correct?"

"It's ours now, and we're renaming it." Greer laughed. "I hope that won't ruin it for locals giving directions. I know how it goes if a landmark gas station gets dozed."

The teacher waved a hand to quiet the kids and her charm bracelet jingled. "Getting her on the right bus is my responsibility, and it's no problem. We only have two buses at the moment. One picks up rural kids, the other takes those living in town."

"Oh, well then." Green leaned over and dropped a kiss on Shelby's head. "You'll ride the rural bus, hon. I'll watch for it at our lane around three-thirty."

Shelby nodded happily and ran off to choose a desk between Brittany and Heather. And that was all there was to putting her daughter in school. Greer suffered the same sort of pang she'd felt the day she brought Shelby to kindergarten. *Third grade.* Her daughter was growing up so fast. The years rolled past, one after the other. Before she knew it, her baby would be heading off to college and Greer would be middle-aged.

A depressing thought. Or maybe not. With luck her business would thrive. Running a guest ranch meant a constant turnover of guests. Interesting people, from all walks of life. But even saying that out loud in the privacy of her SUV, Greer still felt something vital missing from the life she'd planned to create.

Her first stop was Guthrie's Hardware. She clutched Noah's list. "Hi, Myron. I told you I'd be back. Can I get you to fill an order? I have other errands, but I'll come back in about an hour. Oh, who's the best fencing outfit in town?"

"You aren't planning on barbed wire?"

"No, woven. I'll need a company that uses an automatic posthole digger. A lot of my property is granite underneath the soil."

"We only have two companies now. I'd try McPherson first, then Satterwhite."

"Much obliged."

Greer knew Pete McPherson. He used to attend St. Mark's and was a friend of her dad's. She caught him climbing into a truck loaded with lumber, headed for a job. "Hi, Mr. McPherson, I don't know if you remember me. I'm Greer Bell. Robert's daughter. I need to install woven wire between my place and the Four Aces."

The big, ruddy faced man spit a toothpick onto the ground. "Can't help you."

"Myron Guthrie figured you could."

"Nope. Too busy." He heaved his bulk up into the cab of his truck.

"Then will you direct me to…Satterwhite's, I think Myron said."

"Rudy's at the far west end of town. But he won't build your fence, either."

"Why not?" Recoiling, Greer gaped.

McPherson pulled out a new toothpick and clamped it between his lips. "I s'pose you could say that old-timers like me 'n Rudy don't cotton to the way our new mayor's populatin' Homestead." He slammed his truck door and started the engine, forcing Greer to hop back or get hit.

"I hope you don't mind if I ask Rudy myself," she shouted, knowing Pete wouldn't hear or answer if he did.

Satterwhite had a less progressive-looking fence yard than McPherson did. Greer found the owner sitting at his desk in a cubbyhole office, reading a *Playboy* magazine, which he quickly shoved out of sight when she walked in. "Myron Guthrie said you could probably run a woven wire fence for me. My name is Greer Bell."

"No can do." The man rocked his beefy body back in a chair that groaned under his bulk.

Greer glanced around at the signs of neglect. "Too many jobs lined up?" she asked sarcastically.

"Matter of fact, yeah. I'm booked solid to…May. Then the real rush starts."

At first Greer assumed he was joking. But there was something in his eyes that said he wasn't. Something that made her remember the letters she'd received in Denver suggesting she might not want to pick the Dragging F from the town's list of properties. For reasons that weren't totally rational, Greer didn't want to present her back to this man. She eased out of his office without another word.

In her SUV, she fumed to herself. It was a conspiracy against her. Someone—or several someones—wanted to prevent her from turning the Dragging F into a guest ranch. But…who?

Drumming her fingers on the steering wheel, she racked her brain as to what to do next. She noticed a sign across the street for Buddy's Gas and Auto Shop; that would be Callie's dad. Callie had mentioned that he might know of a cook and a ranch hand. Maybe he also knew of day laborers who'd build a fence and handle other odd jobs. Revving her engine, she tore out of Rudy's parking lot and zipped straight across the street to Collins's shop.

Buddy greeted her in a far kindlier manner than the previous two men. Greer dropped Callie's name instead of Myron's, and quickly rattled off her reason for dropping in. "I used to live here," she added. "My folks are Robert and Loretta Bell. I'm on the old Farley ranch, thanks to Miranda

Wright's Home Free project. It seems not everyone in town wants to see those of us in the program succeed."

"I'm *not* one," Buddy responded. "Did Callie tell you the folks I know who need work are Mexican-American?"

"Yes. That's fine, but I'd like them to be here legally."

He pulled a small address book from a drawer. "I can give you the names of two men who'll jump at the chance to do jobs such as fence-building. I'll have to think some more about a cook and all-around ranch hand. Got a couple in mind. The wife was born here, but her husband's a migrant worker. I think he'd like steady work. Their daughter's had some drug problems in the past, but she's enrolled in a good program now."

"I still have a little time. I haven't had business cards made. Let me give you my cell number. As for day workers…" Greer named an hourly rate she was willing to pay. "Myron can deliver my rolls of fencing this afternoon. When do you think these two guys might be available?"

"Anytime. Just tell me when you want them."

They settled on a time that afternoon and Greer left to go and order her business cards. Those, she discovered, she needed to order from the *Homestead Herald*. Hiram Niebauer was the only printer in town. His wife, Millie—Greer recalled too late—was Homestead's biggest gossip. And yet, not even she could offer anything but wild guesses as to who might benefit from driving Greer off Farley's ranch.

"*My* ranch," Greer reminded the birdlike woman for the sixth time in a row. "It would help me if you'd start referring to the place as Sunrise Ranch." Greer pointed to the information she'd written out for her cards. She asked Millie to come out the following week and take pictures to put in a brochure. The woman seemed happy to do so.

Completing her chores in town, Greer drove straight home

to unload the bags and boxes she'd collected on her return trip to the hardware store. Myron even had a date for when she could pick up her gun. Her application had been approved, but he needed the signed form to file before he could sell her the firearm.

Greer fairly bubbled with delight over her progress, and she called Marisa Sanderson to share her news. Noah also heard all about her day when he arrived and remarked on finding two men digging postholes and a flatbed truck off-loading fencing materials.

"Wow, you have been a whirlwind. I don't recognize those guys. Did Pete McPherson hire new help?"

Greer regaled him with her whole story.

Noah listened while she paced and gestured. Worry lines settled on his brow. "Maybe both companies really are busy, Greer. Thanks to Miranda, Homestead's been growing steadily.

"Rudy Satterwhite didn't look busy at all, Noah. His phone wasn't ringing and his fence yard was idle. It was as if he expected me and was prepared to turn me down."

"I don't want to say you're being paranoid, Greer, but.... I can't think who, except Senator Gallagher, has enough influence to command such loyalty. And your fence is to his advantage."

Greer shrugged; Noah was entitled to his opinion. He hadn't talked to McPherson and Satterwhite. She had. Plain and simple, they'd stonewalled her.

Noah dug through the sacks from Guthrie's and pulled out the plumbing supplies he needed to fix the leaks. Greer immediately went to paint the bunkhouse; otherwise she'd have hit him with what her mom had said about his mother's complaint. She should have talked to him about that kiss, too. It was still kicking around in her mind a couple of hours later when Noah stuck his head in the bunkhouse to announce the arrival of Shelby's bus. "I finished both bathrooms and put the lock on the pantry. I have to run, Greer. I'm meeting a young couple at church in fifteen minutes to arrange a christening for their new baby." He brushed a streak of dust off Greer's cheek as he talked.

Her fingers flew to the spot as his fell away. There was a tender light in his eyes that made her heart beat faster. This would've been the perfect time to say something—except that they both saw Shelby skipping down the lane, her jacket dragging. Papers stuck out of her pink backpack. She wore a happy grin, and that was the most important thing to Greer.

"Hi and goodbye, squirt," Noah called as he passed her. Retrieving his keys, he opened the door to his pickup. "Greer, I have a full slate tomorrow and Wednesday morning. Are we still on to drive over to the animal shelter in the afternoon?"

"Unless you cancel," Greer said hopefully.

He wagged a finger. "It's a good time to go there. A receptionist at the shelter told me they have a lot of adoptable dogs. She asked if I'd seen the recent articles explaining that so many single servicemen and women in the National Guard have been called to active duty, often on short notice, and many have no one to take their pets. All shelters have been affected. She said the owners beg them to see their pets placed in good homes."

Greer glanced up from a paper Shelby had given her to read—school rules. "Noah, that's so sad. Those poor animals. The owners must be heartsick."

"Without a doubt. People like us can provide a good home for a couple of dogs," he reminded her as he stepped up on the running board, leaving Greer with that thought as he slid beneath the wheel and drove off.

His pickup had barely turned out of the lane when a black,

crew cab Ford turned in, pulled into the clearing and stopped. A man with jet-dark hair got out. Greer didn't recognize him, and didn't much care for the way he eyed her workmen and gave her property the once-over. Nervous, she drew Shelby against her side and waited for him to state his business.

"I'm Ryan Gallagher," he said without preamble, hiking a thumb toward the neighboring ranch. "My dad was out around the Four Aces earlier. He recognized one of your workers and asked me to come and tell you that Rolando Diaz has been in trouble with the law. Drunk and disorderly, petty theft, I don't know what all else."

Greer shaded her eyes. "Does your dad also know why McPherson and Satterwhite claimed to be too swamped with work to build my fence?" Blocking the sun with a cupped hand, Greer decided that Ryan Gallagher was a cold one. His darkly hooded eyes gave nothing away.

"I have no idea what you're talking about, Ms Bell. The Four Aces has nothing to do with how other people in Homestead choose to run their businesses."

"I won't be harassed off my property. Tell your father that!"

"Dad's aim is to be neighborly. He thought you probably didn't know the history of that man you hired." Ryan dropped his sunglasses over his eyes and strode back to his truck, leaving it at that.

Greer watched him drive off in a crunch of caliche.

"Mama, that's Cody's dad. Don't you like him?"

Greer unclenched her jaw. Why hadn't she told Ryan Gallagher she didn't think screams in the dead of night were altogether neighborly? "I don't know him, honey. Everything's fine. Let's go get you changed into play clothes. Then you can come and see what I've done in the bunkhouse. We'll be ready to pick out rugs and move in furniture soon."

"Can I buy a special rug for the dog I'm getting Wednesday?"

"We'll see about that, okay?"

NOAH WAS ALWAYS prompt. He drove in at the exact hour he'd promised Shelby he'd collect them to visit the animal shelter.

Too excited for words, the child bounced in her seat and asked questions without a break. The shelter was a clapboard structure on the drive to the outskirts of town with wire mesh pens and dog runs on three sides. Several were occupied by big dogs. "Oh, look," Shelby said, leaning as far forward as her seat belt allowed. "Gosh, how will I choose?"

"It'll be tough. Shall we go inside?"

They bypassed the runs and opened the door. The din was horrendous.

A young woman, the attendant on duty, met them as Noah closed the door. "We're here to maybe adopt a couple of dogs," he said over the noise.

"Two?" The young woman's eyes sparked with interest. "Are you familiar with keeshonds? They're purebred, a male and a female from the same litter." She led them to a pen. Two roly-poly silvery-gray and black half-grown pups put their paws on the wire and whined happily. Kneeling, Noah scratched their ears through the cage.

Shelby landed on her knees beside him. "They're adorable. Mama, I think this one already likes me." She let the more inquisitive of the two dogs lick her fingers.

Noah glanced at the attendant. "What's their history?"

"Their owner is a National Guardsman."

"Ah. I heard about that. Maybe it was you I spoke with on the phone."

"Possibly. I'm telling everyone. I especially hope this pair finds a good home soon. They're expensive dogs. And they're on our short list," she admitted sadly. "But it's just not economically feasible for our small shelter to maintain animals indefinitely."

"I know nothing about this breed," Greer said. "They resemble bear cubs, don't they?" She turned to her daughter. "Shel, I was thinking of a dog who's good with sheep. Maybe a border collie. Plus I hear they're good watchdogs." She glanced around at other pens and walked over to one, but neither Shelby nor Noah followed. "I'm also going to have paying guests on the premises, so I'll need a friendly dog," she added as she wandered off.

"Oh, but keeshonds love people. The breed originated in the Netherlands," the girl said. "They're renowned for their sunny dispositions. And they're quick learners. You could teach them to herd sheep in no time."

Greer returned to the cage. "Shelby will be spending some time alone with whatever pet we select."

"Perfect," the attendant said, growing animated. "Honestly, if you read what breeders say about this dog, you'll see that they actually call them canine babysitters. They do have a thick bushy coat that requires a thorough weekly brushing, though."

Noah saw Greer's guarded expression. Rising, he smiled at the eager attendant. "Perhaps you could give us a minute to talk?"

"Sure." She shrugged. "I'll be at the counter if you have questions."

Taking Greer's arm, Noah walked down another aisle, pausing at various cages. "They're a good age to train. Not too young. Not too old."

"It's the weekly brushing, Noah. I expect to be putting in long days as it is."

He placed a hand on the back of her neck, which brought

Greer's chin up and forced a meeting of their eyes. "Make that a condition of Shelby's owning a pet."

"I suppose." Greer found herself resting against Noah's wide palm. "But she is, after all, just a kid."

Sliding his hand down to her shoulder, Noah led her up the next row and the next until they'd walked around the whole facility. Shelby, however, hadn't budged from the keeshonds' cage. She sat there, petting both dogs and talking up a storm.

"What do you think after seeing the other choices?" Noah asked. "Don't forget what the handler said about that particular breed being a reliable babysitter."

Greer caved in and got out her wallet, while Noah set his credit card on the counter. The attendant picked it up first. "So, Mr. and Mrs. Kelley, are you taking both?"

Greer opened her mouth to correct the girl. It was Noah who let it go, merely saying he'd pay for the male and Greer the female.

The young woman tallied the costs for each. "We recommend spaying and neutering now. They're the right age. If you do that, you can pick them up on Saturday."

Shelby, who'd joined them, started to cry. "But I want to take my dog home today."

Greer was reluctant to explain why the dogs had to stay. Noah hoisted the crying girl into his arms. He gave a simple yet forthright explanation that had Greer gazing up at him in admiration. "You did that so well," she murmured after they'd walked out and Shelby scampered ahead to Noah's pickup. "Maybe I'll send her to visit you when it's time for the whole dating issue to crop up."

He studied her seriously for a long moment, then laughed. "It's probably less to do with my expertise with kids and more because I said we'd stop at Callie's Café while we discuss names for our pets."

"You don't think you'd make a good dad?" Greer asked, sticking to the subject.

"I do, yes. Now, let me ask if you think I'd make a good husband?"

Gulping, Greer felt relieved when the attendant raced outside after them, saying they'd forgotten their receipts.

CHAPTER NINE

As THEY DROVE to the café, Noah wondered just how he could show Greer the extent of his interest in her. He understood why she was skittish, why she'd shied away. Or thought he did. But he didn't have a lot of experience with this kind of thing. Maybe he needed help.

Tomorrow, one of his meetings happened to be with Ethan Ritter. They usually met once a month to talk about the progress the special-needs kids were making with their therapeutic riding classes and for Ethan to let him know if any of the low-income kids needed additional support. Funding fell to Noah. After he and Ethan had finished with business, maybe he'd wangle time for a personal chat. Ethan's road to romance with Kayla had been a rocky one. Noah would be open to hearing any advice his friend could offer.

GREER HAD DEBATED trying to talk Noah and Shelby out of eating in town. She worried about the impression it would give if anyone from Noah's church saw them in Callie's Café a second time in as many weeks. But, she didn't have it in her to hurt Noah's feelings or deprive Shelby of a treat.

The last time they'd eaten here, Greer had seen how huge the portions were. Tonight she asked to have the fried chicken dinner split between her and Shelby.

"Is that women's secret for staying slim?" Noah teased. "You split meals?"

"When the meal's this big, it's split or take half home, or waste food. Restaurants would save money if they served less."

"Tell that to Callie. But everything's big in Texas. Including appetites, I guess."

Shelby tugged on Noah's sleeve. "You said we could talk about naming our dogs. I'm gonna call mine Bear," she said, sliding a grin toward her mother. "At the shelter, Mama said they looked like baby bears."

"And so they do," Noah agreed. "I think that's a fine name. Did you hear the shelter attendant say her coat needs a good brushing every week? Maybe your mom will get you a calendar, Shelby. Put an X on every day you brush Bear. It'll keep her coat healthy."

"Okay. Hey, since my dog's a girl, we can share my hairbrush."

Noah laughed. "I'm not making fun of you, squirt. I'm just imagining the horrified look on your mom's face if she caught you brushing Bear with your hairbrush. Dog brushes are more wiry. I'll pick one up for you when I buy mine."

"Thanks, Noah!" Shelby said happily. "Watcha gonna name your dog?"

Their platters were delivered, suspending the discussion for a moment. Shelby got straight back to it, even though she bit into a steaming homemade roll. "Do you remember the woman at the shelter said keeshonds smile? You could call him Happy," she said, her mouth full.

He held his crispy drumstick over the plate and paused before taking a bite. "I like it. Happy and Bear. What do you think, Greer?"

She'd popped grilled veggies into her mouth, so had to swallow before responding. "They're good names. Now, Shelby, settle down and eat." She glanced around to see who might overhear. It struck her how much they resembled a real family, sitting here eating, talking about names for their dogs.

Noah was aware of her sudden tension. "What is it Greer?"

"N-nothing." She took another forkful of carrots, then devoted her attention to sorting through the chicken pieces on her plate.

Noah didn't think it'd been nothing. Something was bothering Greer. He wished he could get to the bottom of these sporadic flare-ups between them.

This time, whatever caused it didn't last. Perhaps because it was difficult to stay on the sidelines around chatterbox Shelby.

"Do you guys know my school's only got two 'puters in the whole place?" That tidbit was a footnote to a longer discourse about her new school. "We had lots and lots of 'puters at my old school."

"Honey, your old school was larger. According to Miranda, Homestead was in danger of having to close its schools when she was elected. I imagine money's still tight for buying extras."

A well-dressed, silver-haired man wearing wire-rimmed glasses rose from a nearby table. He broke into their private conversation. "Pure poppycock," he snapped, looming over Greer. "The name's Arlen Enfield. I'm Homestead's former mayor. Our schools lag behind the times. Our kids need the perks found in bigger schools. If we'd had our eye on the ball, we could've bussed our students to schools with larger enrollments, or consolidated for less money than the Home Free program costs. Chopping up the K Bar C and other ranches will be our downfall, mark my words." He adjusted gold cuff links at the wrists of a soft blue shirt.

Greer didn't know what to make of the stranger's intrusion. Shelby scowled at the man. "My old teacher said little schools are better 'cause kids who go there make friends who'll be friends forever."

"That's another thing. If I had kids, I'd worry about the kind of drifters and no-accounts a program like this is attracting." Green eyes glittered icily as he pulled out a monogrammed money clip and dropped bills on his table.

Greer stood then, too. "Excuse me," she said. "Your description doesn't fit any of the people I've met who've availed themselves of Miranda Wright's program. Furthermore, I'm one of them. It seems to me Homestead benefits from an influx of responsible, well-educated, hardworking families."

You could have heard a penny drop in the formerly noisy dining room.

Noah didn't like to remain seated while Greer faced down a guy head and shoulders taller. Getting up, he casually slid a proprietary arm around her stiffened shoulders. "Arlen," Noah acknowledged the one-time mayor, who was purported to have his eye on Clint Gallagher's senate seat. "The council voted on the proposal. It passed. Most of us think it's time to accept the outcome and move on."

The man's gaze narrowed. "Now, don't we all know the mayor would've lost if your daddy hadn't taken sick and let his woman stand in where a man belonged? Our land's too valuable to hand over to a bunch of squatters. Save your preaching for the pulpit, boy." Brushing by them as if they were pesky flies, the ex-mayor swaggered out.

"Well," Greer murmured, retaking her seat. "That was unpleasant. I'm sorry, Noah. I shouldn't have reacted the way I did, even if he did pounce on us. Obviously I pushed his buttons."

"Don't apologize. It's a hot topic. You spoke your mind and came down on the side of right." One of his crooked grins sneaked out. "Hey, Shelby's tough, too. If I ever get pounced on, I want both of you Bell women in my corner."

"Stop teasing, Noah. If you'd wear your collar, you'd never get pounced on. People would show respect for your position."

"Hmm," he muttered over Shelby's head, his eyes twinkling with mirth. "It'd depend on who's doing the pouncing, Greer. If we had fewer prying eyes, I'd give you a wise-ass comeback and tell you to join me in a private spot and pounce away."

"No—ah!" she groaned, her face erupting in flames.

"I didn't like that man," Shelby declared to no one in particular. She was oblivious to the adults' byplay. "He's wasn't nice, was he, Mama? I'm glad your friend, M'randa, got to be mayor 'stead of him."

"Amen to that," Noah agreed, deciding it was time to let up on Greer. "Are you ready for dessert, Shelby?" He turned guilty eyes to Greer. "Sorry if I'm overstepping my bounds."

She hadn't fully recovered from their last exchange. "A cookie, Shel. Too much sugar's not good on a school night." Greer was happy enough to don her mom-hat.

"One is all? Pooh! Okay, Noah, I want Texas Pecan Kisses. Brit loves them. Her mama got the recipe from Mayor Miranda's mother."

He motioned the waitress over and ordered peach pie for himself and a cookie for Shelby. "What'll you have Greer?"

"Nothing. On second thought, coffee." She glanced at the order taker and discovered to her chagrin that it was once again Janet Kaufman, the same waitress Noah had said was pursuing him. The woman acted cool enough. Icy, in fact, as she left to turn in the order, having delivered several nasty stares at Noah. He either didn't notice or didn't care, Greer thought, as he started a game of tic-tac-toe with Shelby on a napkin.

Greer fidgeted with her empty cup, but the others took their sweet time. Noah lingered over his pie and Shelby munched her way slowly through her oversize pecan cookie. Greer's mind wandered—back to the scene with Homestead's former mayor. If a lot of people in town felt the way Enfield did about Miranda's program, anyone might take it upon himself to make her plan fail. What better way to do that than to scare off recipients in the land program? Quite possibly she'd shot darts in the wrong direction the day she'd said hostile things to Ryan Gallagher about his father.

On the way home, Greer shared her musings with Noah.

"The council's vote did spark controversy. Senator Gallagher was out of town, if I recall. Some people think if he'd been here, the vote might have gone the other way. As far as Clint sending Ryan to warn you about a man you'd hired, I'm sure the warning was genuine, at least on Ryan's part. When was this? You never mentioned it to me. Did Buddy vouch for them?"

"He did. Anyway, what other choice did I have? I didn't say anything because when I said it was suspicious how McPherson and Satterwhite turned me down flat, you sloughed me off. I'm *not* being paranoid. And we didn't imagine those screams."

"A lot of people resist change," Noah said. He was thinking of his parents and the church board in particular. "Since there's been no repeat, I'm assuming Wade's patrols along the river have put a stop to it. He's a good man, and he's competent. I'm sure you can quit worrying."

"You're probably right." Greer absently spun one of Shelby's curls around her forefinger. Her daughter, dead to the world, had slumped against Greer's shoulder.

Noah noticed. "Shelby's a kid who goes and goes full steam, then crashes big-time, isn't she?"

"Yes, but I can't say a lot. I'm pretty much the same."

"You've accomplished miracles at the ranch already. I'll

admit that I thought opening by Thanksgiving was a stretch. But now… What's next on your agenda?"

"Bunks for the bunkhouse. And Shelby and I talked about going somewhere to buy accent pieces, like rugs. I'd like braided rugs, but they're not easy to find. What I need is a craft fair or a flea market to pick up the odd pieces of furniture I need to put finishing touches to the cottages."

"Fredericksburg has everything you could want. I've got an idea. The day after tomorrow, school's only in session half a day. We can drive up there in my pickup, and that way if you find any big items, I'll be able to haul them home for you."

"I saw a note in the stuff Shelby brought home reminding parents of the half day. But I didn't see why they're off."

"A teacher in-service, or so I was told when we were selecting a day for the kids' choir to meet. You haven't forgotten that?"

"Kayla Ritter's bringing Shelby. She and Callie are sharing the car pool."

"Why not you, Greer? You should come and meet some of the other parents."

She looked away and was happy to be saved from answering as Noah turned off the road into her lane.

He felt the walls go up again between him and Greer, and hoped they weren't insurmountable. He intended to start breaking them down. "It's really dark tonight. Have you thought of installing perimeter lights or motion detectors?"

"No, because people go to guest ranches to escape all trappings from the city. Noise. Lights. They want to see the night sky and the stars."

"Hmm. Makes sense. Here, let me carry Shelby inside. That'll leave you free to unlock the front door."

"Noah, I'm used to hauling Shel in to bed alone. Or waking her up enough to make her walk by herself."

"Yeah, but why do that when help is available?"

Her keys in one hand and her purse in the other, Greer had no good answer. She wasn't sure why it bothered her to accept his continued help. Or perhaps she did, but didn't want to admit how much she'd liked having him around these last two weeks.

He placed the girl on her twin bed and smiled when Greer snapped on the night-light he'd bought Shelby. "When does her cast come off?" he whispered.

"Another week. And will I be glad. She's complaining about the itching." She paused. "I need to see about shipping our horses in soon. A cast wouldn't stop her from riding, but I'll feel better seeing a follow-up X-ray before I put her on a horse."

"You need to draw strict boundaries about where she can and can't ride," Noah said. "Clint has those deer leases. I haven't heard of any accidents, but you give some city guys rifles and they'll shoot at anything that moves."

"She and I have already had that discussion. She thinks that when she gets her horse and dog, she'll be able to ride at will. I've told her I don't even want her riding alone to your house, Noah. She figures the two of you will go exploring. But I'm worried about the river. She doesn't swim all that well. And I don't want her making a wrong turn and getting lost in the hills. When my stock comes, I'll hire a ranch hand, and I'll have him help me install trail markers for my guests. Or that's my plan. Then maybe I'll let Shelby ride the marked trail." She'd skimmed off the girl's jeans and shirt and pulled a nightgown over her head. She followed Noah down the hall toward the front door. "Thanks for dinner, Noah. And for taking us to pick out a dog."

"What about Fredericksburg?" They'd left that hanging.

"You think they'll have what I need?"

"Unless you want to drive to Austin or San Antonio. If you haven't been to Fredericksburg in a while, Greer, you'll be surprised by how the town's grown—and yet it still feels like the Old West. There's a butterfly ranch and a bat tunnel. Shelby will like that."

"Oh, fantastic." Greer's laugh came from her belly. They stepped out onto the porch, and a half-moon drifted out from behind the clouds. The light wasn't enough to illuminate the porch, but enough for Greer to lift her arms skyward and make a wish on the stars. "Star light, star bright, first star I see tonight…"

Noah gazed at her raptly. Her defined cheekbones were gilded by silvery light. The picture she made moved him to do something he'd wanted to do since the first day he'd seen her standing in the entryway at Tanner's. Noah slid his arms around her waist, pulled her forward and kissed her the way a man kissed a woman when he meant business.

Her wish smothered by his lips, Greer wedged both hands between them. Maybe she intended to push him away; instead, her fingers curled into the fabric of his shirt. If her original intent in moving her head from side to side had been to break free of his lips, she gave up too easily. Especially after Noah curved a hand around the back of her head and held her in place. She abandoned all resistance and kissed him back.

The fire in his belly burst into flames, warning Noah he was getting too involved too fast, considering he'd caught Greer off guard.

Afraid she'd let him have it with both barrels the minute he released her, he abruptly broke off the kiss. With a whispered goodbye, Noah strode from the porch and made a bee-line for his pickup.

As the engine roared to life, his high beams played over Greer. Noah knew if he didn't get out of there immediately, he'd be in danger of going back. She hovered near her porch swing looking slightly vulnerable—and altogether delectable.

Noah wasn't above praying for control, and also guidance. And as he swung in a wide arc to retreat up her lane, he even crossed his fingers that by tomorrow Greer would be in a forgiving mood. A mood amenable to more kisses. He liked the taste he'd had and didn't want their relationship to end there.

Maybe her past had soured her on dating, but that kiss told Noah he'd made inroads into her resistance.

Greer watched Noah's pickup until the maroon shade melted into the night. She clutched a hand to her still-quivering stomach. Time seemed suspended, and she was at a loss to know how long she'd stood there before she gave herself a solid shake and got moving.

Even after going in, she barely remembered to lock the door. Her plan had been to wallpaper her bedroom that evening, and she made herself do just that. However, wallpapering was fairly mindless, and it left her thoughts free to wander. She hadn't kissed a lot of men before or after her disastrous experience with Dan Harper. Those she'd kissed weren't particularly memorable—nor were their kisses. Chuck Hazlett said straight out that she had a problem in not warming up to being kissed. If tonight was any indication, either the problem had fixed itself or Noah had Chuck beat when it came to kissing, hands down.

As Greer smoothed a brush over paper sprigged with pale yellow flowers, she relived the kiss. Not quite the same as feeling Noah's mouth on hers, but vivid enough to keep the memory alive.

The paper up, she went into the kitchen to clean her tools for storing in the broom closet. She couldn't help it if the window over her sink faced Noah's house. His lay in total darkness. Her place blazed with light. It dawned on Greer that she was probably the only one affected by his good-night kiss. Maybe he'd left so abruptly because he'd come to the same conclusion as Chuck.

But maybe not…

She paused and tried to imagine Noah's parents or hers in a lip lock of the type they'd engaged in. Heavenly days, her mind wouldn't stretch that far. And her mind probably shouldn't stretch that far where the younger Father Kelley was concerned, either. But it did. Boy, howdy, did it!

Climbing into bed, she yawned and extinguished the light. As the room was plunged into blackness, she discovered her mind had a will of its own. In the privacy of her bed, she delighted in the things Holden Kelley said were sinful and wrong. Right before she drifted off, she wondered where Noah had gained all his kissing technique.

With another yawn, she wondered if there was a proper protocol for facing a man of the cloth after he'd kissed you into mindless oblivion. Luckily she had a day and a half until she needed to come up with the answer. Greer wouldn't see Noah again until noon on Friday, for their scheduled trip to Fredericksburg.

But that wasn't the case, she learned bright and early the next morning when her phone rang at seven-thirty. Shelby was in the process of collecting her lunch and backpack to head out and catch the school bus. Greer didn't know who to expect as she answered her cell phone, but Kayla Ritter hadn't occurred to her.

"Greer? This is Kayla. Kayla Ritter? We haven't met, but you'll probably want to kill me. I can't drive the girls to their choir tryouts tonight. Ethan's out of town, and Brad's been throwing up all night. The flu I think. The kids said it's making rounds at school."

"I'm sorry to hear about Brad, Kayla. So, does this mean you and Callie are switching days? If so, that's fine with me."

"There's the real problem. Callie has dental appointments for Mary Beth and Adam. She's rescheduled them once already. Brit was the only one who didn't have a cold last time. Since Homestead has no dentist, Callie can't make it back to town by five. Wade has something on tonight, and Brit's going to his dad's after school. She'll need to be picked up from Jock's house."

Greer kept expecting to hear another option put forth. But as Kayla fell silent and there was nothing but a faint buzz in her ear, Greer belatedly realized what the other two moms saw as the only solution. Her.

Kayla finally spelled it out. "We hate putting you on the spot, Greer. If you absolutely can't do it, well, the kids will just have to miss it."

"Callie led me to believe they'll all be given spots anyway," Greer mumbled in a lame attempt to avoid the inevitable.

"True, as long as they make the first session—the practice plus tryouts. Did you read the note?"

"I must not have." Greer chewed her lower lip.

"It's only an hour. Well, two, counting driving time, which includes picking up the kids and dropping them off afterward. We'll make it up to you, Greer. Callie and I will both invite Shelby over and give you extra free time to work on your ranch."

"When you put it like that, how can I refuse?" Greer wanted to. Oh, how she wanted to. She supposed she could take a book or sit in the Blazer and draw up a final list of chores that needed doing before she held a grand opening or invited guests.

"Fantastic. Callie and I thank you profusely. I can't invite you in, I'm afraid. I'm doing my best to keep Brad isolated. I'd hate to risk his germs infecting anyone. Honk when you get here. I'll at least run out and introduce myself."

Greer discussed where and when to collect the girls. Then she put the unpleasant task out of her mind for the rest of the day. She didn't want to consider how it would feel to drive into the church parking lot after ten years. It was in full view of the rectory where Holden and Ruth Kelley still lived. She believed that had it not been for Holden Kelley's influence, her parents wouldn't have sent her away. Although her dad held his own strict interpretation of right and wrong… He'd proved that by having a fit when her mother wanted to visit her at the time of Shelby's birth. And more recently. According to Noah, her dad had shunned her daughter at church.

They should all have handled the situation differently back then. Everyone except her believed the right and proper thing to do was marry her baby's father. She'd stubbornly refused to even name Dan. Oh—why look back? Why dredge up the old unhappiness? As soon as she had her business underway, she'd drive out to the farm, face her dad and at least attempt to make peace.

Greer expended her restless energy weeding around the house and along the walkways. She was more than tired when it came time to load Shelby in the backseat of the Blazer and drive out to Jock Montgomery's to pick up Brittany. Shelby was so excited she couldn't sit still, and Brit did her share of gleefully bouncing around. As she headed for the Ritters' ranch, Greer thought back to this morning and knew she could never have denied the girls this outing.

Kayla Ritter walked out with her two girls. She and Greer were surprised by the fact that they looked so similar to each other they could have been sisters. Both had auburn hair, although Kayla's was longer. And her eyes were more hazel, like Shelby's, rather than Greer's, which were closer to gold. They laughed about everything they had in common.

"I'm jealous," Greer joked. "If we're related, how come you got four or five inches more leg than me?"

"It's okay now," Kayla said. "But when I was Megan's age I was always taller than the boys in my class. That's no fun."

"Women always have some cross to bear. Too tall, too short. Hair too curly, not curly enough. Eyes, nose, feet. You name it, we obsess over someone else being prettier." The kids laughed uproariously over something, just as Greer said she'd better get going.

Kayla stepped back. "Oh, Callie wanted me to tell you that as soon as you can take a break, she's having us all over for a grand old coffee klatch."

"Sounds wonderful. See you later." The women waved, and Kayla returned to her house, and Greer began the drive into town. She knew the route. And thought she was prepared but discovered she wasn't.

The stone church, built to withstand time and tornadoes—should any swing off course and pass through Homestead—triggered memories both happy and sad. Her baptism, first communion and other personal milestones, marred now by one horrendous misstep. Yes, she admitted as she sat there looking up at the silent bell in the spire of her childhood church, she'd made a series of mistakes, starting the day she'd met Daniel Harper.

Greer clung to the steering wheel, hearing only a roaring in her ears as one by one the girls climbed out. Shelby broke into her private reverie. "Mama, come walk us in."

"Oh, honey, no. I...no, I'll wait here until you're done."

The girls ran back and crowded around the open car door. "None of us know 'xactly where we're supposed to go," Brit said.

"The choir loft? Usually that's where choirs gather to sing."

Megan shook her head. "Father Noah told my dad he's gonna play the guitar while we sing. He's liable to play any old place."

Greer unwelded her hands from the steering wheel. *Noah, play guitar?* Suddenly she felt a desire to see a very different Noah Kelley than the man who came to her ranch in boots and blue jeans. A man who comfortably wielded a screwdriver or a paintbrush. This would be *Father* Kelley on his own turf. She thought nothing was as apt to drive seductive images of him from her mind as seeing him at work, wearing his collar.

She got her notebook, crawled out and locked the Blazer. Then she led the way through a side door of the sanctuary. The mellow sounds of an acoustic guitar floated up a set of stairs to her left. The main chapel was dark except for the late-afternoon sunlight filtering through tall stained glass windows. Guiding the girls behind the pews, Greer herded them toward the artificial light streaming up from the basement, which housed the classrooms.

Partway down, Greer fell behind. The girls burst into the room at the bottom of the stairs, and the music stopped with a sudden twang. Noah's deep voice, greeting each child by name, made Greer go weak in the knees. She heard disbelief in his tone when Shelby announced who'd driven them to church.

Bracing a hand on the cold wall for support, Greer was even less prepared when his shaggy head appeared around the corner of the door.

"Hey, this is a welcome surprise. You don't have to sit out here on the steps, you know. You're allowed to hang out at the back of the room while I run the kids through some preliminary songs."

It embarrassed Greer to discover that her legs had given way, and she was in fact sitting on a middle step. Staring down at him, she was equally shocked to see Noah wasn't a different man here in his own workplace. He still wore holey blue jeans, run-down boots and a casual, open-throat shirt. Funny twitches ping-ponged around in her stomach.

His smile changed to a look of concern when she didn't immediately get up. "Did you slip? Are you hurt?" He unstrapped the guitar from around broad shoulders, put down the instrument and rushed to Greer's side.

"I'm fine," she said, feeling even more embarrassed. "It's just…I didn't expect…well, you to look like…*you,* frankly." Greer clasped her hands in front of her. Until this moment, she hadn't realized they'd gone icy.

He'd been surprised and delighted to see her, and worried. He instantly knelt to gather her in his arms and help her stand, thoroughly baffled as he tried to make sense of her convoluted babble.

Suddenly, they were both aware of an audience—eyes in a solemn ring of faces peering around Noah's broad back. Brittany posed the same question Noah had. "Did Shelby's mama trip and get hurt?"

Self-conscious, Greer scrambled to her feet. She ran a hand nervously through the auburn curls that had fallen over her face. One hand flew to her jumpy stomach, while the other brushed hair away from her face. It was probably better to let everyone think she was clumsy. "I'm such a klutz. Caught my heel on the step. I'm fine. I've got padding," she said, patting her backside. The onlookers lost their worried expressions enough to laugh and disperse.

Noah, too, appeared greatly relieved. "You're sure?"

"I am. I am." She waved him away. Entering the room, she hurried to take a seat clear in the back, right by the wall.

Taking her at her word, Noah clapped his hands. "Okay, kids, gather round." He didn't bother with chairs or any formality, but sat cross-legged on the carpet with his guitar. He motioned for the fifteen or so children to form a semicircle around him.

He struck a few chords and hummed a bar. "Anyone recognize the song?"

Hands were thrust in the air. Oddly Greer remembered the song as an old standby from her youth choir days. That evoked fond memories. In short order, the mellow strumming, combined with the sweet voices of the children and Noah's rich baritone, let her jumpy stomach relax. The hour she'd expected to suffer through slid by, over before she was ready to leave.

But there was Noah, climbing to his feet. He shed his guitar and stood it in a corner. "You kids are all fantastic," he said. "I can picture you kicking off our Christmas service. Hmm. I wonder how you should be dressed.... "

"We want white robes. Like the grown-ups. Please!" The girls crowded around him, dancing on their toes, clamoring all at once. The boys, comparatively few, horsed around by the windows.

Noah studied the eager faces. "White robes?" He stroked his chin, and even Greer leaned forward in anticipation.

"I'll need a commitment from each of you if I invest in robes. Everyone on my team has to learn the Christmas carols and attend practices. Unless you're sick."

All the girls chimed in with promises. Even the boys did. "Okay, let's plan on your first performance being Christmas. White robes for the girls, and dark green for you guys. How does that sound?"

The chorus of yays was deafening.

Greer was impressed by how easily he had the lot of them shouting *yes* as he went down the line exchanging high fives. She saw his smile flicker—a smile that did funny things to her stomach. Clever man, he'd had it planned all along, but let them think they'd talked him into giving them robes.

"From here on, you're the official St. Mark's junior choir.

I'll have song sheets printed for next week. Same time, same place." He grinned. "And by the way, you all passed the audition."

Cheers again. And applause from behind her. Greer turned to other moms at the door. Calling her over, Noah introduced her. The majority of women were her age and they all said they were new to Homestead. She was glad no one there remembered her from high school—or the year after.

The room cleared fast after a petite brunette, Mickie Ferrell, mother of one of the boys, reminded everyone it was a school night. Shawna Jones and her kids followed the Ferrells out.

Shelby and the girls Greer was driving ran up to her. "Mama, can I unlock the car?" Greer had the keys out ready, and she handed them to Shelby, then started to head out.

"Give me a minute to turn down the thermostat and shut off the lights," Noah said. "I'll walk you guys out."

"No need for that," Greer protested.

"I want to." She saw the same light in his eyes as she'd seen last night, on the porch. Greer's calm fled. It bothered her to have such feelings—especially here. She charged up the stairs and bolted out the side door. It was very dark in the parking lot, and she skidded to a stop to gain her bearings. Spotting the Blazer's interior light, she stepped forward, then felt Noah's arms go around her. His breath tickled her neck and she had no resistance against the sudden pleasure of his nearness. Her willpower dissolving, she let him tug her out of sight of the children. He pressed her back against a spreading live oak that stood between the church parking lot and a walkway leading to the rectory.

The kiss he gave her tonight was steamier than yesterday's. The sound of a snapping twig broke them apart, and their heads shot up simultaneously. Greer was horrified to see Noah's mother standing on the walkway not two feet from them. The look on Ruth's astonished face could be termed anything but joyful.

"Mother," Noah said mildly, his fingers continuing to stroke Greer's neck. "Out for a stroll? You remember Greer Bell. I know you do." He exerted pressure to hold her in place, clamping his arm around her waist.

Even though she was much smaller, Greer found the strength to break away. "How humiliating," she muttered. "I've, uh, got kids to deliver," she said more loudly, then literally ran like a rabbit for her vehicle.

She had a head start, but Noah's legs were longer. He caught up to her before she reached the Blazer. Grabbing her arm, he turned her toward him. "What happens between us, Greer, has nothing to do with anyone but us."

"How can you say that? You saw her face. She hates me. So does your dad."

"They can like what I do, or lump it. I understand you have to get the kids home, and I left the church unlocked. We'll talk more tomorrow on the drive to Fredericksburg."

"No. Not with Shelby there. Noah—don't you see, there *is* no us. My past here makes an us impossible."

"No. God makes all good things possible." Leaving it at that, he called goodbye to the girls, whose noses were plastered to the side windows of Greer's vehicle.

CHAPTER TEN

THE GIRLS WERE LESS ebullient on the way home, until Greer put in a Shania Twain CD they all liked and suggested they sing along. Listening to the mingling of voices suited Greer. It gave her time to think about what had happened in the parking lot, and what Noah had said. He certainly hadn't tried to hide her from his mother. He'd chased after Greer and left Ruth standing there.

It was obvious that something was developing between them. Greer just had to decide if she was in favor or not.

The answer was pretty much decided as she relived the pleasure she felt whenever she and Noah were together, as opposed to the emptiness sweeping over her each time he went away.

During what remained of her evening, she resolved to let Noah set the pace. She'd wait to see what developed—see where it took them.

It was just as well she'd done all her decision making the night before, because in the morning things got downright hectic.

To begin with, Millie Niebauer from the *Herald* showed up at about 6:30 a.m. Greer noticed the birdlike woman skulking around outside her kitchen window and went out to see what she was doing.

"Oh, Greer. Didn't know if you were up or not. I didn't

want to bother you, but it occurred to me that we may not have many sunny days left. I want to capture your fabulous sunrise as the focal point for the brochure."

"That's fine, Millie. But I'm not ready to have you take pictures inside the cottages or the bunkhouse. They're not pulled together yet. In fact, I'm going to Fredericksburg today to hunt for rugs, pillows and knickknacks. I need the living quarters to look inviting and homey, if you know what I mean."

"Sure do. I can come back anytime. Phone me whenever." She pulled a folded paper out of her back pocket. I wrote this copy," she said, passing the paper to Greer. "See if I've said what you had in mind."

Greer read it over. "Millie, this is wonderful! Exactly what I want."

The reporter/photographer had turned away to snap several shots of the rising sun. Anything else Greer might have said was drowned out suddenly by three big stock trucks rumbling down the lane.

"What the—?" Greer ran out to meet the driver of the first vehicle as he disembarked. He extended a clipboard.

"Ms. Bell?"

"Yes, that's me."

"Harris and Company out of Denver shipped you a hundred sheep. Tell me where you want them woollies unloaded. There's a horse van not far behind us." He shoved a pen into Greer's limp hand. "Need a signature there."

"Wait. I told Mr. Harris I'd call him with a delivery date."

"Yep, but old Reggie passed away right after you moved. His sons and heirs are liquidating the Colorado holdings. Toby Harris, he's executor of the estate, said for us to ship all existing orders. You're last on the books, Ms. Bell."

Greer's eyes cut to her half-finished fence and then skittered back to the broken-down corral. Shelby came out of the house as the horse van pulled in. She all but knocked her mother down in her excitement.

"Shel, stop. Will you go in quick and phone Noah? The card with his number is on the counter under the phone. Ask if he has room in his barn to stable eight horses. Tell him it's only until I can pull Marcus and Rolando off fence construction and have them repair our corral." She quickly selected the greenest pasture near the house, and told the driver to start unloading his sheep there.

"Mama!" Shelby hollered from inside. "Noah needs to talk to you."

Offering Millicent a shrug, as the woman had come over, still clicking away on her Nikon, Greer rushed in to pick up the phone.

Noah sounded sleepy and no wonder; it was barely seven. "What's up?" he asked lazily. "I couldn't make head nor tail out of Shelby's run-on sentences."

Greer gave him a shortened version of their dilemma. "I have no feed, no door on my barn, and my corral is falling down. Can you board eight horses?"

"I can take three. I'll see if Ethan Ritter has room for the others. Or maybe Ryan Gallagher will let you turn them out in one of their fields. You'll need to call Miranda Wright and order stall shavings. Ask for the ones bagged in Junction. She'll bill you. Tell her I'll swing by Wright's and pick up the order. Oh, and Myron Guthrie may have a barn door in stock. If not, he can order one. I'll call and give him the dimensions."

"Try Ethan first, please—about boarding my horses. I'll pay the going rate. I can't ask Ryan. I didn't leave him with a very good impression of me."

"Ryan won't hold that against you."

"Please, Noah. I wouldn't feel right." With that, she hung up. Making a mad dash across her side acreage, she gestured wildly while talking to her workmen about switching from fence-building to the corral. Her jitters had faded marginally, knowing that Noah was going to help her. His calm attitude made this mess seem manageable.

"Mama, I see my bus. School's only half a day, remember? Can I stay home and play with the sheep, instead? The little ones look so cuddly."

"We have little ones? Don't sheep lamb in the spring?" she said to no one. But, sure enough, there were some ewes with nursing lambs. "Uh, no, Shel, you can't stay home. The sheep will still be here. Run, hurry. Catch your bus. See you at noon, okay? Have a good day."

"Are we still going to that town that has butterflies and bats?"

Greer rubbed at her temples. With all of this, she wasn't sure. "I'll have to check with Noah. It's possible we'll need to cancel."

That definitely was not what Shelby wanted to hear. She not only didn't run for the bus, she dallied, kicking at rocks along the way. Greer was extremely glad the bus driver, a grandmotherly type, exhibited patience, since her own was growing thin.

Turning, she passed the now-crumpled mock-up brochure back to Millie. "This is perfect. Can we just use outside photos of the cottages and ranch for now? Print up a minimum order. I have a few dozen people I want to send advance copies to, travel agents and so on. The names were supplied by my former boss. I'll add inside shots later, in the next version. Like dining room and kitchen. Those attract customers." Speaking of customers, another thing she had to do was hire staff. A bona fide ranch hand, and a cook.

Millie agreed to print fifty trial brochures with color photos. Once she left, Greer searched her purse and found Buddy Collins's card. She stood on the porch, watching the milling sheep, and thought how quickly well-laid plans could turn to chaos.

"Buddy, hi, it's Greer Bell. I'm glad you're in this early. The noise? Uh, I have drovers unloading a flock of sheep. My workmen? They're fine. I'm watching them hammer away on my corral as we speak. Why I'm calling is this, I wondered if you'd been in touch with the family you mentioned? I need someone sooner than I expected. Like today," she said, feeling panic rise.

Dale Collins sounded as if he was rummaging through a drawer. Then he rattled off a name and phone number. "Hang on a minute," Greer yelped. "I need paper and a pen." She gave a last grimace at the sea of bleating, smelly sheep and wondered what had ever possessed her to order so many. At the time, a hundred had seemed reasonable.

Forty minutes later, Noah drove in. His pickup was piled high with bags of a high-grade feed mix, shavings and a new pitchfork. He backed his truck right up to the barn. As he climbed out and pushed his sunglasses up into windblown hair, he saw Greer mucking out who knew how many years' worth of moldy, dirty straw.

He waved to the men knocking down splintered rails, then called to Greer. "Ethan has room for four horses, so I'll make room for an extra. I see you have them hobbled. Are they broken to lead?

She nodded, and he grabbed the pitchfork still bearing a price tag and waded in.

"Noah, you don't have to get all icky and itchy on my account." Greer leaned tiredly on her pitchfork handle.

He waggled his brows, but kept hauling forkloads out onto

a pile she'd started at the back door. "You haven't heard that Texans conserve water by showering with a friend?"

Her mouth went dry. "Why do you make jokes like that? To fit in? To fool people into thinking you aren't who you are?"

Near enough to stare deep into her turbulent eyes, he brushed his knuckles over her dirt-streaked face. "Every time you say that, I wonder who you think I am, Greer. Yes, I'm an ordained priest. But first I'm a man."

"Of God," she muttered.

"A man of the earth, which God created. A man endowed with all the equipment, desires and temptations endured by every man since Adam."

"So that's the itch you want scratched? I wanted to think better of you." Disappointment was evident in her jerky movements as she tossed the next forkful of dirty muck outside.

"No, you didn't, Greer, but you should," he said, not hiding his temper. "And you should think better of yourself."

"Who are you to lecture me? Just what's all that touching and kissing about?"

His temper evaporated. They both recognized the shift as he said quietly, "I don't have any agenda where you're concerned. I react to you, Greer. Not to just any woman, but to *you*. I don't know how else to make that clear." He set his pitchfork against the wall. "I hear Ethan's pickup and horse trailer pulling in next to mine. "You need to come meet him and set terms."

Greer's gloves were damp inside from nerves. Because she'd once again leaped to judgment regarding Noah, she was ashamed. Lengthening her stride, she overtook him before he reached the front of the barn. "Forgive me, please. I project my history with the town, with the church, with other men onto you. You make me feel things I think I have no right to feel."

A tiny muscle twitched along his jaw. "You have a right. We all have a right to happiness. With your permission, I'll hang around until you find that out."

A gamut of emotions crossed Greer's face. The tension between them began to fade, and she gave him a brief nod.

His breath crowded thickly in his throat. Rather than trust himself to give the rebel yell of triumph he was feeling, Noah went out to greet Ethan with a firm handshake that caused his good friend to wince.

Slower to follow, Greer needed an extra minute to compose herself. She peeled off a dirty leather glove to respond to Noah's introductions. Ritter was another tall Texan. Greer had to tilt back her head to talk to him. He had brown hair and clear green eyes, but wasn't as compact as Noah. It was evident Ethan knew horses as he quietly assessed hers for soundness.

"They look good," he said, allowing a small but decided smile. Greer had a feeling he might dispense smiles more readily to loved ones, but strangers had to prove themselves first.

"I appreciate your boarding them on short notice. Myron Guthrie had to order a barn door for me. I have no idea why anyone would steal one. I shouldn't need your space for more than two weeks. A large horse-trailer is another purchase on my list." They talked terms and types of feed. Greer wrote a check, trying not to think about her dwindling bank balance. Noah helped Ethan load the two mares and two geldings into his six-horse trailer.

"They're all docile enough," Noah remarked as they stood watching Ethan leave.

"That's a requirement if a guest-ranch owner takes on the responsibility of trail rides. She pointed out the hills she'd earmarked for trails. "Callie's dad came through for me. Starting tomorrow, George Robles will be tending my sheep. When I open for business, his wife, Lupita, has agreed to be our cook. She doesn't want to do camp cookouts, but recommended a man she thinks might be interested. A cowboy poet. Lupita gave me his address. I wondered if we could stop to see him on our way home from Fredericksburg."

"Ah, you still want to go? I wasn't sure," Noah said.

"Well, it's okay if you've changed your mind." She headed back to the barn.

Noah caught up. "I didn't change *my* mind. But, uh, after our earlier go-round, I decided I'm not suggesting anything you can misconstrue as pressure from me."

"That's fair." She stripped off her right glove again and stuck out her hand. "Noah, I'm Greer Bell. Shall we start over? Be neighbors? Friends. And…see where it takes us?"

His smile was swift as always. And as always it dazzled Greer. He didn't shake her hand, but picked her up and twirled her around and around until she giggled the way Shelby might. "I'm already past the just-friends stage."

"Oh, put me down, you goof. I told myself I couldn't go anywhere this afternoon unless I get this barn cleaned."

"Yes, ma'am. And I'm going to help see that it's spic-and-span."

Considering its age, unless it was bulldozed and replaced by a new barn, it would never fit Noah's description. However, the floor was clean and the whole place smelled better when they declared themselves done. Noah stacked bags of shavings along one wall to be spread out in the stalls later, before she moved the horses in. He had curls of wood sticking out of his hair and shirt pocket. Greer refrained from picking off the pieces, although she wanted to. When it seemed he'd drive off that way, she brushed at the stray shavings with short, impersonal strokes.

"Hey, take it easy." He jumped back with a laugh. "I know I look like I rolled in the stuff, but I'm not finished quite yet. I need to run home, pick up my horse trailer and come back for the remaining four horses."

"This is my gelding, Favor, and Shelby's new mare, Majestic. The others are Lucy and Fan. Darn, if only I had my tack uncrated." She jerked a thumb toward boxes lining another barn wall, "I'd ride Favor to your house and walk back."

Noah slid up his sleeve and checked his watch. "Shelby's bus will be here in half an hour. Otherwise I'd stay and we could break out your saddles and both ride."

"Thanks. I guess we'll save it for another time. Once my work on the place is under control, I'll log plenty of hours in the saddle. Wait, let me get you a check. I insist on the same terms for boarding these as I negotiated with Ethan."

"This is different. I don't board as a business. My stalls are empty. Oh, and once we get our dogs, Shelby and I can start training them to stay a respectful distance from horses' hooves."

"Which has nothing to do with my giving you money. For feed at least," she insisted, writing and ripping out a check.

"Okay, that I'll accept." He slid into his pickup. "Before I forget to tell you, take a light jacket or sweater this afternoon. Shelby's determined to see the bats, and the best time is at sundown when they swarm out of the tunnel."

"I suppose it's not nice to secretly cross my fingers that the bat place will be closed?"

He laughed. "It's an old wives' tale that bats get tangled in your hair, Greer. And I can't believe you'd want to deprive your child of this experience."

She waved him off and went inside to shower with a much lighter heart. She looked forward to the afternoon. Much more so since she and Noah had cleared the air. Greer hoped it was normal female satisfaction that she felt, knowing—as he'd said—that she alone caused his very male responses when he held and kissed her.

In the privacy of her shower, she was free to revel in that. And free to indulge in the hope that good things would follow today's honesty. She'd quit daring to believe she might find a nice man who could be interested in her.

Greer was showered, dressed and waiting in the lane for Shelby's bus. The last horses were gone, she discovered. Noah had left a note on her door saying he'd collected them at eleven-fifteen, and he'd be back at one. That gave her time to give Shelby a snack and let her share all her tales from school. It had become a ritual for mother and daughter to exchange news about their days. Today, Greer had almost as much to impart as Shelby.

"My horse is at Noah's? Can I go riding tomorrow?"

"Maybe. Did I mention Noah plans to pick up Bear and Happy? Maybe you can go over and see how the dogs behave."

"Okay!" She grinned. "I saw the men fixing the corral. Is that for my horse?"

"Partly. We won't get all our horses home until the barn door arrives and someone has a chance to hang it."

"I'll help."

"You will *not!* Next week your cast comes off. We're not risking either of us falling and breaking something vital. It takes strong men to hang a barn door."

"Like Noah? He carried me when I broke my arm. And I saw him lift you down from the ladder when you guys put up the mini blinds. Luke said daddies are strong. Mama, is Noah strong enough to be a daddy?"

Greer caught her breath. She suddenly admitted Noah had

strength to be a daddy in more ways than just physical. But she delayed responding because she recognized a desire in her daughter to have a *real* dad. A full-time dad. Greer didn't know if that was where her relationship with Noah Kelley was headed, even though it was nice to dream. Broken promises had the capacity to hurt more than promises never made. "Honey, Noah's a friend. He's a good, kind man, and he's given us a helping hand. Being a dad is way more complicated than that. Understand?"

She nodded, but her eyes clouded over.

"Hey, speaking of our knight in shining armor. Isn't that his pickup I see turning into our lane?"

Shelby dashed out onto the porch and let the screen slam behind her. From her beaming smile and the way she kept waving madly, Greer knew she'd averted that crisis only temporarily.

The afternoon proved to be more than Greer could have hoped for. Fredericksburg had grown in the past ten years. The place was a bargain-hunter's dream; she bought handmade pillows and bright bed throws. Noah settled a good-natured argument between her and Shelby over whether to buy pictures of scenery for the cottage walls, or ones with horses that depicted a wilder west. Shelby, of course, voted for the horses. Noah, the rat, sided with the kid. "These do have more attractive colors," Greer grudgingly admitted after Noah stowed them in the lockbox in his pickup bed that he'd emptied of tools for this trip.

Shelby went crazy in the bookstore. It had a fantastic children's section. Greer agreed to buy her two, but found out when she was paying that the little monkey had conned Noah into buying two as well. "You're spoiling her," Greer chided him as they window-shopped.

"Ten dollars' worth of books isn't exactly like buying the kid a sports car."

Greer planted an elbow in his ribs, but she still laughed.

Shelby, who'd skipped ahead to look in the window of a shop loaded with Christmas ornaments, ran back to join them. "Is it time to see the bats or the butterflies yet?"

Glancing at her watch, Greer was surprised to see how many hours had passed. "We'd better do that now. I've decided I do want to buy three of those hand-painted blanket chests we saw in that rustic furniture store. Do we have time to tour the butterfly ranch, come back and pick up my chests, then drive out to view the exodus of the bats?"

"I think so, if Shelby doesn't linger over the butterflies." Noah tweaked her freckled nose. "If you do, we'll have to forgo bats for stopping to eat. My stomach is not on the same schedule as yours." That he aimed at Greer.

"I get involved in shopping and I forget to eat. Is there a good place you know of on the way out of town? Remember I want to visit Kipp Hadley. He's the cowboy poet."

"Right. I had forgotten. But yes, there's a really good German restaurant I know of. From there it's maybe forty-five minutes to Mr. Hadley's house."

They did practically have to pry Shelby away from the glass-walled incubators where the Monarch and native butterflies could be seen in various stages of hatching.

Once they drove to the furniture store, there wasn't a parking place to be had. "Greer, you'll have to get out and buy the chests while I drive around the block. Come to the window and give me a high sign. I'll double-park long enough to load them."

"The sun's going down," Shelby wailed. "You said the bats fly out of the tunnel at sunset, Noah. I won't get to see them."

"Yes, you will, squirt." He reached across her and opened Greer's door. "We can do this," he reiterated calmly, and the smile he offered Greer made her believe they could.

They did. They got in just under the wire, paid the fee and

picked up brochures telling them all about the Mexican free-tailed bats that lived in the tunnel. The guide told them where to stand and where to watch. Sure enough, the sun hadn't quite sunk out of sight when millions of bats swarmed from the opening and turned the sky absolutely black.

"Wow," Shelby squealed, stepping back on Noah's toes in her effort to keep the bats in view longer. "That is so cool." Whirling, she flung her arms around Noah's waist. "I've never seen anything like this. Thank you, Noah! Thank you. Wait till I tell my teacher at school."

Noah's eyes met Greer's over Shelby's strawberry-bright curls. They shared a satisfaction Greer thought was probably reserved for parents. She was positive of it when the guide, a Texas park ranger, remarked, "This must be y'all's daughter's first time viewing the bats. She's lucky you came this week. We're only open June through October, but this year it was extended due to warmer weather."

"She is lucky," Greer said, threading her fingers through Shelby's hair. "We're both lucky." She murmured the last, her gaze clinging to Noah's. "I never expected to enjoy the experience of seeing so many bats. It's an amazing rush of adrenaline. I thank you, too, Noah."

He was going to tease her about giving him a hug, as well. Turning the idea over in his mind, and remembering their morning conversation, he merely took her hand instead. He made it seem natural, Greer realized later, for them to stroll hand in hand back to the pickup.

She enjoyed dinner immensely, too. Not Shelby. "What's this stuff on my plate, Mama? It looks gross."

"Sauerkraut," Noah said. "It's a good German staple. You don't have to eat it all, kid, but you do have to try it. Otherwise, how will you know whether or not you like it? You can't always tell how something tastes by how it looks, you know."

The fact that Shelby picked up her fork and took a couple of bites without further complaint astounded Greer. Once again, Greer thought Noah was excellent daddy material. He was persuasive without being heavy-handed. Greer was even surprised when Shelby ate all her ham and the potato casserole, no inducements required.

Replete and happy, the girl nodded off before they'd driven five miles.

"She's quite a kid," Noah said softly.

"You're so good with kids. I saw that the other night when you sang with them at choir practice. At first those boys didn't want to be there. You convinced them, though, and I think they really had fun."

"I like kids. My mother harasses me because I haven't provided her with grandchildren yet."

Greer froze at the mention of his mother. Then, emboldened by the dark intimacy of the cab, she said, "Did Ruth also harass you about kissing me the other night?"

He winced. "She tried. I'll tell you what I told her. I'm thirty-one years old. Far too old to have my mother telling me how to live my life."

"Ouch. That's harsh. I'm thinking ahead to how I'd feel if Shelby said something like that to me."

"Moms and daughters may be different."

"Or not. The other day I wasn't very kind to my mom when she tried butting into my life."

"I thought Loretta liked me." Now he was teasing, and wasn't prepared for Greer to scowl.

"She does like you, Noah. She happens to think your association with me and with Shel will damage your reputation."

"Hogwash! I can't believe—on second thought, I can," he muttered, as he remembered seeing Loretta with his mom last

Sunday. "Ignore them all, Greer. Their beliefs are archaic and old-fashioned."

"Maybe. Uh, Noah, wasn't that the road leading to Kipp Hadley's place? Lupita Robles said Kipp lives in a two-room cabin. I gather he's quite the character, the type to shun all kinds of progress. So, while I'm wary of approaching him, he does sound like the perfect person to treat my guests to a taste of old Texas."

Bent, gnarled and hobbling, Kipp Hadley was all of that and more. He didn't chew tobacco, but judging by how stained his teeth were, Greer figured at one time he had. The Robles name got them in the door. A half-asleep Shelby charmed the old man with her wide-eyed questions about the saddles, ropes and deer heads lining his cabin walls. Kipp got a kick out of regaling them with stories and poems that explained what life used to be like in the state.

Noah spotted the old man's guitar and mandolin. They talked music for a bit, and then Kipp entertained them with a couple of lively songs. Shelby dozed off again, leaning on Noah. Seeing how tired she was, Greer got to the purpose of their visit.

After listening to her offer, Kipp stroked his grizzled jaw. "Seems like the ideal job for an old buzzard like me," he said. "My days get pretty long just sittin' around."

"Once I open, I'll provide cookouts at least once a week. I hired Lupita Robles as ranch cook, and George will herd sheep and handle trail rides. That'll be another two weeks or so. Do you want to think about this and get back to me?"

"No need. I should let you know—I used to have a problem with alcohol, but I've got it licked."

"Good for you." Greer grasped his hand and pumped.

"I have a couple of daughters," he said, his eyes glued to Shelby, whom Noah held, her head pillowed on his shoulder.

"Or I should say *had*," Kipp added. "Hard living and hard drinking lost me my family. I've probably got grandkids and maybe great-grandkids someplace around the state."

"Have you ever tried to locate them?" Greer asked. "Uh, not that it's any of my business."

"'Sokay," he drawled. "I think about it. Guess I don't know where to start."

Noah's eyes darkened in sympathy. "Once you're working for Greer, I'll come around and if you still want to, Kipp, I have a computer program at my church office that might help us track them down." He stood and lifted the gangly girl.

"Really?" The man's faded blue eyes lit. "That'd be nice. If my ex-wife's still alive, I'd like her to see I've gotten half-way respectable." His plaintive words followed them out the door.

After they were in the pickup and on the road again, Greer reached over and placed her hand on the arm Noah used to lazily guide the vehicle down the highway. "That was a nice gesture you made back there. I saw tears in his eyes. Do you think it's possible to find his family?"

"It depends on how much information he has, and how much they have on him. I'm guessing there's a better chance of turning up a grandchild. They'd be about our age." He grasped the wheel with his other hand and turned his palm over. Holding hands in the dark was something Greer found totally comfortable. And if she was content to drive through the night in silence, so was he.

He needed both hands on the wheel to steer the pickup down the rutted lane to her ranch and gently released Greer's.

She sat up straight when she realized how far they'd come. His bright headlights outlined a white square attached to her screen door.

"I wonder what that is," she mused, rubbing her eyes.

"Wait here," Noah said. "I'll fetch it. Looks like some kind of note. You can turn on the cab light."

"I could take it inside. I don't know who'd leave me a note. Unless Millicent came back and it's one of my brochures. That's probably it," she said to thin air, because Noah had climbed out and now had the paper ripped off the door.

"It's from Wade," Noah announced, leaning across the seat to hand it to Greer. "I didn't read your mail," he stated. "Can't miss his signature at the bottom, though."

She read it, gasped and started at the top to read it again.

"What's wrong?"

"Listen to this. He has Rolando Diaz locked up in jail." Noticing Noah's blank expression, she elaborated. "Diaz is one of the two men I hired for odd jobs and to build my fence."

"Oh. Why is he in jail?"

"Clint Gallagher phoned Wade to haul off Rolando. Clint swears his crew caught him illegally hunting deer on one of Gallagher's leases. Rolando insisted one of my rams wandered through a spot that's not fenced. He claims someone, he didn't see who, shot my ram. Clint's crew apprehended Diaz after he ran back to his truck for a twenty-two. He and Marcus Arana mixed it up with Gallagher's men—to find out who shot the ram. Marcus fled when Gallagher's men jumped Rolando."

"That doesn't make sense. Surely Wade has proof Diaz told the truth if there's a dead ram?"

"No. What Wade saw when he arrived is one very dead deer. A doe at that, and no sign of any ram."

Noah shut his eyes and pinched the bridge of his nose. "That complicates matters," he said.

"It certainly does. I have a count on my sheep. It'd be morning before I could do a comprehensive recount. And that's provided I can even do it. I've counted cattle, but sheep all look alike," she lamented.

"I have a question. Do you believe Rolando? Did he see the deer and think it'd be easy meat for his family?"

She bit her lip. "His family is in Ciudad Acuna. He and Marcus work hard." She sighed. "Another problem Wade mentions is Rolando's priors. He's not allowed to possess a firearm. To tell you the truth, I wasn't aware he had a rifle in the truck."

"This is sort of a mess."

"Right. A convenient way to see I don't get my fence built. I say that because I'm sure McPherson and Satterwhite deliberately turned me down, Noah."

"I know you think so." He stroked her hair. "In the morning I'll get Ryan's version. Ordering someone tossed in the clink for trespassing on one of his deer leases is a bit harsh. I can't see even Clint making up charges and exchanging one dead animal for another."

"Thanks, Noah. Speak to Ryan tomorrow. Oh, could you please unload what I bought in Fredericksburg. Stack it behind my porch swing." She retrieved her purse and dug out her car keys, then unbuckled Shelby.

"What are you going to do?" Noah frowned. He watched her awkwardly carry her daughter to the Blazer and open the back door and slide Shelby in.

"I'm going to town to see what it takes to bail out Rolando. Unless I get that fence up, this mess will only be the tip of the iceberg."

"Dammit, Greer! You can't go off to the jail this time of night. Virgil Dunn will be on duty. He's not the brightest bulb in the chandelier, and besides that, he doesn't cotton much to women."

"I'm going," she said, closing the door on her sleeping child.

Sprinting across the road, Noah jerked her keys out of her hand. "Get in. I'm going with you. In fact, I'm driving."

"But my things? Everything I bought—"

"Will be as safe in my pickup as sitting on your porch."

She climbed in slowly. After he'd started the Chevy with a roar, Greer, who'd lain her head back against the seat rolled her face toward him. "My mom and yours are right, Noah. I'm a bad influence on you. I'll bet in the whole of your life this is the first time you've been in a jail."

"You'd be surprised at what I've done in my reckless life," he said grimly, shoving the gears into reverse.

CHAPTER ELEVEN

AT NINE O'CLOCK in the evening, Homestead resembled a ghost town. Most of the weekend action was at the Saddle Up Saloon on the outskirts of Homestead. There were a few cars around the Lone Wolf Bar, but none parked near the courthouse. The path to the sheriff's office lay in shadow.

A marked patrol car sat beneath the single streetlight, and Noah parked close behind it.

Greer opened her car door before he shut the engine off. She started to open the rear door to unbuckle Shelby.

"Let me get her," Noah said. "Have you had any dealings with Virgil Dunn?" he asked Greer, then went on before she had a chance to answer. "To say Virg is the excitable type may be an understatement. You'll get farther with him if you don't storm the jail like some avenging angel."

"I'm mad, Noah. It's so…so small-town to lock up poor Rolando for no reason other than the word of a self-appointed big cheese like Clint Gallagher."

"State Senator Gallagher *is* a big cheese."

She deflated like a spent balloon. "*Soon to be former* state senator, but you're right, his name carries weight. What do you suggest? I'm sure Rolando's been treated unfairly—and not only that, I need him at work tomorrow."

"Then tell Virgil you're here to bail Diaz out. Promise you'll make sure he shows up at a hearing if Gallagher presses charges of trespassing or something."

"That's ludicrous." But when they went inside, Greer followed Noah's suggestion to the letter.

Virgil was a small man with a receding hairline. His eyes were a bit buggy, and to Greer it seemed that he never let his gaze rest in one place for more than a second. He did hitch up his pants and made sure they saw he was armed as he produced the charges.

"Now, little lady," Virgil said with a twang. "Wade didn't say to hand Diaz over to anyone. And it's too late to bother the boss. So, trot along home till tomorrow."

Greer felt herself popping with anger. She planted both fists on Virgil's desk and leaned close. "You cannot hold a man without bail for trespassing."

"There's the matter of the dead deer," the deputy mumbled, rolling back in his chair.

"That's not stated on the preliminary complaint you gave me. Where is the deer? Did you or Wade check to see if the bullet came from Rolando's rifle?"

Virgil jumped up in agitation. "You some kind of lady lawyer?"

"I'm his employer," Greer said tiredly. "It's late and I need him on the job tomorrow. I need a fence strung between my land and Gallagher's. I know citizens have rights, and I don't see here that you let Rolando speak with a lawyer."

Noah, who'd been standing back, moved into the light, still holding the sleeping Shelby. "Virg, it says bond is set at one hundred dollars. If Ms. Bell pays, you'll have to accept her money and let Rolando go."

"Father? Then you're vouching he ain't a flight risk? He won't light out for the border?"

Noah strode to the broad stairs and saw that two of the cells in the basement were occupied, one by a sad-looking Rolando Diaz. The other probably a drunk sleeping it off. "Promise

Virgil you won't take off tonight, and that you'll be at work for Ms. Bell in the morning," Noah called down to Diaz.

"I didn't shoot no doe." Rolando's voice floated up the stairwell. "Someone at Gallagher's killed a fine ram of Ms. Bell's. This whole thing stinks."

"We believe you," Greer hollered, bending to see him. "Noah wants your word that you won't disappear on us if the deputy releases you tonight."

"You believe me?" Getting to his feet, the wiry man wrapped leathery hands around the bars.

"Yes, " she reiterated. "I believe you enough to fork over a hundred-dollar bond."

"That's nice of you. I need the job bad. I got a green card, but my wife, she don't. Most every cent I make I send home. I swear the Four Aces crew…they're lying."

Greer turned back to Virgil and pulled out her checkbook. "Let him out," she said in a no-nonsense voice. "Tell Wade Montgomery we'll talk about this tomorrow."

Virgil opened a drawer and removed a ring of keys. He clattered down the concrete stairs and unlocked the cell. After that, he prodded Diaz up the steps, then handed him a plastic bag containing his wallet and a cheap watch. "Gotta keep your twenty-two in the evidence closet until Wade okays givin' it back."

"It means a lot to me. Tell the sheriff, please, it's all I have of *mi padre*."

Noah murmured to Greer as Diaz signed a receipt for his belongings. "We'll need to give him a lift to wherever he lives. Shall we wait in the Blazer while you finish?"

She nodded. "You don't think he *is* a flight risk, do you?"

"No."

His firm answer settled Greer's flip-flopping stomach. She'd never had to do anything like this. And if she needed to find a lawyer for Rolando, she wasn't even sure how to go about locating anyone competent.

Her part in the process after the men had left amounted to signing forms verifying she'd paid, and that she promised Rolando would show up for any future hearings. "I'd like a receipt," she said when Virgil put her check in the drawer.

He took his sweet time locating a receipt book. But as she pocketed the paper and left the sheriff's office, Greer had a feeling of accomplishment.

If Diaz thanked her once for believing in him, he thanked her fifty times on the drive to a battered trailer on the outskirts of town. A rental, he said.

"You have a ride to work in the morning?" Noah asked him.

"Marcus drives. I, uh, have no license. I'm close to gettin' mine back after a couple of drunk driving arrests. I've been real sober, I swear, thanks to Mr. Collins. Dammit, I hope this don't mess up my record. Uh, sorry, Father."

Noah rolled his eyes. "I've heard cussing before." He sneaked a peek at Greer. "Your current boss said several *I'm mad as hells* on the trip to the sheriff's office."

"I was…*am* so mad I could spit. Is that more acceptable, Noah?"

He held up both hands. "Don't be mad at me." To Diaz, he muttered in an aside, "You don't wanna cross this lady. She's one tough hombre. Or is that hombress?"

"Goodbye, Rolando," Greer drawled in an attempt to end Noah's teasing. "You just show up for work. I'll get this sorted out with Gallagher and Sheriff Montgomery."

With final and effusive thanks, Diaz scuttled out of the Blazer and into his trailer.

"Where to now?" Noah asked, throwing the Blazer into Reverse to back out of the seedy trailer park.

"Home. I probably need to get out a flashlight and walk my property line to be sure no other sheep have made their way across to Gallagher's grass."

Slowing to switch the transmission from reverse to drive, Noah picked up Greer's hand and carried it to his lips for a kiss. "Deal with Ryan Gallagher. It's probably not his fault. His dad, his crew, they're all headstrong. If it comes down to a he-said, he-said kind of thing, you may never get straight answers."

"You mean if Gallagher's men engineered this fiasco, they'll get away with it?"

"It's the kind of dispute that's hard to prove. Jase Farley hunted with half of Clint's crew. He rented cabins to hunters who lease deer blinds from Clint. There was a lot of grumbling when Jase was forced into bankruptcy because the consortium failed."

"Ed Tanner said a lot of locals lost land and money when that happened, including my dad. Was it due to bad management?"

"An extended drought forced the sale of cattle when beef prices were at an all-time low. The rains came too late to help. The collapse of the consortium left good men stuck and bitter, and some think Clint could've done more. Like Ethan Ritter, who blames Clint for his father's suicide. The members all started out as friends. I haven't heard anyone being blamed publicly, but privately there's grumbling and speculation. Some of them believe Senator Gallagher blocked their requests for bank loans."

Greer had been content to let Noah steer with one hand and keep hold of hers. "Miranda said Senator Gallagher wanted the whole parcel, but couldn't raise the capital. You don't think he'd try to force me out?"

"I know he's developed health problems. The Four Aces

had their own troubles. They were fleeced by a former manager. Ryan's done a lot to restore the place to its former success—well, he's getting there, anyway. However, I can't vouch for everyone who might rent a deer lease from them." He shrugged. "I think you should leave it in Sheriff Montgomery's hands."

She thought about that as Noah parked between his pickup and her house. "I appreciate all the help you've given me since I moved in. How can I ever repay you?"

"Would you let go of the past and come back to church? Before you refuse, just listen a minute." Letting the engine idle, Noah slid a hand around her neck, and rubbed away her tension with his thumbs. "If you hadn't wanted to heal old wounds, Greer, nothing would have induced you to leave Colorado and move home."

Closing her eyes, she leaned across the console and touched her forehead to his. "I had high hopes that my dad, especially, could've forgiven me."

"Just be you, Greer. Hold your head high. Our congregation is changing. Come and see, and let everyone get to know you. Callie and Kayla will accept you, the same way I do. Let our feelings influence the old-timers. Your dad will come around."

"You think so? I want to believe you, Noah." She studied him. "I want this move to work for Shelby. And…for us," she said softly, smiling into Noah's warm eyes.

He dragged her body across the console, despite the awkwardness. His kiss drove away every obstacle Greer could imagine. And when he finally released her, she did believe that she and Shelby could make a better life here, one in which Noah would figure prominently.

WADE MONTGOMERY, Ryan Gallagher and Noah all wheeled into Greer's ranch at the same time the next morning, but in separate vehicles. Greer thought privately that they were three of the finest-looking men she'd ever seen. Wade and Ryan both wore Western hats. Noah, a baseball cap. Wade looked official, Ryan like a working rancher in his jeans, boots and dark shirt. Again Noah was the odd man out in gray sweats. He looked ready to hit the basketball court. "That's exactly where I'm going," he said when Greer laughingly made the observation. "One or two mornings a week, I run out to the boy's reformatory where I'm trying to coach a couple of teams. I hope it teaches them to solve differences through athletics instead of with fists."

Greer's nervous gaze followed Wade, who headed straight for Rolando. He and Marcus were busily using heavy staplers on the fence she'd had them abandon to fix the corral. It was half done.

Pushing back his hat, Ryan scanned the sea of sheep munching their way across the field below her house. "They look like a placid lot."

"Yeah, eating is what they've been doing since they got here. I don't know why one ram would've left the flock yesterday. I'm sorry, Mr. Gallagher."

Noah knew it hadn't been easy for her to apologize. He smiled encouragingly.

Ryan accepted with alacrity, but he did say, "My men are sticking to their story. As is Diaz. Before I got involved, both reportedly dead animals had vanished, and without carcasses, it's impossible to prove a crime's been committed. I've let our crew know I won't tolerate anything else of this kind. Should there be another incident of your animals crossing onto our property, our men have strict orders to find me and not take matters into their own hands. It's the best I can do. I got Dad to agree."

It'd been a long speech for a man as buttoned down as Ryan, Greer figured.

"Did you count your sheep?" Noah settled a hand familiarly on Greer's shoulder.

"I tried. Twice. I got ninety-six the first time and one-oh-two the second. Anybody else want to give it a whirl, be my guest. Really, though, I'm okay with dropping the whole thing. As long as the sheriff removes those charges from Rolando's record."

Wade walked up in time to hear. "I told him I've already done that. He really appreciates being given a second chance, Greer."

Ryan turned to her. "Dad thinks you're nuts to hire migrants. Kristin heard from Callie that you've engaged Lupita and George Robles. My wife sends you kudos. I won't tell you what Dad said. There's no proof, but other ranchers have claimed that George Robles is guilty of assisting in illegal border crossings."

"George and Lupita are naturalized citizens. I checked. I have more reservations about their eldest daughter. Denise is just out of drug rehab and hasn't found a job. I agreed to give her a try as housekeeper for my guests' quarters."

"Denise is a good kid who fell in with a bad crowd," Noah said. "I should've thought of her when you were looking for people, Greer. She's been volunteering in our Sunday morning nursery for a couple of months. And I can't side with the senator on George. He and Lupita studied hard and prize their citizenship. Hey, I've gotta take off or I'll be late getting to the reformatory. Greer, I'll see you this afternoon. Don't forget I'm picking up our dogs from the shelter."

"How can I? It's all Shelby talked about before going to school." Greer trailed Noah to his pickup. "Last night you brought up the idea of taking Shelby out to ride. I hated to say anything to her without making sure you meant this afternoon."

"I did. Can you go, too?"

"I'd love to, but I set myself an escalated timetable. If nothing else goes wrong, I'll be able to open on schedule. Thanks to Marisa Sanderson, who sort of jumped the gun, I have some guests lined up," she confided, although a mix of pleasure and worry flitted across her face. "Six Western writers. I know them, and Marisa insists they're perfect for a trial."

Noah, unable to resist, tugged her behind the open door of his Chevy and stole a quick kiss. "If they're Western writers, they're coming to the right place. I predict things will go your way, Greer. In fact, I think they're already starting. It's likely that Gallagher's men were behind those godawful screams, but since Ryan gave them the word, that'll be the end of such tricks."

"I hope so. Will you stay for dinner tonight, Noah?"

"You bet. A preacher never turns down a home-cooked meal." He winked.

Wade and Ryan prepared to leave after Noah did. "Keep the card with my phone numbers, Greer," Wade said as Ryan pulled out first. "I hope we've seen the last of your troubles, but in this business I never say never. I didn't get a chance to tell you, I think you're doing a great job pumping life into this spread. I saw Millie Niebauer at the café. She's enthusiastic about your brochure. She and Hiram want to attract outside visitors to Homestead. They're solidly behind Miranda's program."

"Callie Montgomery suggested I have an open house for locals after my trial opening. I'll experiment on one set of guests, seasoned folks. If it goes well, I'll do a Thanksgiving weekend open house for people in town."

"Say, maybe your open house can take the place of the Saturday Thanksgiving fellowship dinner we talked about having at the church. Ask Noah to dedicate the new name of your ranch at the same time. It'll make the gathering semiofficial."

"Great idea. I'll ask him tonight."

"I hesitate to say it might go over better if you attend church first," Wade said slowly.

"Did Noah put you up to nudging me?" she asked with a laugh. "This conversation is déjà vu. He twisted my arm again last night. And…convinced me to join you all this Sunday."

"Hallelujah!" Tipping his hat, Wade grinned as he drove out.

GREER PUT IN a full day hanging the pictures she'd bought in Fredericksburg and finding the right spots to display the other items. Before she knew it, Shelby's bus dropped her off, and not fifteen minutes later—just when she was sure Shelby was going to drive her crazy asking after Noah—he showed up with the dogs.

Everything stopped while Greer, Rolando and Marcus admired and laughed over the antics of the two fluffy dogs. "Look," Shelby said as Bear and Happy dashed across the field to nip at the heels of a sheep straying from the flock. "They're so clever already, aren't they, Mama? You said this morning it'd be a miracle if Bear could learn how to herd sheep. He already knows what to do."

"It appears so. I stand corrected. I guess the girl at the shelter knew what she was talking about when she said they had a natural instinct as babysitters."

Shelby raced after the pair of dogs, her laughter floating back on the breeze. Greer slid an arm around Noah's waist and rested her head on his wide shoulder. "I love seeing her this happy."

Noah placed a kiss on the tip of her nose. "And I love

watching you this happy. What time do you want us here for supper?"

"Five-thirty? I have another surprise," she said, smiling up into his eyes. "The cable company wired the house and cottages for TV today. I rented a movie and bought popcorn for after supper. It's a kids' movie," she warned.

"Darn, I was hoping for X-rated." Noah enjoyed a laugh when Greer's lips parted. "I'm kidding. But I did mention I'm not the saint you'd like me to be, sweetheart."

Just the way he casually called her sweetheart sent shivers through her. She accepted his sizzling kiss without even glancing around to make sure Shelby wasn't watching them.

That in itself gave Noah satisfaction, and hope. He wanted Greer to become so comfortable with his presence that she'd want him as a fixture in her life. He thought she was beginning to.

For the remainder of the week they fell into an easy pattern. Noah and Shelby rode to the river and back, then gave the dogs a workout with the sheep. Shelby brushed both dogs as she'd promised. In the evenings the three of them either played board games or watched kid-appropriate movies. Noah developed a habit of sticking around until after Shelby fell sleep. He and Greer cuddled on the couch. But after a few nights of that activity, they both ended up panting and clearly frustrated.

Noah always let things go just so far, then he'd suggest a walk outside, to make a last check. Or they'd sit in the porch swing and see who could identify the Southern Cross first. If his control was dangerously near breaking, he made excuses to go home early.

One night as they circled the bunkhouse, Greer said unexpectedly, "What do you suppose makes two people feel so attracted to each other?"

The moonlight played over her serious face, or otherwise Noah might have supposed she was joking. They held hands after exiting the house, but he could still feel faint tremors from their couch activities running through her body. He, of course, had other physical reminders.

"Is this where you tell me you don't believe in love, Greer?"

"Love? Hmm. I wasn't even thinking in terms of surreal emotions. In Colorado a man I dated a couple of times said I had a serious problem with frigidity. I, um, don't seem to have that problem where you're concerned."

He did laugh then. "Sorry, but only a fool would call you frigid. You tackle everything you do with total passion. Maybe he expected too much too soon."

"Maybe. I explained that I hadn't dated very often. I told you the same thing."

"So what you're saying is that we connect. The way two halves go together to make a whole. Incidentally, I don't think love is surreal. It's a very real emotion. Love keeps this old world ticking. It…keeps me ticking." Bending, he kissed her in a different way.

She tried to frown, but her heart tripped madly, leaving her short of breath and slightly dizzy. He couldn't be saying… that…he was falling in love with her. Could he?"

"Don't scowl, please." Nothing clutched at Noah's stomach like seeing her beautiful face contort in distress. Especially distress at the idea of something more intimate developing between them. "I promised we'd take things slow. Let them unfold naturally. So, come on, Greer, walk me to my pickup. Oh, and tomorrow night I have a church council meeting. Saturday I have to carve out some time to put together Sunday's sermon. You won't back out and not come on Sunday?"

His anxious tone spurred Greer to a reckless reassurance,

especially as she had difficulty imagining herself seated in a pew at St. Mark's. "I promised, Noah. I don't take promises lightly. I'll be there."

"I wish you didn't sound as though it's like a trip to the guillotine. I'll try not to bore you, sweetheart."

She did laugh at that and swatted his arm, which relieved the tension that had built between them.

Noah leaned out of the pickup and poured every bit of emotion he had into a goodbye kiss that went on and on and on. Once it did end, he blindly started his pickup and hit the gas to signal that he had to leave. It did his heart good to look in the rearview mirror and see her staring after him, her eyes big and luminous.

SUNDAY, Greer attended St. Mark's for the first time in ten years. She suffered a bad case of nerves on the drive to town, and was afraid she'd throw up as she and Shelby mounted the front steps that led to the main sanctuary. The organ music brought back a flood of memories. Same sounds. Same smell. Same people, including her parents and Clint Gallagher, all sitting in the same pews they always had.

Everyone seemed to take her appearance in stride. Throughout the service, her eyes remained locked on Noah as she clutched her purse in her lap.

Callie and Kayla came up afterward to greet her. Her mom, too, singled Greer out. Loretta beamed as she bent to hug Shelby, who suddenly blurted, "Mama, I left my Sunday school papers downstairs. Is it okay if I run and get them?"

"Sure, hon. Meet me in the car." Greer turned back to her mother. "I see Daddy over by the door. Will you go with me so I can at least say hello?"

Loretta followed her daughter's gaze. "Yes, but please

don't be disappointed. Robert is so…well, you know he's always been set in his ways."

The women approached and Robert Bell broke away from the men he'd been huddled with. He met them without any expression of happiness. "Loretta, you should think about my position on the church board. And, Greer, I see no ring on your finger, which means nothing's changed since the last time we discussed your predicament. At the least you ought to act embarrassed."

Fury swept through Greer. "You wear a ring, Daddy, but that doesn't make you a good human being. It's okay if you can't find it in your heart to forgive me for a mistake I made as a naive, vulnerable girl. But I'm sorry you've let bitterness keep you from knowing a marvelous child like Shelby. She may be the only grandchild you'll ever have." Greer struck out immediately after her outburst, running out a side door. Resentment brought tears. She was angry with her dad and even slightly irritated with Noah, who'd convinced her that showing up here would alter attitudes.

Even in her haste she saw that Noah stood at the front door shaking hands. It was plain from the rapt expressions on the faces of those filing past that he was adored. No one would ever say he was an embarrassment to the town.

Her father had cut through Greer's carefully shored up defenses. Locating Shelby at the car, she drove straight home. The minute she'd changed into jeans, she called Shelby. "Let's go visit Kayla and Ethan. We have horses to exercise there."

The real reason for her haste to leave the house was that she couldn't face Noah after failing to keep her end of their bargain. She'd promised to hold her head high no matter what. Given her dad's comments, there was little hope of the healing she'd longed for. Greer wasn't sure she had the grit to stay, after all.

If Shelby sensed that something was bothering her mom, she didn't bring it up. "I wish we could do stuff like this more often," the girl said three hours later when Brad met them at the barn and helped unsaddle their well-exercised geldings. They spent another half hour brushing all four animals they'd stabled with the Ritter's.

"Next time maybe Brad, Heather and Megan can ride with us."

"Maybe. But today was work, hon," Greer said. "Did you notice how often I stopped to jot down notes? I'm mapping trails for guests to ride. Remember the stand of cottonwoods where we got off and walked to the river? That's a perfect spot for Mr. Hadley, our cowboy poet, to park his chuckwagon and treat guests to an old-fashioned cookout."

"Goodie! Can Bear and me go, too? Or Brad, Heather, Megan and Brit? We can be guides sometimes, like Lindsay Sanderson."

"Honey, Lindsay was fifteen the first time she worked as trail guide. When you're all fifteen, ask me again. Until then, Mr. Robles will be the guide. Tomorrow I'll ride out with him, to set trail markers. I think a big U-shaped trail around the property, with a few switchbacks should allow the riders to reach the chuckwagon in time for a leisurely evening meal of steak and cowboy beans."

"I hate beans." Shelby wrinkled her nose. "Why didn't we wait for Noah? I thought he said we were all going riding this afternoon."

"Really? I assumed he'd be tied up at church. And we needed to check the horses stabled with Ethan. With luck, we can bring them home next week. Mr. Guthrie stopped me before the service this morning to say the barn door Noah ordered is due on Wednesday. He'll deliver and hang it, too."

An hour later, Greer was surprised and a little thrown to see Noah and his dog napping in their porch swing.

Shelby and Bear tumbled from the Blazer, raced up the steps and pounced on the sleepers. The dogs tore around the porch, obviously delighted to be together. Shelby bounced on her knees on the padded seat and regaled a yawning Noah with a blow-by-blow discussion of her afternoon.

His indulgent smile affected Greer as few things did. And when he noticed her mounting the steps and transferred his attention—a different *quality* of attention—the resentment she'd felt earlier died away.

"You guys disappeared after church so fast, I wanted to make sure everything's okay." There was a wealth of concern in Noah's greeting.

Shelby answered, and it was probably just as well. "Me'n Mama went over to Megan and Heather and Brad's to exercise our horses. It was way cool."

"Oh." The one word spoke of his dashed hopes.

Nevertheless, it compelled Greer to explain. "I figured you'd be tied up all afternoon with duties at St. Mark's, Noah."

She knew better from past Sundays. It was obvious that she'd run off to avoid him.

Shelby slid off the swing and chased after the dogs. Noah stood, as well, and reached out to rub his hands up and down Greer's arms. "I saw you talking to your parents. I knew if you made the effort to extend the olive branch, even a tough old bird like Robert would give a little. How could he not, when you and Shelby are two of the sweetest, most beautiful females God ever created?"

Greer felt her resentment erupt again, then instantly crumble. Honestly, only a man who cared deeply about them could be that naive and optimistic. His eyes said it was more than a minister's caring. That was unmistakable when he cleared his throat and spoke. "Greer, I've fallen in love with you. With you and Shelby."

Greer felt as if she were tumbling headfirst down a long

black tunnel. Oddly, it wasn't a frightening sensation. Lifting a shaking hand, she traced Noah's cheekbones, his chin and his lips. She'd fallen in love with him, too. How she wished she could tell him. But the feelings were so new and so overwhelming, the words stuck in her throat.

Noah felt her unspoken emotions flow through her fingertips. He clasped her hands and nibbled light kisses along her knuckles. He assumed her feelings were tied in with her first trip back to church. "I wish I had time to stay, or to take you and Shelby off for another Sunday outing. I have a meeting of the Halloween committee, and I'm afraid it'll run right into the evening service. I won't ask you to come back for that, Greer. Twice the first time out would be a bit much."

"Definitely," she hurried to say. "I need to polish the big old table and chairs I had delivered yesterday from that consignment store. If it cleans up as well as I hope, I'll finally be ready for a grand opening." She told him about Myron promising to bring the barn door. "My first guests told Marisa they're fine with rustic. It'll be a good test."

"That's great." Noah swept her up and whirled her around. He set her down gently.

"Oh—Wade said I should ask you to dedicate our new ranch name and turn my open house into the Thanksgiving weekend fellowship potluck. But…I don't know if that's a wise thing to do."

"I'd be honored. Can you handle feeding so many?"

"I think so. I'll find out how my help handles a crowd, anyway. Lupita and George Robles, and Kipp Hadley go on my payroll tomorrow. Rolando and Marcus are happy to work part-time at odd jobs. They're good and reliable."

"Well, make a list of last-minute repairs that need doing. I can't get by tomorrow, but Tuesday afternoon I'll bring my toolbox."

"You're too good to me, Noah. A woman could get used to having you around."

"I hope so, Greer. In fact, that's what I'm counting on." There was no mistaking he meant what he said. Nor had it escaped him that Greer didn't return his declaration of love. He intended to change that.

After he left, Greer had a hard time getting down to work polishing the table and chairs. Noah said he loved her. But wasn't the next step usually marriage? All evening, Greer let herself imagine how life might change for her and Shelby if a man—this man—came into their lives permanently. And she tried to be realistic. There would, Greer was pretty sure, be pluses and minuses. Except she had difficulty putting anything in the minus column.

The next morning, during an unscheduled run into town— to mail out the brochures Millicent had dropped off—Greer accidentally stumbled upon the most major of all minuses. Coming out of the post office, she ran smack into Noah's mother.

Stepping aside, Greer gave her the briefest nod. She expected Ruth Kelley to pass without a word. Instead, the woman latched bony fingers around Greer's sleeve. "Greer! Greer Bell. Hold up a minute. I've been hoping I'd see you. I missed church yesterday because Holden suffered severe angina most of the night."

"I'm sorry," Greer murmured politely.

"Today, some of the church board came to visit him, which freed me up to run errands. I understand several board members heard you yell at your father yesterday. In the sanctuary. With our congregation all around."

Greer's head came up. "I wasn't aware that anyone but my mother was nearby."

Ruth released her hold on Greer's jacket. "You may not

know this, but I cast the tie-breaking vote that allowed the implementation of Mayor Wright's Home Free plan."

"Ah, well then, I have you to thank."

The older woman's eyes were cold. "Believe me, had I known the problems it would cause, I would've voted no. Young woman, are you aware the church board is at this moment talking of removing my son from his temporary post at St. Mark's?"

Greer couldn't rein in her gasp of shock.

"No need to ask why. I'll tell you. A man in his position can't be too careful when it comes to his deportment in and around a small community such as ours. It's come to our attention time and again how often you two have been seen together. Maybe in a big city a person's background isn't of consequence. Here in Homestead, that's not the case. People know how frequently Noah's pickup has been parked outside your home. And how late," she added with a sniff.

"I fail to see how that's anyone's business."

"A priest's conduct is *always* open to scrutiny, my dear. And thanks to you, these last few weeks Noah has fallen far short of what is deemed acceptable. I don't know how you two feel about each other, but…I do know nothing can come of it."

Greer flinched and drew back.

Ruth narrowed her eyes as she resumed speaking. "I can see you're in love with my son. Not surprising. He's a fine, upstanding man. The question now is, how *much* do you love him? Enough to walk away and let him continue his job? More than a job, really. A higher calling to which he'd dedicated his life before you proved to be too great a temptation. The Bible warns of such women. Holden believes Noah's too blind to see what's right. I'm not one to judge, but it's obvious you hold some kind of power over him that we, his parents, can't combat. So if, as Loretta insists, you came back to Homestead to make a better life for your child, then I beg you as one mother to another…release my son. For his sake."

For such quietly spoken words, they had real power. Too much power for her to fight. "You win, Ruth. Consider Noah released."

It was to her credit, Greer thought later, that she'd managed to excuse herself with a degree of dignity intact, and walk away before she dissolved into tears.

She did cry all the way home. She was barely able to overcome her deep despair and pull herself together in time to ride out and meet George Robles and Kipp Hadley. She carried out the duties of a confident boss as they marked trails, drove stakes and discussed the first cookout. She behaved as normally as if her heart wasn't breaking.

Greer counted it fortunate that she'd been allowed all of Monday and most of Tuesday to fall out of love with Noah Kelley. But then, on Tuesday afternoon, he showed up with Shelby's favorite pizza and his toolbox, as planned. Thinking ahead, Greer had arranged for Shelby to be at Callie's for a play date with Brittany, Adam and Mary Beth.

"Noah." Greer greeted him through a locked screen. "I've had time to do a bit of thinking. Here's the thing—I moved home to build a business. I hope you'll understand, but it's important I do that on my own. And well, something else. Shelby's become too attached to you, Noah. I…don't…want that."

He couldn't conceal his hurt and confusion. "What happened between Sunday and now, Greer? Where's Shelby? I promised we'd take Bear and Happy and go riding today. Are you running away because I admitted I love you?"

Coolly, Greer reached out to shut the door. "On Sunday I saw how good a preacher you are. The church, St. Mark's, is linked to my past. To old sorrows. You've tried to make me see you as a maverick. But Noah, you love what you do. You said you love me, but…you can't. I can never accept that church. I…I'd hoped we could be adult about this. I really hate scenes."

"Scenes? You're the one creating a scene, Greer." He loved her, and he didn't want them to end like this. But when he was prepared to fire an angry response, he faced a closed door.

He lifted a hand to pound on it, but ordered himself to calm down. What words would refute her logic? He did love his job, and it was just as plain that she didn't like what he did at all. And that *was* a big problem. Only God would know if it was greater than the love Noah carried in his heart for Greer Bell.

Inside, Greer slumped against the door. She couldn't even tell him she'd rejected him for his own good. Her tears coincided with the firing up of his pickup's engine.

CHAPTER TWELVE

DURING THE FIRST WEEK, Shelby didn't ask about Noah's absence. Kayla drove the girls to choir practice on Wednesday. Friday night was the Halloween party at the church. Greer arranged a ride for Shelby with Callie Montgomery, by claiming she and Lupita Robles were too busy testing menus and putting together grocery lists for her to leave. It was true in a way.

Sunday presented a bigger problem. Since Greer had driven them the previous week, Shelby expected that to happen again.

"Shel, honey, I simply can't spare the time to sit in church all morning. If you don't want to call one of your friends and ask for a lift, phone your grandmother. Her number's in my phone book."

"Mama, is Noah sick?"

Greer straightened from where she'd just popped a tray of oatmeal raisin cookies in the oven. The day before, she and Lupita had made twenty pints of peach marmalade, and the day prior to that they'd assembled and frozen twelve assorted pies. "Wasn't he at choir practice?"

"Yes, but he was…different. And Mrs. Montgomery said he didn't act like he felt good at the Halloween party. May I ride Majestic to his house and see if he's okay?"

"No, you may not. We've had this discussion, Shel. You

aren't riding alone until I've had a chance to explore our ranch fully and completely."

Shelby flounced over to a chair, sat and buried her chin in her hands. Her arm was pale where the cast had been. "Noah visited me after I broke my arm. Will you call and see if he's all right?"

"Shelby, no. He and I—well, the truth is I can't have him underfoot all the time, getting in my way. He kept me from doing what I have to do in order to be ready for guests."

"When did Noah get in your way? He fixed the bathroom sinks! He helped paint and move furniture. Noah made me promise not to tell, but he fixed the corral."

"Shelby, you know perfectly well Marcus and Rolando rebuilt the corral."

"Not all of it. The afternoon you went to pick up towels for the cottages, Noah sawed rails for the last section and nailed them up. So you could bring our horses home, and it wouldn't cost all the extra to board them with Mr. Ritter."

Stunned, Greer had no comeback. "I'll phone your grandmother," she ended up mumbling, and hurried to the far wall to grab the receiver. "Mom? It's Greer. Would it be convenient for you to swing by tomorrow and pick Shelby up for Sunday school? My first paying guests are due to arrive on Monday around noon. I'm, uh, not going to church this week since there are so many last-minute things to do."

Greer listened as her mother said she'd heard all about the pact her daughter had made with Ruth Kelley. Loretta seemed more than pleased with this development.

"I didn't sever my relationship with Noah for Ruth, Mother. I did it to keep the church board from voting to remove Noah from St. Mark's." Greer was glad when Loretta let the subject drop. They settled on a time to have Shelby ready, then she said goodbye and hung up.

"Mama, what's *sever?*"

Greer spun around. "Uh, honey, it's nothing. Just adult talk. Grandma will give you a lift. While I take this last batch of cookies out of the oven, run and look in your closet for a dress. If you're going to church with my mom, you'd better conform to her standards. That means wearing a dress." Greer held up a staying hand. "No more questions. Just do it because I say so."

Shelby slunk off in a snit. Bear, who'd had a busy morning, loped around the corner after his playmate. As Greer hoped, Shelby was soon distracted and off to play with the dog.

The next afternoon, Shelby returned from church in a happier frame of mind. "Noah said he's not sick," she announced as Greer helped her hang up her good dress. "He said he's been out of sorts. When I asked what that means, he told me it's a different way of saying someone's sad. Why do you s'pose he's sad, Mama?"

Greer handed Shelby a pair of clean jeans and a long-sleeved T-shirt. "I put away most of your short-sleeved shirts. Fall is definitely in the air. And did you notice the sheep are getting woollier? Good for when we have them sheared next spring. Bear, too. You'll have to brush him more often."

"Yeah, but...about Noah being sad. Don't you wonder why?"

"Do you still want to earn money by packing your wagon with wood to deliver to the cottage wood boxes? Our guests will want to use their fireplaces mornings and maybe evenings." Greer had ordered three cords of pine. She'd paid some boys Denise Robles knew to stack it in a shed near the barn, out of the approaching bad weather.

"Wood is splintery, but I'll help 'cause I saw a new saddle I want at Guthrie's."

Greer smiled, and knew she'd have to find more little

chores if Shelby expected to earn money for an expensive saddle. Greer had hoped to buy her the saddle for Christmas, but this was better. Teach her the value of a dollar.

They spent the afternoon hauling wood and rechecking everything in the cottages. Six guests were set to arrive the next day. Greer didn't think she'd ever been so nervous. Yet she knew all the women writers, who were personal friends of Marisa Sanderson's. They were an easygoing bunch. Best of all, their deposit had cleared the bank, although Greer was tempted to frame her first earnings. She'd prepaid a shuttle to pick them up at the airport in San Antonio.

Greer fell into step beside Shelby as they headed for the house. "Tomorrow is the big day, honeybun. Julie Masters, Sandra Bowman, Fran Holmes, Bobbi Jo Pickering, Maggie Johnson and Sarah James will be here to test all your mother's handiwork."

"Yep," Shelby said, skipping along. "You said they're our guinea pigs."

Greer came to an abrupt halt. "Shelby, I realize I may have said that while talking to Lupita. That's just between us, okay?"

"Guinea pigs are cute! We had one in our classroom last year."

"Yes. They're cute little animals." Greer felt tension begin to tighten her neck. Greer was going to have to watch what she said around Shelby.

"So why did you call them that?"

"It's also an expression for—oh, never mind." She couldn't explain how guinea pigs were used in labs for testing vaccines and things. Not right now, Shelby would be too upset.

The phone was ringing when she walked into the house, and she jumped at the chance to end this conversation. Little did she know she'd plunge straight into another, more difficult one.

"Greer? It's Noah. I've been trying to reach you off and on for hours. Since I said goodbye to the last parishioner, in fact. Shelby said something curious today."

Greer darted a quick glance at the girl playing tug-of-war with Bear. Merely hearing his voice made her feel as though her knees would give way. But it concerned her to hear that his call came as a result of something her daughter had said.

Rounding the corner, Greer carried the phone receiver as far as she could to get away from Ms. Big Ears without ripping out the cord. "The last week or so she and Bear have been hanging around watching Marcus and Rolando paint the barn. If she used bad language, I'll speak with her, Noah."

"No, it's nothing like that. In an indirect way, she said you broke up with me to save my job at St. Mark's. Actually, she stumbled through something about your severing our relationship not because of my mother but so the church board wouldn't vote me out of my job. That's why I gave it credence. According to Shelby, she overheard you practically shouting at Loretta. I went straight to my mother, and she refuses to talk to me, period. So I want you to tell me."

Greer raked a hand through her hair. Twice now, the things she'd blurted out in her daughter's hearing had come back to haunt her.

"Greer? Did you hang up?"

"I'm still here," she said wearily, twisting the phone cord around her forefinger.

"Is it true?"

"What's true is that I'm going to have to be much more careful about what I say around Shelby."

"I'll take that as a yes. Listen, Greer. The board can't oust me. I was assigned to this post by the greater area council. St. Mark's was in danger of closing. It will be, and the property sold, unless I increase our membership. Another of my missions is to remove the old governing board and replace it with a more liberal-thinking group. I haven't tackled that yet. I wanted to wait until my father was better. He's quite fond of his current board. But I've already put up with too much. If they try voting me out, I'll have to hand them my agenda as set down by the bishop."

"Noah, I had no idea. Your mother…well, suffice it to say she's completely in the dark about this."

"Tell me what she said."

"Maybe you ought to ask her."

"I did. Like I told you, she refused to answer me. That's why I'm asking you. I can't challenge what I don't know, Greer."

"There's nothing to challenge. I'm glad the board can't remove you from your post, but it doesn't change the fact that you need to date someone more suitable to your position than I am, Noah. More suitable than I'll ever be. I had Shelby out of wedlock."

"So what? How does that affect my mother or, for that matter, the board?"

"You're the church leader. They think you should lead by example."

"Bull droppings! Greer, I'm not going to let them pile this on your shoulders. I thought I'd made it clear to everyone in the church that my life is my own. What I do is my choice. I'll tell them again. Once I'm sure everyone gets it, I'll be knocking on your door. Even before, if you or Shelby need anything. Okay?"

"All right, Noah. We're doing fine. But…I miss you. So does Shelby. I honestly wouldn't have believed I could miss you so much. I…uh…have fallen in love with you."

"I love and miss you, too, Greer. It's affecting everything I do. Listen, Shelby said your first guests arrive tomorrow.

After what you've just admitted to me, I'd come straight over, but Jim Marshall was hospitalized in Austin today. Colon cancer. I promised his wife I'd run over and give them some moral support. I can't get back until late, and you definitely need your rest. When does this batch of guests leave? I want to make a note of it. Expect to see me that night."

Smiling, she lightened her tone. "They're here for a week unless something goes horribly wrong and they check out early."

"Quit that. Everything's going to be great. I have to head out now. But take this to bed with you, Greer. I'll love you forever. Beyond forever."

He hung up without waiting for her to say the same in return. Or maybe he was afraid she couldn't commit herself to "forever." Yes, she'd been stingy with putting her emotions into words. The next time she saw him, that was all going to change.

THE SHUTTLE that delivered Julie Masters and her pals on Monday, caused quite a stir in Homestead. The car Greer had hired turned out to be a black stretch limo. Not only were the writers impressed, they were quite the talk of the town.

Already acquainted with the fun-loving women, Greer hugged each one. After placing their bags in the cottages, she gave them a tour of Sunrise Ranch. It filled her heart with pride to listen to them exclaim in delight.

"Will you look at those gorgeous fat sheep," Maggie Johnson squealed. "I've never written about a sheep rancher. I'm putting dibs on sheep right now. Greer, is there a bookstore in town that might have research material?"

"We have a small library. If our librarian, Frances Hasse, can't locate what you want, it doesn't exist. I've included a trip to Tanner's Market in our schedule. It's an eclectic store that sells everything imaginable. Their book section has local lore."

"We passed a little winery on the way here. I'd love to visit it and maybe include that in one of my books." Sarah gave a vague wave in the general vicinity of Kayla Ritter's Stony Hill Vineyard.

"She's not selling wine yet," Greer said, quickly adding, "But there are other wineries around. Uh, just so you're aware, my camp cook is a recovering alcoholic. And I haven't applied for a liquor license yet, but you may certainly have liquor in your quarters."

Bobbi Jo, the most gregarious of the writers, took that information in stride. "You should probably mention the lack of a lounge in your brochure. Although most everyone knows there are dry counties in Texas. Maybe I could build a story around that. Oh, this trip is going to be so worthwhile."

"I'm burned out. What I need is a getaway," Fran murmured, sinking into one of the soft-padded wicker chairs Greer had placed on the porch opposite the swing. "I'll be content to sit here the entire week and read or simply gaze at the river."

Sarah, who'd chosen to dress in Western garb, announced that she wanted to spend her week riding.

"Oh, good," Greer said. "I've planned a trail ride for tomorrow afternoon. George, my ranch foreman, will lead you on a two and a half hour trek, ending at a chuckwagon designed to provide an old-fashioned cowboy steak fry. I specifically didn't tell Julie, but a real cowboy poet will cook, serve and entertain you at dinner. Then we'll enjoy a leisurely moonlight ride back to the stables." Greer beamed at them.

The oohs and ahs went a long way toward easing any remaining worry. She counted herself lucky to have such an amenable group of seasoned travelers for her maiden voyage, so to speak.

For the evening meal, Lupita fixed soft shell chicken tacos, peppery rice and a big green salad. Dinner was a hit. The women all carried on about how much Shelby had grown. And there wasn't a guest among them who didn't love Bear. The dog was in his element with so many to fawn over him. He went from chair to chair and really did look as if he were smiling at each person who rubbed his ears.

In spite of how well the afternoon had gone, Greer fell into bed that night physically drained. She counted on each day getting easier. So far, she hadn't done one thing that she hadn't also done while working at the Sandersons' Whippoorwill Ranch. The difference, she decided, was the pressure of ownership. The pressure of having no one to fall back on should a crisis develop.

It was a good thing she'd set her alarm because she'd slept soundly. She considered calling Noah to see how Jim was doing, and to update him on her day. But the morning passed in a blur.

She'd driven three of the writers into town early. They'd stopped by Miranda's office so Julie could interview her. Miranda graciously gave them some time, but as usual was up to her armpits in paperwork. "I'm in negotiations to return Homestead to the official Bluebonnet Trail tour," she said. "I hope you ladies have a wonderful time during your stay in Homestead and will pass the word to others."

The three heartily agreed.

By 2:00 p.m., Greer had everyone home again and gathered for the trail ride. The gentlest of her mares, a small dappled gray, bucked off Sandra Bowman, the least experienced rider, almost before the woman had settled her weight squarely in the saddle.

They were all shocked, no one more so than Greer. She ran over to where Sandra was picking herself up out of the dirt. "Sandra, are you all right? I used to ride Powder Puff at Whippoorwill. She was a sweetie. George, what on earth do you suppose got into her?"

"Don't know, Ms. Bell." The man ambled up to the horse, who now stood quietly. "I saddled them at one-thirty, like you said. I tied them all outside the corral while you all were getting ready. They acted fine."

Greer pulled out her cell phone. "Sandra, don't you move. I'll see if Kristin Gallagher can come and check you over. She's the P.A. who set Shelby's broken arm." Greer paced, and suggested George work any kinks out of the mare.

"Kristin, hi, it's Greer Bell. What? No, Shelby hasn't fallen and broken anything else. One of my guests was bounced off a horse. I know you sometimes pick Cody up from school and bring him home. If you're doing that today, do you think it'd be possible to stop here and give my guest the once-over? I'll pay her bill, of course."

She hung up, assuring Sandra, who still looked somewhat dazed, that the P.A. had promised to come by.

Robles led the gray into the corral; everything seemed fine as he stepped into the left stirrup. When he swung his right leg over the saddle and sat, the mare again went berserk. She didn't unseat George, but she only stopped bucking the minute he vaulted lightly to the ground.

Greer, who'd climbed up on the lower rail of the corral to watch, called him over. "Check her saddle and blanket, please, George. I bought it secondhand, and maybe there's something wrong with it. She's acting like a horse in pain."

"Right. But I checked the tack myself. I would've noticed anything sharp enough on the saddle to poke clean through the blanket." He loosened the cinch and dropped the pieces one by one while Greer watched. They both heard something hit the ground with a ping.

George bent and picked up a good-size dried peach pit. "I...I...swear that saddle blanket was smooth as a baby's bottom when I got this horse ready."

She held out a hand and George dropped it into her palm. Greer gazed unhappily at the other horses as she tucked the pit into the watch pocket of her jeans. "George, let's keep this to ourselves for now. Here's Kristin pulling in. While she examines Sandra, could you check the other horses? I know the women were all seated and seemed okay, but I just want to be certain. Uh, could someone have purposely shoved this under the blanket after you tied the horses?"

He rubbed his chin. "The mare was last in line. Hidden from my sight by the barn." They both eyed the fence. "Why would anyone wanna hurt one of your guests?"

Greer thought about the ram incident. More likely, someone wanted to hurt her business. She shook her head. George wasn't privy to the other things that had gone on, and Greer wanted to keep it that way. If rumors spread, they could cause harm to her business. It worried her that someone might have been hurt—worried her enough that she vowed to call Wade Montgomery at her first opportunity.

Shelby's bus drove in while Kristin was looking Sandra over. On the heels of the bus, Kipp Hadley arrived with his chuckwagon hitched to a team of six braying mules, which he'd managed to rent. Fortunately, the others clustered around Kipp and plied him with questions, letting Kristin complete her exam without an audience.

"Sandra's fine. A little shaken, which is understandable," Kristin said, helping the guest up. "Greer, if she still wants to, I see no problem with her riding."

"Sandra, it's up to you. I planned to take Shelby and the

dog and ride out to where Kipp's setting up the cookout. If you'd rather take my horse or go with Kipp on the wagon, I can ride Powder Puff."

The petite woman offered a dimpled smile. "The others are always giving me a hard time about being a wimp. If I dropped out, I'd never hear the end of it. No, I feel fine. Guess it's the middle-age padding," she joked, patting her ample behind.

"Then I see no reason why you can't all get started," Greer said. "We've lost maybe half an hour, but that should still get you to the chuckwagon at a reasonable time. I'll tell Kipp to allow an extra half hour before throwing on the steaks.

This time the group mounted without incident. Greer breathed a sigh of relief watching them disappear over the first rise. She hurried Shelby inside to change into her boots and jeans. As she wrote the check for Kristin's house call, the P.A. remarked, "They're riding just on your land, aren't they? Ryan told me about the debacle with the ram and deer. We're still in the height of hunting season."

Ripping out the check, Greer bit her lower lip. "George and I were very careful to check the boundaries when we marked our trails. I was worried about stray bullets, but Ryan apparently told Noah there are strict rules for hunters on deer leases. They can't shoot toward another rancher's property."

"Then you should be fine," Kristin said, closing her traveling medical bag. "I don't pay a lot of attention to the men when they discuss hunting. So, outside of this minor incident, you're really getting your business underway."

Greer swept a glance over her land and tried to see the improvements through a stranger's eyes. "The Saturday after Thanksgiving, I'm holding an open house for anyone living in Homestead. It was Callie Montgomery's idea, but Millie at the newspaper made me see what a great advertising tool it'll be. Noah's going to dedicate the new ranch name. Look for the invitation, which is going out in next Thursday's *Herald*, okay?"

"That sounds great." She pulled out her pocket calendar. "If you know the date, I'll block the time now."

Greer gave the date. Talk fell off as Shelby and Bear barreled out of the house. "Thanks again, Kristin, for coming on such short notice. I have the necessary insurance, but I never thought I'd have to file a claim the first week I'm open."

"It happens," Kristin said with a slight grimace. "Your authentic cookout sounds exciting, Greer. You should consider having one for local groups and organizations if ever there's a slack time in your business."

"Now, that's a thought. Speaking of cookouts, I see Kipp's getting antsy. I still need to saddle my horse and Shelby's. I don't want to risk another mishap, so we'd better get the wagon to the cookout site pretty soon. I want to be sure Kipp has everything he needs for the steak dinners."

"I'll let you go then. The women seem a fun bunch," Kristin noted in passing. "Sandra said they're all published writers. I'm afraid she didn't want to hear how little time I've had for pleasure reading. But between work and school, it's the truth."

"She ought to be thankful you had the time to read all the medical textbooks you needed to get your certification." The two women shared fleeting smiles before they went their separate ways.

Greer made short work of saddling Favor and Majestic. She'd told Kipp to head on out. They caught up easily to his slow-moving wagon, Bear trotting cheerfully beside them. Pots and pans that hung along the sides, hooked on leather thongs, rattled and clanked musically. "Shelby," Greer said, "you're experiencing a piece of the authentic West. Men like

Kipp trailed herds of cattle going to market. Chuckwagons kept the cowboys fed."

"I like eating in the kitchen best. Mama, don't you miss the suppers we had when Noah came over?"

Greer reined in so that her longer-legged gelding kept pace with Shelby's smaller mare. "What made those evenings so special, honeybun?"

At first Shelby shrugged. Then she turned her head away and said almost too softly for Greer to hear, "I liked it when Noah ate with us, 'cause he made us a family."

"Not really, Shel."

"I know, but it felt like we were. Kids always ask where my daddy is. You know, Cody's real daddy got d'vorced from his mom. So he's got two. That's not fair, when I don't even have one."

Unwilling to talk about Dan Harper, Greer let Favor stretch into a canter. She was glad Shelby didn't continue with the subject after they'd reached the stand of cottonwoods she'd picked for their cookout. Cookouts of this sort were new to Shelby. At Whippoorwill, meals were always served at the ranch, family style. As they waited, Kipp kept her and Shelby entertained with stories about his years as a working cowboy.

The sun tilted toward the west. As usual in the late fall, a brisk wind kicked up. "Kipp, you were smart to pull the cook wagon deeper into the trees." She smiled as Bear flopped down under a big pine. "Mmm. Smell that coffee. And the steak." She rubbed her hands on her thighs. "Everything looks good."

"And near ready. Shouldn't those riders of yours be rollin' in 'bout now?" The bowlegged man limped to the edge of the trees and stared out on an empty horizon.

"I'm trying not to worry." Greer lowered her voice to keep Shelby from hearing. "The guests packed cameras. They're probably driving George crazy wanting to stop all the time. I think we mapped out a really beautiful route."

"Huh. Well, next time I won't be in such a big rush to fire up the grill."

"Everyone in the group knows they're our first customers. I gave them all a nice discount for that reason. If the steak's a little overdone, they'll have to live with it."

"Yeah. Maybe you need a walkie-talkie so George can call in and let us know it's time to toss the steaks on the fire."

"Good idea, but that won't help today." Nor did it help Greer's uneasiness to have Kipp grousing about his meat getting charred. She attempted to redirect his thoughts, as she occasionally did with Shelby. "I've been meaning to ask if you know of a good rodeo in the area, Kipp. The writers asked about one. I'm sure when I start booking families, their kids will be anxious to see a real rodeo."

"Your neighbors, the Gallaghers, would be the ones to talk to about rodeoing. Garrett, one of Clint's boys, used to ride the circuit. Ended up in the money quite often, I think. Not that the Gallaghers need more dough." He hobbled out into the open again, and Greer recalled what Noah had said about a ranch manager stealing from the Four Aces. As well, Clint hadn't been able to raise the capital to buy consortium land. The Gallaghers might not be in such good financial shape even now, with Ryan running the show.

"Where in blue blazes are those riders? It's flat gettin' dark and there's still no sign of 'em. This steak's gonna be tough as shoe leather."

Greer's nerves snapped. "Kipp, if you'll keep an eye on Shelby and Bear, I'll ride out and hurry them along."

"Good idee!"

She'd actually hoped that by the time she tightened the cinch on Favor, her worries would turn out to be for nothing and the seven riders would meander in. They didn't. Greer mounted, wielding her flashlight. The farther she rode up the trail without seeing any sign of them or any recent tracks, the more she began to panic.

She reached a marker she and George pounded into the soil, only to feel completely confused. Dismounting, Greer walked in a circle, hunting for the spot where she was positive they'd placed it. The hole, she found. But the marker now pointed in the opposite direction, into thick underbrush. It directed riders following the arrows back the way they'd come.

She shone her light on a mess of hoofprints. They weren't easy to pick out. Once night got serious here in the hills, it had the same result as shutting off every lamp in a brightly lit room. Dark meant pitch-black until the moon rose.

As best she could, Greer followed the tracks. She reached a point where the riders should have crossed the original trail. That was where she'd supposed George would see the mistake. That marker, too, had been removed and turned.

It hit Greer like a sledgehammer. Someone had come out here after she and George had made their final practice run. The markers were all switched. Heaven only knew how confused the riders could've become.

She capped the top of a rocky promontory. From this vantage point she should've been able to hear approaching horses. She was greeted by silence. Greer was afraid she might vomit. She'd heard stories of ranch owners who'd lost guests for a day or even longer. The results were always the same; word circulated and the ranch went under. She had opened on a narrow money margin. This could kill her.

More than worry for herself was the fact two of her guests weren't seasoned horsewomen. Sandra had already had one mishap. Greer thought maybe she could locate them if she continued to ride. But in the back of her mind lurked the possibility of not finding them. Lord, she hated to call out a rescue party. That, however, was her wisest course, and she pulled out her cell. The phone number that ran through her brain was Noah's. The minute he picked up, and Greer heard his deep, steady voice, her stomach settled. She told him what had happened, the words tumbling over each other.

"Whoa, Greer. Let me get this straight. You've lost your trail riders? And you say someone caused this by moving your markers?"

"Yes. Oh, Noah, I can't find the guests or George. It's really dark. Who'd think they'd get so turned around? But this is his first ride with guests, too. He's not experienced, but I swear, Noah, someone wanted them lost."

"You sit tight. I'm calling Wade. He'll round up some riders. I know that stand of cottonwoods where you say Kipp's set up. We'll start there and work our way out to you. Don't touch those signs, okay? Wade needs to assess the situation for himself. Once and for all, he needs to get to the bottom of this. It's gone beyond mischief."

Greer waited for almost half an hour, sitting atop a granite boulder, before Noah rode in on a white gelding that stood out in the faint light of a newly risen moon. Without thinking how it would look to anyone who might be with him, Greer flew off the boulder and into Noah's arms. He tucked her head under his chin and held her tight enough to feel the battering of her panicky heart. "It's okay, sweetheart. Wade, Ryan Gallagher and five ranch hands from the Four Aces are below checking that last marker. I didn't want you to wait here alone any longer."

She relaxed a bit, just being held by him. "Noah, over there is a cattle path used by Gallagher's men when they move their herd from pasture to pasture. Maybe they're responsible for this."

"If your trail crossed their cattle path, maybe that got George turned around."

"The markers were moved," she insisted. "I'm afraid you left the fox in charge of the henhouse, leaving Ryan Gallagher and his men near markers they probably switched."

"Ryan's men weren't out here doing dirty work. He had to call them in from branding. With a herd that size, I'd bet they've been at it all week."

"If not them, who?"

"Seems we sang this same chorus the night you moved in." Noah pointed across the trail. "Is that another of the markers that's been fiddled with?"

"Yes." Definitely calmer now, Greer led him to where the first hole was clearly visible in the beam of her flashlight. The stake had been moved across the trail.

"Based on the first switcharoo, it appears that your guide and guests are going in circles. Instead of ending up at the cook wagon, Greer, they're heading back to your barn."

"We can only hope," she said, sounding wretched.

Noah used his flashlight, which gave off a larger, wider beam. He knelt and panned the area around both the new and old marker sites. The hills had gotten a bit of rain late the previous week. The edges, where the underbrush held moisture, were still a bit muddy. "You haven't ridden your horse around this stake, have you?"

"What? Oh, no. I went directly to the rock and climbed up to see if I could see George. But it's too dark. Why? Did you find something?"

"Maybe. Listen, I hear Wade and the searchers coming in now. Why don't you ride on back to the chuckwagon? Shelby wanted to come with me, but I made her stay there with the dogs. She's scared that you're lost. Seeing you will reassure her."

"I'll go as soon as I speak with Wade. I want to discuss the fact that I believe the first incident, the dead ram and this mess are all related. Someone's trying to ruin me. I'm telling Wade, in front of Ryan and his men, that I won't be frightened or coerced into leaving Homestead."

Noah saw the determined light in Greer's eyes. "Don't forget to mention the letters you received in Colorado."

"There's that, too. You think the same, don't you?"

"I'd rather not, but yeah." He hadn't found a tangible clue, but he'd picked up on an unusual horseshoe print. A rounded shoe. It was familiar, yet he couldn't place it. Still, Noah had an odd feeling he'd seen it recently. He just couldn't recall where.

Wade and Ryan rode up, and Greer saw they were alone. Wade hailed her. "You'll be happy to hear that we stumbled across Robles and your guests at the last switchback. George figured out the marker mix-up. As soon as the moon came up he was able to get his bearings and began working his way back. Your friends are probably sitting down to one of Kipp's great-smelling steaks right now."

"So, you think that closes this incident?" Greer strained toward the sheriff, hands on her hips. She told him about the earlier incident with the peach pit. "These aren't more simple kid pranks as far as I'm concerned."

"I agree. Tomorrow when it's light, I'll ride out here and see if I can unearth some clues."

Noah gestured at Wade. "Take a look-see at this print. It's a specially shod horse. Who has a gimpy mount that uses such a shoe?"

"Danged if I know. Ryan, you have any idea?"

They all grouped around. Ryan shook his head. "Only a few farriers service this neck of the woods. One of them can probably tell you what horse wears that particular shoe."

Wade slapped his reins against his leg. "That's where I'll start tomorrow. Does that satisfy you, Greer? If it's any consolation, I don't like this any more than you do."

She shrugged. "There's not much you can do in the dark. My guess is you won't have to go far to find answers." She glared at Ryan.

Unfazed, he posed a question in return. "Greer, I know you'd like to pin this on my crew. They were pretty shaken by it. Half a dozen people lost in these hills at night is no laughing matter." He paused. "Maybe this is a touchy subject, but Monty Tyler asked me if Shelby's dad's still in town. I mean, it's your business, Greer, but say the guy's pissed off over you moving back. Might he want to run you off?"

Greer ran nervous hands up and down her thighs. "To my knowledge, Shelby's father doesn't even know she exists. In any case, I doubt he's the type to run around in the dark trying to scare me into leaving Homestead. Good try, but totally wrong. Gentlemen, I'll leave you to it. I have guests to look after. Oh, Wade, get Noah to tell you about some letters I received shortly after I sent in my land application." She swung up into her saddle and trotted off.

CHAPTER THIRTEEN

"WADE," Noah called. "We'll talk later. I'm going with Greer. If I remember where I saw that print before, I'll let you know." He stepped up into his saddle, tapped his heels to his horse's sides and galloped up to Greer as she left the hill and struck out across the valley. "Greer, I suspect you still want to lay this at the feet of Gallagher's crew. Shouldn't you at least consider other options?"

She pulled back on her reins. "Besides the former Senator Gallagher—who's upset because I have a piece of land he tried to buy? Or your folks, who've made it clear they'd like to see me run out of town on a rail? Otherwise, I can't think of another enemy."

They rode for a ways in silence, then Greer roused herself. "Noah, I know you said Callie Montgomery and Kayla Ritter had stuff happen to them after they arrived, but neither had repeat problems like I'm having, right?"

"Ethan Ritter!" Noah yanked back on his reins, nearly sitting his big white gelding on its haunches. "*That's* where I saw that odd shoe print. Outside Ethan's corral the other day when I met him. We stood at the corral gate and talked."

"You think Ethan…?" She just kept shaking her head.

But either Greer's face turned paler at his announcement, Noah thought, or the rising moon leeched color from her sun-bronzed skin.

"You knew Ethan from when you lived here before. I'm sure you told me that." Noah couldn't forget what Ryan Gallagher had said back there about the possibility of Shelby's real father being at the bottom of Greer's troubles. Only now Noah wondered why no one, not even Holden, who'd been furious over Greer's return, had ever put a name to Shelby's father.

Why not Ethan? He was a couple of years older than Greer. And that dark, brooding, macho type always attracted women.

Greer's horse danced beside Noah's. Her gelding wanted to run, but she exerted pressure holding him in. "Surely you don't suspect Ethan? I thought you and he were good friends. Also, what's the likelihood of him having poisoned Kayla's vines?"

"They know who did that. Tolly Craddock's fingerprints were on the herbicide bottles. He denied it, and a big-shot Austin lawyer got him off on some technicality. Tolly worked as a janitor at the elementary school. Kayla and Wade both think he triggered Megan's allergies by putting cat hair around her desk. Back to Ethan…"

"What possible motive could Ethan have? Any fool can see he adores Kayla."

Noah didn't mean Kayla's case. He decided just to ask her. "Shoot me, Greer. But…Ethan wouldn't happen to be Shelby's real dad, would he?"

She shortened her reins so fast, Favor reared, blocking the full extent of her shocked expression. Noah saw enough to know he was barking up the wrong tree. "I'm sorry. It's…I started to wonder why people are down on you, yet no one ever mentions the other half of the equation. Ethan said my dad refused to officiate at Zeb's funeral. According to Ethan, Dad offered a lame excuse for not giving Zeb the sacraments because he committed suicide. I know Dad has rigid views and isn't above making his own rules. I'm sorry, but adding two and two, I'm not coming up with four."

Greer edged her horse practically on top of Noah's. "Stop! You couldn't be farther off base. Poor Ethan! I've got no idea why Father Holden has it in for him. Ethan's *not* Shelby's dad. Her father's name is Daniel Harper. He doesn't live in Homestead."

Greer hated to spare the time, but Noah deserved to hear the whole story. It unfolded in a rush. "There you have it," she said, winding down with a sigh. "I haven't heard a word from Dan in ten years. Nor do I want a man like him around my daughter. I assume he married his socialite girlfriend and returned to Houston where he probably works for his daddy's oil company. I never meant anything to him, Noah. He certainly wouldn't expend the effort involved in sneaking around a town he called Hicksville, U.S.A. I frankly doubt he even remembers my name."

While vastly relieved to learn that Greer hadn't spent the last ten years pining for the man, Noah wished he could hold and comfort her. And if his father and hers were privy to that story, they ought to both be ashamed over how they'd treated her.

"What a jerk. I'm glad you saw through him, Greer. Shelby's lucky, too."

"She's not so sure, Noah. Recently she's asked a lot of questions about her dad. I haven't leveled with her. I think it's a lot for a kid to understand. Maybe I'm not giving her enough credit, but…"

"She is a bright kid." Noah chuckled as they sped up again. "I predict that one day she'll be a take-charge woman like her mother."

"Funny, I barely feel in control, let alone 'take-charge.' Especially since I came back to Homestead. Hardly a day goes by that I don't worry I've made the biggest mistake of my life."

"Not from my perspective."

"I'd feel more confident if some unknown person wasn't trying to ruin my life again."

"We have a hoofprint this time, Greer. First thing tomorrow, I intend to visit Ethan."

"I wish I could go along, but I'm scheduled to take my guests on an outing to Lost Maples. Julie read about the big-toothed maple showing up there when it's not indigenous to this area. If it doesn't rain, I promised we'd hike back and see the trees. Are you going to phone Wade and direct him to Ethan?"

"I probably should. But as you say, I may be jumping to conclusions. I'll speak with Ethan privately about the horse with that shoe before I do anything else."

"Will you call me if you find out anything? I'll have my cell with me."

"You have my promise. Hey, smell that barbecue! And hear all the laughter? I'd say your guests don't seem to be suffering any aftereffects."

"That's a relief. I've been afraid they'd lynch me on sight. Will you stay for supper, Noah? It's the least I can offer you for coming to my rescue. Yet again. You're better to me than I deserve."

He saw the regret in her eyes as they entered the firelight. "I hope we've settled all our misunderstandings," he said quickly, knowing they'd soon be besieged by the others.

"Yes," she murmured, and suddenly recalled what he'd said the day her guests arrived. Noah told her he loved her, and she'd admitted the same. Given another minute, they would probably have repeated those words. But they'd already arrived at the site. They rode into camp as Kipp

Hadley strummed the first three chords of a song on his guitar. He stopped when Shelby jumped up from where she sat cross-legged near the fire pit.

"Mama. Mama and Noah! Mr. Gallagher's men told me you weren't lost, but I was worried they were wrong."

Greer slid off Favor. George separated his stringy length from the chuckwagon to come and take her reins. Greer scooped up Shelby and covered her face with kisses that made the girl giggle and push her mom's face away.

Noah received similar treatment from the two dogs, and wished he could trade places with Shelby. He'd far rather be kissing Greer.

Her second act of the evening was to apologize profusely to her guests.

Julie and Bobbi Jo both waved off her apologies. "We were honest-to-gosh lost, and how many writers can boast of having that firsthand experience? Kipp was nice enough to keep our steaks warm an extra ten minutes so we could all write down our exact emotions while they were still fresh."

Maggie Johnson eyed Noah with interest. "Maybe getting lost was the highlight of Julie and Bobbi's outing. Being rescued by so many big, strong cowboy-types provided me with something better to write about. And here you waltz in, Greer, with yet another good-looking savior."

Greer didn't much like the gleam in Maggie's eye as she looked Noah up and down. Surprisingly it was Shelby who staked a claim on him. She threw her arms around his legs and declared in a gruff voice, "Noah's ours."

He placed a hand over her shiny hair. "The lady is right, squirt. I am a savior of lost souls." Removing his ever-present baseball cap, he grinned engagingly and loved how quickly the Johnson woman backed off when he announced that he was the priest at St. Mark's Church. He didn't elaborate. It tickled him to no end when Greer didn't make a point of mentioning his denomination, either. She handed him a steak, beans and corn bread she'd dished out of the warming tray. After helping herself to another plate, they found seats in the circle and told Kipp to continue with his song.

In his element, the old cowboy played and sang some of traditional country tunes made famous by Eddy Arnold and Hank Williams Senior.

Once Greer took her empty plate and Noah's back to the wagon, Shelby crept between the dogs and sagged against Noah's side where she fell asleep, even though she rubbed her eyes and tried valiantly to stay awake.

How right those two looked side by side, Greer thought. Such an appealing picture. She fought a pain deep in her chest. In not giving Shelby over to some nice couple for adoption, had she deprived her daughter of a father's love? Greer had never truly felt loved by her own father. Odd how clearly she could see that now.

Noah reached behind one of the sleeping dogs and linked his fingers with Greer's. He was struck by everything that was missing in his life. He could be content to sit this way forever with two people he loved. Two people who brought love into a life he realized had been empty of so much before he'd met them.

Kipp rounded out his program with several pithy cowboy poems he'd written himself, which delighted the writers. Several asked if they could copy the words down to use in their books. They promised to give him credit, and he was thrilled.

As the women gathered around the old cowboy, Greer stood. "I hope Shelby can wake up enough to ride Majestic home," she said, studying the sleeping girl.

"I don't mind holding her and riding double if you'll lead her mare. She's plumb tuckered out."

Greer smiled. "I think Kipp's cowboy lingo is rubbing off on you, Noah. Do you know how Texan you just sounded?"

"I am a Texan," he shot back. "So are you, though you might not want to admit it."

"Why wouldn't I want to admit it?"

He struggled to stand without waking Shelby. He had to move the two dogs, who were curled into fluffy balls. "I don't know. Every so often, I catch a certain faraway look in your eyes—like a few minutes ago. Then I worry that you regret coming back to Homestead."

"I didn't say I regretted returning, did I? Only that I'm afraid I'd made yet another mistake. A minute ago I watched Shelby with you and my heart got really heavy. She so obviously feels the lack of a father."

His eyes turned soft. "That's a condition you and I can rectify, Greer. I trust it's evident how much I love you both. I don't want you to go through any more of these incidents alone." He freed one hand to lift her chin. Their eyes met, but she broke contact first.

"Noah...don't. This isn't exactly an ideal setting to discuss personal matters. And there are other major problems I think you're forgetting. My parents and yours are both dead set against our having any kind of relationship. Let alone...marriage."

"I told you it's not for them to decide," he said firmly. "Anyway, I think your mom would come around. And we have to present a united front to convince the others."

"Oh, you dreamer." Greer gave a small shake of her head.

The others began drifting away from Kipp, who'd opened his guitar case to store the instrument. Clearly Noah and Greer's private time was at end.

George Robles led the guest's horses into the firelight. Ladies, I'll help you mount up. Ms. Greer, shall we head back? Are you sticking with Kipp to button things up here?"

"Yes, I'll douse the fire and tie and load garbage sacks while Kipp secures the wagon hatches."

Again the women exclaimed over what a great time they'd had. The outing had, after all, turned out the way Greer had envisioned.

Kipp approached after he'd battened down the loose items, such as condiment bottles. He held out a blanket to Noah. "There's room to make a bed on the wagon seat for the little miss. Ms. Greer can tie the mare to the O-ring on the back. And those sleepy dogs will fit nicely on the floor."

"Noah, that sounds easier on your arms than juggling her in front of your saddle all the way home. I know you said you didn't mind, but she's no lightweight."

"I really don't mind. But she'll be more comfortable in the wagon." Noah also thought it'd give him a chance to resume his conversation with Greer.

But that wasn't to be. She chose to ride abreast of the wagon, presumably to keep an eye on her daughter. Which left Noah to either trail behind or ride on the other side. He elected to do the latter. And greatly enjoyed listening to the talkative cowboy, who had interesting tales of his life on the range. Plus, Kipp asked Noah to run a computer search for his ex-wife and daughters, as Noah had suggested the first night they met. Kipp gave him what information he had. Noah thought it might be sufficient, although he made no promises.

At the ranch, he offered to carry Shelby inside.

"I can't believe she didn't wake up with all the bouncing around on that hard wooden seat. Kids are so resilient." In the next breath Greer lamented, "I probably shouldn't keep her out so late on a school night."

Noah walked sideways down the hallway so as not to bump Shelby's head or knees against the wall. "She had a blast tonight. As you said, kids are flexible." He laid the girl in the middle of her bed and watched Greer remove her boots and socks.

"Oh, shoot," Greer moaned. "I just got sand all over her bedspread."

"It's washable."

"Luckily so is she. I know you'd like us to talk, but I can't let her sleep in sandy sheets. I'll say good night now, and wake her up and toss her in the tub. Thanks, Noah, for all your help."

"If you're serious about sending me home, I'm not going without a decent good-night kiss." Noah didn't wait for her approval. He wrapped Greer in his arms and kissed her. Thoroughly. Passionately.

"That's to tide us both over until we see each other again."

"When will that be?" she asked, her voice none too steady. Her knees weren't too steady, either. She saw that Noah wasn't unaffected, either.

"Soon," he promised, swooping in for a last, deliciously slow kiss. Drawing his fingers through her curls, he finally collected his thoughts. "I'll phone you tomorrow after I talk to Ethan. And then you and I will set a time to talk."

"Okay." Greer was having a hard time thinking in practical terms. "I hope Ethan can provide answers. Or maybe not, Noah. I like Kayla and the kids a lot. I'd hate for anyone connected to them to be behind the attempts to frighten me and my guests."

"It could turn out to be another dead end. Ethan might not have the only horse with an orthotic shoe, sweetheart." Noah held her at arm's length, but his hands flexed around her narrow wrists. "That aside, I'm sure you're right and these have been concerted attempts to disrupt your business. Swear to me, that you'll be extra cautious tomorrow. Where you're taking the ladies isn't exactly Grand Central Station. Stay alert for anything or anyone suspicious. And lock your car doors."

"Noah, now you're scaring me." Greer gave him a little push toward the door, and paused to glance nervously at the girl snoozing peacefully on her bed. "We'll be fine. Whoever's behind these dirty tricks seems to be confining them to the ranch."

Noah's gaze followed hers. "You have George and Lupita here full-time. Rolando and Marcus will be around for a few more days. I don't think the fence will be done by tomorrow. Even with all of that, you'll be home in time to meet Shelby's bus, won't you?"

"That's the plan. We're leaving early. I asked Lupita to fix a late lunch."

"Good. Okay." Noah hated to leave her when she still seemed on edge. And he said as much several times, between three added sets of good-night kisses.

The last left Greer weak as a rag doll. "Noah," she murmured feebly. "If you don't leave now, I'm going to forget about bathing Shelby. And I may haul you back to my bed and destroy your reputation in the community once and for all."

"No reputation is destroyed once and for all." He smoothed back her bangs with shaking hands that showed their feelings were mutual. "I'd never stay overnight given Shelby's age. Besides, I want our first time making love to be beautiful *and* legal," he said, his voice rough with feeling. "Otherwise, it wouldn't take much at all to convince me to stay."

"Noah," Greer said urgently, "you act like we…well, you make it sound as if there being an *us* in the future is a foregone conclusion."

"It is. I feel it in every bone—and plenty of other places," he said in a half-teasing manner. "Get used to it." With that, he let her go and melted into the night.

She had no time to ask any further questions, but saw his left hand whip back around the door to flip the lock. The door shut decisively.

Rattled as always whenever he made bold statements, Greer used the only defense she had. She immersed herself in work. Tonight it happened to be getting her sleepy child bathed and into a clean bed. Considering the day she'd had, that was sufficient to wear her out.

THE NEXT MORNING, after a restless night during which Noah kept an eye on Greer's ranch, his first order of business was to visit Ethan Ritter. He did so, even though it meant ignoring a phone message requesting he stop for breakfast with his father.

Ethan could almost always be found working in or around his barn. Today was no exception. The tall man glanced up from stacking hay bales when Noah appeared. Wiping a sleeve across his sweating brow, Ethan leaned on the handle of his pitchfork. "Hey, Noah, what brings you out into the country today? Turned up a new kid you want evaluated for my program?"

"Today I have a question about horseshoes." Noah produced a picture he'd drawn from memory while having his morning coffee. "I don't claim to be an artist, but I wonder if you'd know anything about a horseshoe that left a print like this?"

"Well, yeah. It's designed for an animal with a defective foot. I have a horse I just bought that has a round shoe exactly like this one."

"When did you buy him?"

"Oh, two, three weeks ago. From Dalton Guthrie. A shirt-tail relative of Myron's. Dalton wanted me to take his mentally handicapped son in a class. The kid's nineteen, and I didn't feel he'd benefit. Basically Stanley rides well enough. I bought the animal because Dalton's having a tough time financially. He said he can't afford the feed and vet bills. They live on a dinky farm and have a passel of kids." He frowned. "What's this about, Noah?"

Noah propped an elbow on the stacked hay. "Any chance Stanley rode this horse off your property, say the night before last or early yesterday?"

Ethan looked surprised. "Matter of fact, the kid almost rode him into the ground yesterday morning. I gave Stan quite a lecture. I even phoned Dalton, because I'm never sure whether or not I'm getting through to the boy. I suspect Stan understands more than he lets on."

"Hmm." Noah unburdened everything that had happened to Greer in the past weeks. "We found prints like this at a junction where Greer's trail markers had been switched. In your estimation, is Stan capable of removing and replacing wood markers mounted on steel shafts?"

"He's a big kid. Muscular. If you're asking does he have the strength, yes. The question would be why? He would've been only nine years old when Greer left Homestead. That act sounds like someone with a vendetta."

"It does, Ethan. I'd like to ask the boy some questions. I could let Wade do it, I suppose. But before I call him in, I'd rather determine if there's cause. It sounds as if Dalton Guthrie's had enough bad luck."

"Let me tell Kayla where I'll be, and I'll take a run out to Guthrie's with you. I need to come to an understanding with him. Stan can't just come get a horse I now own any time he wants."

The men discussed other of Ethan's students on the drive

to the Guthrie farm. It was pretty run-down. The house had shingles missing from the roof and a board over one window. The porch sagged in one spot. Several coon dogs didn't seem to mind the condition of the porch. They rose, stretched and woofed halfheartedly as the men got out of Noah's pickup.

Dalton Guthrie, a stooped man with thinning but overlong graying hair, noticed them. He was running a beat-up tractor in a nearby field. He shut down and hiked across a fallow section. "Boys, what can I do you for?" He shook hands with both of them.

Ethan stated his concerns about Stan taking the horse when it suited him.

"I'm real sorry, Ethan. I'll speak to the boy. Riding and hanging out at the café in town are about the extent of what interests that kid. My wife used to have him do projects. But she's been sickly nigh on three years. Stanley does as he pleases. I'm busy farming all day, trying to make a living. The younger kids are in school. The older ones married and gone. Stanley's slow, but he's not mean."

Noah felt bad for this hardworking man. But if it had been *his* son involved in mischief, he'd want to know. So he plunged ahead with his story once Guthrie stopped talking. Noah didn't exactly accuse the boy of terrorizing a neighboring rancher, but he hinted strongly that Stanley might be involved.

"Father Kelley, I don't know what to say. If Stanley did those things, it'll be the first time he's done anything like that, to my knowledge. He's up at the house with his mama right now. We're a God-fearing family. Baptists, not your faith, but I know you won't hold that against us. This is a serious charge. I appreciate y'all coming to me instead of calling the law."

"Sheriff Montgomery is investigating events at Ms. Bell's

ranch, Dalton. The trail may lead him here. And if Stanley admits to this deed, or others, Ms. Bell may press charges. Ethan and I would like to hear your son's side first."

"Will you wait here while I fetch him? Hearing this will break my wife's heart. Stanley's always been real special to her because birthing him was hard. We delivered him at home to cut costs, and Muriel's sure that caused Stanley's brain injury."

Noah felt doubly sorry for the Guthrie family. He had a gut feeling, though, that the boy, almost a man at nineteen, *was* involved.

Ethan said as much while Dalton hurried up to the house. "Isn't Wade under the impression that what happened to Greer goes back to the incidents at Kayla's vineyard and Callie's house? I know Stanley, and while I think he had something to do with this, can't picture him masterminding a whole series of events. I'd still bet Tolly Craddock figures in somehow."

"Wade's got his hands full, for sure. I think he's more worried than he lets on."

Dalton returned with the boy. Noah had seen the kid around town, but hadn't connected him with the name.

The farmer got right to the point with his son. All three men knew Stanley was guilty as sin before his dad finished spelling out the charge.

"Yep, I did them things to Ms. Bell, Pa." The boy bobbed his head. "A man came out of the café and gave me twenty dollars to set up a little ol' tape player and speakers. He said I had to smash the tape after—so wouldn't nobody find it. You almost did," he said, turning to Noah. "I hid behind that big old cypress waitin' for the woman who bought Farley's ranch to come out. I wasn't expecting nobody else."

"What man, Stanley?" Noah asked gently.

The boy scratched his upper arm and shrugged. "A cowboy. Don't know 'im. Wears a black hat pulled so low can't nobody see his eyes. He sent me a letter in the mail, too, and fifty dollars. Just to play a joke with Ms. Bell's trail markers. Ask Anna Mae. She read me the letter and the directions three times so I'd get it right."

"Anna Mae's my littlest daughter," Dalton said. "She's twelve, almost thirteen."

They questioned the kid for over half an hour, but all came to the same conclusion. The man who'd approached Stanley, a stranger, was dressed like a cowboy. But he didn't work for Senator Gallagher. Stan said he knew the Four Aces crew.

"Son, I don't understand why you'd pick on Ms. Bell. We don't even know the lady."

The kid's face sagged. "I know, Pa. The man said she wasn't gonna get hurt. It was only a little ol' joke. I wanted the money. First time I ever had any of my own. I bought Mama a dress for her birthday. I got it hid till then. Will you take it away?"

Noah took a deep breath and shook his head. "You swear you had nothing to do with killing one of Ms. Bell's rams, and you never put a peach pit under the saddle blanket of her horse? You didn't spray anything on Mrs. Ritter's grape vines? Oh, and you didn't help mess up Callie Montgomery's house?"

Each time Stan Guthrie gave a vigorous shake of his head. "I swear on our family Bible. Those other things, they're really bad."

Dalton, who'd begun to sweat, appealed to Ethan and Noah to recommend leniency for his son with the sheriff.

"Pa," Stanley whined, "can I go back in the house now? Me and Mama always watch this cookin' show on TV." He gestured back toward the house. A woman's pale, anxious face was pressed against a streaked window.

"I'll phone Ms. Bell to let her know the situation, Dalton. Until she decides whether she wants to pursue this, Stanley's free to do whatever. As long as he promises not to play any more jokes on her or anyone else."

Ethan held the boy a moment longer. "Stan, no more taking your horse out without checking with me. Also, if you see that man in town again, the one who gave you the money, I want you to tell your dad, me, Father Kelley or Sheriff Montgomery."

The kid nodded. After thanking the men for letting Stan keep the gift he'd bought his ailing mother, Dalton escorted him to the house, lecturing him along the way.

Noah dug out his cell and punched in Greer's number. The women had finished their hike in to see the Big Tooth Maples, and were heading out of the park to come home. "I've got some information on your trickster, Greer. It's a mixed-up tale. Why don't I meet you at your ranch in an hour? I have a couple of other errands to run."

"I hate being in suspense all that time, Noah."

"If it's any relief, I don't believe you're in any danger from this person."

"That helps. Especially after you had me going through the house checking all the locks last night after you left." She added quickly that they were approaching a deep cut that ran between high mounds of granite rocks. "I'll probably lose cell reception, so I'll say goodbye. One hour, Noah." Static cut off whatever else she said.

"Do you think she'll demand that Wade arrest Stanley?" Ethan asked as they got in Noah's pickup.

"I can't speak for Greer. I know this last incident shook her up. Her guests were good sports, but they could've caused her plenty of grief. Or worse, if anyone had gotten hurt stumbling around those hills in the dark, she'd be liable."

"Yeah. One of her horses could have stepped in a prairie dog hole and broken a leg." For several seconds neither one spoke. Then Ethan blurted, "Kayla asked the other day if I knew who Greer might've been involved with before. But if I'd ever heard who got her pregnant, I've forgotten."

"The guy isn't from the hill country. I don't know if she wants any of this spread around, so please treat it as confidential. I only found out last night. I'm not sure I should admit this, but I even wondered if it was you. After I recalled where I'd seen that odd hoofprint…"

"I'm not flattered that you'd think I wouldn't do my duty by a girl if I got her pregnant. Apparently no one told you I had a vasectomy years ago, Noah. It's a long story, too, and one day I may share it—*if* I manage to forgive you for labeling me the kind of bastard who'd cut and run."

"I'm sorry, Ethan. Accidents do happen. In college I had a close call of my own. And don't look so surprised. I spent some time rebelling against Dad's rigid rules."

Seeming to relax, Ethan uttered a snort. "From what I hear, you still *are* rebelling, old son. Why else would you take up with the town's scarlet woman?"

Noah shifted his gaze off the road. "Rebellion against my father? Is that what his board is saying? They couldn't be more wrong. I've fallen for Greer, Ethan. It hasn't got a thing to do with my dad or anyone else. If she'll have me, I intend to marry her."

"Jumpin' catfish! Kayla said that, but I turned a deaf ear. I never figured you for the type to go against the strict and narrow."

"Now *I'm* annoyed. You know I follow a far less stringent path than Dad ever did." Noah drove onto the road that led to Ethan's property.

"Yeah, I know. You gave my pa a decent send-off. Okay,

so that makes us even. Let's shake on it." Ethan stuck out his hand when Noah had stopped outside Ethan's barn. They did shake, and Noah felt better for having cleared the air. All night he'd been plagued by guilt over wrongfully judging someone he counted as a friend.

Leaving the Ritter ranch, Noah decided he'd have enough time to see what his father wanted before he met Greer.

As he'd done on his previous visit, Noah left his car at the church, walked to the rectory and knocked.

Ruth swung open the door. "My word, Noah, what's taken you so long to get here? Your father's phoned your house and the church office ten times if he's phoned once. Stress isn't good for his heart. It's not like you to deliberately dally."

"My visits with Dad are never very pleasant."

"We're your parents, Noah! We deserve respect."

He'd always softened his attitude toward his mother, because he supposed she put up with a lot from his dad. But Noah was still angry over the way she'd tried to manipulate Greer. So today, he hardened his heart. "Respect is a two-way street. Do you and Pop think it hasn't come to my attention that you've been trying to undermine me in the church and out in the community?"

Ruth drew herself up and pursed her lips. "Honestly, this isn't like you, Noah. It's that Bell girl rubbing off on you. Even her own father thinks she's—"

"Greer isn't a girl, Mother. She's a woman. A woman badly mistreated by all of you when she was little more than a girl. I'll tell you first, and in a minute I'll tell Dad—I plan to marry Greer Bell. And if she agrees, I'll adopt her daughter."

He didn't wait for Ruth's response. Nevertheless, he heard her swift intake of breath as he strode down the hall and shoved open the door into his father's makeshift bedroom.

Noah was met by a scowl that didn't make his father seem a sick man so much as an angry one.

"Boy! Where in heaven's name have you been? If you say you spent the night at that floozie's house, I'll call our regional director myself and have you removed from your post at St. Mark's."

"I didn't spend the night with Greer because I care too much to let her suffer any further disgrace in this town. I am going to sleep with her soon, though. My plan is to marry her. As for having me removed from St. Mark's… If you're strong enough to attack me, you're strong enough to hear the truth." Pacing back and forth at the end of Holden's adjustable bed, Noah imparted the directive he'd received from the regional council—increase St. Mark's membership and improve the church's finances, or the property would be put up for sale.

At first Noah feared the shock had been too much. But the older man rallied. He turned and shouted, "I don't believe you! You're making that up to distract me from reminding you how that woman is turning you into a pathetic excuse for a priest. You should stand at the helm of St. Mark's, above reproach. Joe Carpenter was visiting Senator Gallagher last night when you and Wade Montgomery stopped at the Four Aces. Joe said you were in a frenzy over Greer Bell. He saw what time Ryan came back, and knows how long your horse was tied to Bell's corral. It's disgraceful, Noah. But she'll be gone soon, so it won't matter. If you'd phoned me earlier, I'd have let you know that Robert called me with news while you were chasing over the hills after his daughter. Robert heard from the kid's other grandpa. The way you've acted, I shouldn't give you fair warning, but I am, so now you can bow out before it becomes a triangle. Wouldn't do for a priest—or a son of mine—to get mixed up in a mess like that."

"If Robert wasn't lying, wouldn't you say the joker is ten

years too late with his supposed interest in Shelby?" The news rattled Noah all the same.

"Bah! What it proves is that if the girl had given her dad and me the name of the boy who did her wrong, she wouldn't have been living with the sin of bearing an illegitimate child all these years. She'd have been properly wed."

A red haze of anger burst inside Noah's chest. Turning, he stalked from the room, down the hall and out to his pickup. He didn't calm down until he was almost at the point of entering Greer's lane. Little by little he'd begun to see how unlikely it was that after so many silent years, Shelby's other grandfather would show up out of the blue. And why contact Robert instead of Greer? Before Noah reached her house he decided the story had been manufactured by his father for the purpose of getting him to dump Greer. He was glad he'd had time to work it out in his mind. Now he wouldn't make a fool of himself by suggesting such a preposterous notion to Greer.

When she saw him drive in, she hurried out, shrugging on a jacket as she ran. "Okay," she said the minute he opened his door. "Tell me what you found out about the trail markers."

Relieved to see her, and even more relieved at her sunny smile, Noah gathered her against his chest. He wouldn't let her go, and held her close as he relayed what he'd found out about Stanley Guthrie.

"Oh, Noah. That poor kid. Did you tell Wade? You didn't, I hope."

"No. That's up to you. You should let him know whether or not you plan to press charges, though."

"I couldn't do that to a young man who suffers from a decreased mental capacity. But I will call Wade. One of you—Wade certainly—should have told me about the tape player." She sighed. "Anyway, he'll need to see what he can dig up on this stranger. You say Stanley didn't know him, only described him as an itinerant cowboy?"

Noah released her, but kept one arm locked around her waist. "Might that description fit Shelby's real dad or…his father?"

Greer frowned. "Oh, Noah. You need to drop that line of thinking. What first attracted me to Dan Harper was his snazzy way of dressing. I never met his folks, but I later found out that they've got lots of money. And what oil executive would dress as an ordinary rodeo bum? Or sneak around for that matter?"

Feeling a rush of happiness, Noah dismissed his father's warning as a lie.

CHAPTER FOURTEEN

THE SHERIFF DROVE in before Noah left Greer's ranch. Wade Montgomery set a booted foot on the lower porch step and removed his hat. "About an hour ago, I received an interesting phone call from Dalton Guthrie. Noah, seems to me that you and Ethan decided to take over my job. Did you ever plan to include me in your sleuthing?"

Noah flushed dark red. "As a matter of fact, I've been discussing the results of our findings with Greer. She planned to call you. She's not too happy that we kept her in the dark, especially about the tape player. I'm surprised you heard from Dalton. He begged Ethan and me not to turn Stanley in."

"Yes, well, his wife, Muriel convinced him Stan could be in danger from this stranger. Like, if the guy needs another *favor* and Stanley doesn't deliver. Did either of you think what might happen then?"

"Wade," Greer said. "I did intend to phone you. I can't bear to lodge a complaint against a boy with Stan Guthrie's mental problems. And before you start grilling me, I don't have any cowboy enemies that I know of. Noah said Stan's description was too vague to make any kind of positive identification. And he's sure Stan knows all of Gallagher's men. In fact, Noah said the kid probably knows everyone in town, and this guy's a stranger."

"On the one hand, that's comforting. On the other... I wish

Stan had come to me when he was first approached. Stanley said the man was in Callie's Café. I questioned her staff at length. The heck of it is, about the time you moved here, Greer, it was peak rodeo season. Any number of cowboys stop in town to eat. So it's a pretty useless thread." He sounded exasperated.

"My guests leave the day after tomorrow. For a couple of weeks, Lupita and I will be focused on getting ready for our open house. I've issued a blanket invitation via the *Herald.* If someone in town is bent on ruining my business, that would be a good opportunity…. I'd appreciate it, Wade, if you, Noah, Ethan and anyone else so inclined could keep watch. Maybe someone will act suspicious or try to disrupt the day."

Wade twirled his winter cowboy hat idly around a thumb. "I'd like to catch the sucker in the act, I'd gladly string him up by his ears." He sighed. "This was a quiet town until Miranda launched her grand scheme. Not that I'm complaining. I'd never have met Callie otherwise. It's more that Homestead was peaceful in the old days. These days, my dad swears he never saw so many nice women becoming magnets for a criminal element." A smile said he was just joking.

"If your wife and Kayla were as baffled as I am," Greer murmured, "we're no help at all. Hey, maybe it's not us. Could someone have it in for Miranda?"

"Now, there's a possibility. Her mother, Nan, might have said yes a number of years ago. Miranda used to be a handful. No one would've guessed the wild child of Homestead would turn out to be our dedicated mayor. She's worked her fanny off to make sure this program runs smoothly. Grumblers like our former mayor and a few old ranchers opposed her idea early on, but they're basically blowhards who eventually caved in."

Greer shrugged. "Well, I thought I'd toss the thought on the table. As I said, I've wracked my brain trying to imagine who'd pay—what did you say, Noah—seventy dollars to do me harm."

"Seventy bucks and a tape recorder with high-intensity speakers," he teased, running a finger across her nose.

"Whoop-di-di!" She rolled her eyes. "That tells you what they think I'm worth."

They all laughed, and it was clear Wade had gotten over being angry with Noah and Ethan for sticking their noses into his police work.

"I'll leave you two," Greer said. "The school bus just turned off the highway. The writers want to tour our court-house and then eat at Callie's. I thought it'd be good to include Shelby in the tour. Most of the other kids in her class already know the old building's history."

"You're brave," Noah said. "Kids find historic tours boring."

"I told her she can take pictures and send them to her friend Luke Sanderson."

"Clever thinking." Noah bestowed a big smile on Greer.

Wade's cell phone rang, and he took the call. "Gotta go," he said. "Somebody's Hereford bull is walking down the middle of Farm-to-Market Road 25." Waving, he ran to his vehicle.

Noah ambled down the lane alongside Greer. "I've always thought I'd like three or four kids of my own," he said unex-pectedly. "I've never asked what your feelings are toward maybe having more."

Greer abruptly stopped walking. "I've been consumed with raising Shelby. I haven't given any thought to more children." Standing there inches apart, with Noah gazing down on her with such love in his eyes, Greer imagined what a tender lover he'd be. She pictured growing round with Noah

Kelley's baby. It'd be a vastly different experience than the anxious months when she was carrying Shelby. Rising on tiptoes, she instigated a kiss.

Surprised and pleased, his arms slid around her and clasped her tight. "I told my parents today that I intend to marry you, Greer." Feeling her stiffen and drop back on her boot heels, Noah lightly massaged her back until her tension eased.

"I can guess *that* announcement was met with a lot of resistance."

"Greer, I'd like us to start being seen around town as a couple."

She gazed into his eyes and let a forefinger tentatively brush the middle three buttons on his shirt.

"I know you've held back. And maybe you still have reservations. All I want is a chance to prove that life will be better when we're together than when we're apart."

The doors of the big yellow bus swished open, and Shelby hopped out and ran pell-mell toward the adults.

"Your timing always stinks, Noah. Do you know that?" Greer murmured. "Shelby's a hundred percent in your corner. She believes wholeheartedly that our life is better when you're around. I do love you, Noah. It's—I don't want to be the cause of you being treated badly."

Noah's eyes twinkled. "I forgive them, Greer. Poor souls are out of touch with reality." Grasping her upper arms, he lifted Greer back up on her toes and about the time Shelby reached them, he was kissing her mother into oblivion.

"Noah! Mama! Does this mean you aren't mad at each other anymore?"

The girl's shrill excitement served to break the couple apart. "It means more than that, squirt," Noah said, smiling down on her upturned face. "And I could use your help convincing your mother she ought to marry me."

Shelby's little freckled face turned serious. "Will you be my daddy then, like my friend in Denver got? Rhonda Ann and some other kids were flower girls. When her mama got her a new dad, the flower girls wore really cool dresses."

Noah sorted through all the subtleties. He waited a heartbeat, thinking Greer might jump in. She didn't. "Uh, marriage usually means having a wedding, Shel. If your mom and I get married, I'd be your, ah, stepdad. And depending on the size of the wedding, we might have flower girls who wear really cool dresses."

"All right!" She pumped her fist in the air. "But the part about you being my dad is *way* cool, Noah. I already decided that's what I was gonna ask Santa Claus for. Brittany said Santas don't deliver dads, and Brad called me dumb. He said I was wasting a wish. Wait till I tell him I don't hafta waste a wish now."

Greer broke into her daughter's rambling. "Whoa. Hold it right here, Shelby Lynn. And Noah, too. It's customary for a proposal to precede any talk of a wedding."

"Huh?" Shelby wrinkled her nose.

"She's right." Noah sank to one knee, took Greer's hand and said simply, "Please, will you marry me?"

"She will, she will!" Shelby flung her arms around, shouting.

Greer snatched back her hand and turned Shelby toward the house. "Get up, Noah. I need time to think. I've just made a home. Just opened a business. I have guests waiting to go to town. Once they've gone home, I have to get ready for the open house." Her voice rose, sounding panicky.

"That's in two weeks," Noah said, slowly standing upright. "What better time to announce our engagement to the world? We could fit a wedding in before Christmas, couldn't we?"

Greer's mouth opened and shut twice.

"And another thing, our backyards connect. You can easily expand and rent my house out to larger parties or families. Greer, I believe you love me enough, but you're afraid to take the risk. Please…don't be. I know we can make us work."

"I…you're right. Everything you say is right." She took a deep breath. "Okay, my answer is…yes. Yes, Noah, yes!" She was still gripping Shelby's shoulders, and her voice vibrated with hope—and a little fear.

Letting out a whoop, Noah flung his baseball cap into the air. "So we can set a wedding date. Large or small? I'll find someone to officiate."

"This feels rushed, somehow. I'd, ah, like a medium-size wedding. I know we probably can't hold it at your church."

"Wait! Why would you think that? I never envisioned it anywhere but St. Mark's."

"Really?" Releasing her daughter, Greer reached out. "Oh, Noah!"

He stepped forward and again swept her into a fierce hug. They were interrupted by the arrival of the boisterous writers. On hearing the news, the six babbled excitedly. Julie Masters clapped her hands. "Marisa and Cal Sanderson will be thrilled. Wait until we spread the word. Everyone who visited Whippoorwill loved you, Greer. I hope you plan to invite all your old friends."

Suddenly overwhelmed, Greer grabbed hold of Noah's hand and said weakly, "My mother doesn't even know yet."

Noah calmed the excited women. "We're in the very early planning stages. Our church isn't very big. Greer and I have a lot to discuss. I'm thinking it'd work to have family and close friends attend the service, followed by an old-fashioned Texas brisket barbecue in the park for as many as want to show up."

Greer felt a little like a puppet on a string. Nodding at everything Noah mentioned. It wasn't until she, Shelby and the writers were touring the old courthouse, that Greer had to pinch herself to make sure the day wasn't all just a dream.

THE NEXT TWO WEEKS slid by in near-idyllic perfection. Near but not total. Half of Homestead—people she knew and many she didn't—stopped them on the street to regale them with congratulations. Except for both sets of parents and the church board members.

But neither did Greer phone her mother, although she reached for the phone several times. What stopped her was that she knew word of the wedding was everywhere. Greer felt hurt when Loretta failed to call and ask to be involved.

She and Noah discussed it the day they spent shopping for matching wedding bands in San Antonio.

"Our folks will come around before the wedding, Greer," he said. "I have faith. Give them time to see how happy we are together. I, ah, wonder what you'd think of me asking my father to officiate? I've heard he's up and around more."

A laugh almost burst out of Greer, although Noah's earnest expression curbed the impulse. Obviously this was important to the man she'd agreed to spend the rest of her life with. A man she loved to distraction. Selfishly a tiny ray of hope sprang up; if her parents were to hear that Father Holden was going to perform the ceremony, her dad might agree to attend. She didn't know why that mattered, but it did.

"If it pleases you, Noah, it'll please me," she said, looping an arm through his. "I want our special day to be perfect for both of us, and Shelby. By the way, do you have a problem with her asking Brit, Megan and Heather to be flower girls? I know we said we'd keep the wedding small. but…"

"Medium. We said medium," he reminded with a grin. "How could either of us refuse her when we invited Ethan,

Kayla, Wade and Callie to stand up with us? And I'm surprised but glad that you put Ryan and Kristin on the list to be invited to the church."

"It's right, don't you think, to include them, plus Miranda and her mom, Millie and Hiram Niebauer, and Cal and Marisa Sanderson, with their kids? Oh, and the writers, of course."

Chuckling, Noah leaned over and kissed her right there in the middle of the jewelry store. "Sweetheart, once we get your open house behind us, it'll be smooth sailing to our wedding. I was shocked the other day when Clint Gallagher offered us the use of his big, fancy smoker for grilling the brisket. It's the one I've seen at his election rallies.

"So, have you two decided on this pair of rings?" An indulgent clerk prodded them to make a choice.

"I don't know, Noah. These are more expensive than we agreed to spend."

"Send them to be engraved," he told the clerk. "These are the ones we like best. I'll be in to pick them up two weeks from Monday. I have a fitting for a new suit on the same day." He gave a little shrug. "Wade said the suit I wear to preach in every Sunday just doesn't cut it as something a groom should wear. Ethan thinks I need new black boots. I notice you haven't given a hint as to what your dress is going to be like."

The reason Greer hadn't was because she continued to hope her mom would phone and want to go dress-shopping with her. She'd seen Shelby and Loretta chatting at church, but Loretta seemed to go purposely out of her way to avoid Greer. And she couldn't not know about the wedding, since everyone in town was talking about it.

"I'll settle on something soon, Noah," Greer said listlessly. "Callie, Kayla, Kristin and even Miranda are determined to drag me to a quaint little wedding shop Kristin recommended.

And you've gotta know our mayor isn't one for fancy dresses."

As they walked out into the cooler November air, Noah stopped and buttoned Greer's jacket tight beneath her chin. "You'd tell me if something was bothering you about our wedding plans, wouldn't you, sweetheart?"

"Yes, why?" It was impossible to miss his worried expression.

"You don't seem as ecstatic as other prospective brides whose ceremonies I've been asked to preside at."

She cupped his warm face with chilly hands. "I'm so happy, Noah, that I have this fear that something's going to suddenly rise up and snatch it all away."

He slid his hands over hers, brought them to his lips where he dropped a series of kisses on each slender finger. "I'm in your life to stay, Greer."

She let the euphoria from that promise carry her through the whole next week and into the weekend, where more people than she'd expected turned up at her dedication and open house. At first she was sure Lupita had prepared way too much food, yet by midday it was evident every scrap would likely be consumed. Her face hurt from smiling perpetually. Likewise she'd shaken so many hands, Greer thought her fingers would fall off.

Greer noticed the house was finally empty. Only Noah, Wade, Callie and family lingered. The adults watched the kids play with Happy and Bear.

"No sign of anyone making trouble for you today, Greer," Wade said as they stood together on the porch.

Miranda pulled slowly around the house from where she'd parked near the barn. She rolled down her window and called, "I had fun. It was a great day, Greer." She started to drive off, and Wade whistled her down. He gestured Noah over to her pickup. "Sheriff, are you planning to give me a ticket?" Miranda laughed and tossed her glossy ponytail over one shoulder.

"I've been adding up the annoying pranks taking place of late." He sketched out what Noah had told him about Greer's letters. "It's growing ever clearer that someone's targeting Home Free participants."

Miranda and Noah both nodded their heads in agreement. "Why?" Miranda asked, nose wrinkling. "What's to be gained? We're making good progress."

Wade stroked his chin. "I figure someone in Homestead's carrying a big grudge. But it must be costing them some bucks to make it appear like an outside job."

"Good point." Noah squinted into the fading sun. "You sound like a man with a plan. Do you need my help?"

"I'll let you know. I'm thinking of bringing in someone from out of town who may be freer than I am to nose around without arousing suspicion."

Miranda gunned her engine. "If you'd like to read the early council minutes or Home Free planning committee notes, my secretary will run off copies for you, Wade." She glanced at her watch. "Sorry I have to dash. I'm off to welcome another new family."

Wade tapped her pickup door. "Okay…for now, let's keep this between us. Since more stuff has happened to Greer, I especially want to be sure Noah's on the lookout."

"Sounds good," Noah said. "I hope you ferret out answers, and soon. Bye, Miranda. Wade, shall we join the others?"

They did. The kids were still chasing after the dogs, whose coats had been brushed into wild fluff that resembled dandelion down. Happy wore a green satin bow around his neck for the festive occasion, and Bear had on a matching red ribbon. Greer told Shelby to remove them before the dogs got caught on something. The children all tried to help, which made for laughter all around.

The chore was eventually accomplished, and Callie said they had to get home. She brushed a kiss near Greer's left ear. "Less than four weeks until your *really* big day," she whispered. "About that dress…" She let the sentence hang.

"How about if we meet at the shop Kristin recommended the day after tomorrow? Noah can meet Shelby's school bus then. He's going to San Antonio tomorrow. And I'll be busy cleaning up. I'd hoped my mom…" The words had no more than slipped out than Greer caught her lip hard between her teeth.

Noah thought he knew then what was behind Greer's frequent sighs. Neither his mother nor hers had turned out for the open house that had seen almost everyone else from the church. Well, not the Steffans, Fentons or Joe Carpenter, either.

Over the course of the day Noah had given out stacks of the new brochures, and even booked two cottages for over New Year's. Shaking up his folks and Robert and Loretta just moved to the head of his to-do list. Noah had put off asking Holden to officiate at their wedding. He'd held out, hoping the stubborn old goat would step forward and offer on his own. *Yeah, right!*

Noah hung around as late as he dared that night without endangering the promise he'd made to himself and Greer— that they weren't going to end up in bed together until they were husband and wife. Holding off, no matter how great the frustration, was Noah's most precious gift to Greer. They'd also decided to forgo a honeymoon in favor of forging a family routine with Shelby.

Heaving a ragged sigh, he got up off the couch, tugged Greer to her feet and straightened her sweatshirt, which had ridden high when he stroked the soft flesh underneath. "If I don't leave now, sweetheart, I risk several things, one of which is not getting on the road to San Antonio bright and early in the morning."

Sliding an arm around his hips, Greer walked him to the door. "It'll be late when you hit town tomorrow night, Noah. Are you sure it's no problem to come over the day after to meet Shelby's bus? Lupita will be here cooking up a storm again. Shelby could spend the afternoon with her. I just thought it'd be good for you and Shel to have some private time together. And…uh…you might get in the swing of being a dad by explaining why she can't wear the red cowboy boots you bought her with the pink dress she'll be wearing at our wedding."

He tossed back his head and laughed deeply. "Thanks." Dancing Greer in a circle, he two-stepped her out the door and kissed her soundly as they stood beneath the porch light. "If this is some kind of daddy test you've devised, I'll pass with flying colors. Maybe if you come back from the bridal shop swearing you bought the prettiest dress in the store, I'll tell you how I accomplished the feat of getting our daughter to abandon her boots for girly shoes."

Greer's heart did a funny, happy little jig at Noah's easy ability to call Shelby his daughter. "Noah, you've never brought up wanting to adopt Shelby. Is…that, uh, a sometime possibility?"

He stopped their silly dance and held her still. "Are you kidding? I'd like nothing better. It's a privilege I thought you and she ought to talk over and decide. A privilege I wouldn't presume to take for granted."

"I'll talk to her in the next few days. You know, she's always been Shelby Bell. Her biological dad isn't a subject I've ever needed to bring up with her. She's never asked.

She's recently expressed the desire for a father, but she hasn't shown any interest in learning who, specifically, he is."

"Some day she may want to look up her real dad."

"He's not a *real* dad in any sense of the word, Noah. Dan Harper did nothing more than donate sperm." She stepped back and flipped a falling curl out of her eyes, crossing her arms as if to ward off unpleasantness.

Noah watched her grow rigid and recalled the day his pop threw out some remark about Shelby's other grandfather getting in touch with Robert Bell, or vice versa. So, as he'd assumed, Holden was just blowing smoke. But that didn't mean Shelby wouldn't be curious one day. "I hear what you're saying, Greer. You prefer to forget that this guy, Harper, even exists. Me, too, but I know from working with foster kids in Austin, that at some point abandoned kids often develop a need to search for their roots. I want you to know I'm not opposed."

"I am. Vehemently. And it's not a subject I care to discuss. I will talk to Shelby about taking your last name, Noah."

"Good, and tell her I'd be honored. Now come here and give me a proper send-off kiss. I don't want to leave you looking so disturbed."

She walked into his arms and one kiss led to two. Two led to three. But when they finally made the break and Noah trotted out to climb into his pickup, he left Greer floating on clouds once again.

AROUND TWO the next day, Greer and Lupita stood at the kitchen counter poring over cake-decorating books. They were trying to pick a pretty, two-tiered cake that would be symbolic of Greer and Noah's wedding. It would be cut into tiny slices for guests to freeze and bring out on the Kelleys' first anniversary. Because of the large number of people expected at the reception in the park, they'd serve sheet cakes.

Suddenly the loud whop-whop-whop of helicopter rotors over the ranch house interfered with the women's ability to hear each other.

Lupita went to the window to see what was going on. "It must be Señor Gallagher going or coming."

"I thought Kristen said they were going to sell the helicopter." Greer listened as the noise filled the kitchen. Curious, she joined Lupita at the window. "Darn, whoever's flying, he's sure scattering my sheep." Greer yanked open the back door and ran out into the field.

The machine, big, shiny and silver, hovered above the ground a short distance away. Then it dropped, and big as you please, sat down. Whining blades flattened grass that was meant for Greer's sheep to consume. Woollies ran every which way.

"What's that idiot doing?" Lupita yelled, rushing out as well.

"Beats me." Greer shaded her eyes against the afternoon sun. "Maybe they developed engine problems. I wonder if I should call Kristin."

"Ms. Greer, I don't think that's Señor Gallagher's helicopter."

"Huh?" Greer frowned as she faced the older woman.

"I see two men climb out, and I have never laid eyes on either one."

"Quick, Lupita, grab my guest book. It's under the phone. Could I have listed guests for the wrong week? I'm positive I didn't talk to anyone who said they'd be flying in, not before the wedding anyway."

Two men crossed the field, taking long, purposeful strides as they headed for the front of the house. The rotors had begun to slow, but still carried enough wind to whip the graying hair of both strangers. One glanced up and saw the women. Both switched course.

Not only did Greer not care for surprises, but she didn't like the way the men studied her and Lupita. As if they were little more than dirt under a microscope lens.

The men wore expensive silk suits, conservative ties and black shiny shoes that put Greer in mind of the IRS or undertakers. As they approached, the taller stepped forward.

"Quit gawking. One of you run and fetch the ranch owner. We're here to see Ms. Greer Bell." There was power in the voice, combined with a coldness in the lake-blue eyes that sent a shiver up Greer's backbone.

"I'm Ms. Bell," she said haughtily, or at least that was her aim. "Are you gentlemen in need of a repairman? You're welcome to use my phone. Otherwise, I can't say I'm altogether happy with your pilot for scaring the heck out of my sheep. If any of them stepped in holes and broke their legs, you can expect a bill."

"Feisty, huh?" The tall man's upper lip curled. "I'm Barnaby Manville, private attorney for Troy Harper. This is Troy. We understand you had a child nine years ago with Daniel Harper. That would be Troy's granddaughter."

The words slapped her like an uppercut to the jaw. Greer felt the wind from the river blow cold, then hot. Her knees began to knock, as a cry that wanted to be a scream of denial rose madly in her throat.

"Well," snapped the lawyer, "did you or did you not have Dan's baby?"

Though her mouth had become cotton dry, Greer managed to squeak out a weak, "Yes." Feeling Lupita Robles grasp her arm bolstered her. "How, how…more to the point…*why* did you find me? Daniel's last words to me were, 'I don't give a damn what you do, Greer, get rid of the kid. It'll be nothing but a major inconvenience to both of us.' He threw a hundred-dollar bill on the table. I ripped it up and threw back in his face. Then he walked out. I haven't seen him since, and I don't want to."

The shorter, solidly built man came toward her. "I'm Dan's father. Two weeks ago I spoke with Robert Bell. He directed me here. I meant to come the next day, but an emergency arose at one of my companies that required my attention. I'd already wasted time chasing false leads. Dan gave a Colorado address for you. I should explain that until then, I knew nothing of you or the child. Daniel married three times and none of those marriages produced an heir." The dark eyes clouded and his voice choked up. "My son was critically injured in a sports car crash five months back. He passed away without leaving intensive care. During my wife's last vigil, the night he died, Dan confessed he'd fathered a child. He admitted he'd ordered you to abort, but said he hadn't trusted you to keep your word. So he paid someone to track your whereabouts for five years—a ranch outside Denver. Since you never attempted to contact him or us for money, he quit paying to have you followed."

"I'm sorry for your tragic loss, Mr. Harper," Greer said stiffly. "Sorrier still that Dan felt a need to say anything at all. I meant nothing to him, and after our final encounter, he meant nothing to me. If you and your lawyer are worried I might try to collect something on my daughter's behalf, don't be. Shelby and I have survived for almost ten years without anything from the Harpers. We can survive twenty, thirty, fifty more."

"You don't understand, Ms. Bell. On top of the grief I endured from burying my only child, I…I—" Harper choked again and couldn't finish. His lawyer jumped in.

"Troy has lung cancer, Ms. Bell. If a grandchild exists, and of course we'd need proof through DNA, the Harper family will move heaven and earth to bring such a child to Houston to take her rightful place in the family business. Your daughter will be given legitimacy—which, according to your dad, is important to your family. At age eighteen, Shelby will inherit a piece of the Harper fortune. Other than Daniel's child, the only family left, if Troy passes, will be Troy's wife, Lucille, and his elder brother Daniel, for whom Danny was named."

Greer raised an eyebrow. "And what about Dan's three wives?" she asked sweetly.

The lawyer again responded. "Of no consequence. We negotiated generous settlements on them, as we've come prepared to do with you, Ms. Bell."

"Wh-what do you mean?" Greer felt faint.

"Oh, I'm sure your dad thought you'd be part of the package. If I hadn't let him assume so, I doubt he would've helped me locate you. The truth is, Ms. Bell, as young Daniel said ten years ago, you're an inconvenience." He reached inside his suit jacket and pulled out some folded papers. "Read this over at your leisure. I'll be back in touch in, say…three days. There are provisions for DNA tests. I'm sure you'll find the settlement more than adequate to improve this ranch. I did some checking and learned that you began your business on little more than a shoestring. Troy and Lucille are prepared to set you up for life. In turn, you will relinquish complete control of the child. And you must promise to stay out of her life as well.

At Lupita and Greer's simultaneous gasps, he pressed the papers into her fluttering hands and smiled an oily smile she didn't think she'd ever forget.

Troy Harper had more finesse. "It may seem harsh now, Ms. Bell. But I'm sure you'll come to realize you'll be affording your daughter the opportunity of a lifetime. She'll be a multimillionaire at age eighteen, with the probability of one day standing at the helm of a major international oil firm.

She'll attend the finest schools and universities, and meet young men of the same caliber," he said with a hint of disdain.

Greer longed to weep and rage. She longed to throw the men off her land. She wanted to scream at them that money had done nothing to shape the caliber of Daniel Harper. And if it had, Shelby would be better off as a pauper.

"Oh, one other thing," the lawyer said softly. Or maybe it seemed soft because Mr. Harper had begun to cough violently. "I should add that Troy is prepared to battle you in court if need be. As you can hear, his time to see the child settled may be short. Should he sue, Ms. Bell, we will win, and you will forfeit every penny of our original offer."

They turned back to the helicopter. "You dirty rotten sons of bitches," Greer shouted, then winced, thinking Noah would counsel her to forgive them. She probably lived up to what they thought of her, swearing like a stevedore. But she wanted to say so much worse. She wanted to run after the men and pound them into the earth.

Instead, she sank to her knees in spite of Lupita's trying to hold her up. Greer sobbed fat, wet tears all over Harper's stupid, insulting contract.

"Ms. Greer. Get up. Stop this now! Don't let those bastards see they have the upper hand," Lupita ordered sharply. She tugged until Greer did get up and stumbled into the house.

Lupita sat Greer at the kitchen table and hurried to the stove to put on water for tea. Ten minutes later, when Greer still hadn't touched the tea, the other woman paced the kitchen wringing her hands. "Aren't you going to call Mr. Noah?" Lupita shoved Greer's cell phone under her limp hand.

"Why, what can Noah do? What can anyone do?"

"You can *fight*. Mr. Noah can fight."

Greer shook her head. She'd experienced this sick fear one other time in her life. She was alone again. Helpless in the face of power stacked against her. Last time the power had been her folks and Father Holden Kelley. This time, it was the Harper family and their mountain of money. Once again she'd been betrayed by her mother and father. This was the worst betrayal of all.

As nothing else could, that fact got under Greer's skin. "Maybe you're right, Lupita. When this happened before and I got shuffled off to Denver, I had nothing and no one on my side. Now I have Noah."

She grabbed the phone. It almost slid out of her damp hands, but she managed to punch in Noah's cell number.

"Hi, sweetheart," he said. "I didn't think we'd talk today." The urgency in her tone and her words frightened him as he attempted to sort through her sobbed-out sentences.

"Dammit to hell! So my father was telling the truth!"

Greer frowned at the phone. "Noah, what does your dad have to do with any of this?"

"Maybe nothing. Maybe everything." In fits and spurts, Noah repeated what Holden had shouted after him that day in anger.

"And you didn't mention it to me? Something this important? How could you not?"

Noah heard her pain. "Greer, I honestly thought he'd made it up to try and get me to stop seeing you. He was furious over us, and what I'd told him about the greater church council threatening to sell off St. Mark's. Listen, I'm on my way home. Wait until I get there to do anything, unless you want to start looking for an attorney to take our case. Greer, I know you feel Harper has the upper hand because he's rich. What's more important here is the fact that Shelby's biological dad—who had nothing to do with her while he was alive, and who didn't contribute one red cent to her welfare—is dead. Time and again, I've read that grandparents have lost cases when they go up against a biological parent. Furthermore, maybe Harper's lawyer isn't as smart as he thinks. I believe that with DNA, you could sue them on Shelby's behalf for her portion of her father's estate."

"I don't want their money, Noah. I want Shelby. That's all."

"I know."

"Noah, how do I go about finding a good lawyer? I don't have a lot of money to give them. Don't I have to pony up a retainer or something?"

"Not always. Call Miranda Wright. I heard that she engaged the advice of some pretty crafty lawyers, former friends of hers in Austin, before she wrote the land grant agreement."

"I will. I'll call her right now. I need to postpone my dress-shopping trip, anyway. Oh, Noah, hurry home. I wanted to be mad because you knew about Troy Harper and didn't tell me. But I love you and I need you beside me if I have to fight him."

"Like I said, I'm on my way. Listen, Greer, I have two stops to make on my way to Sunrise Ranch. One, I'm going to pay your mom and dad a visit. Two, I'm stopping by the rectory. What I have to say will probably give my father apoplexy or worse."

"Don't. It's taken me a while, but carrying around a buck-etload of grudges is no way to live. Let them go, Noah. Some-where, some time, my parents, yours, Dan Harper and his folks will have to answer for what they've done."

"Boy howdy, will they." He sucked in a sharp breath. "I intend to give them all sneak previews of how a litany of their sins will read when they reach the pearly gates. Before we sign off, Greer… As long as you're phoning Kayla or Callie to postpone your dress-shopping, see if Shelby can stay with one of them until we sort this out. No sense getting her upset."

"You're right. I should've thought of that, but I'm too rattled."

"Of faith, hope and love, the greatest is love, Greer. Between us we have enough to beat this."

"Yes," she declared without faltering. "Yes, we do. Drive carefully, Noah. I love you so much."

CHAPTER FIFTEEN

THREE HOURS AFTER he'd hung up from talking to Greer, Noah's tires spit gravel roaring down her lane. Bear barked like crazy to announce his arrival.

Greer opened the door to his knock, and in spite of tripping over the dog, flung herself straight into Noah's arms. "I didn't expect you so soon," she sighed against his warm, solid chest.

"I didn't stop to see our folks. I started thinking about it on the way home and decided we should visit them together. Hear me out," he said when she sputtered a protest. "Your dad avoids us. Your mom tries to walk a tightrope between you and him. I've blown up at my parents separately, but they're not getting the message that we love each other. This nonsense has to stop. We're getting married in a few weeks, Greer. They can like it or lump it. But I want them to know once and for all that any attempt to split us up won't work, so they'd better give up."

"Maybe siccing Troy Harper on me is payback, Noah. None of them wants us to be married. Especially not at St. Mark's," she said miserably.

"We are going to be married at St. Mark's and that's final."

Greer had never seen Noah look so angry or so like an avenging angel. Her heart had frozen in a cold lump in her chest with Harper's visit. Warmth stole over her now and she felt the lump melt. All the other times Noah had said he loved her, it hadn't fully sunk in. Hadn't seemed real. Right at this moment, she believed. Empty years of longing for love, longing for acceptance from people who might never change their minds, no longer mattered. Noah loved, accepted and wanted her as she was. She cried then. Cleansing tears. "We *are* ge…getting m…ma…married? I…really don't have to deal with Mr. Harper alone," she sobbed, the words muffled because Noah held her so tight.

When her tears finally eased, he raised her head and swept damp curls off her cheeks. "We will exchange our vows before man, woman and God in His house, Greer. In my church. As for Harper, he can go jump in the gulf. He's not getting his money-grubbing hands on Shelby. She's going to live right here with us where she belongs."

Turning her lips into his palm, Greer had never been more at ease. She was confident their wedding would proceed, just as Noah said. She finally began to believe she wouldn't lose Shelby to Daniel's parents.

"Shelby's riding with Megan, Brad and Heather. I told Kayla I'd come for her at five. That gives us two hours." Greer blotted her eyes with the snowy white handkerchief Noah pulled from his pocket and handed her.

"Let's hop to it." He steered her toward his pickup as she blew her nose.

"I must look a mess."

"You look beautiful," he assured, boosting her into the passenger seat. He shut the door, got in and started the pickup. "Did you find an attorney?"

Greer glanced up from fastening her seat belt as he backed down the lane. "Miranda gave me the name of Abigail Winslow. She and her husband, Kirk, work as a team. I felt better after talking to them. I am a little worried about the cost, though."

"Hey, I'm good at fund-raising."

Her eyes brimmed with tears again. "Abigail had me phone Colorado to ask for affidavits from people who could vouch for how well I cared for Shelby. Marisa Sanderson promised to fax a statement, and so did the head counselor at the group home for unwed mothers. And Cal, bless his heart, phoned me. He's contacting a bunch of their customers and getting them to reserve with us to prove I can still provide for my daughter. Our spring calendar is nearly full."

"Hey, great! There are people here who'll stand behind you, too."

"And some who won't," she murmured, nervous again once they'd reached her family's farm. She felt surer when Noah came around and helped her down, taking her hand as they started up the walk. Her mom had planted chrysanthemums in the window boxes, and the walkway was lined with fall marigolds. Two big old mulberry trees stood sentinel at the corners of the clapboard house. Greer's steps grew hesitant.

Noah tightened his grip on her hand, tugging her nearer as he knocked.

Loretta opened the door. She saw who it was, saw Noah's determined expression and clutched the front of her dress. "Rob," she called shakily, "we have guests. Father Noah, and...Gr...Greer."

Noah barged past her. He strode down the short hall and unerringly found the man. "Robert," Noah spat, intending to be gruff. "Don't get up. We've come to deliver a personal invitation to our wedding. Three weeks from Saturday at St. Mark's. One o'clock. Your daughter would like you to walk her down the aisle. I'll be marrying her, with or without your consent."

Robert, who'd clearly been napping, blinked like a frog.

"I, ah, was under the impression, Greer, that you and the girl would be joining the Harper family in Houston."

"How did you find out who fathered Shelby?" She clenched her fists. "I never listed his name anywhere, Daddy, for this very reason. I knew you or Father Holden would contact Daniel's parents. Why? Why couldn't you have let it be?"

"What are you going on about? I didn't contact anyone. Harper's attorney phoned me. He offered your girl a last name, and it sounded as if you'd both live in the lap of luxury."

"What if he wasn't who he said? Did it occur he might have been a…a murderer or something?"

"I didn't tell him anything at first. Especially 'cause your mother pitched a fit. I called Holden. He knew ways to check Harper out. After the guy turned out to be legit, we agreed it'd be sinful to block such an opportunity."

"Opportunity?" Greer's eyes shimmered. "Oh, Daddy, their idea of opportunity is to pay me off and take Shelby away."

Behind them, Loretta cried, "Oh, Robert…no!" She rushed around the couple still standing in the entry to the living room and beseeched her husband. "You can't let this happen! Shelby's our granddaughter."

He climbed slowly out of his recliner. "The man on the phone never hinted at that." He grabbed his wife's fluttering hands. "I—we—Holden and I and the church board have always governed by example. You know that, Greer. We tried to get that through your head years ago. If you cared enough for the Harper boy to sleep with him—to have his child—I fail to see why you won't just marry him."

"For one thing, he's dead. But if he wasn't, I'd have had to stand in line. He's had three wives, Dad. Dan took advantage of me. I was barely seventeen. I never understood and never will, how legitimacy meant more to you than my feelings."

Noah kept Greer from fleeing. "Robert, you need to examine what's in your heart. I hope you haven't killed all the love that should be there, because if so you'll die a lonely man. I'm giving Greer my name, and if Shelby lets me adopt her, she'll legitimately become a Kelley. Monday, I'll be appointing a new board to serve until the church members vote in representatives who care more about people than appearances." Unmoved by how deflated Robert suddenly was, Noah began their retreat.

Loretta ran after them. "Wait, please," she implored. "Greer, darling, I let Rob convince me this was best for you and Shelby. He said I'd be selfish to want you to stay in Homestead. I can't think why you should forgive me, but more than anything I want to attend your wedding. I want you and Shelby in my life."

"Oh, Mother!" Noah let her go so Greer could meet her mother's embrace halfway. He noticed Robert shuffling like an old man to the door, where he gaped at the reunion.

"Noah," the elder Bell called out, "Holden still sets the rules for St. Mark's."

"No. God sets the rules, Robert. And I think he'd expect you to apologize to Greer."

Robert descended the steps, a hesitant, stoop-shouldered man.

"I forgive you, Dad." Greer's lips trembled. "The offer remains for you to walk me down the aisle."

Seemingly choked up, Rob let tears trickle down his cheeks, but he said nothing and ended up turning away.

"Lord knows you've got no reason to, but give him some time to reflect on this," Loretta begged.

Greer gripped Noah's hand. "It's up to him, Mama.

Uh…tomorrow I'm going with some girlfriends to choose my wedding dress. I was going to postpone, but I didn't. I know it's a school day and you have to teach, but I'd like you there."

Loretta's hand flew to her mouth. "Truly? I have plenty of personal days that I've never taken. What time? Where? I've dreamed of this, Greer. Wild horses couldn't keep me away."

Greer gave her the particulars. She wore a faint smile after she and Noah climbed back into his pickup.

"Are you okay?" he asked. "We can skip visiting my parents."

She sighed deeply. "Did I let him off the hook too easily, Noah?"

Leaning across the console, Noah kissed her. "Not at all, sweetheart. For a priest, I was kind of rough on Rob. I've been planning to appoint an interim board for weeks. It really wasn't tied to our visit."

"God will get you for that, Noah Kelley." She punched his arm lightly.

"I warned you not to put me on a pedestal, Greer. I'm very much just a man. So…do you think Rob will come to the wedding?"

She shrugged as he swung the parking lot at St. Mark's. "Noah, maybe we *should* skip talking to your folks. After all, your dad's not well."

"He survives confrontations when he instigates them. Besides, I saw Dad's cardiologist. He says the old dog is tougher than he lets on. And Dr. Cooper said something else that was interesting. He told me Dad knew the church was mired in debt, but couldn't seem to correct it. I suspect he used this last stroke to his advantage, as a way of avoiding the issue."

"Maybe he's not aware of how manipulative he is," she said as they approached the rectory. Noah opened the door and walked right in.

Holden wasn't alone when they burst into his room. Three church board members sat around his bed. Ruth stood at the foot. All feigned surprise when Noah and Greer appeared, but it was apparent that someone, obviously Robert Bell, had given them a heads-up.

Greer let Noah talk. And he didn't hold back. He finally wound down, saying, "You've made Greer a scapegoat because your mother treated your father badly. Admit that it's way past time to leave the judging to God." Afraid Greer might bolt in the middle, he clamped her to his side. Following his second announcement of their intent to marry, Noah again gave the day and time.

Holden swung skinny, blue-veined legs off the bed. "Noah, stop this nonsense."

Ruth pressed her husband back. "Holden, I've only ever gone against you one other time, when I voted with Miranda Wright to save the town. Now I'm siding with my son. Take a good look at him, Holden. Noah's happier than I've ever seen him. I attempted to discourage them as you asked. That obviously didn't work. All I've ever really wished for Noah is that he find happiness in his life. I don't care what you say, I'll be attending our son's wedding."

Joe Carpenter and Harvey Steffan glanced away and fidgeted. Ralph Fenton rose, mumbling, "I'd better be goin' home, Father Holden."

"Thanks, Mom," Noah said softly. "You'll be most welcome at the ceremony." Extending a hand, he blocked Ralph's exit. "Stay! It's a good thing you're all here. Saves me calling you in on Monday to thank you for serving on the board as long as you have. St. Mark's will be holding elections in January. Until then, I'm appointing Wade Montgomery, Ethan Ritter, Max Beltrane and Myron Guthrie to finish out your terms."

"Father Holden!" Joe demanded, "can he just up and do that?"

The elder Kelley slumped back against his pillows and covered his legs with the sheet. "Yes, Joe, he can." He cleared his throat. "I've got a confession. St. Mark's has been sliding for five years at least. Noah told me weeks ago that the area council considered selling the church and all the property. I didn't want to believe him, even though in my heart I figured he could be right. I phoned headquarters in Austin, and yes, every word's true. But Noah's already produced results. Bishop Weems sang his praises."

Holden's guilty eyes sought his son's. "You never said churches all over the state are using a computer program you designed to keep their budgets straight." He clasped his hands and lowered his eyes. "Ah…the bishop offered me a retirement package. I've, uh, that is, Ruth and I discussed it. We, uh…it's a good offer."

Greer, who had an arm lock on Noah, felt a ripple travel through him.

"Effective when?" Noah's query held both compassion and concern.

"January first. Your mother's already begun to pack. The bishop said they'll renovate the rectory since you're not interested in living here. Apparently you can use the space for an after-school teen club. They'll convert this house into counseling rooms, a rec center, an outdoor basketball court and oh, I forget what all." He waved a liver-spotted hand.

"I'm sorry. I hadn't heard that. Where will you and Mother go?"

"I voted for Florida. But Ruth won't hear of leaving Homestead. Especially not now, when at long last she thinks there's a possibility of grandchildren."

Noah couldn't resist hugging Ruth with his free arm.

Turning again to his father, he murmured, "Sir, as your last official duty, I…Greer and I wonder if you'd perform our wedding ceremony?" His words were jerky and left the older man blinking rapidly. But it was to Greer that Holden Kelley turned.

"Little lady, I could never stand before God in good conscience and join you in holy matrimony with my son—" Greer felt Noah tense, and she ran a hand up and down his arm, waiting for his father to drag in a breath and finish, which he did. "—unless I first beg your forgiveness. Noah's right. I'm guilty of letting my moral judgments overrule the…Word. I'm…sor…sorry, so if you'll forgive me…"

The man deserved to be kept hanging. But Greer wasn't mean-spirited enough to do that to Noah. She loved him with her whole heart, and if he wanted his dad to preside at their wedding, so did she. Snuggling closer, she felt Noah's approval after she smiled and nodded her head.

Leaning toward Ruth, Greer whispered, "Tomorrow my mom and a few friends, including Miranda Wright, are helping me pick out a wedding dress. Although," she added wryly, "I had to twist the mayor's arm, plus promise her lunch. Be that as it may… If you can get away at ten o'clock, I'd like you there. Lupita is serving us lunch at noon, by way of celebration."

"I'll believe you can pick out a dress in two hours when I see it," Noah scoffed, breaking the tension that still hung heavy in the room.

"Ha! It's bad luck for you to see the dress before the wedding. You'll have to take my word that I even have a dress until you see me at the church."

Ruth accepted without so much as a glance at her husband. Oddly enough, the board members mumbled congratulations. Greer and Noah left feeling a sense of accomplishment.

THE NEXT DAY Greer would have been the happiest bride-to-be alive had she not had Troy Harper's threat dangling over her head. But amid prodding and laughter from everyone gathered at the dress shop, she found the perfect gown. Fitted ivory satin, with spaghetti straps and tiny bows at the shoulders that her friends said would drive Noah crazy wanting to untie them.

Loretta and Ruth pretended not to hear that portion of the younger women's banter. Ruth fussed with the hem and Loretta fitted her with a headpiece and veil.

Greer was worried about the lunch gathering at her home, but it turned out to be successful. Everyone got along and had a good time.

TWO WEEKS LATER, ladies from the church held a combination shower-fund-raiser, designed to help Greer pay the lawyer. The event was well-attended, but still drew fire. Several letters to the editor showed up in Wednesday's *Homestead Herald*. The main gripe seemed to be aimed at the Home Free program. One letter said it was supposed to add to the city coffers, but had plainly attracted people who were so broke, church members had to kick in money to help them.

Millicent hand-delivered Greer's copy. "We just print the news, Greer. I don't want you to think Hiram and I side with any of the mealymouths who sent in gripes. But that's only part of why I dropped by, Greer. The other is to see if you'd like me to take pictures of your wedding and reception next weekend."

"Millie, I'd love it! I never gave a thought to photographs. I should have, because Kristin Gallagher gave us a beautiful album at the shower. But it's not an elaborate wedding, you know."

"Don't you worry, all weddings have a way of being gorgeous." Millie drove off, leaving Greer to hope she was right.

The saving grace over the ensuing days was that so much needed to be done in preparation for the wedding and the much larger reception, it cut down on the time she had to worry. And worry she did over the out-of-court negotiations going on between Abigail and Kirk Winslow and Troy Harper's weasely lawyer.

One really good tidbit of news came as a welcome surprise, midweek before the wedding, when Wade summoned Greer and Noah to his office. "I think we got a break," he said, snapping his chair forward as they both sat across from him. "Stanley Guthrie burst into my office this morning. Claimed the guy who paid him to play those tricks on Greer was getting into a black pickup. It was pure luck that I was able to run the plates. Registered to a guy by the name of Darrow. The junior Darrow."

The name meant nothing to either Greer or Noah, who both shrugged.

"I'll follow up. I just wanted you to know. Henry, the father, is the developer who built your ranchette, Noah. He lost big when the drought killed the boom he predicted would come to Homestead. Rumblings are that he's a man who doesn't like to lose."

Greer glanced at her watch. "I hate to leave in the middle of this, but I have a dress fitting. Wade, this sounds promising, don't you think? Someone like that could easily get information on land applicants. I think Stanley deserves a reward."

Wade grinned. "Possibly. We'll see. The detective I told you I wanted to hire is due to roll in here Friday or Saturday."

The happy couple left feeling they had one less worry. But the day prior to the wedding, all the bridesmaids fretted over an impending threat of rain. By nightfall, the dark clouds had passed by. Greer started to relax, then her mother phoned. "Guess what? Robert had me buy a new white shirt to go with his best blue suit. He hasn't said, but I think you can expect him at the wedding."

"To walk me down the aisle? But I asked Cal Sanderson…."

"Oh. Well, what can Rob expect since he wouldn't commit until it was too late?"

"That's right. Cal and Marisa came to my aid in Colorado when I had no one. Tell Dad he's welcome, but that I have someone else to escort me." They chatted a bit longer, but that was how they left it.

When the big day dawned with one of the most gorgeous sunrises Greer had ever witnessed, she gathered Shelby, Lupita and anyone else within earshot to come and see. In spite of what Noah had once said about not believing in omens of any kind, Greer counted the sunrise as a very good one.

She'd given Noah orders to stay away, but at ten, his pickup bumped down the lane. Greer spoke to him through the door. "I will not do a single thing to tempt bad luck today," she declared. "Can you wait a minute? There's my phone."

Noah heard her crying and all but broke down the door getting to her, bad luck or not. She dropped the receiver and spilled tears all over his starched white shirt. "Noah, Mr. and Mrs. Harper caved. His chemo is apparently shrinking his cancer. He may have years rather than months. Abigail said they've requested to meet Shelby, but will agree to supervised visits. They'd like also to give Shel a photo album of Daniel— sort of a record of his life. I said we'd discuss it. I know we said that after the wedding, we'd host your family and mine at Christmas. Do you think after the New Year we could drive to Houston and let the Harpers give Shel the album?

Somehow, before then, you and I can explain to her about her biological dad."

"You know I'll help any way I can, sweetheart," he said, kissing her forehead. "I'm closing my eyes and backing out of the house, so I'll take any bad luck with me."

"I'm so happy now, nothing would dare spoil our special day"

AND NOTHING DID. The ceremony went off without a hitch. Holden looked splendid in a gold-trimmed white robe. The happy couple glowed. The flower girls couldn't have been cuter. Shelby fairly floated down the aisle, looking smug as could be. She wiggled in to stand between her mom and her brand-new dad.

And they let her.

Robert and Loretta Bell sat next to Ruth Kelley. Greer saw both her parents take out white handkerchiefs, and she found that touching.

The service seemed far too short for all the time it had taken to make the arrangements. "I suppose we have to go to the reception," Noah growled in Greer's ear as they turned to be presented as husband and wife. Among the guests smiling at them were George and Lupita Robles, Rolando Diaz and Kipp Hadley, who'd brought his youngest daughter and her family. Noah had found Dina via the Internet. Kipp's ex had remarried and moved on, but even she had agreed to open an e-mail dialogue with her ex.

Greer gloried in feeling the tremors pass from Noah's muscular frame to her body. There was no mistaking what went through his mind during the requisite kiss—a long, satisfying kiss. Greer wouldn't have imagined that she'd anticipate her wedding night by counting the hours until they could be alone. But…she *was* counting. They'd arranged for

Shelby, along with the two dogs, to have her first sleepover at Greer's parents. Loretta was so excited. She'd rented kid movies and Rob had reportedly bought microwave popcorn.

"There's hope for our folks yet," Greer quietly confided to Noah after they'd changed out of their finery and headed to the park for the barbecue.

The band was setting up, and someone asked how long they should play. "One hour or till dawn if people want to dance all night," Noah said. To Greer, he muttered, "I have other plans. I vote we stay a respectable length of time to meet and greet. Then, wife, we're going home to drink champagne, eat chocolate-dipped strawberries, and—" he wiggled his eyebrows "—consummate this marriage."

If he expected to hear an objection from Greer, none was forthcoming.

They ate, and danced, and laughed with friends like the Sandersons, Dale Collins and the writers who were busily making notes. All the while, Noah edged them closer to Greer's Blazer. His pickup held their clothes from the wedding. He'd hoped to confuse anyone who might decorate the getaway vehicle, but predicting such a move, friends had slipped off and decked out both vehicles.

Millicent rushed up, requesting a quote for the *Herald*. Noah deferred to his wife. Greer blushed hotly. "Just say…our wedding's perfect, Millie. A blend of old, new, borrowed and blue."

"Speaking of old, did you see who's back in town?" Millie motioned with her pencil toward a very tall, lean man with short, straight brown hair, who stood nursing a beer, well apart from the crowd grouped around a keg.

Greer followed her pencil to Ethan Ritter's older brother, Jud. They watched him limp over to a tree. The lights set up for the band glinted off his face, making his fierce focus seem a bit sinister. However, this wasn't a day Greer wanted to think of threats, past, present or future. Especially since Wade had said earlier that they had a good tip on where to locate the younger Darrow.

Noah's fingers slid up and down the back of her neck. "Ethan's had a lot of tragedy in his life. I hope his brother's sudden visit bodes well."

"Jud Ritter can't seem to take his eyes off our Miranda."

Noah and Millie shifted so they were better able to see the mayor, who for the past hour had stood alone beneath one of the big live oaks dotting the park. She looked quite pensive.

Greer said worriedly, "Noah, I don't think Miranda's enjoying the party."

"Well, she has every reason to kick up her heels and celebrate with us. We're a testament, don't you think, to the success of her long-range plan for repopulating Homestead?" Grinning like a fool, he trailed damp kisses up Greer's exposed neck.

She blushed more profusely and rammed an elbow in Noah's ribs. He grunted, but hoisted her up and over his shoulder, caveman style. She only laughed. "Excuse us, Millie," the groom said, winking. "It's time for the bride and groom to exit stage right!"

"Hold on," Greer implored. "Maybe you should go introduce Miranda to Jud Ritter. See if you can get something going between them."

"I've got plans to get something going, all right," Noah said, placing her in the Blazer. "Jud Ritter's man enough to march over and introduce himself."

"You're probably right." Greer gave up trying to see through the words sprayed across her window in shaving cream—something to do with wed and bed—that she couldn't read backward. Which was probably just as well. She wanted

Noah to make it safely home, where she'd put satin sheets on the bed and set candles in the fireplace, instead of pulling off the road into some layby. Heaven knew he didn't need the added incentive of a primitive suggestion scribbled on the window. She could tell he had enough ideas of his own to last a lifetime.

Smiling contentedly, she reached over the console and looped a possessive arm around her husband. The word *husband* had a wonderful ring.

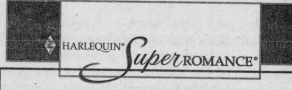

HARLEQUIN® *Super* ROMANCE®

Home to Loveless County...
because Texas is where the heart is.

Introducing an exciting new five-book series set in
the rugged Hill Country of Texas.

Desperate times call for desperate measures. That's why
the dying town of Homestead, Texas, established the
Home Free program, offering land grants in exchange
for the much-needed professional services modern
homesteaders bring with them.

Starting in October 2005 with

BACK IN TEXAS

by Roxanne Rustand

(Harlequin Superromance #1302)

WATCH FOR:

AS BIG AS TEXAS
K.N. Casper (#1308, on sale November 2005)

ALL ROADS LEAD TO TEXAS
Linda Warren (#1314, on sale December 2005)

MORE TO TEXAS THAN COWBOYS
Roz Denny Fox (#1320, on sale January 2006)

THE PRODIGAL TEXAN
Lynnette Kent (#1326, on sale February 2006)

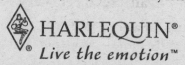

HARLEQUIN®
Live the emotion™

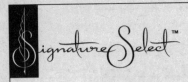

**Firefly Glen…
there's nowhere else quite like it.**

National bestselling author

KATHLEEN O'BRIEN

FIREFLY GLEN

**Featuring the first two novels in
her acclaimed miniseries
FOUR SEASONS IN FIREFLY GLEN**

Two couples, each trying to avoid romance,
find exactly that in this small peaceful
town in the Adirondacks.

Available in February.

Watch for a new FIREFLY GLEN novel,
Quiet as the Grave—coming in March 2006!